Annie came into the living room, ashen, shaken. "They've issued a life directive, Jack."

"Life directive? What the hell are you talking about?"

"If you don't begin processing and I continue living with you, they'll cut me off from Transformationalism. Totally."

Weller's composure shattered utterly. "That does it!" he shouted. "I absolutely, categorically, totally forbid you to see any of these maniacs again!"

"Jack! Stop it!" Annie screamed. "Don't you see that you're confirming everything they said?" Tears began to form in her eyes. "If you won't come for processing, I'm getting out of here this very minute!"

Then she slammed the door behind her, leaving Weller transfixed in the center of the living room, his body frozen in rage, his mind roaring with emotional white noise.

He stood there for long moments trying to force rationality back into his screaming brain, trying to break the shocked, stunned, raging stasis that held him in emotional and physical paralysis.

But before he could move, before he could get himself to the door, he heard the engine of her car start in the driveway. Then, with a roar, the metallic scream of a missed shift, and the howl of an engine revving toward redline, she was gone. . . .

Other books by Norman Spinrad

Novels
THE SOLARIANS
THE MEN IN THE JUNGLE
AGENT OF CHAOS
BUG JACK BARRON
THE IRON DREAM
RIDING THE TORCH
PASSING THROUGH THE FLAME
THE MIND GAME
A WORLD BETWEEN
SONGS FROM THE STARS
THE VOID CAPTAIN'S TALE
CHILD OF FORTUNE

Short Story Collections
THE LAST HURRAH OF THE GOLDEN HORDE
NO DIRECTION HOME
THE STAR SPANGLED FUTURE

Non-fiction
FRAGMENTS OF AMERICA
STAYING ALIVE: A WRITERS' GUIDE

Anthologies (editor)
THE NEW TOMORROWS
MODERN SCIENCE FICTION

THE
MIND GAME

Norman Spinrad

BANTAM BOOKS
TORONTO · NEW YORK · LONDON · SYDNEY · AUCKLAND

THE MIND GAME
A Bantam Book / published by arrangement with
the Author
Bantam edition / August 1985

ISBN 0-553-25061-2

Published simultaneously in the United States and Canada

Bantam Books are published by Bantam Books, Inc. Its trade-mark, consisting of the words "Bantam Books" and the por-trayal of a rooster, is Registered in U.S. Patent and Trademark Office and in other countries. Marca Registrada. Bantam Books, Inc., 666 Fifth Avenue, New York, New York 10103.

PRINTED IN THE UNITED STATES OF AMERICA

H   0 9 8 7 6 5 4 3 2 1

Order is the enemy of Chaos. But the enemy of Order is also the enemy of Chaos.

—Gregor Markowitz

One

Sweat plastering the back of his shirt to the seat of his Triumph, eyes burning from San Fernando Valley smog, brain throbbing with dulled exhaustion, Jack Weller turned off the Ventura Freeway onto Moorpark. *Another day, another ten minutes of Monkey Business in the can, another piece of my lifeline sold for a hundred dollars and my name flashed across the boob tube as the director of a peculiarly mindless kiddie show,* he thought. *But don't get me wrong, I love Hollywood.*

Down Moorpark—gas stations, Burger Palaces, supermarkets, giant drugstores—left, right, left, and onto the street where he lived. Endless anonymous ticky-tacky ranch houses inadequately veiled by trees and thick shrubbery. *Oh, the towering feeling?* He turned up the driveway and parked behind Annie's ancient red Porsche sitting in the open garage. *Image, image, the price we pay for image!* If a would-be up-and-coming young director or an aspiring actress wanted the comfort of a closed, air-conditioned car, it had to be a late-model Cadillac or at the very least a fancy Buick—anything less said "poor," and that was the kiss of death. So two sports cars it was, acceptable image on the cheap.

Inside, Annie was waiting for him in the living room, lithe, blond and lovely in a flowering caftan but tired and empty around the eyes, poor baby. "Hi, babes," she said. A brief pro forma kiss with no juice in it.

"How did it go?" Weller asked, going to the bar and getting out the Martini fixings.

Annie sighed. "The usual," she said. "Next week Harry's lined up an audition for a part in a perfume commercial. And some writer client of his is working on an original screenplay which might have something for me in it if it ever gets sold. How's the monkey business?"

Weller poured two Martinis, handed her one, sat down on the couch beside her, and took a long cold swallow. "More fun than a barrel of producers," he said. "Our warm, wonderful father figure came in with a hangover, the kids were into

1

playing practical jokes on each other today, and the damned chimp crapped on the set twice."

"But don't get me wrong, I love Hollywood," Annie chorused along with him. They laughed and relaxed closer to each other.

The air-conditioner was beginning to cool him off, and the Martini was beginning to loosen a few of the knots in his gut. There are those who would say I've got it made, Weller reflected. A more or less steady five-hundred dollars a week directing a network show, even if it is kiddie stuff. Twenty grand of equity in a house, even if it is in the Valley. A beautiful wife who loves me, even if we do have our problems. One man's ceiling is another man's floor.

"What's for dinner?" Weller asked, feeling like any nine-to-fiver coming home to the little woman, and hating it.

"Chinese spareribs and corn on the cob," Annie said. "Pour me another and I'll go take a look."

Weller's stomach sent pleasure messages to his grumbling brain. It was one of his favorites, and Annie's fixing it was always a little flash of the love between them that still seemed to survive despite her frustration with an acting career that was going nowhere and his frustration at clinging to the bottom rung of a long, long ladder, no closer to directing feature films or even prime-time segments than he had been two years ago. At least we haven't gotten to the point of taking it out on each other, he thought, pouring two more drinks. *Not yet*.

Annie went into the kitchen, and Weller sat back down on the couch, sipping his drink and contemplating the furniture. How he hated the wall-to-wall carpeting, the Danish-modern junk, the big color TV console, the Middle American-ness of it all! Five years, and he still couldn't think of this house as home, as something permanent. Home was a big, lavish place in the Hollywood Hills, with a swimming pool, a huge garden, and a sauna; home was where they were going to live when Annie was a star and he was a big-time feature-film director. The only thing that could be worse than the transient feeling of this house would be accepting this place, this life, as something they had arrived at, rather than a place along the road to the top. I'm only thirty-one, he thought, and Annie's only twenty-nine. We're not old enough to be stuck where we are.

"Come and git it!" Annie called from the kitchen. Weller tossed down the rest of his drink, his attention drawn from these heavy musings to the dinner-sized hole in his stomach, and he went into the dining room happy to be thinking of little else but ribs and corn.

By the time he had put away two butter-drenched cobs of corn and a plate of crackling sweet-and-sour spareribs, Weller was feeling more mellow, and he and Annie leaned toward each other across the table over coffee, looking into each other's eyes and beginning to feel cozy. They would probably make love before settling down in front of the tube tonight.

Despite everything—a couple of brief bouts of experimental swinging, three desultory orgies, and a few sneaky side affairs along the way—they could still please each other in bed. In fact, after the transitory thrill of unwrapping a fresh new body, Weller had found the other women he had had during their six-year marriage ultimately and rapidly boring compared to Annie. Annie had always told him that other men left her with the same feeling, and nothing in their life together had signaled to him that this was a kind lie. They had been totally faithful to each other for over two years now, having learned, if nothing else, that their sex lives together were not the source of their mutual nagging frustration, that bedtime adventures were no cure for lack of career satisfaction.

"Love you, lady," Weller said, reaching across the table and touching his palm to her cheek.

"We're lovely people," she said. They touched, and they eyed, and they kissed, and then they went into the living room, shucking clothes as they walked, and made love on the green velvet couch, dissolving away the tedium and frustration of the day, at least temporarily, into the mindless melding of bodies.

But inevitably after a time it had to be over, and they found themselves once more lying naked against each other on the couch, dully watching television.

For the Wellers, as for two hundred million others, the tube was an artificial release from boredom, from the need to chew over things that had been said to each other a thousand times before just to fill dead air. But for them it was also an instrument of self-flagellation. Weller watched the prime-time dramatic shows knowing that they were formula garbage, contemptuous of the directors who had made their secure careers in big-time TV and who no longer burned to do features. And yet each time a director's credit line appeared on the screen, it was a little knife in his gut. For the nobodies

3

who directed these turkeys were still a long step up the ladder from Jack Weller and his Saturday-morning monkey show, and he never saw a prime-time segment that he could admire, that he didn't *know* he could do better. And Annie compared the face and figure of every featured actress to herself, unable to understand why they were getting the work while she had to scramble and scheme just to get an occassional commercial or walk-on.

"Full shot, close-up, full shot, close-up," Weller muttered, seeing whatever it was only in terms of the formula blocking.

Weller wondered why he watched so much of the damned stuff—there was certainly nothing to learn from it. But what had they done during those intermittent periods when they righteously swore off watching TV? Lots of movies, which made the envy even worse. Middling Hollywood hangouts which led to swinging which led back to middling Hollywood hangouts. Rounds of parties with people who were mostly worse off than they were, where *they* were objects of envy. Earnest heart-to-heart talks which petered out into dull staring contests which left them hating each other and blaming each other for the deadly boredom. What was missing from their life? It didn't take a shrink or a marriage counselor to figure it out for them. *Success*, that was what was missing, and there was no substitute for it.

"Look at her," Annie said. "She's walking through it like a zombie. Maybe I should shop around for a new agent—"

The ringing of the phone cut through the television trance. Annie got up and answered it.

"Hello, Bob—"

"The what—"

"It is?"

"I'll ask him. Hold on."

Standing by the phone table, Annie said: "It's Bob and Susan Shumway. They're going to the Transformationalist Celebrity Center tonight. Bob wants to know if we'd like to meet them there."

Bob Shumway was a fairly successful television writer. Bob and Susan and Jack and Annie had had a brief swinging number three years ago which had quickly faded out into a kind of distant friendship. Bob was something of a Hollywood trendie, always trying to be "where it was at," a great believer in going to the right parties and meeting the right people. Weller admired his style, though only in small doses.

"What's the Transformationalist Celebrity Center?" Weller

4

asked. He had heard of Transformationalism, dimly. It was one of those consciousness-raising cults, like Arica, EST, or Scientology, of which he had a low and jaundiced opinion. Somehow it didn't seem like much of a Bob Shumway number.

"Bob says it's a kind of private club run by the Transformationalists. Free drinks. Very Beverly Hills."

"You want to go, Annie?"

She shrugged. "We don't have anything better to do."

"Let me talk to him," Weller said. He went to the phone. "Hi, Bob. What's happening?"

"Thought you might like to meet us at the Celebrity Center, babe. It's only been open a couple of months, but it's an interesting scene."

"Didn't know you were into guru games, Bob."

"Hey, you can just tune out the Transformationalist scam. Point is, Transformationalism has mucho bread, and this center is designed to attract the Hollywood heavies."

"So?"

"So? So they've set up a groovy place, and they ply you with unlimited free booze. And such being the case, a lot of people are starting to hang out there. Contacts, boy! The movers and shapers. Beautiful people. Take a look. Might be the place to make the Big Connection. What do you say?"

"Just a minute, Bob." Weller looked at Annie. "Want to see if we can meet someone who can make us stars at this guru den?" he asked sardonically. "At least we can lap up the free booze," he added in a W. C. Fields voice.

"Sure," Annie said, much more earnestly. By the look in her eyes Weller could tell that she was already fantasizing a chance meeting with Joe Levine. Hope springs eternal, he thought, feeling just a little sad, a shade protective.

"Okay, Bob, we'll meet you at about eight thirty."

"Make it eight thirty sharp, and we'll meet you in the parking lot."

"Roger."

"Ten-four, babe. See you there."

The Santa Monica Mountains march east-west to the sea, a natural barrier between the suburbia of the San Fernando Valley to the north and the glitter and flash of Hollywood and Beverly Hills at their southern feet. From Mulholland Drive, running along the crest line, Weller could see the vast nightscape of Los Angeles spread below them, a brilliant carpet of light. Driving up over the ridgeline and down the defile of Beverly Glen Boulevard toward Beverly Hills, whipping around the curves in the open sports car with Annie's golden hair streaming in the fragrant night air, he lived for the moment in the Hollywood persona he longed to capture and hold. Beverly Hills, Bel Air, Malibu Canyon, Topanga, Laurel Canyon—these hills were the habitat of those who had made it; this was where they belonged.

Out of the hills and onto the flat streets of downtown Beverly Hills, the streets largely empty of pedestrians even at this hour, the action taking place very privately, behind closed doors. Weller pulled into the parking lot of the Transformationalist Celebrity Center. There were about two dozen cars in the lot—Jags, some older Porshes, a couple of Cadillacs, but also some of the cheaper sports cars, and even one VW van. Weller parked alongside Bob Shumway's vintage Aston-Martin. Bob and Susan were leaning against the car, Bob slightly paunchy in a cream-colored leisure suit, Susan dark and full-bodied in midnight-blue capris and a bare midriff red blouse.

"Hi." "Hi." Kiss, kiss.

"Been here often?" Annie asked as they walked out of the parking lot.

"A few times," Susan answered.

"It's only been open awhile," Bob said. "Just starting to catch on. The real heavies should just be starting to appear. The only free saloon in town."

By this time they had reached the entrance: a brown door in an otherwise featureless building front. A small bronze plaque identified it as "The Transformationalist Celebrity Center."

Immediately inside was a small blue-walled reception area. Facing them was another closed door with another bronze plaque. This one said:

Transform the transformers and transform the world.
Transform the world and transform your own lives.
—John B. Steinhardt

Beside the door was a small desk, and behind the desk was an intense-looking young man with a clipboard of papers and a ball-point pen.

"Good evening and welcome to the Transformationalist Celebrity Center," he said earnestly. "Please sign in." He handed

Weller the clipboard and pen. The form on the clipboard had places for name, address, phone number, and whether or not he had visited the Celebrity Center before. Weller shot Bob Shumway a narrow look, thinking, here I go onto one more mailing list, filled out the form, and handed it to Annie.

After they had all filled out the form, the attendant held the door open for them, and they walked into a large room with a cream-colored ceiling, red flocked wallpaper, and a dark hardwood floor. A bar with a mirror behind it ran the length of one wall, and there was a small, low stage in the middle of the opposite wall. The rest of the room was filled with small café tables. On the far wall was a huge black and white photograph of a heavyset man in his fifties with long, thinning gray hair and a bushy gray moustache. There were thirty or forty people scattered about the place, a few of them sitting at the bar. Anonymous soft music played, far in the background.

They took a table near the bar. Bob Shumway ran his eyes around the room. "Couple of TV producers, few actors, there's Eddie Berger from GAC, what's-his-name who writes half the cop shows in town, film critic from *Los Angeles*, nothing much. Looks like a slow night so far."

A waitress appeared, wearing a white blouse and black slacks, again with that intense look about the eyes. "What's your pleasure, folks? All refreshments are courtesy of Transformationalism. May you enjoy your evening and leave transformed." The little spiel reminded Weller of a living television commercial. The waitress took their orders and departed toward the bar.

"Weird," Weller said, cocking his head in her direction.

"Yeah," said Susan. "They remind me of the Salvation Army, all bright and clean and wide-eyed."

"But they run a good place," Bob said, perhaps a bit sharply. "So how are things with you kids?" he asked.

"Still got a contract for fourteen segments of *Monkey Business* a year," Weller said. "Annie's auditioning for a commercial next week. . . ." He gave Annie a sympathetic look and gilded the lily a bit for her. ". . . and she's up for a major part."

"In an unsold script," Annie added somewhat wearily.

Bob shook his head. "Chimp shows. Agent's bullshit. What's wrong with you kids? You've got the talent, all you—"

"*Bob!*" Susan hissed. "Will you leave them alone? Bob forgets that if he hadn't gotten to Arnie Palucci in a drunken

7

moment, he'd probably still be back writing cartoon shows."

"For Chrissakes, Susan, that's the whole point. It's not what you know—"

"IT'S WHO YOU KNOW," the other three chorused.

The waitress arrived with their drinks. She set them down with a little bowl of nuts and four copies of a lithographed brochure. On the cover was the same photograph that hung enlarged on the wall and the words, "TRANSFORMA-TIONALISM AND YOU!"

"Who is this guy?" Weller asked.

Bob lifted his glass and toasted the wall photograph. "Our host and benefactor, John B. Steinhardt," he said. "Guru of Transformationalism and proprietor in absentia of this noble saloon."

"Weird-looking duck," Weller opined.

"He used to be a science-fiction writer, I think," Susan said. She gave Bob a little false smile. "All writers are crazy."

"Hey, Bill, over here!" Bob had caught the eye of a balding, middle-aged man drinking at the bar. As he lurched over to their table, Bob whispered to Weller: "Bill Wallenstein, story editor on *Harrison & Company*, make the most of it, Jack baby."

Wallenstein sat down, none too steadily. "This is Jack Weller," Bob said. "He's a director."

"*Yeah?* What's he directed?" the story editor said with a certain shit-faced belligerency.

"And this is Jack's wife, Anne Weller, she's an actress."

Wallenstein beamed a woozy smile at Annie. "Ah yes, I believe I know your work," he lied transparently. Annie gave him a sickly smile and pointedly began leafing through the brochure. A story editor on a TV series usually had about as much to do with hiring directors as the script girl and even less to say about casting. Which, however, did not always prevent them from using the old casting-couch come-on.

"So . . . ah . . . how's it coming, Bill?" Bob said, a shade uneasily.

"Ah, the usual," Wallenstein grunted. "We've got a backlog of a lousy two scripts, and Irv wants me to knock out two myself this month, in between rewriting the crap we've got. Say . . . how about you doing one for us, Bob?"

"No way," Bob said. "I'm doing a TV movie, and I'm happily booked up."

"*Lucky bastard*," Wallenstein muttered. "Say, Mrs. Weller,

maybe you'd like to come down to the studio and maybe I could introduce you to Irv. . . ."

Oh, brother! Annie didn't bother to look up; she continued reading the brochure.

"Mrs. Weller—?"

"Annie—?"

"Huh?" Annie finally looked up. "What . . . ? Sorry. . . ."

"I said maybe you'd like to come down to the studio and I cound introduce you to my producer."

Annie smiled sweet-sour at him. "I'm tied up for the next few weeks, maybe I'll give you a call after that," she said, and pointedly went back to reading "TRANSFORMATIONALISM AND YOU!"

"*I'd* be glad to come to the studio and meet your producer," Weller said, giving Wallenstein a somewhat toothy smile as he put a slightly fey lilt into his voice. "You wouldn't happen to be bi, would you?"

Wallenstein cringed woozily. Bob looked aghast. Susan tried to choke back giggles. Annie kept reading, ignoring the unseemly scene.

"Good evening, ladies and gentlemen, and welcome to the Transformationalist Celebrity Center." Mercifully on cue a tall, gray-haired, almost regal-looking woman had mounted the small stage and was speaking into a small throat mike slung around her neck. She carried herself like an actress, and her cold, unblinking green eyes dominated the room.

"Uh-oh," said Bob, "here comes the commercial."

"For those of you who are here for the first time, let me tell you what this place is all about. Candidly, Transformationalism wants *you*!" She pointed at the center of the room (deliberately?), mimicking the famous Uncle Sam poster.

"And we want *you* to want Transformationalism! Transformationalism has centers throughout the United States and the Western world. As many as twenty million people have had some Transformational processing, but *this* is something *new*. John has decided that it's time to reach out directly to people like yourselves who mold public consciousness. Our goal is to *transform* the mass consciousness, to raise the total consciousness of the human race to ever-higher levels. *You* are in key positions to further this great cause, and *we* can transform *you* into happier, more successful, more highly conscious human beings. . . ."

As the dull rap went on, Weller's attention began to wander.

His eyes moved around the room, and way over at a corner table he thought he saw Marsha Henderson. He had known Marsha when she was in the children's-programming department at CBS, they had gotten along well, and now she was a hotshot studio executive overseeing a whole stable of prime-time shows. Maybe she'd remember me, he thought. Maybe this evening won't be a total loss.

"—to give you a real feel for what Transformationalism is about, our founder, the first Transformed man, the highest consciousness on the planet today, John B. Steinhardt."

The lights dimmed slightly, and a section of the wall behind the stage slid upward, revealing a giant-screen television set, a full five-by-seven job. A moment later the face of Steinhardt appeared on the screen, approximating the pose on the wall photograph and the brochures, but in full color. His complexion was ruddy like a Colonel Blimp, and his eyes were blue and somewhat watery. Looks a bit like a rummy, Weller thought.

"Hi, I'm John Steinhardt, and I've served my time in the entertainment racket too, written three hundred science-fiction stories and a shelf of books as long as your arm, you probably never heard of. But that was many moons and many transformations ago. I remember what it was like to crank out wordage at peon wages, working like a maniac just to survive, never even having enough time to think about why the hell I could never get anywhere, why a so-called creative person had to run at top speed all the time just to keep from slipping backward like the Red Queen. Yes, friends, I know your problems and your dreams and your frustrations all too well. . . ."

Steinhardt spoke in a gravelly voice with the speed of a used-car salesman doing a thirty-second commercial, yet Weller found the performance instantly capturing his attention. Steinhardt didn't come off like the usual slick guru; he had the ability to project himself as one of the boys, to give this video-tape spot the immediacy of beery barroom rap.

". . . The world moves so fast these days even those of us who fancy we're *leading* public consciousness can't keep up with the changes we're creating every day. Politics, media, the stock market, our own kids—zip, zip, zip, everything transforms itself faster than we can follow it. You have to be a moron not to realize that none of the old rules describe reality anymore. But a lot of otherwise smart people fall into the contemporary trap of believing that somewhere, somehow,

10

someone or something is going to give you a new set of rules and simple step-by-step instructions for putting Humpty Dumpty together again. . . ."

The man had energy. Weller saw that most of the people in the room were paying attention, Bob nodding over his drink, even Annie staring at the screen and toying unconsciously with the brochure. This good old boy sure could sell snake oil!

". . . Synanon, Arica, est, old-time religion, the world is full of outfits that claim they can navigate you through all the whirlpools if you'll follow their instructions. Well, not Transformationalism, I kid you not, friends. Transformationalism faces the truth, and the truth is that the human race has evolved to the point where ongoing change has become permanent. There will *never again* be a set of rules or a fixed consciousness that will make sense out of the world for you, because the only thing that's certain is that anything that describes how reality works today will be obsolete tomorrow. . . ."

Over in the corner Marsha Henderson was getting up and walking toward the ladies' room. Got to find some way of introducing myself before she leaves tonight, Weller thought.

". . . So I'm not trying to sell you rules or sets of perception or a static road map of reality but a series of processes designed to give you *Transformational Consciousness*, to free you from the trap of seeking permanent perceptions of *anything*, to evolve your minds into instruments capable of *riding the changes*, transforming the world as the world transforms you. So take a look around, ask questions, see if you don't want to get involved in what's happening here. In the meantime the drinks are on me!"

Steinhardt saluted the room with his hand in the manner of your genial host; off went the TV set, up came the lights, and onto the stage came the woman who had introduced the taped speech. "Upstairs we have demonstrations and detailed literature for those of you who are interested. Any of our people here will be glad to assist you."

She left the stage, and the room was immediately transformed back into a bar. Drinks were ordered, people resumed their conversations, and over in the corner Marsha Henderson was standing beside her table talking to her party.

"Well, what did you think of *that*?" Bob Shumway asked.

"He could sure move used cars," Weller muttered distractedly, looking over his shoulder at Marsha Henderson who looked as if she were preparing to make her exit. Can I just

11

walk up to her and say, "Hi, you remember me, I'm Jack Weller. . . ?"

"He was kind of impressive, wasn't he?" Annie said.

"Good line of bullshit," Wallenstein woozed.

"Well, it made some sense to me. According to this brochure they claim they can make you as psychically together as he is, and *he's* sure got charisma. If they can really teach you to *project* like that. . . ."

I could wander down the bar, maybe order a drink there, Weller thought. Then I casually turn, catch her eye. Say . . . pardon me, you look familiar, aren't you . . . ah . . . er. . . . That would be subtle enough; it wouldn't seem too gross. I really don't have anything to lose.

"They say this organization is worth hundreds of millions," Bob said. "And lotsa tentacles."

"There's no business like the guru business."

Yeah, I'll do it! Weller decided. He turned his attention back to the table and started to rise. "Uh, if you'll excuse me, I'll be right back. I have to—"

"Hello, I'm Tanya Blaine. May I join you for a moment?" A well-built redhead, about twenty-five, wearing a white blouse and black slacks, had appeared beside Weller and was already pulling up a chair.

"I'm one of your hosts at the Celebrity Center," she said, "and I'd be happy to answer any of your questions about Transformationalism." Her voice was professionally friendly, yet also coldly insistent, and her eyes had a repellent rodential quality. Here was a beautiful woman who gave off no sexual vibrations at all.

Weller tried to ignore her and continue his move, but Annie spoke up immediately, and he couldn't walk out on her line. "Just what do you do to . . . uh, process people?"

"We use many techniques," Tanya Blaine said. "Role reversal. Gaming it through. Block auditing. Meditative deconditioning. It's quite a complex technology, and we're developing more every day."

Marsha Henderson turned away from her party and began slowly walking toward the exit along the length of the bar.

"—demonstrations of some of the techniques upstairs—"

"—maybe later—"

Damn it! Weller thought, as Marsha Henderson disappeared through the door while Tanya Blaine and Annie continued to babble about Transformationalism. I've blown it. So near and yet so far, the story of my life.

12

"Well, it's been nice talking to you," Tanya Blaine said, finally getting up to leave. "If you want any further information, feel free to come upstairs. If you'll excuse me. . . ."

"*You're excused*," Weller snarled in frustration. Tanya Blaine's composure cracked for just a flash at the tone of his voice; she gave him a puzzled look, shrugged, then departed.

"What the hell was that, Jack?" Annie said angrily. "Why was it necessary to be rude to that woman?"

"*I* was rude? That woman barged in here and screwed everything up, and *I'm* rude?"

"What are you talking about, Jack? Screwed up *what?* What's gotten into you?" Annie was looking at him as if he were nuts, and Weller suddenly felt very foolish, and he knew that he would feel even stupider having to explain it in front of Wallenstein. There was a long tense moment of eyeball-to-eyeball silence.

Fortunately Wallenstein, even through his booze haze, managed to pick up on the vibrations. "If you'll excuse me," he said, "I've got to see a man about a turkey." And he lurched off in the general direction of the bar.

"Well?" Annie demanded.

"Yeah, Jack," Bob said. "What the hell was all that about?"

"Ah, I'm sorry," Weller said sheepishly. "I saw Marsha Henderson over there—you know, the production executive —and I used to be fairly friendly with her years ago when she was doing kiddie shows at CBS. I was about to go over and see if I couldn't subtly do myself some good when Little Miss Sunshine came along. Now Marsha's gone, and I've blown it."

"Gee, I'm sorry, Jack. I didn't know," Annie said.

"Of course you didn't," Weller said distantly. Their eyes met, clashed, looked away.

"At least you're learning, boy," Bob Shumway said. "You're learning. There'll be other chances, if you just put yourself in the way of them."

"Yeah," Weller said. "Yeah, you're right. Maybe this place does have its possibilities."

"Told you it did."

They sat around for another hour or so, having two more rounds of drinks and talking of the inconsequential. Bob Shumway spotted two more low-level producers, but Weller's energy, or his nerve, or both, were at too low a level for him to contemplate introducing himself, especially since these were people he didn't know.

13

They called it a night at about eleven, and the Wellers drove home largely in silence, Weller concentrating on his driving, thinking about his lost opportunity—if a real opportunity it had been—and Annie sitting quietly beside him, fingering the brochure she had taken from the table.

As they drove down Moorpark, past eerie empty Valley sidewalks, Annie finally spoke. "Maybe we ought to go back there soon."

"Yeah. I was thinking the same thing." There did definitely seem to be a goodly number of producers drifting through the Celebrity Center. No real heavyweights, maybe, but if we hung around the bar by ourselves, we might be able to strike up a conversation with someone who could put us onto some prime-time segment work. And that's certainly a step up from where we are.

"What did you think of it?"

"Seems like there are some useful people hanging out there," Weller said.

"I mean what they're doing there," Annie said. "Steinhardt. The processing."

Weller pulled up into their driveway and looked over at her quizzically. "Steinhardt? Transformationalism? I wasn't paying much attention to all that stuff. Why, were you?"

Annie seemed to draw into herself slightly. "Oh, not really. I looked through that brochure while that creep was trying to come on to me. Kind of interesting." She showed it to him as they left the car. "I brought it along, if you want to take a look at it," she said.

"Uh-huh," Weller mumbled, already thinking about tomorrow's shooting, another long, tiring, tedious, essentially pointless day of *Monkey Business*.

They got ready for bed quickly, and Weller began to drift off to sleep almost immediately thereafter, going through tomorrow's shooting sequence in his head, which for boredom certainly beat counting sheep. As he dropped off, Annie lay on her back beside him, staring at the ceiling and thinking her own private thoughts.

Two

Feeling tired but more emotionally up than he usually did returning home from work, Jack Weller closed the front door on the late-May heat and sucked up the first cooling blast of the air conditioning.

For once the shooting had gone smooth as butter, and he had even gotten a little ahead of schedule. A nice dinner, and then later maybe we'll go to the Center and see what we shall see.

They had gone to the Center four times in the last three weeks, and while no hard contacts had yet been made, they had become familiar-enough faces to talk casually with anyone there without seeming to come on too strongly. Weller hadn't seen Marsha Henderson again, but he had had a few brief and casual conversations with two prime-time producers and a director who was getting regular work on a cop series. He hadn't come on as an assignment-chaser to any of them, but at least now there were some potentially valuable people who knew who he was. And it seemed only a matter of time before some random talk drifted onto the subject of his directing career and from there to a "come see me at the studio." Maybe tonight would be the night.

He went into the living room to make a drink. Annie wasn't there. "Annie? I'm home!" he shouted in the general direction of the kitchen.

No answer.

"ANNIE?"

Nothing.

He went into the kitchen. No Annie. Nothing on the stove. She must be in the john, Weller thought. Then he noticed the note on the kitchen table, secured under the sugar bowl.

"Dear Jack," it said, "I've gone to the L.A. Transformation Center, and I won't be home for dinner. There's some salmon salad and vegetables in the refrigerator for you. Be back about eight. Love, Annie."

"Goddamn it!" Weller snarled, crumpling up the note.

What the hell is all this about? Reflexively, he looked in the refrigerator and saw a big mound of salmon salad on a platter, artfully surrounded by lettuce, tomato wedges, cucumbers, green onions, and endive. There was a small cruet of fresh salad dressing next to it. But his hunger had evaporated. What in blazes is she doing at the Los Angeles Transformation Center? Just what *is* the Los Angeles Transformation Center?

He closed the refrigerator door with an angry slam, stood there stupidly for a moment, then went into the bedroom, where, he remembered, Annie had been collecting a pile of Transformationalist literature on her night table over the past couple of weeks.

He had not been paying much attention to it at the time, but during their last two visits to the Celebrity Center, Annie had spent some time upstairs while he was making conversation at the bar and had come home with pamphlets and flyers stuffed into her pocketbook. They had gone upstairs together on their second visit to the center; the come-on hadn't impressed Weller much then, and he had paid no further attention to it. But come to think of it, Annie *had* seemed to be interested, now that he remembered it through hindsight's eyes.

They had been standing at the bar with an out-of-work production executive named Harry West. West had been standing on the unemployment line for a while, but he had produced four reasonably long-running series and had also done three or four television movies, so he seemed like a good guy to get to know. Sooner or later he would get another assignment, and when he did, having gotten friendly with him when he wasn't working could turn out to be a double advantage.

Unfortunately all West seemed interested in talking about was Transformationalism. "I've only had a few months of processing, but I can sense the changes in my consciousness already. They're really onto something, I tell you. I'd be in bad shape without it."

"*Really?*" Annie said. "You really feel different?" At the time Weller had assumed that Annie was just playing the game, that that look of earnest interest was part of the act.

"Well, when *Dog Days* got canceled, I found myself without regular work for the first time in years," West said. "The entire pattern of my life was fractured. Two weeks on the unemployment line and I was starting to panic without knowing why. Then I ended up here, went upstairs, and got talked

16

into trying some processing—gaming it through, role reversal, block-auditing, a little meditative deconditioning, just the basic stuff. After awhile I found my whole perspective changing. I was trying to cling to a previous pattern that had already been destroyed instead of riding the changes. That's where the panic was coming from. I was trying to cope with *now* in terms of *then*; my behavior reflexes were stuck in the previous reality."

"And now?" Annie asked.

"Now at least I'm riding the wavefront," West said. "I don't perceive myself as an out-of-work producer. I'm a creative individual with certain skills, certain contacts, a certain track record, all of which are intrinsic factors that I carry along with me as I evolve through the now. But I'm not trying to hold together an obsolete instantaneous personality, I'm open to my further personal evolution."

The Transformationalist jargon made West begin to seem like a brain-barble case, and it took a certain effort for Weller to refrain from pointing out that all this advanced consciousness hadn't gotten him another job. Fortunately Annie was carrying the ball, so he was able to just lay back and shut up.

"I've got a feel for what you're saying," she said, "but I'm not sure what you mean by 'instantaneous personality' or 'riding the changes' or any of that stuff."

West's eyes widened. "You mean you kids don't know anything about Transformationalism?" he said. There was something definitely unwholesome in his eager tone of voice as far as Weller was concerned.

"We've only been here twice," he said.

"Never been upstairs?" There was a bit of the school-yard pervert in West's expression now.

"Nope."

"Well, come on. You *must* let me show you."

"Okay," Annie said brightly, "I'd like to." Weller caught her eye with his protesting vibrations. Annie looked back at him with that cool, determined set to her eyes that always meant it would be less hassle to do things her way than to follow his own instincts which were now telling him that this Harry West was a blown-out turkey. But Annie apparently still felt that he was worth humoring, and maybe she was right; certainly they had nothing to lose.

So they let West lead them up a flight of stairs near the stage to a cool blue hallway with five open doorways leading off it, and they took the quickie tour.

In the first room a guy was hooked up to a complicated-looking brainwave-monitoring machine and a male Transformationalist was studying an oscilloscope as he read off a series of words. "Mother . . . prick . . . boss . . . faggot . . . communism . . . Adolf Hitler . . ."

"Block-auditing," West whispered. "Measures direct brainwave reaction to loaded words, locates areas of psychic blockage quickly and scientifically. . . ."

They just peeked into the next room, which was given over to tables of literature, some of it free, and some of it for sale. In the third room, a female Transformationalist was engaged in what seemed like a very weird argument with a well-dressed middle-aged man in front of a small audience.

". . . I won't do it, I don't like the taste," he said.

"You don't have to taste it if you take it all the way back in your throat," she said.

"It's too big. It'll choke me."

"If you haven't tried it, how do you know you won't like it?" she said.

"You're just saying that because *you* enjoy having it sucked."

Out in the hall a bewildered Weller turned to West. "What the hell was that?" he asked.

"The role-reversal game," West said. "She plays him, he plays her. I think they were role reversing a blow job." He grinned sheepishly. "They ran that on me once," he said.

"Jesus Christ!" Weller had to admit that it was funny, in a sardonic way, but it seemed to him that this kind of thing went too far, that there was a deliberately nasty element of humiliation in it, viciousness for its own sake.

But Annie burst into infuriating giggles. "*Very interesting,*" she said in a mock German accent. Weller felt a surge of genuine anger toward her. A feminist she was not, but she was not above occasionally using the stance to irritate him with a gamester feminine superiority. It was as if this role-reversal game was an outside sanction of the aspect of her personality that he found least pleasing, a wedge inserted into their solidarity as a couple, an unpleasant reminder that no male-female relationship was quite as unified as either mate would like it to seem. The fact that he took it more seriously than she did only added an extra edge of gall.

In the fourth room four people were being put through a standard psychodrama, apparently set in a Nazi concentration camp, with a man and a woman playing gas-oven victims and

18

two men playing guards. Even more vicious, Weller thought, but a lot less closer to home.

The fifth room was just a recruiter behind a desk laden with sign-up forms and charts explaining the cost of various processing package deals, and Weller managed to get them out of there fast.

The whole setup had seemed like just a reasonably slick con to Weller. He had naturally assumed that Annie, being an intelligent person like himself, had taken it the same way, that her approval of the blow-job role-reversal game had just been a superior female amusement of the kind he was used to, that her apparent interest in the psychodrama had been professional.

But now, sitting on the edge of their bed and leafing through all the Transformationalist literature she had brought home, he realized that he had been pigheadedly blind to what was going on, that he had taken old level-headed Annie too much for granted, which was an occasional nasty habit of *his*. It was always hard for him to realize that really different things could be going on inside her head when they were in the same situation together. Parties that he wanted to leave when she turned out to be in the process of making a connection, that single stupid orgy which had Olympianly amused him and disgusted her . . .

And now this. Every time they had been at the Center, he had been so absorbed in hustling people that he had just *assumed* that she was attracted to the place for the same reason; he had been too inside his own head to notice the way this Transformationalist garbage had been capturing his own wife's attention.

Some director you are, Weller! he thought, scanning the stuff Annie had been reading right there in bed beside him. Some husband, with your head stuck up your own asshole while your wife was drifting off into a whole other trip! What *was* this stuff that was doing this to her?

"TRANSFORMATIONALISM AND YOU!" the basic sales pitch, complete with a list of famous Transformationalists including a baseball player and a couple of minor actresses, but no one else Weller had ever heard of. A brochure on the Los Angeles Transformation Center, describing the processing that was available there. Something on a Transformational Desert Retreat. Little booklets on "BLOCK-AUDITING," "GAMING IT THROUGH," "ROLE-REVERSAL," and "MED-

ITATIVE DECONDITIONING." A flyer pushing TRANS-FORMATIONAL MAN, a science-fiction novel by Steinhardt, a $7.95 hardcover self-published by Transformationalism.

Weller disgustedly tossed the literature back onto the night table. I should've noticed, he thought. Goddamn, I should've noticed. He checked his watch. Five after six.

Might as well eat, he decided, going into the kitchen, taking the salad out of the refrigerator and sitting down at the kitchen table. As he picked at the food, he ran through the past week in his mind, and in retrospect, he realized that the signs had been there, if only he hadn't been too bloody self-involved to notice.

Last Wednesday, when Harry called Annie and told her she hadn't gotten that commercial part, there had been no tirade, no tears, no talk about looking for a new agent, just a dull acceptance of the inevitable. "Why am I even wasting my time going after commercials?" she had said. "Do we really need the money that badly? Am I really going to be discovered in some stupid perfume commercial? It's just playing out a tired old pattern, Jack, jumping at whatever dull crap I think might come my way. If I want to act in features, I should be going out for feature parts and stop kidding myself that the rest of it means anything."

That hadn't seemed like the usual old Annie, Weller thought. In the past that kind of attitude had been a signal of her boredom and frustration, foreshadowing things like a bout of swinging or an argument or a rap about going to New York and becoming a *serious* stage actress. But he had been too damned pissed off at how badly the shooting had gone that day to pay any real attention to it. And all the hamburgers she's been serving up lately, he thought. The Colonel Sanders Chicken. Annie cared about what she put on the table—except when she was signaling dissatisfaction with him, and then the slovenly meals were deliberate gestures, at least on a subconscious level.

Weller's appetite deserted him again. The half-eaten cold supper became an affront to him, a chastisement, a symptom of what had been going on, unnoticed, under his very nose, for at least two weeks. He put the remains back into the refrigerator, went into the living room, thought about making himself a drink, decided against it, put on the news, and immediately ignored the drone of the television set, pacing around the living room, into the hall halfway to the bedroom,

20

back to the living room again. Damn, damn, damn! Schmuck that you are, Weller!

The jargon that had crept into her vocabulary! Now, with the house echoing to her absence, he could see it. They were both forever grumbling about how much television they found themselves watching, but what had she said only two days ago . . . ? "It keeps pumping out the same cultural matrix, the whole country sucking up the same static brain-freeze, including the people who create it." It was what they had both thought of the tube all along, so he hadn't noticed that the words came from somewhere else.

What had she said when her friend Sally came over to bitch about her old man's reaction to her consciousness-raising group? "Game it through, Sally. Get into his head. He's confronting a discontinuity." And that business about the new network guidelines. "You've got to ride the changes," she had said, "not let them wash you over."

Oh, it's insidious stuff! Weller thought, perching for a moment on the arm of the couch. That Transformationalist jargon slides into what you're thinking about, and without realizing it, you start thinking in *their* terms, and then you're thinking *their* thoughts, thank you Marshall McLuhan! No wonder I didn't pick up on what was happening. They add a little this and a little that to your vocabulary, and while you're not looking, it soaks into your brain.

Weller turned off the television set angrily, hyperaware, indeed almost paranoid now, about being caught and programmed by random, unnoticed word patterns. He spent the next forty-five minutes in silence, trying to clear his mind for the inevitable confrontation ahead.

Finally he heard the rumble of Annie's Porshe pulling into the driveway. Vibrating with tension, he met her at the door.

"Hi Jack," she said brightly, looking cool, casual, and relaxed. "How was your day?"

"*How was my day?* Is that all you've got to say?"

She did a short take, a look of puzzlement. "Oh," she said, striding ahead of him into the living room, "you want to hear about my processing." She sprawled on the couch, kicked off her sandals, put her feet up on the coffee table. "Well, it was very interesting," she said. "They start you off on block-auditing, you know, they hook you up to a brainwave monitor, feed you key words, and map your brainwave reactions so they finally end up with what they call a 'psychomap' of—"

"Wait a minute. Wait a minute!" Weller shouted, standing in front of her listening to this goop, not knowing how to start, not even knowing precisely what it was that he wanted to start. "That's not what I want to know."

"Then what do you want to know?" she asked, looking up at him evenly. "What's the matter with you?"

Already feeling somewhat foolish and impotent, Weller hesitated, his body locked in tension, then collapsed onto the couch beside her. "What I want to know is why you went to the Transformation Center," he said slowly.

"To try some processing. They don't do it at the Celebrity Center."

Mentally Weller counted to ten as he studied Annie's calm, untroubled face. *Game it through*, he told himself sardonically. We're obviously not on the same wavelength, and it's at least as much my fault as hers. I can't let this alienation I feel escalate into a shooting match. But there was still that feeling of talking to a stranger as he said, with tense exaggerated patience: "What I want to know is why you wanted to try Transformationalist processing."

"Oh," Annie said. She thought quietly for long moments. "Well, as we both know, we don't exactly feel satisfied with our lives. We're still knocking on the same doors and getting the same wrong answers. So I figured, maybe it's not the world, maybe it's me. So why not give Transformationalism a try?" She looked at him, touched his cheek. "Oh, you're upset about dinner," she said. "I'm sorry."

"Why did you just go off and do it?" Weller asked. "Why didn't we talk about it first?"

"It was a spontaneous decision," Annie said. "Besides, I've sensed that you're not too receptive to the whole idea. Am I wrong?"

"No," Weller said. "I think it's all an insidious crock of shit."

Annie nodded. "That's what I thought. So I figured that if I went by myself and you saw it was doing me some good, then I could get you to try it."

"And you plan to continue?" Weller said unhappily.

"I've signed up for the four-week trial course," Annie replied.

"Oh shit!"

Annie reacted by drawing away from him, into a cool, annoyed, slightly superior shell, an attitude toward him that he had rarely experienced before from her. "I don't see why you're acting this way. I'm trying to do something to better myself. Just because you—"

"How much is this four-week course costing?" Weller blurted, and instantly wished he could take it back. It immediately put the whole thing on the tackiest possible level.

"For Chrissakes, Jack, it's only two hundred fifty dollars for eight sessions, which is a lot cheaper than the usual forty dollars for two sessions."

"Two hundred and fifty bucks! Forty dollars for two hours! For crying out—"

"This is certainly a new side to you, Jack Weller! I've never seen you as Uncle Scrooge before. Besides, it's my own money."

"Oh, now it's *your* money and *my* money, is it? What happened to *our* money? Besides, it's not that we can't afford it . . ."

"Then what *is* it?"

"I don't like watching my wife being ripped off by a scam like Transformationalism," he said. "Can't you understand that?"

"Now you're going to forbid me to spend my own money for my own good? From Uncle Scrooge to Porky Pig!"

"Damn it, don't try to run that number on me. You know I wouldn't forbid you to do anything even if I could, which I can't. I'm just trying to tell you in my chauvinist way that I think you're being conned, that this whole thing smells."

A curtain of clear, impenetrable tranquility descended across Annie's face. "Why are we shouting at each other?" she said. "Let's—"

"I know, I know, *let's game it through*." They both laughed, fracturing the tension at least temporarily if somewhat artificially.

"Just listen to us," Annie said. "Listen to you. Don't you really think you might benefit from—"

"*Please*," Weller said, holding up his palm resignedly. "Peace. But *please*."

"Okay," Annie said. "For now let's be civilized and just agree to disagree." She snuggled up to him, kissed him lightly on the lips. "No need to get so serious about it anyway, is there?" she said.

"If you ask me, Jack—and you *are* asking me—you're taking it too seriously," Bob Shumway said, sipping at his drink. "That's what women are like, is all."

23

They were sitting at the bar at the Celebrity Center, and for once Weller wasn't even noticing who was and who wasn't in the place. He felt spooky and strange discussing Annie with Bob. He had never been one to chew over his relationship with his wife with one of the boys, considering it a kind of treason to the primary loyalty in his life. But lately he had come more and more to feel the need to share his troubles with someone, particularly since Annie's growing obsession with Transformationalism was beginning to seem like the same kind of treason to the primary loyalty she owed *him*. So here I am, he thought, crying in my beer with Bob at the Celebrity Center while Annie is downtown being processed by the same people who run this place. It had a kind of awful symmetry to it.

"If you notice," Bob said, "it's women who tend to get involved in these mind games more than men. Est, Arica, Esalon, the ladies get involved in it first and drag the old man along for the ride. Why, you may ask?"

"Why, I may ask."

"Because while we're out working and home worrying about work, they've got all those empty hours to fill."

"That sounds like obsolete piggery to me," Weller said. "Besides, Annie isn't a bored housewife; she's got her career."

"Which at this stage consists mainly of sitting around waiting for her agent to call, right?" Bob said.

"Sorry. You can't sell me Annie as a victim of the bored-hausfrau syndrome."

"Okay, then look at women's lib—"

"You can't sell me Annie as a women's libber either."

"Well, then," Bob said out of the side of his mouth, "would you like to buy a duck? Seriously, Jack, what I mean is that women have been cut loose from their old housewifely roles, and they're thrashing around trying to figure out how the world works now, so they try their consciousness-raising groups, this guru, that guru, Transformationalism, whatever. It's a phase, it'll pass, you're taking it too seriously. After all, what's Annie really doing? Going to the L.A. Transformation Center twice a week. Big deal. Believe me, better that than she should be hanging around with bull-dyke storm-trooper feminists; that I have lived through."

"It's not the lousy two nights a week at the Center," Weller said, "it's living full-time with the deathless words of John B. Steinhardt." Only last night it had even penetrated the bedroom. . . .

24

Sexually, things had been screwed up lately to begin with. *Something* had been keeping them from making love on nights that Annie went for processing. Weller could not bring himself to make an approach. It seemed to him that Annie was putting out totally turned-off vibes, as if what went on at the center was absorbing the same kind of energy that went into sex, or as if his attitude toward the processing made him an object of distaste. Of course, it could also be that his resentment drove the possibility of intimacy from his psyche, but whatever it was, never-on-Tuesdays-or-Thursdays was becoming an iron-clad rule.

It was the first time in their marriage that their lovemaking had ritualized into pattern. Spontaneity was lacking, and when they did make love, Annie had trouble coming, or was punishing him by making it difficult, withholding her passion and moving her body from some deep inner distance. And Weller found himself having trouble lasting, or caring less and less about satisfying her. Sex had become an ambiguous battlefield.

Last night they had reached the pits. Weller found himself lying atop her, flesh moving on flesh in a strange, passionless silence, and all at once he perceived himself as a machine, pumping away on another machine to produce a mechanical response. On and on it went, in, out, in, out, like an oil-field pump doggedly working a dry well, and he felt an anger building within him, a trapped weariness not of the flesh.

Finally he got petulantly tired of waiting for her to come; he just didn't give a damn, and he let himself go in an orgasm that was a mere relief from sexual constipation, even an act of self-involved aggression. Then he rolled off her, and they lay side by side glaring at each other in the semidarkness.

Annie finally broke the awful silence. "Don't you think it's time we finally talked about this?" The very reasonableness of her voice made Weller sick inside. They had never gone into sexual postmortems before; they had never had to. *Talking about it* seemed to be a terrible confrontation with the possibility that something between them might be in mortal danger.

"We've really developed a block in the sexual area," Annie went on relentlessly. "I've completed my psychomap, so I know where my blocks are. Creative commitment. Motherhood. Competitiveness. But my processor hasn't uncovered any blocks in the sexual area, so it's got to be something *you're* generating, Jack. I really think you should begin

25

processing now. It's beginning to seem essential to our relationship."

"Listen to you!" Weller exploded. "Listen to how you're talking about *us*, like some goddamn Transformationalist textbook, like we were bugs under John Steinhardt's microscope! It's unreal, it's inhuman. Can't you see that it's this Transformationalism garbage that's causing the trouble in the first place?"

"Your *reaction* to Transformationalism is the problem," Annie said. "You're blocking on my Transformation. You feel threatened, left out, even jealous." Her calm, clinical voice spouting the damn jargon was totally, patronizingly, infuriating.

"How long is this crap going to continue?" Weller asked. "Aren't the four weeks up this Thursday?" After that, he hoped, things would get back to normal.

"I've signed up for the next six weeks at the regular rate," she told him.

"Jesus H. Christ!"

"I know you're blocking on this," she said in a tone of maddening sympathy, "but try to understand. I've completed my psychomap, so we know where my blocks are, but I've just started working on them with meditative deconditioning. If I had some disease, you wouldn't want me to stop going to the doctor as soon as it had been diagnosed. You'd want me to keep on till I was cured. Otherwise, what's the point?"

"What's the point indeed!" Weller snarled.

She laid her head on his bare chest. "Won't you give it a try?" she cooed softly. "Even without a brainwave monitor I can feel the block you have on my Transformation. A processor could map it in a single session. I'm transforming, Jack. I feel that I'm near the takeoff point where transformation becomes permanent and ongoing. I don't want to look back and see you trapped in the same old instantaneous persona while I keep growing. It would break my heart. Don't you want to know *why* you're reacting this way to my Transformation? Don't you want to get rid of the block?"

Weller stroked her hair, feeling sad, feeling shut out, and yet at the same time determined not to be sucked in. Poor baby, he thought, what are they doing to you? "I want to get rid of this whole business," he said. "Can't you just forget about it? For me. For us."

"No, I can't," she said. "Not even for you. Not even if I wanted to. If only you'd try it, Jack, you'd see what I mean. . . ."

26

"It's even screwing us up in bed," Weller told Bob Shumway softly.

Bob frowned sympathetically. "Have you tried putting your foot down?" he suggested.

"All the way to the floor."

"I mean making it a me-or-it proposition," Bob said.

A bubble of chill formed in Weller's gut. "I think maybe I'm afraid to do that," he said. "Besides, it's not the way I feel."

Bob's expression brightened artificially. He glanced around the room, bobbing his head at a couple of attractive women. "Well then, maybe a little fresh pussy," he said. "Make you feel livelier, and the smell of it on you just might put the old lady back on her toes."

Weller grimaced distastefully. "I'm not into playing those games," he said.

Bob Shumway laughed brittlely. He looked down into the depths of his drink. "You *do* have a problem, boy," he said.

"—no, Harry—"

"—I don't care—"

"—well, maybe I *should* look for a new agent—"

"—all right, if you want to talk—"

"—not till next Wednesday—"

Annie hung up the phone and walked back to the kitchen table where Weller was finishing up the remains of his big Sunday brunch. "What was that?" he asked.

"Harry," Annie said. "The actress who was cast in a refrigerator commercial they're shooting Tuesday got appendicitis, and he got me the assignment to fill in."

"Great."

"*Great?*" Annie said, taking a sip of coffee. "I turned it down."

"*What?*"

"I had to. I've got a processing session on Tuesday, and I would've missed it. Besides, I've decided that there's no point in expending energy on something as meaningless as a commercial."

Weller leaned back in his chair and stared at this strange creature his wife was becoming. "Don't you think this has gone far enough?" he said. "Now you're turning down a part because you don't want to miss a processing session and making up an artsy-fartsy rationalization. Don't you think you've lost your sense of proportion?"

27

"There's a rule that you're not supposed to miss a session unless you're sick," Annie said. "It would show a lack of commitment."

"What about your commitment to your career?" Weller snapped.

"To *what*?" Annie said. "To making meaningless commercials? To doing walk-ons in stupid television segments? It's all ego, Jack. I'm beginning to understand that now. It's nothing. A maximized person has to have a sense of commitment to something beyond ego-feeding games, to something of absolute value. That's why they have the rule, and it makes sense."

"Annie, Annie," Weller sighed, "can't you see what's happening to you? I'm really getting worried."

"So am I. About us. I think we're in danger of drifting apart."

Hearing her voice his own formless dread sent a pang of fear through Weller. Through career frustrations, swinging, arguments, occassional bad sex, money problems, it had never come to this. Breaking up had never before been a possibility in their universe. However bad things had looked, the assumption had always been that they would work through it together. At the same time, having it out on the table gave him a certain hope. Maybe she was finally ready to face up to what was going on. "It hurts me to hear you say that," he said, "but I'm glad you're at least facing the problem."

"Game it through from my side," Annie said. "I'm beginning to ride the wavefront. I'm working through my blocks, which means I'm changing, and I can't stop changing. I love you, and I look back and see you frozen in the same old static matrix. I'm moving, and you're standing still. How can we not drift apart? You've *got* to begin Transformational processing, Jack. You've got to open yourself up to the changes I've opened myself up to. Don't you see how your block on the subject is just a sign of how desperately you need processing? I don't want to have to travel on alone, but I've *got* to travel on. I don't want to lose you, I want you to share this with me."

Her voice was so tender, her face so sincere, and the thought of losing her to this thing such an ache in his chest, that Weller made the effort to see it through her eyes. What if it were really true? What if her personality really *were* expanding and deepening and he was fighting it out of some mingyness of the soul? What if it were *his* head that was screwed on crooked . . . ?

28

He wrenched his mind out of that mode, for that was exactly the kind of thinking they used against you. Doubt your own center and you were lost. For facts were facts, and the fact was that Transformationalism was doing real damage to Annie. If only their relationship were suffering, he might be able to persuade himself that it was some failing in himself, a lack of courage to dare the leap into the unknown. But here was Annie turning down a part, becoming indifferent to her career, maybe losing her agent. And none of that had anything to do with *his* head. Reality had to be dealt with and since she was incapable, he was elected.

"And if you had to choose between me and Transformationalism?" he said.

"Don't say that! You don't understand. It's not a matter of choice. I can't go back, I can't be the person I was any more than men can go back to being monkeys. You've got to come to me, there is no way on Earth I can go back to where you are. Don't fight it, Jack. Don't get left behind."

When Weller was ten, a group of his friends had gathered in the school yard to plan a childish shoplifting spree. His whole circle of close friends was in the group, and they all urged, indeed demanded, that he go along. But some moral stubbornness in Weller would not let him do it. They had called him chicken, faggot, ball-less wonder, everything boys can inflict on a kid whose courage is called into question. But Weller had stood his ground, and eventually they left him, alone and friendless in the empty school yard. They'll change their minds, he had thought, through gathering tears, but not really believing it. And eventually they had. After a few days they accepted him back into the group again.

But now Weller felt like that little boy standing alone in the school yard; knowing what was right and feeling forlornly abandoned for his goddamn virtue. It had passed then, and he told himself it would pass now, but a part of him didn't believe it. A part of him already felt that he might end up standing there forever, little boy lost in the empty school yard.

It had been a week since Weller had set foot inside the Transformationalist Celebrity Center. As Transformationalism's tendrils insinuated themselves deeper and deeper into the masonry of his marriage, the place had become an object of loathing to him. Indeed he had even begun to conceive a certain irrational dislike for the basically innoccent Bob

Shumway who just happened to have introduced them to the Celebrity Center.

But when Annie told him that her processor, Clyde Franker, was going to be there tonight and wanted to meet him, that was more than enough to make Weller willing to invade the enemy's ground. Face to face, no third-rate used-guru salesman can be a match for me, he thought, sitting at a table alone with Annie, nursing his drink and waiting for Franker to arrive. I'm a trained director and I'll show this prick up for the phony he is.

Annie sat there nervously, not touching her drink, looking sidewise at the entrance every few minutes. She hadn't really told him what this was about, only that Franker was interested in meeting him and that she felt it was important to her for him to agree. But that was all right with Weller; he didn't care what number the processor thought he was going to run, his adrenalin was flowing, and *he* was going to direct this little charade.

"Clyde! Over here!" Annie was waving at a tall, thin, gray-haired man in a tan suit who had just entered the room. He walked over to the table, nodded to Annie, handed Weller a somewhat moist palm.

"Hello, Mr. Weller," he said in a smooth bass voice, "I'm Clyde Franker." His hair was barbered to the point of sculpture, his aging skin looked pink and scrubbed, and his blue eyes radiated insurance-salesman frankness. He looked like a television announcer to Weller, and in fact Weller wondered if he might not have seen him in a local commerical or two.

"Annie's told me quite a lot about you, Jack," Franker said.

"Has she?" Weller said, glancing at Annie, whose eyes were shifting nervously back and forth between Franker and himself.

"Indeed," Franker said. "As her meditative deconditioner, I would naturally learn something of her external environment, of which you, of course, are a major part."

"Of course," Weller said evenly.

"And Transformationalism seeks to deal with the whole person, not just the mind in isolation," Franker said. "So we must concern ourselves with the objective life of the member in addition to the subjective mental reality."

Weller had deliberately let Franker's hype ramble on, waiting for the processor set himself up. Now, he thought, this nerd has gone just about exactly far enough. "It seems to me you've made a real mess out of Annie's objective life, *Clyde*,"

30

he said tersely. "You've fucked up her attitude toward her career, and you're on your way to fucking up our marriage."

"*Jack!*" Annie cried, a look almost of terror on her face. "Don't—"

But Franker cut her off with a raised palm, a cocking of his head, exhibiting a degree of control that Weller found frightening and infuriating. "Such is your perception, Jack," he said calmly. "But I hope we can alter that. First, because your attitude is seriously interfering with the progress of Annie's processing, and second, because we want to help you too."

Franker paused, as if waiting for a response, for the straight line.

Weller let him wait a good long time, breaking the rhythm. Finally he said: "You might as well make your pitch."

Franker hesitated, as if he had been thrown off-stride. But he recovered quickly. "Your attitude is not uncommon," he said. "We know what it is, and we know how to deal with it. Annie has achieved a significant degree of Transformational consciousness. You, without processing, are frozen in a lower evolutionary state. It's as if both of you had lived together as high-school graduates for years, and then suddenly Annie went to college and got an advanced degree. Surely you can see that that is an unstable situation. Annie's Transformation makes you feel insecure and threatened—which is not paranoia but an accurate perception of reality—and your lower state of consciousness acts as a drag on Annie's progress."

Franker paused, smiled ingenuously at Weller, got a fish-eyed stare back, then continued, trying to stare Weller down as he spoke. "Experiments have shown that for the first two years of life a human being and a chimpanzee can be raised as equal siblings. However, once the human begins to talk, to develop an inherently higher state of consciousness, such a relationship is no longer possible."

Weller hardened his stare. "Are you calling me an ape?" he said in deliberately threatening tones.

Franker broke eye contact and laughed, a canned sound, straight off a laugh track. "Quite the contrary," he said. "The difference between a human and an ape is intrinsic; an ape can never achieve human consciousness, so such a relationship is doomed. But it would be quite easy for you to evolve to Annie's level and thus make your marriage viable once more."

"All I need is a little Transformational processing, I suppose," Weller said.

Franker beamed. "Exactly," he said. "What's more, we could put Annie's processing in what we call a 'holding state' until you catch up, which could be done in a month—less if you cared to double up on your sessions. I'm sure Annie would be willing to make such a temporary sacrifice for the sake of your domestic harmony."

He turned to Annie and lowered his voice half an octave. "Wouldn't you, Annie?" he said, making it sound like a command.

"Uh . . . if you think it's best, Clyde," Annie muttered. She was like another person, withdrawn, fearful, submissive.

Weller felt a rising wave of protectiveness toward her. He felt his gorge rising; he had had just about enough. "Are you finished?" he said. "Are you quite finished?" Franker started to say something, but Weller cut him off with voice and hand. "Don't bother," he said. "I'm telling you. You *are* finished. You are quite finished. I'm warning you, there are recourses. In fact I've got half a mind to drag your ass out into the parking lot and—"

"Stop it, Jack! Stop it!" Annie cried. "You don't know what you're doing!"

"Shut up, Annie!" Weller said, surprising himself.

"Really, Mr. Weller," Franker said, "these juvenile threats—"

Weller half rose, his hands balled into fists. "Get away from us," he said. "Get away from this table. Get out of our lives. Leave my wife alone, or I'll screw your goddamn head off!"

Franker cocked an eyebrow at Annie. "This is worse than I thought," he said. "This will require environmental alteration."

"Clyde, *please*—"

"We'll discuss it at our next session, Annie," Franker said, rising.

He turned to stare at Weller with a cold, measured gaze. "Jack," he said, "you will neither believe nor understand this now, but you are a person gravely in need of our help. And you are going to get it. For a time you may think of us as your enemies, but that will pass. One day, you will be thankful. Try to bear that in mind."

"Clyde—"

"*At our next session, Annie,*" Franker snapped, cracking his cool for the first and only time, then departing.

Across the table Annie leaned on her hands, on the verge of trembling. "Why did you have to do it?" she whispered. "Why did you have to do it?"

Warm and weak with the backwash of adrenalin, Weller said, "Because I love you."

"I love you too, Jack, but I think you've made a terrible mistake. For both of us."

"What are you talking about?"

A shiver went through her body. "I don't know," she said softly, "but you shouldn't have acted that way. I just hope to God I'm wrong. . . ."

"Wrong about what?"

But she crawled into a totally uncommunicative shell and categorically refused to discuss it any further.

Weller sat in the living room glumly picking at a platter of cold cuts, waiting for Annie to get back from her processing session. For two days, ever since the confrontation with Franker, she had refused to do anything but make small talk, totally cutting off the subject of Transformationalism. It was a return to normalcy that seemed as abnormal to Weller as anything could be; a cold, unreal Disneyland simulacrum of their previous life together, as empty as wax-museum figures of themselves, as brittle as glass.

All during that ominous period Weller had endlessly contemplated forthrightly forbidding her to go to the Transformation Center, but he couldn't see how he could make it stick, and a part of him lacked the courage to disturb the artificial calm. This morning he had half decided to do it anyway, but Annie remained fast asleep until it was time for him to leave for work, as if anticipating the scene on an unconscious level and willfully cutting off the possibility.

So there he sat in the silent gloom, nibbling fitfully at his supper, waiting for some unnameable ax to fall.

Finally he heard the sound of Annie's Porsche rumbling into the driveway. Then a long, pregnant silence during which Weller stifled the impulse to meet her at the door; there was no point in putting more weight on this moment than it already had.

Then Annie walked into the living room, ashen, shaken, yet also projecting a manic determination. She walked across the room toward him like a zombie, without saying a word, and sat down on the edge of the couch beside him.

"Jesus, what's wrong?" Weller asked.

Annie looked down into her lap. "Clyde issued a life directive," she said in a tiny voice. "He gamed it through with Benson Allen himself, and they both made the decision."

33

"Life directive? What the hell are you talking about?"

Still not meeting his eyes, Annie said, "They've decided that it would be evolutionarily regressive for me to continue to live with you unless you begin processing immediately."

"*What?*" Weller hissed, barely containing the impulse to scream it in rage. "What the fuck are you talking about?"

Annie began picking at the cuticles of her right hand with the nails of her left. "If you don't begin processing and I continue living with you, they'll cut me off from Transformationalism. Totally. Disobeying a life directive would make me a regressive. They'd cut me off and it would be permanent—it's policy set by Steinhardt himself."

Weller's composure shattered utterly. There were no words to express the enormity, the outrageousness, the monostrosity of what she was saying; indeed he could not even feel an emotion that seemed adequate to the situation. An anesthetic curtain descended over the rational centers of his mind. All he could feel, all he could express, was total, blind rage.

"That does it!" he shouted. "I absolutely, categorically, totally forbid you to see any of these maniacs again! I'm going to get me a baseball bat, and I'm going to break it over Clyde Franker's fucking skull! Then I'm going to take what's left and shove it up this Benson Allen's ass till he's shitting splinters!"

Annie leaped up off the couch like a startled deer. "Stop it, Jack, stop it, stop it, stop it!" she screamed. "Don't you see that you're just confirming everything they've said? You've got to go for processing! You've just *got to!*"

Weller bounded off the couch and roared into her reddened, contorted face, blood pounding in his temples. "Processing! I'll give them processing! I'll process them into dogmeat! I'll kick their nuts down their throats!"

"You're raving like an animal!"

"I'm raving like an animal? You're gibbering like a lunatic!" All semblance of Weller's restraint was gone; his true feelings were exploding through him in a volcano of relief. He sucked up his own rage, welcoming it, almost enjoying it.

"I can't give it up! I'm not going to!"

"THE FUCK YOU WON'T!"

Tears began to form in Annie's eyes. Her face was an ugly mask of rage that only fed Weller's fury. "You're not going to tell me what to do with my life!" she screamed.

"I'm telling you, all right. *I'm goddamn well telling you!*"

"I won't listen to this, I won't take it!" Annie shouted, her

34

hands balled into fists. "If you won't come in for processing, I'm getting out of here this very minute!"

"BULLSHIT!" Weller shouted. "RAVING LUNATIC BULL-SHIT!"

"It's no bullshit, Jack," she shouted over her shoulder as she ran out of the living room toward the front door. "I mean it! It's real!" Opening the door, she said, suddenly more calmly, "I'll talk to you in the morning when maybe you'll have come to your senses."

Then she slammed the door hard behind her, leaving Weller transfixed in the center of the living room, his body frozen in rage, his mind roaring with emotional white noise.

He stood there for long moments trying to force rationality back into his screaming brain, trying to break the shocked, stunned, raging stasis that held him in emotional and physical paralysis.

But before he could move, before he could get himself to the door, he heard the engine of her car start in the driveway. Then, with a roar, the metallic scream of a missed shift, and the howl of an engine revving toward redline, she was gone.

All at once there was nothing but the echo of the Porshe engine Dopplering away to nothingness in the night, and the ghosts of their shouting voices filling the living room, reverberating in Weller's throbbing skull.

Three

Taking long gulps from his third mug of instant coffee, Weller paced the house, red-eyed and sour-stomached, trying to figure out what the hell to do. He had been up till nearly three the night before doing likewise. Call the Celebrity Center? Go to the L.A. Transformation Center? Call the police? No course of action seemed viable. Calling the Transformationalists would be pointless. What could he tell the police, that he had had a fight with his wife and would they please find her? Even if they would try to track her down, which they wouldn't, even if they could find her, which they couldn't, they certainly couldn't arrest her, and even if they did, it would certainly only serve to turn Annie more against him.

He had finally knocked himself out with sleeping pills, gotten maybe four hours of fitful, sweaty sleep, then called the studio and told them he had a stomach virus, and was barfing his guts out, and couldn't come into work. They had screamed and moaned about the schedule, but obviously they couldn't expect to get work out of a director who was puking every fifteen minutes.

He had chosen the stomach-virus schtick because that particular bug usually lasted about twenty-four hours, and he just couldn't believe that this nightmare wouldn't be over before tomorrow morning. This wasn't real. Annie hadn't seriously left him; they had just had a fight, and her car would be pulling into the driveway any minute now.

In the meantime there was nothing to do but wait and go slowly crazy.

Through the living room, down the hall, into the mocking, empty bedroom, a shudder, and back down the hall into the living room again. Maybe this will turn out for the best, Weller told himself. Maybe when she calms down and comes home, realizing what insanity this Transformationalism crap led her to last night, she'll come to her senses and this whole mess will finally be over. Sure, a scene like that is just what it takes to—

The phone began to ring.

Weller pounced on it like a hungry hawk. "*Hello?*"

"Jack? It's me." Annie's voice on the other end of the wire was leached of all nuance, any hint of emotion.

"Are you all right?"

"I'm fine."

"Where are you?"

"I can't tell you that."

"*What?*" Weller shouted, snapping right back into last night's screaming match. He quickly regained control; the worst possible thing he could do would be to pick up the fight where they had left off. "Never mind," he said, with some semblance of calm. "Just come home; all is forgiven."

"I can't come home, Jack," Annie's distant electronic voice said. "I'm not coming home. You have to come to me."

"All right, all right. Where are you?"

"I can't tell you that."

"Jesus—" Again Weller caught himself, forced an icy calm. "You're not making sense, Annie," he said. "How can I come to you if I don't know where you are?"

"I'm going to work for Transformationalism," Annie said, "and I don't know where they're sending me. I won't be allowed to contact you again, except maybe for a letter under certain circumstances. But Benson Allen himself has assured me that we can be together again as soon as you've had enough processing to evolve to my level. A month or two, Jack, that's all. This isn't good-bye, just so long."

"Annie! Get ahold of yourself! You can't—"

"I can't talk any longer, Jack, I have to hang up. It's a whole new life for me now, doing work that really matters. The only thing I miss is you. I hope you'll join me soon. . . . I love you, Jack, I do still love you."

"Annie—"

But the phone clicked loudly, and a moment later the dial tone was buzzing emptily in his ear.

Woodenly Weller hung up the receiver, forcing himself to think calmly, mechanically, logically. All his shouting, all his emotion, all his pleading had gotten him nowhere or worse than nowhere. I can't afford to kick and scream and throw things, he told himself. I've got to act. In order to be able to act, I've got to figure out what I can do.

The first step had to be to find Annie. Could the call be

37

traced? No, not after she had hung up, and the phone company wouldn't do it for anyone but the police anyway. Is it time to call the cops?

Wait a minute!

"Benson Allen himself has assured me that we can be together again . . ." she had said. Allen is the head of the Los Angeles Transformation Center. He'd damn well know where she was.

And I'll damn well get it out of him! Weller told himself. He felt the panic that he had been holding back receding, his artificial calm firming up into cold resolve. All I have to do is get it out of Allen. They can't seriously believe that they can get away with this kind of crap. All I have to do is call his bluff.

The Los Angeles Transformation Center was a small converted hotel in Hollywood, just south of Sunset Boulevard and just west of Cahuenga, not too far from several studios. A fading tan stucco building eight stories high with a dirty red-tiled roof; a brand of cheap hotel common to the area. In the Golden Days of Hollywood it would have been in good repair and filled with bright, handsome young people slinging hash and waiting on tables while they tried to break into the movies. These days such places were inhabited by sleazy failed pornographers, down-at-the-heels hippies, homosexual hustlers, the flotsam and jetsam of seedy downtown Hollywood.

This was definitely not a location chosen to attract the elite, and from the outside the building had none of the tone and class of the Celebrity Center. A rather crudely lettered sign above the entrance was all that identified it as the "Los Angeles Transformation Center." And Weller had to park on the street, for the Center had no parking lot—usually a sign of a second-rate operation in car-dependent Los Angeles.

Sleazo! Weller thought as he walked up the short flight of stairs and through the unlocked outer door.

He found himself in an open area that had been the hotel lobby. There were benches along three walls, the lime-green paint was beginning to peel and crack, and there was the inevitable giant photo of John B. Steinhardt hung high on the left-hand wall. There seemed to be no central air conditioning, for the lobby was hot and sticky. About a dozen people were sitting around the lobby—mostly under forty, mostly tackily dressed, a lot of long hair and an unusual amount of bad skin for Southern California. Hollywood losers, Weller thought contemptuously.

A steel fence had been erected across the lobby, cordoning off the flight of stairs and the bank of two elevators that gave access to the rest of the building. Beside the only gate in the fence was a desk with a burly young man behind it, dressed in the informal Transformationalist uniform of white shirt and black pants and presiding over a clipboard, piles of Transformationalist literature, and a house telephone. Two other big bozos, similarly dressed, lurked by the elevators.

As far as Weller was concerned, the placed reeked of sleaze and grease, but was not without an aura of tight security, which made him wonder whether it was really going to be so easy to bull his way through to Benson Allen. Certainly force was out of the question.

Weller approached the man behind the desk. He was about twenty-five, hawk-nosed, with short black hair, and a redneck–cop look around the eyes. "Yes, sir," he said with the cold politeness typical of the Los Angeles police. "May I help you?"

"I want to see Benson Allen," Weller said.

"Do you have an appointment?"

"Not exactly."

"*Not Exactly?*"

"Mr. Allen may be expecting me. My name is Jack Weller."

The man behind the desk looked through some papers. "No," he said, "there's nothing here. If you'll tell me what it's in reference to, I'll direct you to the proper official. Mr. Allen sees no one without an appointment."

"My business is with Allen, it's a private matter," Weller said. "He'd better see me."

The Transformationalist frowned. Something cold, hard, and threatening seemed to exude from his unwavering eyes. "That's a regressive attitude," he said.

"I don't care what kind of attitude it is," Weller said. "Allen had better see me, and he had better see me now. Use that phone and tell him I'm here."

"Transformationalism does not respond to threats," the man behind the desk said somewhat loudly. The men by the elevators came to alert.

"Let me put it this way, Charlie," Weller said. "I know that Allen will want to see me, and I know he's going to be pissed off at you if you don't tell him I'm here." He paused,

39

picked up a certain wavering of the Transformationalist's assurance, and then, off the top of his head said: "And *John* isn't going to like it either." And gave the seated man a disdainful stare of his own.

Surprisingly the man almost immediately broke off eye contact, and his whole demeanor seemed to change. He picked up the phone. "Benson Allen," he said. Pause. "Benson? This is the desk. There's a Jack Weller to see you. He doesn't have an appointment, but—" Another pause. Then he hung up the phone and looked up at Weller with respect, submissiveness, perhaps even a little fear.

I wish I knew what I just did so I could do it again, Weller thought as the Transformationalist at the desk signaled to one of the men at the elevators.

"Karl, show Mr. Weller to Benson Allen's office." Karl opened the gate for Weller and closed it behind him like a hotel doorman.

Whatever I did, it sure worked, Weller thought as he was led to the elevator. He began to feel a little more on top of things. Instinct, so far, had served him well.

The elevator went all the way up to the eighth floor. Here the hallways were paneled in walnut, there was dark blue plush carpeting on the floor, and the light came from modern fixtures set flush in the ceiling. Executive country, for sure— a sharp contrast to the peon region below.

His escort opened a door at the end of the hall and closed it behind him with a flourish as Weller stepped inside.

Benson Allen's office had a rich patina of Peter Max hippie elegance. The ceiling was tented with emerald velvet. A huge Persian rug covered most of the floor. There were two big corner windows. There were large op-art paintings, all psychedelic swirls and zigzags of primary colors, festooning the peach-colored walls. There were two low white plush couches and three leather beanbag chairs. Allen's desk was a kidney-shaped swirl of loud paisley patterns. It was all too much, too much like a set, too unreal.

The man behind the desk wore a fancy paisley velvet shirt and white pants. Allen had very carefully styled shoulder-length blond hair, and soft, warm puppy-dog eyes set in a beachboy face gone ever so slightly to fat. He looked about thirty-two—a rich, aging flower child. It was hardly what Weller had expected.

"Sit down, man," Allen said in a casual, all-too-mellow voice. "I knew you had to make it here."

Hesitantly Weller perched uncomfortably on the edge of a beanbag chair in front of the desk. "I'll bet you did," he said. "Where is my wife?"

"Everything's cool, Jack," Allen said pleasantly. "She's at one of our residential dorms. She's fine. No need for hostile vibes."

"Then if you'll just give me her address, I'll leave."

Allen leaned back in his chair. He smiled softly. "You know that's not in the program," he said.

"Surely *you* must know you can't get away with this," Weller snapped. "I'm her husband. I'll . . . I'll go to the police. I'll sue you. . . . I'll. . . ."

Allen laughed, an infuriatingly mellow sound. "We're a very heavy outfit," he said. "Man, you think we haven't had to deal with this trip before? You think we don't have lawyers telling us what's cool? You think we would do this kind of thing if we didn't know it was legal? Try to sue us, try the police, if you want to run that program. No bad vibes in that. Your old lady is an adult, and she left of her own free will."

"I'll go to the newpapers," Weller said. "I'll go to the district attorney. I'll have your whole organization investigated." But his words sounded futile, even to him.

Benson Allen looked at him sadly, almost sympathetically. "Be real, man," he said. "You can't threaten us. We're too heavy. We're too powerful. We're legally righteous. If you can get into this life situation instead of running paranoia scenarios, then we can rap about what can *really* be done."

"All right," Weller said. "For the moment I'll let you do the talking."

"Groovy," Allen said. He reached into a drawer, took out two manila folders, and laid them down on the desk top. Leafing through one of them, he said, "Anne Weller has had five weeks of processing. Her psychomap shows blockages in creative commitment and career satisfaction, which externally translates into dissatisfaction with an acting career that hasn't made it and probably wouldn't result in eptifying her consciousness even if it did." He put down the folder and smiled at Weller. "Good news for you, Jack," he said.

Weller looked at him blankly.

"Nothing in here about blocking on *you*, man," Allen said. "Most of these kind of cases show heavy marital dysfunction. But according to the psychomap a fully transformed and eptified Anne would still love you. The relationship would not dissolve. Other things being equal."

41

"So what the hell is all this about?" Weller said. "If that's what you believe in your vast wisdom, why won't you tell me where she is?"

Allen began leafing through the other folder. "Because according to your file—"

"*My file?*" Weller shouted. "You've got a goddamn dossier on *me?*"

"For sure," Allen said mildly. "We always start one when somebody signs up at the Celebrity Center. And of course we've added the data we've gotten from your wife's processing. We have to be into our members external environment if we're going to epitify their lives, don't we?"

"Of all the—"

"*Now dig it,*" Allen said more loudly, overriding Weller without cracking his facade of sympathetic cool. "Your file show's that you're a heavy regressive influence on Anne. You've got a very negative attitude toward Transformationalism which you've been laying on her. Your head is full of blocks. You've got a low career-satisfaction index, so we can predict that you would get down on her if her satisfaction index started to go up. And of course this factor comes down very heavily on the evolving state of her Transformational consciousness. In your present state it just bums you out. The relationship could only stabilize if you dragged her back down to your level."

Allen paused, leaned forward, gave Weller a warm, concerned look. "Or," he said, "if we brought you up to her level."

"Which brings us back to square one," Weller said.

"We never left it," Allen said. "You can dig that our first concern must be for Annie, our current member. We can't let you bring her down to your regressive level of consciousness. But we also care about *you.*" Again he fingered Weller's dossier, probably for sheer effect.

"Jack, you've got heavy problems," he said. "Can't you see that? Your work is bumming you out, you can't find a way to change your karma, and you probably couldn't dig it even if you did. Game it through, man: what if your problem isn't with your luck but with your head?"

"What?"

"Get behind *why* you're afraid to try Transformational processing," Allen said. "Your blocked personality is what's afraid because it doesn't want to be transformed into something else, it's afraid of dying in a way. Man, it's the most common

42

syndrome there is; your kind of hostility to processing almost always turns out to be a badly blocked personality matrix fighting to keep control of your head."

"What a crock of shit!" Weller said. "Because I don't want you people messing around with my mind, I'm crazy?"

"No," Allen said, "because you're crazy, you don't want us to process your mind. I mean, look at your scenario. You want to get back together with your wife. Now the only way that is going to happen is for you to agree to processing. Run whatever number you want, you're gonna find that out. So you've got everything to gain and nothing to lose, but you still fight it. Now is that *really* having your head on straight?"

"*Nothing to lose?* What about a little thing like money?" But that rang falsely to Weller even as he said it. I wouldn't spend a few hundred dollars to get Annie back? Can I kid myself that that's really the reason?

"Okay, man, if that's your cop out, I'm going to take it away from you," Allen said. "I'll show you that you're your only enemy in this scenario. I'll authorize a free introductory lesson and demonstration for you. It usually costs fifteen dollars, but you can be my guest."

Weller felt as if he were slogging through glue. Threats had proven useless, and now Allen was working on *him*, being so totally helpful, benign, and sympathetic that there was no way of coming on hostile without feeling like a nerd and an ingrate. But in the process he was not only closing off every possibility save his agreeing to be processed, but rolling out the red carpet to Room 101. Why *don't* I just play it their way? he asked himself. If it's not going to cost me any money, what's really stopping me?

He studied Allen's benign, assured, puppy-dog face, and he had the sudden urge to smash it with his fist. This son of a bitch thinks he has me trapped! he thought. He's sure he's in control. And that, Weller realized, was why he couldn't agree to processing. If Allen were able to dictate this first step, *that* was frightening. Weller finally had to admit that he was afraid of being processed by Transformationalism. Annie, after all, was an intelligent, perceptive, reasonably together person, and look what had happened to her once they got their hooks in. And that business about how he felt about his career had cut too close to the bone, had given him a taste of his own potential vulnerability.

"Well, what do you say?" Allen said. "You've got nothing to lose."

43

"The first shot is free, kid, is that it? The price only starts to go up once you're hooked."

Allen sighed. "That's really lame," he said.

"*Is it?*" Weller snarled.

"You really *are* resistant, Jack," Allen said, perhaps with a hint of petulance.

"You bet your ass I am!" Weller said. "In fact, that's exactly what you're betting. We'll see what the police really have to say about this! And the district attorney, too. How do I know you didn't really kidnap her? How do I know you didn't have a gun to her head when she called me?"

"Oh wow," Allen said, with a disdainful little laugh.

"*Oh yeah?*" Weller said. "Seems to me if I made such a charge, they'd at least have to investigate, and then they'd have to question Annie, and if you didn't produce her then, you'd be obstructing justice." It began to sound plausible to Weller himself.

"Oh man," Allen said softly, "you've got to run it all the way up that blind alley, don't you? Maybe you'd feel better if you went ahead and gave it a try."

"Don't think I won't!"

"I can see you will," Allen said benignly. "That's cool. Maybe it's for the best. Just remember that there won't be any hard feelings. My offer will still be there when you're ready to take it. We want to straighten you out, Jack, and we will. We will."

Weller stood up. "Your last chance, Allen," he said. "If I walk out of here now, I go straight to the police."

Allen just smiled, opened his arms, and shrugged.

"Good-bye, Mr. Allen," Weller snarled, heading for the door.

"Not good-bye, Jack," Allen said. "Just . . . later."

Steaming with rage and frustration, Weller slammed the phone receiver back onto its cradle. The police had given him the politely sympathetic stone wall, and now the district attorney's office had in effect told him to get lost. When it had come down to it, Weller had been morally and psychically incapable of feeding either the police or the district attorney's office a cock-and-bull story about a kidnapping. It had sounded all very well as a threat in Benson Allen's office, but when he got the cool, authoritative desk sergeant on the phone, he found himself telling that impersonal voice the unvarnished truth. The thought of inflaming the Los Angeles police with a phony kidnapping charge was more than he could contemplate in a real-life situation.

"When did you last see your wife?"

"Last night."

"Did she give any indication that she was being held against her will?"

"No, but I have reason to believe she's been brain-washed. . . ."

"Look, Mr. Weller, to tell you the truth, we get lots of calls like this these days. Not just about Transformationalism, either. Est, the Jesus Freaks, the Moonies, people get involved with them, and their wives or their husbands or their parents don't like it, so they call us. If you're talking about an underage minor, sometimes we can do something, consider them a runaway and at least try to track them down. But when it's an adult, it's just not our business. No crime has been committed. You don't have any evidence of a crime being committed, do you? Mail fraud? False advertising? Anything?"

"No, but—"

"Well then, I can't help you. I'm sorry."

"But this whole Transformationalist racket—"

"If you think you've got a consumer-fraud case against them, you can try the DA. Okay?"

Weller had hung up, feeling, in a curious way, as he had in Benson Allen's office. The police too had a procedure for cutting off your avenues of possibility, for forcing you to accept their interpretation of the situation, for controlling your possible responses. Any bureaucracy interfaced with the individual on its own terms, and there didn't seem to be any way to get it to accept your viewpoint on reality.

So he had tried the district attorney's office, and what he had gotten there was even worse. Yes, we have had many complaints of this sort against Transformationalism. Yes, we have looked into their operation. Three times in the last five years. No, we have never uncovered grounds for prosecution. No, we won't start another investigation. Why? Because we've already wasted tens of thousands of dollars of the taxpayers' money investigating Transformationalism. Because getting involved in another investigation would be a political liability, Mr. Weller. Because we have no evidence of any illegal activity, and neither do you. Good-bye, Mr. Weller.

It seemed to Weller that there had been something else going on too, some strange undertone of uneasiness in the voice of the assisstant DA, as if he were slightly afraid to even talk about the case, as if the line he was handing Weller had been the Word passed down from on high. Could Transformationalism have political connections at City Hall?

Well, maybe that's an angle to try, Weller thought, dialing the number of Johnny Blaisdell, a press agent he had had some dealings with. I've done Johnny a few favors, maybe he can do me one.

He got Blaisdell on the line, and laid out the whole story. Johnny started out interjecting questions, making little comments, like his usual bouncy self, but before Weller was more than half through, he was talking to dead silence on the other end of the line.

"So what do you want me to do, Jack?" Blaisdell asked dubiously when Weller had finished.

"Call up some of your press contacts. Have someone from the *Times* come and get my story. Maybe instigate a little good old-fashioned muckraking reporting."

"Oy," Blaisdell said, "I love you like a brother, Jack, but you don't know what you're asking. Better you should ask me to plant some gossip-column items on the sex lives of Mafia dons."

"What's that supposed to mean?"

"It means," Blaisdell said, "that presswise Transformationalism is poison. Let a line about them appear in print, and they sue—the paper, the writer, the writer's doctor's dog. It doesn't even matter if you can prove what you're saying, they just nibble you to death with court costs on nuisance suits. There isn't a reporter in town who will go near them."

"You're kidding," Weller said. "You've got to be kidding."

"Har-har," Blaisdell said in a sepulchral voice.

"You can try. . . ."

"Yeah, I can try," Blaisdell said. "But don't expect me to succeed. Like they say, don't call me, I'll call you. And Jack—?"

"Yes?"

"Be careful, man, be really careful," Blaisdell said, and hung up.

Weller collapsed onto the couch. That son of a bitch Allen was right, he thought. The police won't help, the district attorney won't do anything, and even the press won't go after them. He felt small, powerless, and isolated—one man going up against a huge monolith of an organization without a friend or ally. Without even Annie to back him up.

But the other side of that sense of impotence was frustrated rage, and he flipped back into it almost immediately. Fuck you, Transformationalism! he thought. Fuck you, Benson Allen! Fuck you, John B. Steinhardt! You're not going to do this to me, not to Jack Weller, you don't!

He picked up the phone. There was still one more thing to try—Wally Bruner, his lawyer. Wally was a sharp guy; maybe he could come up with a legal angle.

"Wally? Jack Weller. Look, I feel like I've told this story a million times already, so pardon me if I give it to you as quickly as possible."

"Shoot, Jack," Bruner said crisply. "You really sound upset."

"I am. To make it short, Annie has gotten involved with Transformationalism. They've got her brainwashed. They ordered her to leave me if I wouldn't join the club, and she did. I don't know where she is, I have no way of contacting her, they won't tell me, and the police and the district attorney have told me to get lost. What the hell do I do?"

There was a long silence on the other end of the line; Weller could all but hear the gears grinding in Wally's head. He'll think of something, he's got to.

"Well," Bruner finally said, "if the police won't get involved and the DA won't get involved, charges against Transformationalism are a legal dead end."

"There's nothing I can do?" Weller asked plaintively.

"I didn't say that, Jack. There is one thing we can try, but I warn you, it's heavy."

"What could be heavier than what's already going on?" Weller said. "Let me have it."

"Speaking as your lawyer," Bruner said, "I'd advise you to file divorce proceedings against Annie on the grounds of abandonment."

"*What?*" Weller shouted. "That's crazy? I'm trying to get her back, and you tell me to divorce her?"

"I'm talking as your lawyer," Bruner said. "If you filed against Annie, sooner or later she'd have to appear in court or let the divorce go through uncontested. It's the only way I know of to force her to contact you."

"And then what?" Weller snapped. "I drag her into court against her will, and that's supposed to convince her to come home? That's crazy, Wally. She probably wouldn't even show up. And what would I have then—a divorce I didn't want."

"I can only give you legal advice, Jack," Bruner said. "I'm a lawyer, not a shrink."

47

Weller found himself folding up inside. He wanted to scream and run around the house breaking things. He wanted to go after Benson Allen with a sawed-off shotgun. He wanted to cry. And he knew that all of those impulses were just hallmarks of stupid, trapped, impotent frustration.

"Oh shit, Wally," he whispered, half sobbing, into the phone. "Oh shit. . . ."

There was dead silence on the other end of the line. Had his own lawyer hung up on him too? "Wally?" he demanded. *"Wally?"*

"Huh . . . ? Oh sorry, Jack, I was thinking, trying to remember a name. . . . Bailor, yeah, that's it. Garry Bailor!"

Bruner's rising voice was a life preserver in a hopeless sea. "Who's Garry Bailor?" Weller asked hopefully. "What can he do?"

"I'm not sure what he can do," Brunner said, "but he *is* an expert in these matters, a 'deprogrammer,' he calls himself. He works mostly with parents of kids who have been gobbled up by the Moonies or the Jesus Freaks, I think, puts their heads back together, so to speak. But I think he may have done some work with refugees from Transformationalism too."

Weller rose off the couch on a wave of hope. Good Lord, he thought, there's an expert in fighting these bastards! A hired gun! Who would've thought it?

"That's beautiful, Wally," he said. "I love you. Can you set up a meeting?"

"I should warn you that this guy is no philanthropist. He'll cost you. It'll cost you a hundred bucks just to talk to him."

"Screw that," Weller said. "Can you arrange a meeting for tonight?"

"I think so," Bruner said. "You don't mind if I'm not there?"

"Huh? I guess not. But why—?"

"Let's just say that Bailor's operations walk a very thin legal line," Bruner said. "In fact, let's say that he walks both sides of it. As a lawyer there are certain things it's better for me not to know about. If that doesn't scare you off . . ."

"Hell, no!" Weller said. Bailor sounded like just what the situation called for, and as far as Weller was concerned, the dirtier he played the better. "Do it, Wally," he said, realizing that he was committed to going all the way, and feeling better about himself for it than he had all day. If there were anything that one man could do, he was going to do it, and to hell with legal niceties. Benson Allen, watch your ass!

* * *

The address that Bruner gave Weller for Garry Bailor turned out to be a seedy-looking apartment house in southeast Hollywood—three stories of motel-like apartments around a grim looking concrete central court. According to directions Weller arrived promptly at eight o'clock and rang the bell marked "Larry Jonas." He was buzzed into the building, climbed two flights of stairs, and knocked three times at the door to apartment 3C, feeling a bit dubious about all this hugger-mugger.

A wiry man in his late thirties answered the door. A thin, angular face, suspicious eyes like hooded ball bearings, and a strange, anachronistic military haircut, almost a crew, straight out of the 1950s. Again following Wally's bizarre instructions, Weller handed him a check for one hundred dollars and said, "I'm Jack Weller."

"Garry Bailor," the man said, pocketing the check. "Come on in."

Weller followed Bailor into a small living room furnished in standard Southern-California-motel modern. There was no television set, no radio, and the only thing on the wall was an awful floral painting that obviously came with the apartment. No personal touches at all; the place looked totally unlived in.

"Sit down," Bailor said. "Have a beer. Included in the price."

Weller sat down on the slablike couch as Bailor disappeared into the kitchen and came back with two open cans of Coors. He handed Weller one can, took a swallow from the other, and sat down on the couch beside him.

"Okay, Mr. Weller," he said. "What's the mission?"

Weller was beginning to feel this was a mistake—the phony name on the bell, the tacky apartment, the cans of beer, it all added up to a total effect that did not exactly inspire his confidence. "Do you . . . uh, live here, Mr. Bailor?" he blurted.

"Hell, no, I don't live in this shithole," Bailor said. "But in my business you don't want clients or anyone else to know where you live. It's smart to keep your personal life in another drawer, so to speak. You can't help making enemies in this business, you know."

"Just what *is* your business?" Weller asked. "Wally didn't make that too clear. . . ."

"I'm a deprogrammer," Bailor said. "You won't find me in the Yellow Pages. There are a lot of people these days making money by programming people's minds. I make mine by

49

eradicating that programming to order. The culties brainwash, and I debrainwash, you might say. It keeps the money in circulation."

Weller found Bailor's up-front mercenary attitude disquieting. It did not exactly inspire trust. "Uh . . . what about your qualifications?" he asked. "Are you a trained psychiatrist?"

Bailor laughed contemptuously. "There isn't a shrink in the country who can do what I do," he said. "Try to find one! My qualifications? My training? My man, reality was my training. I've been through them all. I've been a Scientology auditor, I've worked for Esalon and Arica and EST, I've flunkied for all the scams. Each time I thought I was going to make my fortune, and each time I found out that the *organization* was making the real money and the lower-level people like myself were only marks of a slightly higher quality. So I found myself broke and with experience and training in the various mindfuck games. It was either this or set myself up in my own cult, which seemed like an overcrowded field. There are too many outfits in the programming racket, but deprogramming is a sellers' market, in case you haven't noticed."

"That all sounds pretty cold-blooded . . . ," Weller said.

"It's a cold-blooded business," Bailor said. He shrugged. His expression softened slightly; he seemed almost embarrassed. "Of course, there is another side to it," he said. "As a deprogrammer I sleep better at night knowing that I'm freeing people's minds instead of enslaving them. They take your bread, and you're hooked, I take your bread, do a job, and get out of your life. And the money is good enough so that I can do my untroubled sleeping between silk sheets. But you're not paying your money to hear my life justifications, Mr. Weller. What about your problem?"

Weller found Bailor's stark candor somehow a little more reassuring, though there was still a certain cynical edge to the scene that made him nervous. "Wally probably told you something about it," he began.

"Yeah," Bailor said. "Your wife got programmed by Transformationalism. What I gather, she got a life directive to leave you, and she split. Pretty standard stuff."

"*Standard stuff?*" Weller said.

"You think not?" Bailor said. "The Jesus Freaks, the Moonies, Scientology, Transformationalism, Nichiren Shoshu, they all run some variation on this 'life-directive' number. Hell, the Communist Party was doing it in the thirties. So relax, you're not alone; it isn't all a plot concocted specifically against you."

"You've been successful in this kind of situation before?" Weller asked hopefully. "With Transformationalism?"

"A few times," Bailor said. "A lot easier with minors, my main business. There you can just have the parents snatch them, and then I kind of get inside the programming and destroy it from within. I mean, you name the cult, I know as much about it as the people working the scam."

Weller took a big slug of beer, feeling much better now. "So you think you can deprogram Annie?"

"I can deprogram anyone," Bailor said flatly. "Kids are a snap because you've got them in parental custody. With an adult it's trickier because holding them against their will is kidnapping. So we have several possible approaches in your case. I can pose as a friend and begin the deprogramming on the sly, or you could have your wife declared mentally incompetent and hold her that way, or if none of that works, I might be willing to risk the kidnapping charge and deprogram your wife against her will, trusting that she'll thank me later. For a substantial extra fee, of course."

I'd risk that if I had to, Weller thought. He felt quite confident now. This guy really seemed to know his stuff, his self-confidence was impressive, and the fact that he seemed cynical and hard as nails about it might be repulsive but also seemed like the kind of strength that was needed for the task.

"Okay, Mr. Bailor," he said. "As far as I'm concerned, you've sold me. You're hired. What do we do now?"

Bailor seemed to measure him with his eyes. "There's the matter of my fee . . ." he said.

"How much?"

Bailor looked at Weller speculatively over the top of his beer can. "Sounds like this is going to take a couple of weeks," he said. "Three grand for the complete deprogramming, fifteen hundred up front and fifteen hundred on successful completion."

"Jesus," Weller said, "that's a lot of money."

"So is what Transformationalism sucks out of its victims," Bailor said. "Someone who's really sucked in can be shelling out a grand a month to them. Besides, I'm in a high-risk business."

"You're really serious?"

"I can't afford not to be."

Weller sipped at his beer and thought about it. Bailor was the only hope he had, and he seemed like a total pro: cold, hard, confident, and competent. He didn't have much more than fifteen hundred in the bank, but he was making two thousand a month. It would be tight, but what was the alternative? It's like being hospitalized for a major illness, he told himself. You can't afford to do it, but you can't afford not to.

"All right," he said. "You win. Three thousand it is. Now what?"

"Well, I'd go with the old-friend technique before we get into anything heavier. So what you do is invite me—"

A chill burst through Weller's balloon. "Didn't Wally tell you?" he said.

"Tell me what?"

"That Annie left me. That I don't know how to get in touch with her."

Bailor whistled, shook his head, and said, "Uh-oh. Bruner told me she had left you but not that they were holding her incommunicado. This does make life difficult."

"Oh shit," Weller said. "I thought you'd know how to handle it. . . ."

"I didn't say I couldn't," Bailor said. He took a drink of beer, contemplated the ceiling, then looked at Weller. "This isn't standard," he said. "Transformationalism usually likes to keep a channel open so they can use the one they've got to rope in the frantic spouse. Pleading phone calls, tearful visits, the whole bit."

"They've told me that Annie can't communicate with me till I've been processed to her level," Weller told him.

Bailor frowned. "Heavy," he said. "That's a new one on me. Hmmm . . . how did you say your wife first came into contact with Transformationalism?"

"At their Celebrity Center in Beverly Hills."

"Ah!" Bailor said. "This going after the elite is a new twist; none of the other cults have tried it yet. So it looks like you're getting special treatment. The chain-letter technique among you media types. Hook Jack Weller's wife, use her to convert Jack Weller, use Jack Weller to convert his producer, build up an ever-widening network in the media. So each link in the chain has personal importance to them, no mass-marketing techniques on this one! A lot like the way the Communists operated in the thirties. . . ."

"Jesus," Weller whispered. "But . . . but what do we *do*?"

Bailor put his feet up on the coffee table, finished his beer, put it down. "They've called the game," he said. "You've got to go along with them, let them process you long enough for

52

you to play a true convert credibly. Long enough so they'll let Annie get in touch with you. At which point I can take over."

A sour bubble of beer burst in the back of Weller's throat. Jesus Christ, he thought, back to square one again! But now, sitting in the tacky living room with his last possible hope, the narrowness of his choice was finally sinking in. Either I give up and admit that there's nothing I can do to stop these bastards from taking my wife away from me, or I play Bailor's game with them. Either I let them get away with it, or I fight them. Fuck it! he thought. So I blow another few hundred bucks— it's gonna cost me three grand anyway—and let the assholes run their stupid numbers on me. I should be a good enough actor to pull it off. What am I afraid of? What choice do I really have?

"Okay," he said. "If that's the way we have to play it, that's the way we have to play it."

Bailor eyed him narrowly. "Look," he said, "you'd better understand what you're getting into. These people aren't stupid, and they're going to know exactly where you're coming from. They're going to know why you're doing it, they won't believe in any instant change of heart. They're going to use all sorts of techniques on you, and they know what they're doing. They're going to know you're resisting and they're going to know you're trying to con them into believing that you're becoming a true convert against your will. You've got to convince them that they're converting you without actually being converted while they do their damndest to make it real. It's a heavy game you're getting into."

"I *am* a director, after all," Weller said. "I do know how to handle actors, which means I've got to know a few things about acting myself." Then, much more uncertainly: "You don't think I can handle it?"

Bailor thought about it for long moments. "Maybe you can," he finally said. "You being experienced in the acting game. And of course, you'll have a session every week with me. You tell me what numbers they're running, and I feed you the proper responses for a true convert. And, hopefully, erase any programming that might be taking hold in your mind."

He grinned at Weller. "You might say I'll be *your* director," he said. "That should be interesting."

Weller smiled wanly. "Ready when you are, C. B." he said.

"Uh . . . now the matter of money. . . ."

"I thought we had settled that," Weller said.

"That was before I found out we had to get to your wife before I could do my stuff," Bailor said. "Now there's more of my time involved . . ."

"Don't you have any heart?" Weller snapped. "Are you a total mercenary?"

Bailor laughed. "Not a *total* mercenary," he said. "But I'm not in this racket for my health, either, believe me! Tell you what, though. You give me the fifteen hundred up front, and then you pay me a hundred a week until we get to Annie, and for that, you have my unlimited services. Could be worse, right? Cheaper than a shrink . . ."

"I guess so," Weller admitted. He was depressed by the growing hole forming in his pocket, by the way Bailor rubbed his nose in the fact that he was hiring a money-grubbing professional, not a committed ally. But there was also a certain elation in the sense of dedication that came from the total commitment of whatever resources he had. At least I'm fucking well going to *do something!* he thought. He felt a strange new sense of vitality, almost as if he were getting the chance to direct that forever illusive first feature. How, he wondered, could such a good feeling come out of such rotten circumstances?

"When do we start?" he asked.

"You might as well call them now and set it up," Bailor said. "Then I'll brief you on how to handle your first session." He studied Weller, and for the first time Weller sensed a certain unpaid human concern. "You're *sure* you want to go through with this?" Bailor said. "You're sure your marriage is worth this much to you?"

Weller sighed. He took a slug of beer. "Yeah," he said. "I mean, how could I live with myself if I didn't? And to tell the truth, the fact that it scares me only makes me want to do it more. I mean, the fact that these bastards can do what they've done and then even have me thinking that maybe they're too heavy to fight . . . That *really* makes my blood boil. You know what I mean?"

"Who could know better?" Bailor said dryly. "Believe me, Jack, I understand where you're coming from a lot better than you do."

"Yeah, maybe you do," Weller said. He paused, hesitated, then went to the phone and dialed the number of the Los Angeles Transformation Center.

Four

Weller walked into a beige room with about twenty folding chairs arranged in rows facing a large video playback unit at the front. A dozen people were already seated, mostly in uneasy isolation, waiting for the introductory lecture to begin. A few of them were middle-aged, a few well dressed, but mostly they were in their twenties and thirties and looked like either counterculture refugees or lonely people working dead-end jobs. Except for the fancy video equipment, the atmosphere was tacky and de-energized, and from what Weller had seen of the Los Angeles Transformation Center, only the executive country on the eighth floor escaped this aura of sleaze. Yet Benson Allen's opulent office and the expensive video equipment gave Weller the feeling that the dinginess and lack of flash here might be a carefully calculated effect.

He sat down in the middle of the room and waited. He had forced himself to go to work, slogged through a slow day's shooting like a zombie, grabbed a quick hamburger at a Denny's, and then driven here, feeling the nervous tension building in his gut. Now his nerves were twanging like piano wire. Benson Allen had been totally neutral on the phone when he set up the appointment, and this lack of any overt reaction at all to his quick turnabout made Weller more uptight than anything else could have. He wondered if that too might be a calculated effect, and, thinking that, began to wonder if he wasn't getting a wee bit paranoid.

Finally a blond young woman wearing the white blouse and black slacks that seemed to be an informal Transformationalist uniform entered the room and stood in front of the video console. "Good evening, ladies and gentlemen, and welcome to the Los Angeles Transformation Center," she said. "You're all here to find out if Transformationalism is the answer for *you*." She smiled a plastic smile, but her eyes broadcasted a fanatic sincerity. "By the time we're finished tonight, you'll be able to judge for yourself, and I hope you'll all choose to join us in the greatest of all adventures: the exploration of the beyond within."

She paused, looked around the room as if counting the house or estimating their bank balances. "Tonight each of you is going to get the chance to actually try one of our processing techniques. You're going to meet Benson Allen, director of this Center, and one of the earliest Transformed men. But first you're going to see an initial orientation tape prepared by John B. Steinhardt himself at his headquarters at the Transformational Research Institute."

She pulled down the shades, doused the lights, and fiddled with the video console. After some multicolored static and a few protesting feedback screeches, the face of John B. Steinhardt appeared on the screen—florid, mobile, and already talking.

"In the beginning," Steinhardt said, "there was nothing but a bunch of rocks orbiting balls of gas, as deterministic and invariant as a rigged slot machine in Vegas." Stock footage of planets and stars appeared on the screen, looking as if it had been clipped from *2001* or *Destination Moon*. Some more stock footage, this of lightning flashing above a primeval sea.

"Then in the seas of Earth a funny thing happened. Chemical compounds started combining with each other to form ever more complex molecules until finally one of these molecules developed the ability to form replicas of itself out of the surrounding organic *minestrone*. This was the DNA molecule, the gene, the virus, the beginning of life."

Back to Steinhardt's talking head, the big mobile mouth, the expressive eyes, the rubber features. "From the virus to the amoeba to the fish to the dinosaur to the monkey is a long, boring story I won't bother you with," Steinhardt said. "Because until man came on the scene, all these bugs and beasties were creatures responding directly to the environment, basically as predictable and invariant as those rocks circling the suns. If you could feed all the environmental data into a good enough computer, it could just about predict what every one of those creatures was going to do at any given moment. A great big cosmic pinball machine."

A series of quickly changing still shots cribbed from old encyclopedias: cavemen, horse barbarians, African natives, knights in armor, sailing ships, medieval cities, cowboys.

"But man had something new," Steinhardt's voice-over said. "A mind. Between the input of the environment and the output of response there was now psychic space. Inside that hairy skull were memories, internal processes, crazinesses, kinks, and uncertainties, so that no longer could a super computer predict the creature's behavior from a complete picture of the external environment. Good-bye, environmental determinism!"

Steinhardt's face appeared on the screen again. "But not exactly," he said. "As soon as he had a mind, man started changing the environment. He built tools and cities. He started jabbering and writing cheap novels. He invented politics and agriculture. Now there was a man-made environment, premodern culture. Man reprogrammed the environment, which in turn reprogrammed him into reprogramming the environment which was reprogramming him. What is called a direct-feedback relationship. From environmental determinism we evolved into cultural determinism. Language programmed our thought patterns. Religion programmed our moral patterns. Ideology programmed our perception of an official reality. And all of that programmed our behavior. Things were pretty damn stable because each individual was caught in a total cultural matrix which only changed very slowly because the individuals who could change it were pretty well programmed by it already."

More stills flashed across the screen: Chinese paintings, medieval tapestries, Japanese scrolls, Hindu temples, Aztec relics, Byzantine icons. "And that's what all human civilizations were like up till about last Tuesday on the cosmic time clock. Slow moving, stable, long lasting, catching those folks in a total cultural matrix that made them what they were, told them how to think, and determined their actions."

Back to Steinhardt's talking head again. "But from about 1945 on, that brain-freeze has been shattered. Radio, TV, H-bombs, computers, drugs—human culture finally got to what I call the Transformation Point, where *we* started reprogramming the environment faster than it could reprogram *us* to deal with the changes. We're changing the total environment so fast that it's changing us faster than the cultural matrix can evolve to accommodate the changes. The situation has become permanently Transformational. So we've got people whose personalities were formed in the twenties, the thirties, the forties, the fifties, and the sixties, all trying to make sense out of each other and the seventies—which *no one* is programmed for—and not making it, because they're as different from each other, cultural matrixwise, as Ancient Chinese, Middle Ages serfs, Aztecs, and Classical Greeks."

A crazy montage of images flashed across the screen faster than Weller could make sense out of them. Hippies, FDR, helicopters, Donald Duck, the Pepsi Cola Girl, the Beatles, God knows what. Then Steinhardt reappeared, slowly dissolving into the picture out of the chaos.

"That's why you need Transformationalism," he said. "Your mind has to evolve to match this permanent situation of permanent change. You've got to get rid of that instantaneous personality that was frozen in a previous cultural matrix that no longer exists. You've got to learn to ride the changes as they come and change with them. Otherwise your kids will always seem like foreigners, you'll never be able to figure out that crazy boss of yours, and you'll stumble through life forever like a South Seas cannibal on Times Squares. The future belongs to the Transformational Man. Anyone else is already a creature of the dead past. We've got the techniques, we've got the organization, we've got the knowledge to give each and every one of you the Transformational Consciousness to cope with a Transformational World. And all the other wise guys who are peddling enlightenment these days are just whistling "Dixie." Give us your mind, your time, and a few bucks, and we'll give you the world!"

Steinhardt saluted the screen with an almost silly grin, and then the tape ran out. After a few moments of hissing static the attendant turned off the video player and turned on the lights.

Weller blinked, dazzled by the sudden light and by what he had just experienced. Amateurish as the stock-footage cutting had been, the tape certainly had impact. What Steinhardt had said seemed to ring with an essential truth that set off harmonics of agreement in Weller's mind, that seemed to get to him on levels he didn't even know he had, though the details were already fading like the memory of a vivid dream or an acid trip.

Of course, that might be illusion, Weller thought. For Steinhardt had enormous raw media presence—crude, rambling, unfocused, but enormous just the same. Star quality in the raw, as strong as Weller had ever seen it, a visceral onslaught that almost made logical argument totally irrelevant.

"Now that you've been introduced to the basis of Transformationalism by John himself," the attendant said, "here to tell you more about it is Benson Allen, director of the Los Angeles Transformation Center."

58

Allen entered the room, wearing a white ice-cream suit and a red shirt. He walked to the front as the young woman faded away to one side. Theatrically dressed as he was, Hollywood handsome though he might be with his long, flowing blond hair, his presence was still muted and pale in contrast to the immediate memory of Steinhardt. Weller wondered if he realized this, and if so, how he would cope with it.

"Well, that's *John*," Allen said with a boyish little smile. "I'm sure you're all a little knocked out, but man, not as knocked out as I was when I first met him. The only way I can try to tell you how much that dude changed my life is with my own little Transformational story."

Very good, Weller thought. Playing off it, not against it, and that's the only thing he can hope to do. At the same time it seemed to him that Allen was really sincere, that he really *was* in awe of Steinhardt. As well he might be!

"In the early sixties," Allen said, "I was a San Francisco hippie-dip, smoking lots of dope, reading lots of science fiction, and otherwise just goofing around. Then I picked up on a science fiction novel by John called *Transformational Man*. Deep stuff. We have it on sale downstairs for seven dollars and ninety-five cents, and I hope you will read it. In this novel John wrote about a small group of people who were really into what you just heard him talk about and who set out to teach it to the world and who called themselves Transformational Men."

Allen paused, gave his audience a strange, almost embarrassed puppy-dog grin and a little wry shrug. "Now I was loaded most of the time, and this was San Francisco when there was a new guru peddling a new world coming every month, and man, *anything* seemed possible," he said. "Dig, I knew *Transformational Man* was just a science fiction novel, but what John was saying about human consciousness in that story was heavy and deep and true, and it seemed to me that the processes he described in the book would really work. So I started writing letters about it to all the science fiction fanzines, and I went to science fiction conventions and crash pads and rapped about it, and soon I was a little guru myself. I started a little tribe, took some of the techniques from *Transformational Man*, and we began processing people. That was the beginning of Transformationalism."

He looked out over the room, letting it sink in, smiled, nodded. "Uh-huh," he said. "*I* started Transformationalism, not John. After a year or so we had maybe a hundred and fifty members and a little house in the Haight, and that seemed to be as far as it could go. And then one day John B. Steinhardt himself showed up like a psychedelic grizzly bear, showing everyone what a *real* Transformational personality was like."

Allen shook his head ruefully. "For sure, I didn't like it when he showed up. No one was going to accept *me* as the leader of anything with *John* around. John himself was absolutely knocked out at what I had made out of his novel. To him it had just been a good story."

Allen shook his head, as if really remembering those days with a mixture of awe and fading jealousy. To Weller it seemed either genuine or a magnificent performance. "But a head like John's doesn't stay bonged for long," Allen said. "It adapts instantly to the reality it finds itself in. He saw immediately that Transformationalism was the real thing. Dig—I had been transformed by his novel, and he was put through his own transformation by seeing what his own story had created through me, and *that* convinced him Transformationalism was valid, pow! in a flash!"

Now Allen's eyes seemed to look off into some distant yonder; there was no more undercurrent of jealousy, just undiluted awe. "At that moment John had a tremendous vision of how Transformationalism could change the world, of how my little group could be transformed into what Transformationalism is today. So John took over leadership of Transformationalism from me and built it into what it is now."

Allen pulled a folding chair to him and sat down on it with the back of the chair to the audience and his arms folded across it, making the motion into what seemed to Weller like a gesture of fealty to the unseen presence of John B. Steinhardt.

"Dig it," he said. "John didn't rip off the leadership. He took it because he was the Man. If he had had to ask, which he didn't, I would've given it to him. I didn't feel ripped off, I was glad he had taken over, because I knew that this was a greater man than me, that he could do things with Transformationalism that I couldn't even dream about. Not only that, but with John running things, I knew I could become a more fully Transformed man than ever I could when I was the head honcho. I trusted him, I believed in him, I gave him what I had made, and he never let me down."

Allen hunched forward and gazed earnestly at the audience with that unblinking intensity that Weller was beginning to think of as the Transformationalist Stare. "That's my Transformational story," he said. "*That's* how much I believe in what we're doing! That's why I *know* that Transformationalism is the answer for *you*, too! That's why I'm so happy to see you here tonight. That's why I want so much for you to join us. Transformationalism is *real!*"

Weller studied Benson Allen's face, trying to catch some hint of deception, some sign of insincerity, and failing. He was all but convinced that Allen believed every word that he was saying, that his devotion to Steinhardt was honest and total. Steinhardt's sincerity, on the other hand, seemed like a fish of a different odor. It wasn't too hard for Weller to picture Steinhardt totally snowing the stone-out previous incarnation of Benson Allen. But clearly there was more depth to Transformationalism than he had supposed, if someone on Benson Allen's level could be a genuine true believer.

Allen rose from his chair, breaking the mood. "Now each of you is going to get the chance to try one of our processes," he said. "Some of you will try gaming it through, others will have a block-auditing session, and some will have a chance to do some role-reversal. Ms. Henderson here will read you your room assignments. Good luck, and I hope this will be the beginning of a new life for all of you."

Allen left the room and the attendant began reading off names and room numbers. "Hilda Bernstein, room two-oh-three, Harry Adler, room two hundred. . . ." Weller wondered whether the choice of who was going to get what kind of introductory processing was random, or whether they were trying to pick what had the best chance of hooking whom. Judging from the rest of the operation, he suspected the latter. . . .

"Jack Weller, room four-oh-five . . ."

Well at least it isn't Room 101, Weller thought. *Or is it?*

Room 405 was a small cubicle, bare and empty except for two white cushioned chairs and a white formica table between them. The walls were cream-yellow, and the light came from a harsh overhead fixture. It had the feel of a Gestapo interrogation cell, though the man waiting for him, about forty, with calm gray eyes and a bland characterless face, looked more like a supermarket clerk than a secret-police interrogator.

"Hello, Jack, I'm Don, your processor," he said in a flat midwestern voice. "Have a seat. We're going to try a little role-reversal. First, to get us started, I'd just like you to tell me why you came here tonight."

Weller came to tense attention. Bailor had told him to

assume that anything he said would get back to Benson Allen and that anyone he would be dealing with would have access to any information Transformationalism had on him. So he couldn't present a neutral persona; he had to present the reality of Jack Weller, who was here because he was forced to be in order to get into contact with his wife. At the same time this was the opening act in his campaign to convince Transformationalism that he was becoming a genuine convert.

"My wife has joined Transformationalism," he said slowly, "and we've fought about it. In fact she's left me and refuses to even talk to me again until I've had some Transformational processing."

"And she was issued a life directive to that effect?" Don said.

Weller nodded. So Bailor was right, this guy had probably read the whole dossier. He really had to watch himself.

"So then, Jack, you're basically here against your will. Not because you're really interested in Transformationalism, but because you want to be reunited with your wife?"

This is the critical point, Weller realized. I can't deny it, but this is where I have to start laying in the background for a phony conversion. And I had better be subtle about it.

"Yeah," he said grudgingly. "I've got to admit that. . . . And also, I suppose, I've got some curiosity about what this business is all about. I mean, Annie and I were together for a long time, and I thought we knew each other pretty damn well. Now this Transformationalism thing has come between us. I guess I'd be pretty stupid if I didn't want to find out what it was that took my wife and made her into a stranger."

Don nodded. His face remained totally neutral, totally bland. This guy doesn't seem to have too much on the ball, Weller thought.

"And that's all?" Don asked.

"What do you mean?"

"Well, surely you must have some negative feelings about Transformationalism under the circumstances. Strong feelings."

"Sure I have some negative feelings," Weller said carefully. "Who wouldn't?"

"Would you like to talk about them?"

"What's the point?" Weller said uneasily. "I'm pissed off that you've taken my wife away from me. I'm skeptical about any outfit that would do such a thing. I think you charge an awful lot of money. I think you might be phonies. Do I really have to tell you that?"

"It's useful to have those feelings voiced, that's all," Don said. "But now we'll really get down to what we're about tonight. Now we'll play role-reversal. Now *I'll* be Jack Weller and you'll be me."

"Huh?"

"It's really very simple," Don said. "You play the part of a Transformationalist processor interviewing Jack Weller, and I'll be Jack Weller reacting to the processor."

"But I don't have any idea of what a processor is supposed to do or say. . . ."

"Of course you don't. That's the whole point. I get inside your skin and you get inside mine. That's why I asked you a few questions at the beginning. You can start by simply asking me the questions I just asked you and play it by ear from there. Don't worry, I'll be helping you along."

He paused, looked earnestly at Weller, and said, "Try to really get into it. Be merciless. Try to really experience yourself from the outside and react honestly to what you're hearing. And don't be afraid to say whatever you might imagine a processor would say to Jack Weller under the circumstances. Now let's begin. Jack Weller has just sat down, and you ask him why he's come here tonight. . . ."

Weller found it hard to mask his contempt. This nebbish is going to play Actor's Studio games with *me?* "Hello Jack, I'm Don, your processor," Weller said, broadly parodying the man's own voice. "Have a seat. What we're going to do is try a little role-reversal. First, to get us started, I'd just like you to tell me why you came here tonight." Chew on that, you nerd!

"My wife has joined Transformationalism, and we've fought about it," the processor shot back in a fair imitation of Weller's voice. "She's been issued a life directive never to see me again until I've been processed. So I'm here to con you assholes into letting me see her."

What? Suddenly the silly little game took on new levels. Weller had the feeling that he had really been suckered into something, but he didn't know what. Well, if that's the way we're going to play it. . . .

"What makes you think you can do that, Jack?" Weller said. "If we're smart enough to take your wife away from you, don't you think we're smart enough to know where you're coming from?" Jesus! he thought. Why did I say *that?*

"Because I think you people are stupid enough to think you're smart enough to use my own motivations to suck me in

63

and convert me," Don said, plastering a sardonic smirk across his face.

Man, I've got to think this through better, Weller realized. This son of a bitch is seeing right through me! Wheels within wheels!

"Are you so sure you know your own motivations that well, Jack?" Weller said. There, that's better, let him do my work for me.

"What do you mean by that?" the processor said confusedly, and Weller sensed that he was off-balance both as "Weller" and as himself.

"You're a director," Weller said. "You think you know how to manipulate people. Don't you think this is something of a challenge to you, a high-stakes game? Is your head stronger than Transformationalism or is Transformationalism stronger than your head? Don't you think part of the reason you came here is to find out the answer to that one?"

Weller's head was aching with the convoluted tensions of this little exercise in mind-fuck. What he had said was carefully calculated, but even as he said it, he realized that it was also an essential truth. Moreover he was in some way *enjoying* this game; he felt himself filling with energy, he was really cooking. Try this number on a *pro*, will you?

"Maybe you're right," Don said. "One thing is sure, I'm not here because I think I really need Transformational processing. And your job is to convince me I do."

Old Don seemed to be walking right into it, Weller thought. Whether he knows it or not, he's letting me set up the character of "Weller" as a prideful shithead who can be led along into Transformationalism by his ego. Just the rationale I want them to have for the first step of my "conversion!"

"You flatter yourself," Weller said. "Transformationalism has millions of converts. What makes you think it's so important for us to snare *you*?"

"Because I'm a challenge to you," Don said. "As a director I'm the kind of person it should be hardest for you people to get to. And I've come in here hostile and combative. I've got my own strong motivation for conning you into believing that I'm really becoming Transformed while I'm really just playacting. If Transformationalism can really get to me under *those* conditions, it'll really have proven something, won't it?"

Weller paused, studied the processor, and tried to fathom what was really going on. It seemed to him that Don was really throwing down Transformationalism's gauntlet. He was being told that Transformationalism knew exactly where he was coming from and didn't care. That they were so bloody self-confident that they could know his game and tell him *their* game and *still* be sure they would get to him in the end. On the other hand, he himself had at the very least collaborated in setting up that dynamic; it was the only credible motivation for Jack Weller that he could feed to them. Moreover, it was essentially true. Who the hell was conning whom?

"So you see all this is a game between Transformationalism and yourself?" he said, trying to draw out the answer. "The winner is the one with the stronger head?"

Don smiled at him. "It's the king of games, isn't it?" he said. "The mind game. If I win, I get Annie back on my terms; if you win, you've got me as a willing convert."

"But if we win, you win too," Weller blurted. "After all, you get your wife back either way." Now why the hell did I say *that*? Weller wondered. Jeez, I must really be getting into this part!

"It depends on what you mean by winning," the processor said.

"But also on what you mean by losing, Jack," Weller found himself saying without quite knowing why. For sure he had gotten totally caught up in this game for its own sake. He had gotten caught up in playing the part of the processor to the point where he had been speaking off a processor's motivations, even when they ran contrary to his own. Technically, as an acting exercise, the number that had been run on him fascinated and impressed him. More pragmatically and less happily, it gave him new respect for the psychic cunning of Transformationalism.

Don leaned back, seemed to visibly pop out of character, and revert to his supermarket-clerk persona. "You're very good at this," he said.

Weller felt his body relaxing, though his mind continued to spin through the wheels within wheels. "So are you," he said.

"Has this little demonstration shown you that Transformationalism has something to teach you?"

For a moment it seemed as if they were back playing something like the role-reversal game again. He was going to say yes because he had too—and perhaps incidentally because it was true—and he knew that Don knew what he was going to say, and he knew where it was going to lead, and he knew that the processor knew that he knew. . . . Who was really seeing through whom?

"I've got to admit that it does," Weller said.

Don looked at him neutrally. "Do you think you'd like to sign up for the one-month course?" he said. "It's twice a week for only two hundred and fifty dollars. . . ."

Weller groaned inwardly, then psychically collapsed toward the inevitable. The outcome of all this convoluted fencing had been preordained before he had even sat down, and they both knew it. Enough of this bullshit already!

Weller gave the processor the old Transformationalist Stare. "I think you've made me an offer I can't refuse," he said.

But he knew, and not without a certain twinge of self-loathing, that there was a considerable part of him that had been seduced by the role-reversal game, not forced by circumstance. The game itself *was* fascinating, no matter why he found himself playing it. It was as if he were exercising psychic muscles, an aspect of his talent, that hadn't been extended to the fullest for too long a time. He liked the feeling, he didn't want to lose it, and the fact that he was playing this acting game for keeps only added a keen existential edge to the contest.

Don had said it, speaking as "Weller" himself—it *was* the king of games.

Five

"The same thing as the first session," Weller said, looking at Garry Bailor. "He just plugged me into the brainwave monitor and shot words and phrases at me for an hour, no pattern that I could figure out."

Bailor sat there on the couch beside him, rocking back and forth imperceptibly, encouraging Weller to go on only by his silence. Although Bailor just silently studied him like a bug under a microscope while Clark Burns, the block-auditing processor, droned on incessantly during the sessions, Weller was beginning to get the same feeling of tense boredom that he had experienced during his two block-auditing sessions. The lack of human feedback response was the same, and so was the feeling of two people in a room together locked into their own private universes.

Burns was a balding, colorless little middle-aged man, and that first night he had simply introduced himself, fitted an electrode band on Weller's head, plugged it into the brainwave monitor, sat down, and given his brief instructions as if he were reading them off an idiot card, as if he were merely an extension of the machine.

"This is a brainwave monitor. It measures four channels of your brainwaves. I'll read you a series of words and phrases and note your brainwave responses on the chart. Since I'll be reading your brain's responses directly off my oscilloscope, you don't have to respond verbally, though you may do so if you wish. Are there any questions?"

The brainwave monitor was a gray console, about the size of a portable television set, on the table between Weller and Burns. Facing Burns was an oscillosocpe and a series of knobs and switches. All Weller could see now was the top of Burns's head, down to his eyes, peering at him over the featureless back of the machine. Burns had a clipboard and a ball-point pen poised to fill in the spaces on Weller's "psychomap." It all seemed cosmically silly somehow.

"No questions," Weller said, though he would have liked an explanation of the circuitry of the device. But he had the feeling that the brainwave monitor was as much a mysterious "black box" to Burns as it was to him, and he doubted that the processor would have explained anything technical to him even if he could.

"Good," the processor said. "We'll begin. Try to clear your mind of any strong emotional thoughts so I can get a level reading. . . ." Burns's eyes, looking strangely disembodied with the rest of his face hidden by the machine, glanced down at the scope. "Good enough," he said, and started reading from a form on his clipboard.

"Mother. . . " A pause, a glance at the scope, something jotted on the form. "Father. . . ." Pause, glance, scribble. "Fuck. . . . Kill. . . . Shit. . . ."

It only took a few minutes of this brainless procedure for the process to seem interminable to Weller and infuriatingly boring. "A large dog is barking on your lawn. . . . Cock. . . . One hundred thousand dollars. . . . Heil Hitler. . . ."

Just the eyes above the console, glancing at him, the scope, the form, and back again, in a regular, mechanical rhythm, and the flat voice mouthing random words—sometimes obscene, sometimes meaningless, sometimes downright silly. After awhile Weller began to feel that they were *both* just extensions of the machine, lumps of flesh plugged passively into the electronic circuitry. At first this feeling was infuriating, then it became somewhat frightening, but finally it just helped him melt into the mindlessness of the whole process.

"Wife. . . . oral sex. . . . middle age. . . . gum disease. . . ."

Weller felt his mind drifting in a sea of total boredom. The words and phrases that kept coming at him had just enough intermittent momentary meaning to prevent his mind from floating off into any extended reverie about anything outside this cosmically boring situation, to interrupt any coherent train of independent thought that might be starting to form. He tried to keep himself alert by looking for some kind of pattern in the words Burns was reading, but although most of them were loaded with emotional connotations in the heavy areas of sex, death, love, fear, success, age, and money, they seemed to jump back and forth; there seemed to be no pattern, no trend, no line of development.

"Transformationalism. . . . Cunt. . . . Sigmund Freud. . . ."

For a while Weller tried giving verbal responses, as if it

were some classical Freudian word-association game.

"Toothache pain. . . ."

"Jackhammer. . . ."

"Bank loan. . . ."

"Feature film. . . ."

"Syphilis. . . ."

"Orgasm. . . ."

But Burns didn't respond at all. Just the eyes looking at him, looking at the form, a word or phrase, a glance at the scope, back to the form, flick, speak, flick, flick. Flick, speak, flick, flick. He soon gave up on talking back to the process and simply endured the boredom of what was going on like a good soldier.

". . . four score and seven. . . . black leather underwear. . . . you're fired. . . . pregnant. . . . the phone is being disconnected. . . ."

"It seemed to go on for a century," Weller told Bailor, "just like Tuesday. And afterward he just told me that the session was over and he would see me next week."

Bailor continued to study Weller with his cold ball-bearing eyes. "*Well?*" Weller demanded. He was beginning to get thoroughly pissed off with robotic nonresponses in general.

"There had to be some trends in the words he was using," Bailor suddenly said sharply. "That's the way it works."

"I *told* you there weren't any," Weller snapped irritably.

Bailor drummed his fingers annoyingly on the coffee table. "Maybe you're not catching it. Though it *could* be too early. Nobody seems to know what the brainwave monitor really does, or even if it does anything. But the whole point of the *process* is programming through boredom."

"Huh?"

Bailor stood up suddenly and began pacing in small circles, snapping off his words like strings of firecrackers. "Whether they really map areas of resistance in the mind doesn't matter," he said, "because that's just a front for the programming. Bored out of your mind, weren't you? Literally. The only input you get is those random words, but you're getting that continually, so you can't concentrate on anything else either. Creates a suggestible state. Boredom is a powerful hypnotic device, especially when it's being used to focus your attention on a single controlled input. Get it?"

"Yeah . . ." Weller said slowly. "I'm beginning to see what you mean."

Bailor suddenly stopped pacing, stood directly above Weller, pointed a finger at him, and quizzed him like an irate schoolteacher. "So *think*! There *had* to be a pattern—"

"I told you—"

"Hold!" Bailor snapped, cutting him off. He began to pace again. "Forget the simple first-order sequence. If they're programming you, the goal has to be to affect your attitude toward Transformationalism, probably through your sense of self-esteem. The words in between would be just so much static, designed to distract your conscious attention from what they're planting subliminally."

He paused halfway across the room and looked back at Weller. "Now think—just the words relating to Transformationalism and self-esteem, blocking the other stuff out of the sequence. Any pattern *there?*"

Weller looked at Bailor blankly. What does this guy think I am, a fucking computer? he thought. But, obediently, he strained his mind, trying to remember some pattern, something from the second session. "Processing . . . hemlock . . . home . . . cunnilingus . . . garbage . . . grace . . . baby . . . Red China . . . high school . . . helplessness . . . beer saloon . . . Steinhardt . . . elephant . . . power . . . grandfather . . ." Was *that* it? Was there really something there, or was Bailor just making him paranoid?

"Processing, home, grace, Steinhardt, power, grandfather," he muttered. "Do you think that's a meaningful sequence? I think I remember that right, with the other words taken out. Or am I just creating a pattern where none exists?"

"If there's a pattern in your head, there's a pattern in your head," Bailor said. He sat down on the couch, studied Weller. "Do you notice any change in your attitude toward Transformationalism?"

"Yeah. In addition to everything else, it's starting to bore the piss out of me."

Bailor frowned at him disapprovingly. "This isn't funny," he said. "You've got to keep your mind alert during processing. If you let yourself drift, that's when you start to pick up programming."

"Jesus Christ," Weller said, "I'm not in a paranoid enough situation, you've got to get me picking patterns out of endless strings of random words?" He had a terrible vision of a world in which *everything* had an onimous subliminal meaning—random bits of conversation, radio commercials, the sequence of parked cars, every third word in newspaper headlines.

"Don't worry about picking out patterns," Bailor said. "The important thing is just to be aware of the possibility and not let any programming take hold. You've got to assume that these people are out to capture your mind, and paranoia is therefore your best ally. It's an accurate perception of your reality."

"My God. . . ."

"Don't worry," Bailor said much more softly. "You're doing okay. You don't have to concentrate on all this consciously. What we've discussed tonight will stay with you. Kind of a 'clearing program' I've put in your head to help filter out whatever your processor will be trying to plant. Just stay alert, stay skeptical, and let what I've planted work."

"Shit . . ." Weller muttered tiredly. The whole thing was turning into an insane nightmare—the processing sessions, the absence of Annie, this dingy dump, and a guy telling him that he was being counterprogrammed to counteract the Transformationalist programming, that paranoia was an accurate description of reality. And yet the block-auditing *had* gotten to Annie. And Bailor *was* an expert. If the whole thing *were* insane, the insanity was not in his mind or in Bailor's but in the life situation itself.

"Is this all real, Garry?" he asked quietly. "Secret patterns? Programming ? Counterprogramming?"

"Welcome to modern reality," Bailor said dryly. "Yeah, it's real. It's all around you. Transformationalism. TV news. Advertising. Political propaganda. Movies. Books. Magazines. We're swimming in a sea of mind-programing. *Everything* has programing hidden in it, especially when the content *seems* to be random. Even the language itself programs our heads. It's always been like that—the difference now is that there are people out there like Steinhardt who know it and know how to use it. Aside from the money why do you think I'm in this racket? Because I don't like the situation any better than you do."

Weller looked at Bailor speculatively. For what he had said was strangely like the line Steinhardt himself had spouted on the orientation tape: free the mind from the total matrix of cultural programming. In Steinhardt's case that seemed to boil down to substituting new programming of your own. And wasn't that what Bailor was really doing too? Could you really deprogram the mind by using programming techniques? Or

71

was that like lifting yourself by your own bootstraps?

Now Bailor seemed to be studying *him*. "Something wrong, Jack?" he asked sympathetically.

"Nothing," Weller sighed. What was the point in creating more paranoia in this paranoid situation?

"Okay," Bailor said, "so go home and get some rest." Bailor smiled at him quite warmly, clapped him on the thigh.

"Okay, Garry," Weller said, getting up and walking toward the door. "So long. See you next week."

"*Jack?*"

Weller turned to look at Bailor, who stood in front of the couch, waiting expectantly for something. "What is it?" he asked.

Bailor shrugged, gave him a slightly embarrassed grin, held out his right palm. "You owe me another hundred dollars," he said.

"All right now, let's get this damned shot in the can so we can go home," Weller said, mopping sweat from his brow with the back of his hand. He checked his watch: almost seven o'clock. *Shit!*

The *big* processing session, the *terminal* session, was at eight tonight. Bailor had told him that the four-week course was designed to make the mark feel bad about himself, to make him feel that some unformed question was gnawing at him and that Transformationalism was the answer. Well, the four weeks were up tonight, and they were going to ask him to sign up for meditative deconditioning at a fat forty dollars a session, the sinking of the hook into the baited brain. And he was going to tell them it was quid pro quo time, enough was enough, they *had* to tell him where Annie was.

He *had* to make tonight's session, but this shot *had* to be finished today because this week's shooting was already nearly half a day behind. They'd have to shoot till eight tomorrow anyway to wrap up this week's segment in time to keep a gaping hole from forming in the air schedule. There had already been five blown takes, each one lousier than the last, so this one had goddamn better well be *it!*

Weller checked out the setup one more time. Hal Leer, who played Daddy Carson, was sitting in the big overstuffed chair on the basic living room set, looking pissed off at Weller and thirsting for his long-delayed first drink of the day. Barry Greenfield, the obnoxious little brat who played Timmy Carson, was waiting at the right of the set to make his entrance, shuffling back and forth as if he had to pee. Beside him

72

hunkered Scuffles the chimp, looking mean and morose in his white ballerina outfit, while Lindstrom, the trainer, whispered whatever it was you whispered to a temperamental ape into the creature's ear. It was really such a simple shot—Timmy enters from the right into an establishing shot, delivers his line, cuing Scuffles, who pirouettes into the shot with the pie, the camera moves with him as he dances toward Daddy, and pow, right in the kisser!

Such a simple shot, but first the ape had dropped the pie, then Timmy blew his line, then Scuffles pissed in the middle of the take, then Leer blew his line, then the goddamn chimp had ground the pie into the top of Leer's head, screeching and baring its yellow teeth. Tempers were getting hot. Leer had been his usual hung-over, temperamental self all week, and Weller, with random patterns of block-auditing words and phrases whirling through his brain when he wasn't thinking about Annie, had had no patience for Leer's crap and had told him so on several occassions. The last take, with Leer red-faced and screaming with pie ground into his hair, hadn't helped matters. Barry the Brat was already whining about how hungry he was and had to have candy bars shoved into his face after every take to shut him up, and the loathsome Scuffles was, well, behaving like an ape.

". . . transcendence . . . blood . . . nightmares . . . steak tartare . . . orgasm . . . virgin . . . urine . . . masturbation . . . God . . . changes. . . . " Yeah, that was the sequence that kept running over and over again through his memory. It seemed to be the kind of programming Bailor had warned him about, and he had been alert to it, but he still couldn't keep it from repeating in his conscious mind, grinding its way into the deeper levels. And there were other sequences like that, dozens of them these past four weeks, that he couldn't keep out of his head, as if someone were murmuring them over and over again in his ear.

Bailor would analyze the sequences that stuck in his head, but he couldn't analyze them to death. The interpretations of the program only served to make him remember the sequences, and maybe the sequences were even picking up meaning from the so-called deprogramming. To think of Annie was to think of Bailor saying, "This one's building up Annie as a goddess in your mind," was to hear murmuring over and over again, "love . . . Cadillac . . . Annie . . . 747 . . . Athens . . . springtime. . . . "

It seemed to be getting more obvious as the block-auditing

progressed, but it was also getting heavier—such a crude but powerful form of brainwashing that even being able to watch it work didn't stop it dead in its tracks. My God, if I had never met Bailor, if I had staggered into this like an ignorant schmuck. . . .

"Jack? *Jack?*"

"Huh? What?" Weller blinked back into reality. The cameraman was looking at him with barely contained exasperation. "I was telling you I was ready to get this damned shot over with," he said.

"Oh yeah, sure," Weller said. Damn it, he had been spacing out into running block-auditing sequences again when he had to concentrate on getting this damned day's shooting finished. Screw up your marriage and then screw up your job, is that it, Weller? Hold on, he told himself, maybe this whole thing will be over tonight.

And it was already seven-ten.

"All right," Weller shouted. "Lights . . . sound. . . ."

On came the shooting lights, and the cameraman hunkered back down behind his camera, shaking his head and moving his lips in a silent mutter. Snap! went the clapboard.

"*Monkey Business*, scene thirty-four A, take six!"

"Speed," said the chief sound man.

"Action," Weller called, dully and mechanically.

Barry the Brat minced onto the set from the right. "Look, Dad, Scuffles has taken up ballet, too!"

The trainer grunted "go" at Scuffles, and the chimpanzee, after a nerve-shattering hesitation, toe-danced toward Leer in its tutu, balancing the pie over its head on the palm of its hand. Leer rose from his chair to marvel at this piece of monkey business, but as he did, Scuffles lurched suddenly closer and dropped the pie in the crotch of his pants.

"Motherfucker!" Leer screamed as Scuffles gave him a ripe raspberry, and Barry the Brat covered his ears in wounded mock innocence.

"Cut!" Weller shouted. He stared at the mess on the set without saying anything else for a long moment. The trainer was recovering control of the ape, but Barry the Brat was trying to taunt it into some new outrage, and Leer was snarling at the wardrobe people who were mopping at the pie-encrusted front of his pants. Weller looked at his watch: seven-twenty. There just wasn't time to get the set in order, change Leer's pants, do another take, and get to the Transformation Center by eight. And no guarantee that the next take would work, either.

"All right, that's a print," Weller finally shouted. "We'll have to use that take."

"WHAT?" Leer howled. "You're going to use *that*? A chimpanzee dropping a pie in my pants?"

"I thought it turned out funnier than the script," Weller said. "Your reaction was beautiful, Hal. It saved the take. Your expletive can be deleted from the sound track."

Leer brushed away the wardrobe people and came toward Weller. "What's the matter with you, Weller?" he said when he had reached confidential earshot. "You seem to give even less of a damn than usual lately. You can't turn in footage like that."

"Since when did you consider *Monkey Business* a serious artistic show, Hal?" Weller asked.

"*Artistic?* Are you kidding? Forget what an idiot I look like in that shot, you can't give them a pie in the crotch on a kiddie show. Network continuity will never pass that."

"Then that'll be *their* problem later," Weller told him. "They can always tell me to reshoot it, but in the meantime we'll have this segment in the can on schedule tomorrow. Or would you rather stick around here another hour or two to get the damned thing right?"

"Boy, do I love television," Leer sighed, and then took off in the direction of the nearest bar.

Weller checked his watch again. Another five minutes gone! Not even time enough to grab a hamburger on the way to the Center. Just what I need, to face tonight with a head full of *Monkey Business* and an empty stomach!

Weller arrived at his processing room on time, but Clark Burns wasn't there. Instead he was greeted by a slim, dark-haired woman in her late thirties, with hard piercing eyes and an angular face that would have been attractive if it weren't such a mask of ice.

"Who are you? Where's Burns?"

"My name is Sylvia Paoluzzi," she said, barricaded behind the brain wave monitor. "I'm a meditative deconditioner. Please sit down, Jack. I've got good news for you."

Weller lowered himself into the hot seat. *Good news? Are they finally going to let me get in touch with Annie?*

"We've completed your psychomap," Sylvia Paoluzzi said.

75

"That's why I'm here instead of Clark. Tonight we're going to introduce you to meditative deconditioning."

Weller was caught off-balance. "Look," he said, "before we get into any of that, I want to talk about my wife."

"*Your wife?*" She looked genuinely puzzled. She glanced through some papers on her clipboard, then looked up at Weller with new comprehension. "Oh," she said. "I see."

"I'm glad you see," Weller said irritably. "This is the last session of my four-week course, and I was promised I could see my wife when I had been processed."

"*Been processed?*" Sylvia Paoluzzi said. "You mean you think you've *been processed?*" Her tone was not so much sarcastic as incredulous.

"I've been plugged into this damned machine two nights a week for a month," Weller snapped. "What the hell would *you* call it, Miss Paoluzzi?"

"*Sylvia,*" she said with synthetic geniality. "And what I would call it is psychomapping. Meditative deconditioning is the first step in real *processing,* and that's what we're going to begin tonight."

"What the hell are you talking about?" Weller said. "I've spent two hundred and fifty dollars for these eight sessions, and now you tell me it's nothing, that I haven't even *begun* processing?"

Sylvia looked at him with a hard, unwavering gaze. "We're arguing over words," she said. "Of course, four weeks of block-auditing isn't *nothing*; it's an absolutely essential preparation for meditative deconditioning."

"Well, what about seeing my wife?"

"That's not my province," Sylvia said. "Meditative deconditioning is. You have a scheduled meeting with a life counselor after this session, and you can discuss your life-situation problem with him. Now you *have* already paid for this first deconditioning session, so shall we begin? We've already wasted the first five minutes."

Weller studied the woman barricaded behind the brainwave monitor, behind the stonewall of her refusal to discuss anything beyond the procedure she was impatient to begin. Could she really not discuss Annie or was that just part of the game? Either way he knew that he was going to have to get through this session before he got to confront the life counselor, whatever that was.

"Okay," Weller said resignedly, "you win."

"Very good," Sylvia said crisply. "Now as you know, the

purpose of block-auditing is to prepare a psychomap of your areas of psychic blockage. It's basically a *diagnostic* technique. It tells us what areas we now have to work on with meditative deconditioning, which is a *treatment*, in medical terms, or a *process*, as we like to call it. Now do you see what I mean about your processing having not yet begun?"

Weller nodded. First they screw up your mind under cover of their so-called diagnosis, then they sell you the cure for the mess they've made of your head. No wonder there's a special low price for block-auditing! It's the come-on; they suck you in with it and then sell you "meditative deconditioning" at forty bucks a session! Very cute.

"Well now," Sylvia said, "meditative deconditioning is in a sense the reverse of block-auditing. Now that we know in what psychic areas your brainwave plot deviates from the optimum pattern, we concentrate on eliminating those blocks."

She fitted the electrode band onto Weller's head, plugged it into the brainwave monitor, and sat down behind the machine again. "Even an untransformed mind functions at optimum at certain times," she said. "During successful lovemaking, during creative work, in a relaxed meditative state, and so forth. Just as the brainwave monitor detects blocks by variations in your brainwaves, it can also identify optimum mental states. A fully Transformed mind remains in an optimum state in any life situation, independent of the external environment. The ultimate purpose of meditative deconditioning is to eliminate all blocks, to reach this optimum state, to give you what we call a 'fully eptified consciousness.' Do you follow all this?"

"I think so," Weller said. The theory made sense, assuming that the brainwave monitor did what they said it did. But block-auditing used the same rationale to cover some heavy brain-washing games, and he wondered what numbers they ran under cover of this "meditative deconditioning." Well, I'm about to find out, he thought warily.

"Excellent," Sylvia said. "What I do is give you a series of 'life scenarios' keyed to blocks on your psychomap, imaginary situations designed to concentrate your consciousness on specific areas of blockage. You meditate on the scenarios as I give them to you and attempt to reach a calm, meditative, eptified state of brainwave activity in your blocked areas. Once you have succeeded, the block will be gone, and once all the blocks have been processed away, you'll have reached a fully eptified state of consciousness, able to function optimally in any life situation."

77

"Question," Weller said, raising his hand sardonically, like a schoolboy. "Just what are the areas of blockage on my psychomap?"

"Your relationship to your wife. Your attitude toward changing your consciousness. Your creative functioning. Your difficulty with identifying with anything beyond your own egoistic ambition."

"I see," said Weller. Brother, do I see! They're zeroing in on why I'm here and my resistance to Transformationalism. Not to mention my dissatisfaction with my nowhere career. This sounds like it's going to get very heavy.

"One more question," Weller said. "Just what am I supposed to do? How do I make my brainwaves calm in fantasy situations designed to make me uptight?"

Sylvia glanced impatiently at her watch. "I can't really answer that," she said. "You must develop your own technique. Continued confrontation with your blocks will force your mind to learn how to eptify itself in negative life scenarios. It's like learning to ride a bicycle, a *feel* thing . . . Please, Mr. Weller, may we begin now?"

Weller shrugged. "I guess I'm as ready as I'm going to be," he said.

Sylvia fiddled with the controls of the brainwave monitor. "All right," she said. "Here's your first scenario. Your wife has told you that she's signed a contract to play a starring role in a major film that's going to be shot in Spain. She'll be gone for four months, during which you must remain in Los Angeles to work on your childrens' television show."

"Jesus," Weller whispered. The dirty bastards had really keyed into his most shameful fear! How many times had he listened to Annie's end of a phone conversation with her agent, fearing just such a moment? A few times such a role had appeared to be a remote possibility for a while, and during those periods the question had run through Weller's mind over and over again: what's going to happen to *me*? What's going to happen to *us*? How could a star stay married to a failure? And just thinking that way made him loathe his own smallness of soul. He couldn't tolerate the idea of Annie being more successful than himself, and he couldn't stand the shame of his own true feeling.

Sylvia's hard, cold eyes peered at him over the brainwave monitor. "Now try to control that reaction," she said. "Hold the thought in your mind but try to erase your negative feelings about it."

78

"How am I supposed to do that?" Weller snarled.

"Try to imagine the best possible way of facing the situation," Sylvia suggested. "Try to imagine where your mind would have to be to do that and put it there."

Despite himself Weller found himself trying to play the game. All right, Annie, congratulations, you've got your break. I dig your happiness, I'm proud of your success. Yeah, and if you can do it, it proves that I can do it, doesn't it? And if you become a star, you'll have power, and you can use it to help my career. What's so terrible about that? Wouldn't I do the same thing for you? Couldn't you accept it from me? Only stupid male chauvinist ego makes me feel that there's something wrong with that, that a real man doesn't ride his wife's coat-tails, that a real woman couldn't respect a man who did. What good does that do anyone? It cuts us off from half the possibilities of helping each other along through life. . . .

Aw, what a pack of shit all this is! Weller thought, looking across the monitor at Sylvia and wanting to knock the machine off the table and stomp it to bits.

Sylvia looked up from the scope. "Not bad for a first try," she said. "There actually was some change in the readings for a while. Let's try another one."

She paused, then read off a sheet of paper on her clipboard. "You've gotten the chance to direct a major film. But only because the male star is a homosexual who is strongly attracted to you. And his production company is making the film, so he's also your boss. And he's telling you how to direct. And he doesn't know what he's talking about. If you do things his way, the film will be a failure. If you fight him for creative control, he can fire you."

"What the hell is this?" Weller shouted.

"It's a life scenario," Sylvia said evenly.

"It's a piece of slime!"

"It's not beyond the realm of possibility, is it?" Sylvia said slyly. "Is that how you would cope with it? By throwing a temper tantrum? Do you walk away from all of your creative problems?" All the while she was studying the oscilloscope, where Weller could picture his damned brainwaves jumping all over the place. He glared at her. She did not look up at him.

"Try," she said. "Imagine yourself riding with the change, adapting your creative powers to the situation, overriding your emotions, using yourself at optimum, eptifying the situation."

Weller closed his eyes and tried to disengage his mind from the anger that was coursing through him. All right, we'll play your little game. That's all it is, after all, a silly mind game. It couldn't happen, Weller? The fuck it couldn't! If it were a female star, you'd tease her pussy throughout the whole shooting. You'd lock into that sexual energy and twist it around yourself, you'd use it to get what you wanted like a fisherman playing a marlin on light tackle. And you'd ball her, if that was what it ended up taking, wouldn't you? Annie or no Annie. Or don't you have what it takes? Because that is what creativity is all about—turning yourself into your own instrument and doing it with utter ruthlessness. Transmuting whatever lousy raw material you're stuck with into what you want. . . .

But a *faggot.* . . . Weller felt his flesh crawling. He'd never let himself be violated like that. Yet he also felt a flash of shame, for a part of him was saying, maybe you would, maybe you should. Because if you were in deadly earnest about your creative commitment, you had to detach yourself from your own personality, you had to let yourself burn, you had to be a monomaniac. . . .

"Very good," Sylvia said, looking up from the scope. "Very good indeed. You're an excellent subject."

Weller became aware of the fact that he was sweating. His body was vibrating with fatigue, but it was a triumphant, almost sensual sort of fatigue. He felt very much as he did during those rare peak moments when he was really cooking on the set, when he could feel the camera, the actors, the very film moving behind the lens, as extensions of his own being. It felt something very much like creativity itself.

"Quite a little game you've got here," he admitted grudgingly, half hating himself for responding to it the way he had. This was not at all like a block-auditing. It didn't make him feel confused and scattered; it actually did seem to focus his consciousness, to put him more fully inside his own mind. Jesus, he thought warily, I could get to *like* this. I had better watch my ass!

Sylvia's eyes seemed to smile for the first time, though her full expression remained enigmatically hidden behind the brainwave monitor. She glanced at her watch.

"We have time for one more," she said. "This time you're a crippled beggar in ancient Jerusalem, a man of no faith, no belief in anything beyond himself. Jesus has just touched your lame leg and commanded you to rise. You get up, and your body is whole and healthy. You look into His eyes, and you are confronted with a clearly transcendent being, a creature superior to you in every way who loves you and has made you whole. Your skepticism is no longer tenable because your own body proves the reality. You worship him, you are transfigured and transformed."

Weller regarded Sylvia sourly, suddenly brought down from that energetic creative state. This was just a little *too* transparent. Superior being, huh? Transfigured and . . . *transformed*, huh? My skepticism is no longer tenable, huh? Jesus B. Steinhardt, huh?

"This one is just a little too silly for me," he said.

"Is it?" Sylvia said evenly. "That's funny, you're reacting very strongly to it. It really makes you uptight."

"Oh, come on . . ."

"Come on yourself, Jack. You're really blocking. Are you so afraid of such a concept that you don't even dare fantasize about it? Does the concept of a man who is greater than you terrify you *that* much? Is your mind so rigid you won't even try?"

"Oh, all right," Weller said. I've put up my resistance, he thought, so maybe this is an opportunity to plant the sort of thing they're looking for. If I can show that I'm wavering, that somewhere a tiny part of me wants to worship John B. Christ. . . .

He tried to imagine that he was looking up at a Jesus who had just healed him, that he believed, that he worshiped. . . . But it was impossible to even think about it with a straight face. Maybe I should try what they're *really* after, he thought.

Okay, I'm sitting in a room with John B. Steinhardt. Annie and I have been reunited and I've got a fat contract to do a feature film, all through the good offices and wisdom of Steinhardt, who has helped me despite my own worthless self. Wouldn't I love him? Wouldn't I think he was hot shit? Wouldn't I just sit there grinning like an ape and basking in the munificent wonderfulness of his being?

Weller tried to hold this ludicrous concept in his mind, to impress it upon his brain deeply enough to affect the brainwave traces Sylvia was studying while trying to discern how he was doing by reading her expression from the top half of her face. Talk about Method Acting! he thought. Am I getting through? Good old wonderful John, who has given me wealth, success, by wife back, a Transformed mind in a healthy body, sweet breath and clean white teeth. . . . *Ah, shit!*

"How am I doing?" he finally said when he could take it no longer.

"About as well as could be expected at this point," Sylvia said, looking up at him with unreadable eyes. She checked her watch. "I'm afraid our time is up," she said. "You see the life counselor now—Mr. Rohrer in room two-oh-six. About signing up for meditative deconditioning. And you *did* want to talk to someone about seeing your wife. . . ?"

"Yeah," Weller said, blinking himself back into hard reality, remembering what it was that had brought him here in the first place. He tried to recapture the determination to force an immediate showdown that he had carried with him into the center tonight, but it seemed very difficult to connect with that mundane reality at the moment. For something new and unforseen had happened. Sure, the last scenario had been an obvious brain lavage, but the other two. . . . They had turned him on, gotten his mind moving along new parameters. *This* goddamn process really worked! As advertised. And now, despite himself, he felt an unwholesome fascination toward it.

"I'll be seeing you next week, won't I?" Sylvia said with a knowing little smile. "Mr. Rohrer will handle the details of scheduling."

"I guess so," Weller muttered. Now he realized that there never had been any chance that they were going to let him see Annie at this stage. After this one session it was clear that everything up till this point had been low-level stuff designed to lead him into meditative deconditioning, had only been the baiting of the hook. Because this stuff really seemed to work the way it was intended. They had won round one. They had gotten him interested in the game for its own sake. He sensed that some positive change in his life might come out of this meditative deconditioning thing.

He shuddered. If *that* power were really there, what other, deeper, more subtle, and less benign changes could this process unfold in what he had once supposed was his immutable soul?

Rohrer was a pasty-faced little man in his forties, and his office was little more than a cubicle; his persona was that of a paper shuffler, a low-level functionary who just filled out forms. He listened to Weller's opening demands to see Annie

82

with a bureaucratic weariness that no amount of verbiage could penetrate, letting Weller go on till he simply ran out of steam.

"Really, Mr. Weller," he finally said, "my job is to arrange your meditative deconditioning, not discuss life directives which are a matter of policy set at a much higher level. Besides, from what's in your file it's perfectly obvious that you're not going to be allowed to see her until you've been processed to her level. So shall we get down to what we're here for, eh?"

"I'm not signing up for any meditative deconditioning until I see my wife," Weller insisted, but with little internal conviction.

"And you're not going to see your wife until you've had meditative deconditioning," Rohrer said. "We seem to be at an impasse."

"So we do," Weller said wearily.

Rohrer stared off into space for a moment. Then a lightbulb seemed to come on in his head so transparently that Weller was sure it was some kind of act. "I almost forgot," he said, reaching into a desk drawer. He pulled out a white envelope and placed it on the desk top with his palm over it. "This may make a difference," he said.

"What is it?"

"It's an authorized communication from your wife," Rohrer said. "My directive is to give it to you after you've signed up for meditative deconditioning."

Weller leaped half out of his chair and reached for the envelope. Rohrer looked startled, but slickly and quickly slipped the envelope back in the drawer. "Give me that or I'll—"

"You'll what?" Rohrer said. "Violence will be entirely counterproductive from your point of view. You don't imagine you can overpower me and get out of this building with the letter do you? And to what end?"

Weller slumped back into his chair. The wormy little bastard was right. They really had him. They knew he would *have* to see the letter. Of course, he could sign up for the course, get the letter, and then refuse to pay them . . .

"Shall we get on with it?" Rohrer said.

"All right," Weller sighed. "Let's discuss my meditative deconditioning. How long is it going to take me to reach the level where you'll let me see my wife?"

"That depends. . . ."

"On what?" Weller snapped.

"On how well you respond. On how many sessions a week you have."

"Goddamn it, can't you give me a straight answer? How many sessions is it going to take me to be processed to Annie's level?"

"The usual range would be twenty to thirty sessions," Rohrer said. "On the other hand, your wife will be continuing her processing in the meantime, so how long it takes you to catch up will also be a function of how rapidly you take the necessary processing."

Good God! Weller thought. Thirty sessions at forty bucks each is twelve hundred dollars! At two sessions a week, that's fifteen weeks, and another fifteen hundred dollars!

"Do you realize what you're saying, man?" he said. "Twelve hundred dollars! Fifteen weeks before I get to see Annie! Money aside, don't you people have any heart?" The future spread out before Weller in an endless bankrupt headache throb.

"It's not as bad as all that," Rohrer said blandly. "You seem to assume that we're limiting you to two meditative deconditioning sessions a week. If the time factor concerns you, I'd suggest you sign up for the crash course."

"Crash course?"

Rohrer nodded. "You can have a session every night in the week if you want to," he said. "That way, the whole process would only take about a month. In fact it's our experience that people who take the crash course finish the process in fewer sessions. You get into it more deeply that way. You might achieve fully eptified consciousness in as little as twenty sessions in as little as three weeks. Possibly at a savings of four hundred dollars."

Weller did some fast mental calculations. Seven sessions a week would cost him two hundred and eighty dollars, plus another hundred for Bailor. He was making five hundred dollars a week, so that would leave him four hundred and eighty a month to meet the mortage payment and live on. He should be able to squeeze through. And he would save almost fifteen hundred dollars in the long run.

More to the point, he might be able to handle this situation for another four weeks, but *fifteen weeks more* was unthinkable. There was no way he could endure that!

"And at the end of the month I can see Annie?" he asked plaintively.

"I have no authority to tell you that one way or the other," Rohrer said.

"Oh, for God's sake. . ."

Rohrer leaned across the desk and seemed to crack his bureaucratic persona with a man-to-man smile that seemed totally bureaucratic in itself. "Well then, just between you and me, off the record, you understand," he said, "it's been my experience that in a case like this the life directive would usually be rescinded once you complete meditative deconditioning. Does that help?"

Weller nodded. He sighed. There was Annie's letter locked away from him in the desk drawer. I *have* to have that. There's no way I'm going to leave here without it and only one way I'm going to get it. He thought of tonight's session, the strange mixture of crude brainwashing and . . . and something else, something that had held an almost morbid fascination for him at a deep, deep level. Who are you kidding? he thought. You knew you were going to sign up before you came in here, before you even knew about the letter. This little fencing match was just a sham from word one. Get it over with, and get that letter!

"All right," he said. "I guess you've sold me the crash course." Like a man struggling in quicksand, every move he made just seemed to suck him in deeper.

Weller rushed out of the Transformation Center with the still-sealed envelope burning in his hand. He had resisted the impulse to tear it open the moment Rohrer handed it over; whatever was in it, reading it in this place would be more than he could bear.

He ran the two blocks to his car, got in, and tore open the envelope. Inside were two sheets of Transformationalism, Inc. letterhead covered with perfect electric typewriting. Annie could not type worth a damn. Son of a bitch! It meant that someone had read what she had written, passed it, and retyped it—if Annie had really written the damn thing at all.

His hands trembling slightly, Weller began to read:

Dear Jack:

How are you, love? I know you must be feeling better because I wouldn't be allowed to write this letter unless your processors knew they had put you through some meaningful transformations.

I've been going through some heavy transformations

85

myself. I'm feeling better and stronger and more myself every day and the only block was missing you and worrying about you being left behind.

But now I've been told that you're on your way home to me, and it's given me the strength to go on and endure the waiting with a happy heart.

Knowing you, I know that you must still be confused and uncertain. You started your processing out of love for me, not because you thought you really needed it; we all know that. But by now you must see that something inside you has drawn you to Transformationalism for its own sake. I was enough to get you started, but now you're not sure why you're going on.

I hope it isn't making you doubt your love for me. I hope you're not thinking you're somehow betraying our love by continuing for your own "selfish" reasons. I also hope that you're not hiding your real reasons from yourself out of some guilty, twisted loyalty to me.

Because there is no selfishness here. When two people love each other, they both want each other to be the best possible persons they can. What enhances your self enhances us, and so enhances me. I had to leave you for a time because you didn't understand that in relation to me. Now, love, you must be feeling what I felt. So no blame, no guilt. What you do for you, you do for us.

So take care, love, feel free, do what you have to do for *you*, knowing that I understand you're doing it for us. Take heart in knowing, as I do, that we'll be back together soon—enhanced, fulfilled, eptified, a better you, a better me, a better us.

Much love,
Annie

Carefully, mechanically, Weller folded the letter and slipped it back in the envelope. The signature in ball-point pen at the bottom of the letter had unquestionably been authentic. So whether Annie had written the letter herself or not, she had definitely at least read it and at least to that extent collaborated in its writing.

But in another way it seemed like a Transformationalist document, another carefully calculated piece of brainwashing, even if every word had come straight from her heart. The timing was too perfect, what the letter had said was too close to what he had been feeling. It was all too perfectly crafted to psychologically reinforce the tentative decision he had just made for it to be just a random personal letter from his wife.

Wearily he started the engine and put the car into gear. The letter that had seemed to be so much before he had read it now had proven to be nothing at all. Nothing was changed; he knew no more than before. Except, perhaps, that even his own motives might not be what they seemed, maybe he couldn't entirely trust himself either.

Six

Hal Leer, red-eyed and ashen-faced even with the benefit of the best possible makeup, lurched around on rubbery knees in the center of the set while Barry the Brat and Scuffles, wearing matching Little League uniforms and baseball gloves, tossed the ball gently back and forth to each other—left, right, left, right.

Weller, standing behind the rolling camera, watched the take with bleary, hostile boredom. Stupid brainless garbage! he thought. Like life in prison without possibility of parole, like life without Annie, like night after night of meditative deconditioning, the same brain-bonging routine over and over again. Start a segment on Monday, be half a day's shooting behind by Wednesday, work like a maniac on Thursday and Friday to catch up, accepting any crap that was halfway usable as a print, wrap it up on Friday half-dead on his feet. And for what? So he could begin at the top of the cycle again on Monday morning. So he could collect his lousy five hundred dollars and pay out three hundred eighty dollars of it to Bailor and the Transformationalists. So he could keep going in order to keep going. He felt like a creaky robot, badly in need of oil, on an accelerating treadmill to nowhere.

Only during his sessions with Sylvia did he feel really alert, and that was a state of heightened awareness almost too convoluted to bear. Bailor's so-called counterprogramming only seemed to crank up his paranoia a turn of the screw tighter. Knowing what was going on only made it worse. . . .

"They're ping-ponging your head," Bailor had told him. "They feed you scenarios keyed into your fears and guilts and dissatisfactions designed to drop your self-esteem through the floor, and then they hit you with a superman fantasy that lets you feel like the king of the hill. They move your sense of self-worth from your life as you've lived it into the whack-off fantasies of the life scenarios. Soon you want to be *that* Jack Weller, not the nerd sleepwalking around in the real world. The classic cult program."

"So what do I do?"

"Give 'em what they're looking for," Bailor had said. "Stop asking about Annie. Talk about your work problems. Throw in a few questions about Transformationalism here and there. But do it grudgingly and slowly—you've got to convince them that you're coming around against great internal resistance."

"But how do I keep it from becoming a self-fullfilling prophecy? I mean, what's the difference between meditative deconditioning and what you're telling me to do? You're giving me a goddamn life scenario too!"

"You know what scenarios to watch out for. The true-believer stuff. The seeker-after-higher-consciousness stuff. So when they run one of those on you, play *your* game, not theirs. Concentrate on something different, something that will put your mind in the so-called eptified state of consciousness they're looking for, but with *different* content. Like if they run a number about dedicating yourself to the church, think about shooting the last scene of a successful movie. Get it?"

"You mean run my *own* life scenario on top of theirs? I'm glad you're not suggesting anything too complicated . . ."

So the meditative-deconditioning sessions had become games within games within games. Run his own scenarios within Sylvia's scenarios, split himself in half, or was it in thirds? It was getting to the point where he looked forward to certain life scenarios—the creative fantasies, the scenarios where he and Annie were reunited—as the only moments when he could bring himself together, let himself experience the totality of Jack Weller and feel good inside his own skin. Everything else was a paranoiac acting exercise or sleepwalking. He had reached the final irony—he only felt real, authentically himself, during unreal fantasy situations! If only he could reverse fantasy and reality, if only he could live out the life scenario of Jack Weller, the committed creator, if only. . . .

Oh, my God! Weller suddenly realized that he had been tripping out into his own head games on the set again, and this time right in the middle of a take! How long had Scuffles and the Brat been tossing that baseball back and forth? Well screw it, they can just cut away as much of this lead-in as they want to. He brought his right hand up and dropped it sharply, cuing Hal Leer.

Leer seemed to give Weller a look of pure poison before he delivered the line. "Here, let the old man have it. Let's see if Scuffles can hit the old curve ball."

The Brat tossed the baseball to Leer and went down into a catcher's squat as Scuffles picked up the bat and took a

89

right-handed hitter's position, thumping the bat on an imaginary home plate and ad-libbing ape grunts.

Leer went into a woozy, ludicrous double-pumping pitcher's windup, then brought his arm forward with the pitch. But at the moment of release, he seemed to get tripped up in his own stupid feet, and he stumbled forward, half falling down.

The ball hit Scuffles right on top of the head, a perfect beaner.

The ape screamed in feral outrage, bared its yellow teeth, and shambled across the set toward Leer with blood in its eyes. Leer snarled and balled his hands into fists.

"Cut!" Weller screamed. "Stop that goddamn chimp!" He dashed forward as Scuffles leaped at Leer, who sidestepped clumsily and hit the chimp a glancing, ineffectual blow on the shoulder as Scuffles, chittering, slammed into his left side and knocked him on his ass.

Then the trainer and two grips grabbed the howling ape from behind, pinned its arms behind its back, and dragged it, screeching and kicking, away from Leer.

Weller reached Leer, took him by the hands, and tried to help him to his feet, but Leer angrily pulled away from him. "Get your filthy hands off me, you imbecile!" he shouted.

At the right of the set the grips were still holding onto Scuffles while the ape struggled and gibbered, and the trainer tried to calm him with soft sounds in his ear. Barry the Brat stood nearby, taunting the chimp by pretending to throw phantom baseballs at its head.

Weller exploded in a fit of blind rage. "Cut that shit out, you little bastard, or I'll break both of your arms!"

"*Up yours!*" the Brat screamed and stomped off toward his dressing room.

Weller stood there confronting a red-faced Leer. Aside from the gibberings of Scuffles, there was dead silence on the set. Cameramen, grips, and sound men were staring at Weller as if he were a maniac.

"Weller, you are without a doubt the—"

"Shut up, you goddamn drunken sot!" Weller shouted in Leer's face. "You show up drunk or hung over on this set again and I'll have your ass canned!"

The intake of breath from the crew was all but audible. Still red-faced with anger, Leer spoke in clipped, tightly controlled tones. "You'll have me canned, will you, Weller? *You'll* have *me* canned? We'll just see about that. We'll see who gets fired after this little exhibition."

Weller took a deep breath, then took half a dozen quick steps backward, the director commanding the set. "We will break for lunch now," he announced loudly. "After which we will continue today's shooting, and we will get it right. I hope all of you have got that straight."

The crew continued to stare at him with unconcealed, silent hostility. "Scuffles is through for today," the trainer said. "I only hope that's the worst of it."

"Then we'll shoot around him this afternoon," Weller said grimly. "And tomorrow he had better be ready."

"*Or what?*" the trainer snarled.

"*Or else,*" Weller shot back at him, and stalked off in the general direction of the commissary, unable to bear looking at the mess on the set a moment longer—the glowering Leer, the contemptuous sullen eyes of the crew, the stinking goddamn gibbering ape.

That does it! he thought. I can't take another week of this! I've got to get out of here, I can't stand it any more. I'm going to quit this fucking job. I'm going to quit Friday. I can't bring back Annie, I can't get my head out of this quagmire, there's only one thing I can do to try to make my life endurable, and that's get rid of this miserable cretinous insanity. Enough is enough! I've had it! I'll sell my car, I'll take a second mortgage, I'll dig goddamn ditches, but I can't take any more of this.

By the time he had reached the Transformation Center, Weller's energy level was about an inch off the floor, and his will was drained dry. After he had choked down a hamburger at the commissary and returned to the set, the idea of quitting his job had become just another unreal life scenario.

Sell the car? Maybe he could get two grand, but how long would that last at three hundred and eighty dollars a week for processing and Bailor, not to mention mortgage payments and minor matters like utilities and eating? And if he walked out on his contract, no one would ever hire him again; he'd be broke, unemployable, and wheelless, which in Los Angeles was like having three broken legs. A second mortgage on the house? Fat chance, if he couldn't even show a bank enough income to carry the first one! Dig ditches? Sure. Wash dishes? Right. The town was just full of shit jobs that would pay an out-of-work director four hundred dollars a week.

So he had slogged through the afternoon's shooting in even more of a trance than usual. The crew was sullen, silent, and agonizingly slow, as if they were punishing him for the morning's outburst, as if they wanted nothing more than to get his ass off the set. Leer came back with booze on his breath, but Weller dared not openly notice it; as it was, the necessary conversation was conducted in grunts and snarls, and shooting was hopelessly behind already. Barry the Brat he could at least intimidate into working with implied threats of violence; he at least had enough authority left as an adult for that. But throughout the endless afternoon a slow funeral going seemed to be beating in his head; he felt dead inside, and indeed cultivating that anesthesia of mindless zombiehood was the only way that getting through the day seemed possible.

He slunk into the Transformation Center, took the elevator to the third floor, walked into the processing room, and dropped his bone-weary body into the chair in front of the brainwave monitor like a sack of potatoes. Even cold, clinical Sylvia was able to feel his trapped, defeated, exhausted mood.

"Are you all right, Jack?" she said, with *You look awful!* written silently across her face.

"No," Weller said sullenly.

"Would you like to see a life counselor?"

"No," Weller said. Yet another brand of mind game was hardly what his present mood called for.

"Do you feel you'd like to cancel tonight's session?"

"No," Weller said automatically. Did I drag my ass here for nothing tonight, you nerd? Besides, tripping out into a harmless scenario or two might be some kind of relief from the awfulness of reality.

Sylvia snapped back into her robotic persona. She fitted the electrode band on his head and plugged him into the console. "Well then," she said brightly, turning on the machine, "maybe tonight's session will do you some good."

"Maybe it will," Weller said, half surprising himself with the sincerity he heard in his own voice. "I could do with forgetting about what's happened today."

Sylvia favored him with a tiny smile. "That's the right attitude," she said. "Move along the time track with the changes. What's past is memory, don't let it become a block."

Weller nodded. A tiny ray of light pierced his clouds. For the first time today he felt as if he had accomplished something, a little piece of role playing that had advanced him some infinitesimal distance toward Annie. If that were what it was. He tried to force his tired mind further toward full alertness, sensing that he had set the stage for a session that might go a long way toward convincing them that he was moving swiftly toward true conversion. You were zero as a director today, Weller, let's see if you can at least act.

"All right now, ready for your first scenario?" Sylvia said. "Your wife has just had a baby boy. She's gotten an offer to do an important supporting role in a movie. In order for her to accept, you must stay home all day for three months to take care of the baby. She'll be making good money, so that won't be a problem, and you've decided to make the sacrifice for her sake."

Weller could all but feel his brainwaves going wild. This was one that he and Annie had gone through a dozen times, and it was why they had made the cold-blooded decision not to have children, at least not now, not until they had both made it, not until it wouldn't interfere with Annie's chances to advance her career. The idea that *he* might stay home to take care of a baby had never even been discussed; it was unthinkable.

But here was the sacrifice-for-Annie motif again, and with a vengeance. He had to give them what they were looking for, tonight of all nights, when the attitude he had walked in with had already established a lot of credibility for his making the "major breakthrough" in his processing that they were watching for.

And, he realized, Bailor's advice would work like a charm here; all he had to do was apply a little reverse English in his mind.

So he imagined the exact opposite of the scenario Sylvia had given him. Annie had had a baby boy, and *he* was working on a feature film while *she* stayed home to take care of the child. Every evening he came home from a successful day's shooting to a wife mellowed by motherhood. As the boy grew, so did his film, his reputation, his creative powers, his feeling of at last being on top of the Hollywood heap. And Annie was content, because she knew that once the finished film was released to critical acclaim and socko box-office figures, he would be in a position to give her career a boost up, just as the baby was ready for a daytime nurse, just as they reached the point where they could afford it. It would be all they had wanted, all they had dreamed about, and now it was happening. . . .

Sylvia looked up from the scope and wrote something on the form on her clipboard. For a moment Weller got a glimpse of her full face, and he thought he saw the ghost of a satisfied smile—smug, perhaps, but satisfied. Only then did his control waver and a wave of sadness break over him. For after all, what he had constructed in his mind was a fantasy within a fantasy, an ironic negative image of the true reality—no Annie, no child, no feature film, just the awful aloneness and the endless grinding days of *Monkey Business* spiraling down, down, down. . . .

"Very good," Sylvia said. "I think we're really making progress in that area."

Weller smiled a wan eat-shit smile. It was the first time she had actually betrayed a reaction, and she was eating it up. It *was* possible to fool the bastards. At least in this one thing he wasn't a total failure.

"Let's see if we can keep it up," Sylvia said, and Weller felt even more strongly that his processing was entering a new phase, that they were buying his act, that Bailor's strategy was working.

"Now then," Sylvia said, "you've been asked to direct some commercials for a presidential candidate. The candidate is a true man of the people, so the political and economic establishment are all against him, and his campaign is financed strictly by the dimes and dollars of poor people, and every dollar counts. He's offered to pay you a small salary, but the man is so sincere, so dedicated, such an underdog, and so obviously what the country needs that you can't accept even that. Because you know that people all over the country would be missing meals to pay your salary. So you tell him that you're honored to work for him, but you can't accept any payment. It's got to be your own personal sacrifice for the cause."

Oh brother! Weller thought. John B. Steinhardt for President? Our Peerless Leader in the White House off the nickels and dimes of the poor? It symbolized the whole Transformationalist setup. The poor schmuck so dedicated to the cause that he wants to work for nothing is exactly the kind of follower the bastard wants. And exactly the kind of schmuck I've got to convince them I'm becoming.

So he imagined that a long-forgotten great aunt had died and left him five million dollars. He was going to finance his own film with part of the money. He had gotten a great script written by one of the top writers in Hollywood, and every agent in town was calling to push the greatest stars alive for parts in his movie. He was having trouble deciding between Paul Newman and Robert Redford for the male lead—they were both so pathetically desperate for the part—but he had already cast Annie as the female lead. And now he was walking into the office of Morris Fender, producer of *Monkey Business*, and he had the latest awful script rolled up into a tight cone in his hand, and he was going to tell Fender exactly where he could stick it. Then he was going to buy Scuffles the chimp and sell him to a dogfood factory. . . .

"It's quite surprising, Jack," Sylvia said. "You're doing very well tonight, though you came here in a very deenergized mood."

"Yeah, well maybe when you don't want to think too much about what's going on in your life situation, it's easier to get your head behind alternate life scenarios," Weller said truthfully.

"When you can accept your current life situation with the same optimized consciousness you achieve during the scenarios, you'll find that starting to improve too," Sylvia said. "After all, that *is* the ultimate goal of meditative deconditioning."

"Do you really think I'm getting there?" Weller asked in as humble a tone as he could muster.

"You're progressing, Jack, you're progressing."

"I really wish all this was helping my life situation more," Weller said, continuing to string her along.

"When you've achieved a fully eptified consciousness, you'll find that the Transformation will automatically improve your interaction with the external environment."

"I hope so," Weller said quietly.

"Shall we get on with your processing?" Sylvia said. Weller could sense a certain edge of impatience. He had run this little number just about far enough. I've eptified the current situation, he thought sardonically.

"Sure," he said, with what he hoped was just the right tone of subtle, subdued enthusiasm.

"All right now, you've reached the end of your current contract for the show you're working on, and the producer has told you that it's been canceled. You're out of work, you have no immediate offers, and all you have to live on is what savings you've accumulated, enough to keep you going for a couple of months."

Sylvia's words knocked the psychic wind right out of Weller, flung him right back into the bottomless pit of *Monkey Business*—today's fiasco, Leer's threats, the hostile eyes of a crew whose respect he had lost, the futility and frustration dragging on and on forever, the funeral gong peeling in his head.

Good God, do they know? But that was sheer paranoia, that was impossible. . . . *or was it?* How long *was* their reach?

Sylvia looked up from the oscilloscope, frowning. "You're blocking very heavily," she said disapprovingly.

Get ahold of yourself, Weller, get ahold of yourself! Don't blow this too! Desperately, he tried to come up with a counterscenario that would move those readings toward optimum, but he came up dry. His mind was clogged with memory images of today's shooting, and nothing could drive them out.

"Let me help you," Sylvia said. "You're obviously fixating on the negative aspects of this scenario, and that's very regressive. I'm surprised at you. Look at the other side, ride with the change, try to fix your consciousness on the positive aspects. They're there, reach for them. . . ."

With an audible sigh Weller closed his eyes and gave up trying to play the countergame Bailor had taught him. It just wouldn't work in this situation. This scenario was too close to reality. *Too close?* It *was* reality, or only an inch away. It was how he had felt this morning, when he was determined to quit the goddamn show. All those feelings came rushing back. Quit the damn job! Dig ditches! *Get rid of it!* This life scenario was *him*. It's where you want to be, Weller, admit it to yourself. Use this process to learn something for once.

He let himself float down into the center of the scenario, playing the meditative-deconditioning game in earnest for the first time. Reach for the positive aspects? Well for one thing, Weller, you hate every bloody minute on the *Monkey Business* set. And it's not taking you anywhere near where you really want to be. It's making you hate the act of directing itself, isn't it? It's ruining you for anything better. Every day on that set is an extended act of cowardice that chips away at the Jack Weller you want to be.

Anger began to wash over Weller's despair. *Cowardice?* Isn't that it? You don't have the balls to quit! You were ready to do it this morning, but you lost your courage over a greasy commissary hamburger. You want out, but you don't have the balls to do it yourself.

Reach for the positive aspect? If the show were canceled, I'd be out of there, that's the goddamn positive aspect! I'd be broke, I'd have to do God-knows-what to keep up this processing—do porn, maybe—but I'd be free. Free from Barry the Brat! Free from Leer! Free from directing a fucking ape!

A blast of energy went through Weller as he imagined life without *Monkey Business*. His mind soared like an uncaged bird. *I'd get off my butt, find my own center again, do work that mattered or nothing at all, the way I always promised myself I would. I'd have one hell of a huge monkey off my back!*

"Very good," Sylvia said. "You found it, didn't you? See, you *can* do it."

Weller opened his eyes. He blinked. The life scenario was run and over, but that wonderful energetic feeling remained. He felt great. He felt better than at any time since Annie had left him, since God-knows-how-long *before* Annie had left him.

I don't want to lose this feeling, he thought. *I won't lose it. This one was my life, I won't let this slip away. I was right the first time! Quit the fucking job!*

"Jeez," he said, "something happened there, it really did." What he was putting out synched perfectly with the act he was supposed to be putting on, but it was also him; his act was synched into his true self for the first time in longer than he could remember.

Sylvia smiled at him. "You appear to believe you've made a Transformational breakthrough," she said. "And I think you may be right."

"If this is Transformational Consciousness, it's okay, it's sure okay," Weller said, feeding her the line, conscious of projecting the desired effect, but at the same time feeling his current instantaneous personality resonating with the truth of what he was saying. *Is it really true?* he wondered. *Can this stuff really work for me if I let it?*

Entering his semidarkened living room, thick with dust, cluttered with old pizza cartons, stacks of unread newspapers, and unwashed sticky glasses, Weller felt a jarring discontinuity between what he felt like inside and the midden that his external life had become. He hurried to the phone and dialed the emergency exchange number that Garry Bailor had given him. A metallic female voice answered on the fourth ring. "Garry Bailor's exchange. May I help you?"

"This is Jack Weller. I have to talk to Mr. Bailor immediately. Will you please give him the message?"

"Will you please give me the number you're calling from."

Weller gave her his number, hung up the phone, and waited nervously. More of Bailor's security paranoia. He wouldn't give out his home number, afraid that someone might find out where he lived from the exchange digits, even though the number was unlisted. The only way to contact him without a scheduled appointment was to call the exchange and hope he'd call back. And Weller couldn't wait. He had to talk to Bailor *now*.

When he left the Transformational Center, he had known he was going to quit his job tomorrow, but on the drive home he had begun to distrust his own head. The center of his being vibrated with the rightness of the decision he had made. Contemplating life without *Monkey Business* felt wonderful.

But where and when had he made that decision? During a processing session at the center! How could he completely trust this wonderful feeling? The move *seemed* to be his, he had made it once before today, but how could he be sure he was in control even of what *seemed* like his essential center? He was the focus of conflicting fields of psychic energy that bombarded him with programming and counterprogramming on every level. Could he really be a creature of his own free will, or was what he felt just the interface between conflicting programs? He had been through too much to believe with total confidence in the existence of an untouched core of free will at the center of all that psychic determinism. Is the me who thinks he's his own man *really* his own man?

He desperately needed some external anchor, and Bailor was the only person in the world who could understand the nature of the problem, who could give him an outside-observer's viewpoint on his own inner workings.

Finally the phone rang. Weller snatched it up before the first ring of the bell had died. "*Garry?*"

"Yeah, Jack. What is it?"

"I've just come from the Center. I've had quite an experience. I think I'm going to quit my job tomorrow."

"*What?* What in blazes did they run on you to make you do *that?*"

"It's my own decision," Weller said. "At least I think it is. . . . I mean, that's why I called you. There *was* a life scenario, but. . . ."

"You sound spaced," Bailor said. "Give me the whole story sequentially, from this morning on." Even over the phone, Weller could sense Bailor's skeptical, analytical, merciless attention. It helped him organize his own confusion. Bailor was like a psychic computer: feed him all the data, and he would organize it logically and extract the pattern, the implied conclusion. Weller poured the whole story into the phone, in cold, logical, clipped chronological order, feeding in the data without attempting to analyze it.

When he had finished, there was a long silence on the other end of the phone. Weller could all but hear the relays clicking.

Finally, Bailor spoke. "They've gotten to you," he said flatly.

"What do you mean, *they've gotten to me?*"

"You've been programmed," Bailor said. "Can't you see it? You're about to make a real life decision on the basis of something that happened to you during a processing session. Isn't it obvious?"

"But why would they want me to quit my job?" Weller asked defensively. "That doesn't make sense." Wondering just what it was he felt compelled to defend.

"But they don't even know about that, now do they?" Bailor said sarcastically.

"Then what are you talking about?" Weller said, feeling some nameless dread cracking his well-being like ivy crumbling a stone wall.

"Before you got into this, you would never have quit your job, would you?"

"No. . . ." Weller said grudgingly, beginning to see where Bailor was going.

"So your head has been changed during processing," Bailor snapped. "*By* processing!"

Woodenly Weller peered silently into the mouthpiece. Was it true? Could such a feeling of rightness be false? An illusion? Something that had taken control of him?

"That's called programming, isn't it, Jack?" Bailor said. "Something in your mind has been altered."

"You could be right . . .", Weller admitted. "But isn't learning the same essential process?" he said more strongly. "Learning something about myself and then acting on it."

"Will you cut the shit?" Bailor said in exasperation. "Look at the damn *content* of the reprogramming, will you? Can't you see what's happened?"

"You tell me," Weller snapped irritably. "That's what I'm paying you for."

"That's right, buster," Bailor said coldly. "So listen and get your money's worth. You're now ready to abandon about all that's left of your previous life and leap into some etherealized ego-trip pipe dream. Are you stupid? Don't you see what that

99

adds up to as a mind set from the Transformationalists' point of view?"

"Oh shit," Weller said, feeling like a schmuck but also feeling as if he had just been robbed of something he was learning to treasure.

"That's right, Jack. Suggestibility. Ready to follow a program that was *accidentally* implanted. Ripe for the picking when they throw the real thing at you."

Bailor's tone of voice changed, became distantly sardonic. "Of course, you could look on the bright side. At least your act is working. If I can keep you from picking up programming like this well enough to make sure it *stays* an act until they buy it, we're gonna get there."

Weller could see it now, he could see the whole infernal thing. And yet wasn't it possible to make the right decision for the wrong reason? Couldn't his own best interest coincide with the head space they had brainwashed him into? Maybe quitting his job was the right thing to do even if he had been brainwashed into believing it. Wasn't blindly opposing anything that happened to float through his mind during processing a perverse form of mind control too? *Bailor's* brand of brainwashing?

"But that doesn't mean I shouldn't quit, does it?" he said. "I've always hated that damned job."

There was a pause at the other end of the line, and when Bailor spoke again, his voice was like a razor. "Right. Quit your job. Then where do you think you're going to get the money to continue processing, huh?"

Bailor paused again, and once more his voice changed; now it was sinuous and coaxing. "Now that we're really getting somewhere, you don't want to throw it all away for some silly whim you've gotten into your head. Are you forgetting why you got yourself into this in the first place? You've got to hold on, man. You've got to keep making money. When we've gotten Annie back and deprogrammed, *then* quit your job, if that's still your thing. But doing it now would be totally self-destructive."

Bailor's words were like a bucket of ice water in Weller's face. Of course he was right. Pragmatically right. Totally right. Inescapably right. Heroic gestures were something he simply just couldn't afford now, and Bailor had effectively rubbed his nose in it. He had to keep working because Transformationalism wasn't on credit cards. And neither, he thought angrily, is Bailor.

"And, of course, you also have a financial interest in my keeping my job, don't you, Garry?" he snapped.

"You get what you pay for," Bailor said diffidently. "You knew that when you hired me."

"So I did."

"Well, Jack, are you going to stick it out, or has it been nice knowing you? My dinner is ready."

"You know damn well I have no choice," Weller said wearily.

Bailor's tone lightened immediately, became friendly in a mode that Weller now perceived as hacked out of plastic. "No hard feelings then, Jack. This is a heavy game, and feelings get upset, and tempers get tight. See you on Saturday, right?"

"Yeah, Garry," Weller grunted. "No hard feelings."

But when he hung up the phone, he found himself hating Bailor. Not only because Bailor had let the mask slip and bluntly reminded him that he was just a paid mercenary who would be with him just as long as the money held out. But for raining on his parade, for taking away something vague that he had always wanted, that had been just within his grasp. For leaving him with this sullen, angry feeling of having been robbed of the first bit of something good that had drifted into his life since . . . since Annie had left. For this undefined but quite real sense of loss.

Fittingly it was raining the next morning when Weller drove to work, a leaden Southern California downpour that matched his mood perfectly. He parked the Triumph in his regular space just in front of the sound stage, but by the time he had dashed inside, his clothes were already damp and a lock of hair was plastered to his forehead.

Perfect, he thought, just bloody perfect, as he wiped the wet hair off his face with the back of his hand and walked past stacks of old scenery toward today's shooting set.

Then he saw that the set was empty.

The flat of the kitchen set was set up, the furniture, the props, the cameras, sound equipment, and lights. But no crew. No actors. No Scuffles. No trainer. Just the dead, empty set, tiny and forlorn, dwarfed by the shadowy gray vault of the sound stage, like a section of a bombed-out abandoned city, moldering in the cavernous graveyard silence of the huge empty building.

Then Weller saw that the set was not quite empty. A short, balding man emerged from the shadow of a stack of flats and walked toward him, his footsteps echoing hollowly in the

101

silence. It was Morris Fender, the producer of *Monkey Business*.

With his heart sinking toward his rubbery knees, Weller walked toward Fender, and they met alongside the main camera. Fender looked at Weller with utter disdain on his tanned, wrinkled face; his lips were clenched in tightly controlled anger, and behind his air-force-style glasses his eyes were hard as marbles.

"I'll make this short, but it won't be sweet, Weller," he said. "You've ruined our goddamn chimpanzee. The trainer is threatening to sue the studio. Leer refuses to work with you again, and Barry's mother doesn't want the kid around your foul mouth. The stuff you've been turning in for the past few weeks has been garbage, and it's been late. Ordinarily I'd fire you."

Weller stood there awash in Fender's anger and disgust, unable to react, unable to even feel what was happening. Bong, bong, bong, went a deep-throated bell in his head.

"The good news," Fender said, "is that I don't have a show left to fire you from. It'd take weeks to get another chimp ready for the part. Three of your last segments can't be aired without extensive reshooting. So *Monkey Business* has been canceled. You're a lucky man, Weller."

"Lucky . . . ?" Weller muttered inanely. *Lucky?*

Fender nodded. "This way you haven't been officially fired. Your credit list won't have 'this bastard was fired' in big red letters, since the show you would've been fired from has been canceled. But don't expect to ever work for this studio again. Don't expect to work on a show on the same network. Don't expect to work for any producer *I've* ever talked to."

Weller could say nothing. His brain felt like frozen mud. I'll quit, I won't quit, I'll quit, I won't quit—and now this! Elation? A sense of freedom? He felt as if he had been hit over the head with a baseball bat.

"Now take anything you've got here and get off this lot," Fender said. He turned, shook his head to himself, and walked off toward the exit.

Only long after Fender had disappeared into the shadows did Weller begin to react to what had happened, and the first thing he felt was anger. At himself. How many times have I wanted to tell that creep to get stuffed? he thought. How many times have I rehearsed my parting shot to that little bastard in my mind? And now what do you do, Weller? Do you punch him out? Do you tell him what you think of him and his lousy show?

No, you stand there stupidly like a lox. You don't say a damn thing as he fires you. You take it like a clumsy servant being dismissed by the lord of the manor.

"Fuck you, Fender!" he shouted into the emptiness. "Fuck you, you wormy little bastard!" It only made him feel even more foolish and futile.

Woodenly he collected his few things and walked outside to his car. The cloudburst had subsided and water was steaming off the hood above the still-warm engine. The sky remained gray and threatening.

Weller leaned up against the side of the car, not caring that the wet metal was soaking his already-damp pants. What am I going to do now? he wondered. Now that the life scenario had become reality, there was no sense of freedom, no surge of energy and determination. Under the ominous gray sky what it boiled down to was that Transformationalism had cost him both his wife and his job. What was next, the house and the car? His sanity?

He felt empty, husked, drained. How was he going to keep going? And what was he supposed to keep going *for*?

The only meaningful thing left in his life was the wan hope of someday, somehow being reunited with Annie, and even that was vaguing out into an abstraction as it receded further and further into the future, became more and more . . . divorced . . . from his day to day reality.

And in a week or two he would no longer be able to pay for his processing, and then even the hazy hope of seeing Annie again woud be gone.

He got into the car and started the engine. Through the seat of his pants the throaty rumble infused his body with a faint artificial vitality. At least that! he thought. They've *got* to let me see Annie now. Why shouldn't they? There's no money left; they've sucked me dry.

He released the emergency brake, slammed the car into gear, and roared toward the gate trailing a rooster tail of foam. I'll go see Benson Allen, he decided. I'll wheedle, I'll threaten, I'll beg if I have to, but this thing has got to end now, today.

It *will* end, one way or the other, he realized bleakly. I just don't have the money to go on.

As he drove through the studio gate, the skies opened up again, and a fusillade of hard rain spattered off the hood like machine-gun bullets, momentarily obscuring the windshield behind an impentrable veil of water.

and nodded a good deal. Beyond that, he was being friendly enough. Welcher done it in this one way visible ... somehow once had some extra problems, Allen said ... this was about it? Perhaps I should ... as somehow somehow somehow ... Here being my couple ... Problem still. I've had my work to do on ... have finished and to realm ... some government door and Here dot while and ho And a deep-gut ... something else my way! ... saw the touching that prided all ... stood very strong

Seven

Getting into Benson Allen's office proved to be easier than Weller had anticipated. He got by the desk by asking to see Rohrer, the life counselor, and Rohrer quickly got him in to see Allen once Weller made it clear that the problem concerned his inability to pay for any more processing. Perhaps his disheveled state and the confused bewilderment he was more or less projecting had something to do with it too. Bureaucrats like to get rid of messy-looking maniacs as quickly as possible, he thought, as he entered Allen's office, and if they can't pass the buck down, they do their best to pass it up.

But whatever the reason, here he was, and he knew that he had to keep himself under tight control and do the best and most important piece of acting of his life.

Allen was sitting on one of the white plush couches, eating some concoction of nuts, fruits, and yoghurt with a spoon. In his white shirt and pressed blue jeans he looked strangely out of place in the Hollywood-elegant office, as if he were the hippie houseboy of the absent owner.

Weller found his perception of the man strangely altered. Sitting there surrounded by the Persian rug, the big paintings, the garishly lavish furniture, Allen didn't seem like the all-powerful head of the Los Angeles Transformation Center but like some blond beachboy type who had lucked into something way beyond his depth. I can handle this guy, Weller thought. I really think I can handle this guy. From the pit of his current hopeless position, he found himself drawing energy, an irrational sense of his own power and competence. He had hit the bottom, there was nothing left to lose, and now he was going to turn the corner, because the only way out was up.

"Sit down, man," Allen said. "Have some of this stuff. Give you energy." Without waiting for an answer, he filled another bowl from the tureen on the teak table in front of the couch and handed it to Weller as he sat down.

Allen watched Weller silently until he had tasted the goop

and nodded a *pro forma* approval. Let us break bread together? Weller thought. Is this another gambit?

"So you've got a problem," Allen said. "Tell me about it. I'll do what I can."

"It's pretty simple," Weller said. "I've lost my job and don't have the money to pay for any more processing. So you've got to let me see Annie now. I don't have the money to go on, and I don't imagine you're giving any scholarships."

Allen nodded, ate another mouthful. "That's right," he said, "no free rides. Too bad, because you would've completed your meditative deconditioning in another couple of weeks. They tell me you've been really cooking lately."

"Well then, why can't you bend a little and let me see Annie now?" Weller said cautiously, not wanting to fracture what seemed like the down-home atmosphere at this point.

Allen studied Weller speculatively. "You really want to go on with your processing, Jack?" he said slowly. "I mean, other things being equal?"

It seemed like a non sequitur, but Weller could sense the question's importance, as if Allen were on the edge of relenting, as if all he needed now was to see into Weller and be satisfied that what processing he had already had had taken hold. This was proving much easier than Weller had anticipated. But don't overplay it now, he told himself. Don't overact. Stay convincing.

"I guess so. . . ," Weller said with deliberate uncertainty. Then more firmly, "Sure. I've got to admit that I'm learning things about myself. Sure I was forced into it, but, well, maybe it was the right thing for me. . . ." He frowned sadly. "But what's the point?" he said. "I'm tapped out. I'm broke. And frankly I don't have any immediate prospects. So. . . ."

Allen gazed unblinkingly into his eyes, the old Transformationalist Stare. Weller stared back, focusing his eyes on a point in front of Allen's nose, so that Allen's face became a featureless blur, psychologically neutralizing the power of his unwavering gaze, giving Weller more than an even hand in the staring contest. Whatever was going on, it certainly wasn't the confrontation that Weller had anticipated.

It was Allen who finally looked away, shrugged, and then spoke. "Shit man, if it were my decision, I'd say okay, you can see your wife. I just don't get those hostile vibes off you now, and you've had some bad karma, so what the hell . . ."

Weller went up, then down. "But . . . ?" he said. "There *is* a but. . . ." Allen was saying no softly, he was being friendly about it. What turn was the game taking now?

Allen grimaced. He shrugged. He nodded. He seemed genuinely embarrassed, even nervous. "Thing is, it's now up to the Monitors," he said.

"*Who?*"

"Look, Jack, what I can tell you is that your old lady is now working for us in a position with a security lid on it, which means all her life directives now come directly from the Monitors. Out of my hands. All I can do is present your case. But you'd have to pass a Monitor life analysis to see her, and without even completing your meditative deconditioning. . . ." Allen threw up his hands.

"Who the hell are the Monitors?" Weller snapped, losing some of his control. This was like trying to pick up a mound of jello with your fingers.

"I can't get into that," Allen said, and now he really did seem nervous, perhaps even a little frightened.

I've had just about enough of this shit, Weller thought. Enough cute little games. I can't take much more.

"So what you're telling me," he said coldly, "is that I can't see Annie now because I can't pass something called a Monitor life analysis. And you can't even tell me who or what the Monitors are."

Allen nodded. He seemed unwilling to meet Weller's eyes. He seemed really put down, somehow. And he was suddenly looking like much smaller potatoes inside Transformationalism. Who the hell were the Monitors? Why did the head of the Transformation Center himself seem to be afraid to even talk about them? Weller studied Allen for a moment, and it seemed to him that Allen's attitude toward the Monitors might be some kind of hole card.

"So what am I supposed to do now?" Weller said plaintively, reaching for Allen's sympathy, setting him up. "I'm broke, I've got no job, I can't continue my processing. . . ." He put a slight edge into his voice. "And now the head of the Los Angeles Transformation Center tells me he'd like to help, but it's all in the hands of the mysterious Monitors, and he's powerless."

"I didn't say I was powerless, man," Allen said, with a slight whine in his voice.

"Didn't you?" Weller said with open contempt.

Allen looked up with what seemed like a genuine defensive expression on his face. He put down his bowl. His face

106

creased with thought. "Look," he said, "maybe I *can* help you. Yeah. . . ."

Allen seemed to recover some of his energy and authority. "How would you like to work for us?" he said.

"*Huh?* First you tell me I can't even see my wife, now you tell me you want to make me a processor?"

Allen laughed. "Not as a processor," he said. "In your own line of work."

"As a director?" Weller asked incredulously.

"Like that," Allen said. He got up, walked across the room, and stood behind his enormous sweep of paisley-painted desk. The geometry of the situation was abruptly transformed from whatever it had been into some kind of crazy job interview, and Allen had suddenly seized a more powerful persona—the producer barricaded behind his impress-the-peasants furniture. Intentional or not, Weller had to admire at least the blocking, on a technical level.

"Transformationalism is into a lot of things that I never even thought about when I started it," Allen said. He shook his head somewhat ruefully, or so it seemed. "Getting like some damn conglomerate; we own a lot of things that don't seem to have anything to do with anything. Harry Lazlo, our secretary-treasurer runs all that shit. He used to be a literary agent, and now he wants to play Hollywood wheeler-dealer."

Allen sat down behind his desk. He shrugged. "Not my scene at all," he said. "But Harry's always been on this show-business trip. He likes hanging out with show people, and he's moving us heavily into media. We're doing commercials, and we're producing internal training and educational films, and if I know Harry, his wet dream is to get into movies and TV. We sure have the bread to let him do it. He's hiring a lot of people—crew, directors, who knows—and I don't think many of them are really pros like you. Think you might be interested?"

Weller got up and took a seat immediately in front of the desk. "Are you serious?" he said.

"Sure. I could call him this afternoon and make an appointment for you. Harry would probably dig you." Allen leaned back in his chair, steepled his hands. "Not only that, but full-time paid employees of Transformationalism get free unlimited processing," he said. "Like a fringe benefit. And to get beyond the lowest levels in the media end, you'll have to go through Monitor life analysis anyway."

Weller stared at Allen, trying to let the whole thing sink in.

Transformationalist production companies? Commercials? Even feature films? "Let me get this straight," he said. "If I go to work for Transformationalism, I get free processing, and you let me see Annie?"

Allen nodded. "Once the Monitors have approved you for a permanent position," he said. "I mean, if you're both working for the movement, why should we keep you apart?"

Weller sat there quietly, trying to be logical, trying to evaluate, while everything inside of him told him that he had no choice, that in his present circumstances this was a godsend. A job with what sounded like a bunch of well-heeled amateurs, where he could rise swiftly to a position of creative control. Free processing—no more money down the rathole. A clear path to Annie guaranteed. It sounded to good to be true.

And that, of course, was the kicker. *I walked in here canned, broke, and desperate, and now they hit me with an offer I really can't refuse. The alternative is no Annie, no processing, no job, and no hope. Jesus Christ, I wish I could talk to Bailor right now. What's going on here?*

"Well, what do you say?" Allen asked, moving his right hand over the top of the desk toward the telephone. "You don't have anything to lose by rapping with Harry, do you?"

I don't have anything left to lose at all, Weller thought. *And you know it. What would Bailor—?*

Screw that! he thought. *I'm sick of being told what to do as if I were a brain-damage case, and maybe I've been trusting Bailor too much anyway. If I can't make a decision like this without that bastard holding my hand, I might as well hang it up.*

"How can I say no?" he said.

Allen smiled. "Yeah, you'd be crazy if you did," he said. "It would be heavily regressive, even without the processing you've had. I'll call you tonight and confirm the appointment." *Had there been a subtle edge of threat in Allen's voice? Or was that just more paranoia?*

Weller left Allen's office wondering if he had been conned again, if this whole thing had been a setup, even down to Allen's uneasiness at the mention of the Monitors, whatever they were. Or was what he had so far experienced just the tip of the Transformationalist iceberg?

The address that Benson Allen had given Weller turned out to be one of the sleek glass towers on the western end of

Sunset Strip. Weller parked his car in the underground garage, picked up a parking validation ticket, and walked around front to the lobby. Allen had told him to look for Lazlo's office under "Utopia Industries, Inc." According to the building directory Utopia Industries, Inc. had three full floors. In addition to Lazlo's office the sublistings included about a dozen companies—Colby Publications, radio station KRUR, the Narcon Foundation, Sunrise Books, the Delta Agency, Changes Productions, Carmel Properties, the Regency Corporation, United Data Control, Farside Group, Inc.

Weller stared at the directory in amazement for long moments. He recognized several of the companies apparently controlled by Utopia Industries: a magazine chain, a publishing house, a radio station, a narcotics-rehabilitation outfit, a PR agency. None of them was a flagship company in its field, but all of them were solid second-line outfits, and together they made up quite a corporate empire. Not to mention the companies with which he was not familiar. If all this were really owned by Transformationalism, its tentacles were really pervasive, and its net worth must be well in excess of one hundred million dollars! In that league producing feature films was no idle fantasy.

Lazlo's office was on the fifteenth floor, within the overall headquarters of Utopia Industries, and the elevator deposited Weller in a large and lavish—if neutrally bland—reception area. Walnut veneer paneling, matching modern furniture, deep-pile blue carpeting, half a dozen huge but unobstrusive abstract oil paintings, a big salt-water fish tank, and a sleek Hollywood receptionist shining with well-varnished asexual handsomeness.

Weller gave his name to the receptionist and waited while she buzzed Lazlo's secretary, soaking up the sense of corporate power, all very Hollywood establishment, impressively anonymous in its eradication of personality with expensive showroom decor. It looked like a movie set of a plush corporate headquarters—like most such corporate country in Los Angeles, it mimicked the cinematic version of itself.

Another woman appeared through a door in the paneled inner wall, this one older and wearing a tweed pants suit. "Mr. Weller? Mr. Lazlo will see you now."

Weller followed her through the door and down a long hall. She opened a door at the end of the hall for him and closed it softly behind him as he stepped inside.

Harry Lazlo's office occupied a corner of the building, and

two big picture windows overlooked the Hollywood Hills and the grand smoggy sweep of lowland Los Angeles. There were brown leather couches and chairs, a wall lined with expensively bound books that looked as if they were glued in place, and about half a dozen large signed photographs of minor celebrities, none of whom was John B. Steinhardt. The desk was a great stark cube of mahogany, and the man behind it wore a powder-blue suit with a white shirt and a wide black tie. He was balding, with short gray hair above his ears, an Acapulco tan, and lightly tinted Italian glasses. He was even smoking a trim dark brown cigar—the perfect image of the successful Hollywood entrepreneur.

"Ah, yes, Mr. Weller, do sit down, Benson's told me all about you," Lazlo said in a throaty New York voice but lightly overlaid with Los Angeles smoothie.

He rose as Weller approached the desk and offered him a pudgy hand, with a massive gold signet ring on the third finger, which Weller was constrained to shake as he sat down. The smell of *Canoe* wafted across the desk, mingled with a rich Havana aroma.

"Uh . . . pleased to meet you," Weller said.

"I've had your credits checked out," Lazlo said. "Not a hell of a lot, really, except for *Monkey Business,* which I understand has just been canceled."

Weller's reaction must have shown on his face, for Lazlo laughed, and waved his cigar grandly. "Don't worry," he said. "I know the whole story. And I also have had some acquaintance with that schmuck-and-a-half, Morris Fender. Forget about it. We don't want our creative people wasting their time with drek like that, not when there's *real* work they can be doing for us."

Weller found himself warming to Lazlo, despite the heavy veneer of Hollywood phoniness, or perhaps because of it. He didn't seem like some Transformationalist creep; at worst he was a Hollywood creep, a type Weller felt more or less at home with.

"Tell me, Jack, can you handle a camera?" Lazlo asked.

"A *camera?*" Weller said dubiously. He had done some camera work years ago, but he had supposed that Allen had made it clear that he was a director, not a cameraman. "Yeah, I can handle a camera, but I'm a *director,* Mr. Lazlo."

"Sure, sure," Lazlo said. "All things in time." He puffed explosively on his cigar, "Look, maybe I should first tell you something about our operation," he said. "What Transformationalism has got coming out of its ears is money. One of the things I want to do with that money is move us into major-league TV—films, commercials, the whole schmear. What we've got in that area right now is Changes Productions, which mainly makes TV commercials, which are mainly local-station stuff fed to us by Delta, which is our advertising agency. Now what you are thinking right now is, hey, this guy is insulting me, talking about hiring me to work on lousy commercials when I've got network TV credits, right?"

"Well . . . yeah, right," Weller said. Lazlo had indeed been reading his mind. Even from a Saturday-morning kiddie show, local commercials were a long step down.

Lazlo laughed. "Now, do I look like a guy who's mainly interested in making commercials?" he said. "Of course not! We're also making some internal films and some contract industrial stuff, but that's not where I'm mainly interested in going either. No, in a few years, I see Changes Productions getting into series television production, feature films, first-line stuff. We could be the next Universal. Why not? We've got the capital, and we've got the connections." He frowned. "But you want me to tell you what we don't got? What we don't got is the talent."

"I don't understand," Weller said. "If you've got the money, this town is full of film people who are looking for work. All you have to do is go down to the Bevery Hills unemployment office and take your pick."

Lazlo sighed. He chewed on the end of his cigar. "If only it were that simple," he said. "But it's not. You see, I can't hire anyone who hasn't at least gone through meditative deconditioning, and I can't give anyone a permanent appointment until they've passed a Monitor life analysis. Which narrows things down considerably. I've got to hire Transformational talent. Now there are millions of people who are into Transformationalism, but how many of them do you think are screen writers, actors, cameramen, or directors?"

"Not many," Weller ventured.

"Not many," Lazlo said. "So I end up hiring just about anyone the Monitors will pass who can do anything around film production. Loxes you wouldn't believe. It's a son of a bitch getting together a pool of people who could handle anything more than what we're doing now, and that's what's been holding us back. Which is why, a guy like you, with real network credits even if it is a monkey show, I was ready to hire sight unseen before you walked in the door."

"I see," Weller said. "Or do I? Why do you make it so hard for yourself?"

"*Me*?" Lazlo exclaimed. "You think this *mishigass* is *my* idea?"

"You're the secretary-treasurer of Transformationalism, aren't you? You're the head honcho of Utopia Industries . . ."

"That I am," Lazlo said. "But I'll tell you what I'm not, and that is John Steinhardt or Fred Torrez."

"I don't understand."

"Money matters, I run," Lazlo said. "John has no head for business, and he knows it. I was his agent, you know, and even in those days it was disaster to let him get his hands on a checkbook even. Without me he'd still be broke, and Transformationalism, Inc. would still be operating out of a storefront in San Francisco. So I run the business end, period. I made this company what it is."

Lazlo puffed on his cigar, shrugged his shoulders. "But the bullshit, the processing, the personnel, that's John's baby. Aside from the economic end, he keeps control of everything, and he sets policy. And he only wants dedicated Transformationalists working on what our media companies put out. I'm stuck with it. And of course, you can see his point. Media molds consciousness, and molding consciousness is to Transformationalism as fried chicken is to Colonel Sanders, so you've got to have the right cooks in the media kitchen. The USIA doesn't hire Communists, and you won't find John Wayne working in Russian movies."

"And the Monitors . . . ?" Weller asked. "I keep hearing about these Monitors."

Lazlo waved his cigar, as if brushing away the importance of the Monitors. "Auditors," he said. "Boys from the home office. They just keep an eye out to see that everyone is doing things John's way. You know, like the guys from network continuity."

"But they have to clear everyone you hire . . ."

"Yeah, yeah, it can get to be a pain in the ass sometimes," Lazlo said. "Like you, for instance. Now I know damn well you're probably a better director than anyone we've got now, but the directive is that nobody works as a director until they've completed meditative deconditioning and passed a Monitor life analysis. So all I can offer you is a provisional appointment as a cameraman at two hundred a week."

"Cameraman?" Weller exclaimed. "A lousy two hundred dollars a week? Now you *are* insulting me. That's not even

112

scale." If this son of a bitch thinks he's going to hire me as a cameraman for a stinking two hundred a week. . . .

"Take it easy, take it easy!" Lazlo said. "Believe me, once you complete your meditative deconditioning and pass the life analysis, you'll get a permanent appointment as a director. Absolutely. My word of honor. As for the salary—when you figure in the free unlimited processing, that doesn't look so bad either."

"I don't know . . ." Weller said uncertainly. But, of course, he did know. Two hundred a week was two hundred dollars a week more than nothing, and the unlimited free processing made it come out to more than he had been netting off *Monkey Business* at the end. But *cameraman* on some schlocky amateur commercial unit? Jesus. . . .

Lazlo stuck his cigar in his mouth and looked squarely at Weller as he bit off his words around it. "Look, it depends on what you think of yourself," he said. "I've told you what we've got, and I've told you the kind of people we've got working for us now. If you don't think you can rise to the top in a setup like this faster than hot shit through a tin horn, then I don't want you working for us either. You're not the man I thought I was looking for."

"When you put it that way. . . ." Weller said. They did have money, and Lazlo did seem like a man who really was determined to have his production company move on to bigger and better things, and he certainly was right about the situation. If I can't become the main man in an operation like *this*, I ought to look for another line of work.

"How long will it take me to stop being a cameraman and start being a director?" he asked.

"A few weeks at most," Lazlo said. "You think I want to waste a real talent longer than I have to, things being what they are?"

"Okay," Weller said, "you've got yourself a cameraman."

Lazlo grinned. He stood up and once again shook Weller's hand. "Welcome to the family," he said. "You're not going to regret it. Couple of years, and we'll both be up there collecting our Oscars together."

Lazlo sat down. "Okay," he said, "now I've got to get back to work. My secretary will call you tomorrow and give you the details. Your producer will be Sara English, pretty okay, all things considered. Good luck."

And that was it. Weller left Lazlo's office bouncing on the balls of his feet. Hot damn! he thought. I've got a job! A job with a future! I'll be the best damn cameraman they ever saw. And once they let me direct, I'll show them who's going to do their first feature! Energy flowed through him, he was riding the wavefront of destiny, he could hardly wait to begin.

Only when he had reached the garage and realized that the other thing he could hardly wait to do was go home and celebrate his good fortune with Annie, did he remember that there was no Annie waiting for him. That he had not even thought of her once during the whole interview with Lazlo. That even the features of her face were becoming slightly hazy in his mind's eye.

What changes I've gone through, he thought uneasily as he climbed into the familiar Triumph. And what changes are yet to come?

Eight

Changes Productions turned out to be an old, converted porn-printing plant in the nether reaches of the San Fernando Valley, an area of trailer camps, small industry, junkyards, and used-car lots steaming in saturation smog. Weller parked his car with a certain sinking sensation in his stomach and walked in through the street entrance. He found himself in a tiny reception area facing a glassed-in booth containing a switchboard operator and a heavy, hard-faced man wearing a white shirt and black trousers. He gave his name to this bozo, who checked it against a list, and handed him an ID card sealed in plastic.

"Keep this with you at all times," he was told. "You need it to get in. I'll get someone to take you inside."

Weller waited uncomfortably in the unfurnished reception area which had all the inviting charm of a prison cell. This was already not quite what he had expected. There was something not merely tacky but greasy about the face that Changes Productions showed to the world, a strange combination of porn factory and cut-rate military-industrial complex, light-years from the Hollywood veneer of Harry Lazlo's office.

With a loud buzz the steel door at the other end of the cubicle opened, and a short fat woman in her twenties stood there, holding the door open for him. "I'm Arlene Harris," she said, "Sara English's assistant. Come with me, and I'll take you to the set."

Weller followed her inside, directly into a large hangarlike space divided up into offices, storerooms, and cubicles by raw plywood partitions. At the other end of this maze a series of six large, totally enclosed boxlike rooms had been constructed under the high factory ceiling, like outsized dressing rooms in a real studio sound stage. "These are our sound stages," Arlene Harris said proudly. "We have six of them—three for video and three for film. We also have two editing rooms and two sound-mixing stages." Weller was not impressed; the whole operation looked amateurish, and the waste of space seemed tremendous.

115

Arlene Harris opened the door to one of the sound stages and led him inside. Weller groaned inwardly, for the shooting lights were on, and the crew inside was in the middle of a take. He would have crucified anyone who barged into a shoot like that.

A young man and woman costumed in army-surplus hippie gear and caked with scrounge makeup were lying on a messy bed. The girl was nodding out, and the boy was in the process of shooting himself up with a dirty-looking needle. Behind them was a flat of a dingy bedroom wall filthied with miscellaneous graffiti. A single video camera was shooting the scene under harsh rudimentary lighting that gave no dramatic shadows or undertones. A red-bearded young man in his thirties stood by the camera, apparently directing. A script girl and two male grips stood nearby, all young, all wearing jeans and work shirts.

Against one wall stood a striking redheaded woman in a tight tan pants suit that tantalizingly displayed her superb upright breasts and erect dancer's carriage. Across the room a dark-haired balding man in black pants and a black turtleneck stood with arms folded, watching with a lidded, self-contained detachment.

"Okay," the director said, "cut. Let's get ready for the close-up." The actors sat up, and the cameraman began to reposition for the next shot, but no one bothered to kill the shooting lights. *Kill those damn lights!* Weller wanted to shout.

Arlene led Weller up to the redhead. "Sara, this is Jack Weller."

The redhead turned to regard Weller with big green eyes that went straight to his groin. She was in her early thirties, and quite beautiful, though there was something strangely cold even in the sexual vibrations that seemed to surround her. "Welcome aboard," she said. "I'm Sara English." Their eyes met and something flashed between them; Weller felt the stirrings of long-surpressed treasonous desires. She smiled at him. "Let's go outside and talk while they're setting up. Arlene, you keep an eye on things here."

She led him out of the sound stage, with the man in the black turtleneck tracking them all the way with cold eyes like radar antennae. Once outside she leaned up against the wall of the sound stage, thrusting the nipples of her unfettered breasts against the fabric of her jacket, a posture that seemed both deliberately enticing and coldly commanding.

116

"We're shooting a spot for Narcon in there," she said. "That's our narcotics-rehabilitation program, pretty important to the movement. It gets us a lot of state and federal funding." She paused and flipped through some papers on her clipboard. "I generally oversee all the shooting," she said. "All our kids are dedicated, high-consciousness people, but we're kind of short of technical expertise." She gave him a smile that would melt glass. "I'm looking forward to working with you," she said. "Someone like you will have an opportunity to provide a great service to the movement. I'll show you around first, and then we'll pick a spot for you. You might as well get into it right away."

Weller followed at her heels as she took him on the quickie tour of the various sound stages, saying little, trying to ignore her powerful physical presence, trying to soak up and evaluate the situation. What he saw was pretty impressive on an activity level but quite appalling on a professional level. In addition to the Narcon spot, they were presently shooting commercials for Sunrise Books and a housing subdivision being put up by Carmel Properties, outfits which he recognized as being owned by Transformationalism through Utopia Industries. But they were also doing stuff for a savings and loan in East Los Angeles, a line of vegetable choppers, and a health-food company all of which seemed to have nothing to do with Transformationalism.

This struck Weller as odd, because the level of what was being done was the pits, from what he could see. No one seemed to have the faintest idea of how to really use lighting effectively. The actors were stiffs. He saw three blown takes in the space of ten minutes, one because the damn camera ran out of film in the middle of the take. A boom mike nearly beaned one of the actors. A director tried to take the same sequence three times before he realized that a line of dialogue was missing from the script.

Why would anyone hire these jerks unless they had to, unless they were owned by Transformationalism?

"Well, what do you think?" Sara asked him as they stood outside the health-foods-commercial set. Should I tell her? Weller wondered. Should I really tell her? But she was looking at him so warmly, and her eyes were so bright and confident, that telling the truth seemed like a stupid, pointless cruelty.

"Uh . . . you certainly seem very busy," he said.

Sara nodded. "We've got more work than we can handle," she said. "It comes in from everywhere. Our advertising

117

agency uses us exclusively, and of course there's Narcon and Sunrise and all the other movement businesses, not to mention Transformationalists in outside companies who are under life directive to give us their business. TV commercials hit the public in a particularly open state, so we don't like to turn anything down. Every commercial is another chance to get the message through to hundreds of thousands of people."

"The message?"

Sara looked at him peculiarly. "The Transformational message," she said. "You don't think we're doing this just for the *money*, do you?"

"Uh . . . of course not."

"Well now, let's see, where can we fit you in?" Sara said, thumbing through the papers on her clipboard. "Hmmm . . . We could use a new cameraman on the Sunrise commerical. Harrison just isn't working out. How does that sound?"

"Good as anything," Weller said. "But I don't want to come in with bad vibes . . ."

"Bad vibes?"

"Taking someone's job."

Again Sara gave him that peculiar look. "Harrison won't object," she said. "Why should he? If you can optimize the shooting over him, he'll be glad to see you take over. He's as dedicated to the movement as you or I."

"If you say so," Weller said. I've got a lot to learn about this setup, he thought. Maybe almost as much as these nerds have to learn about getting decent footage in the can.

"Come on people, get in sync, eptify yourselves, let's feel that wavefront moving through us all together now, and get this right."

Georgie Prinz, the so-called director, was hunched over in front of the set, trying to inspire the author of *Land of Milk and Honey* with Transformationalist jargon while Weller peered blearily through the viewfinder on the camera, waiting irritably for them to try to get their shit together one more time. The shooting day had been an infinity of contemptuous boredom, and Weller had spent most of his endless waiting time praying for it to be over.

As a Transformational lesson in humility, starting him as a cameraman was a dismal failure. Compared to this mess, *Monkey Business* was *Citizen Kane*, and he was Orson Welles. The best that could be said about the crew was that they knew their equipment well enough to turn it on and off and more or less point it in the right direction. The author, Deke Clayton, was an ex-junkie who had been cured by Narcon and written a book about it which was published by Sunrise Books, just to keep it all in the Transformationalist family. He had a wooden nervous, uptight bearing, and spoke with a bug-brained manic fervor.

Georgie Prinz's idea of camera direction was to tell Weller "close-up" or "medium shot" as if he knew what he was talking about and then give him a lecture about the "energy dynamics" of the shot in gobbledygook about "wave forms" and "rhythms" and "transformations" like some kind of Junior Steinhardt on speed.

What should've taken an hour or two to shoot was taking all day, and to compound the agony, all these turkeys were so intensely sincere that it made his teeth ache.

"Roll 'em!"

"Sound okay . . . I mean *speed!*"

"*Milk and Honey*, scene two, take five."

"Action, people, sync those vibes!"

Weller focused a medium shot on Clayton; a somewhat skeletal figure in a blue suit, with short-cropped hair, steel-rimmed glasses, a burned-out complexion, and eyes that glowed with such unnatural health that they seemed to be in the wrong face. Clayton had his left palm planted on his book as he spoke, as if he were swearing on the Bible.

"I was . . . the lowest junkie in creation," he stammered loudly, straining his memory to recall every other word in the script. "But a miracle called Narcon . . . restored . . . saved me from the . . . pit, and I lived to tell the world about it. . . ."

Weller found it difficult to imagine what idiot had conceived this commcercial. An author talking about his own book was pure death, even if it were Norman Mailer or Gore Vidal, and this character could hardly remember the stupid script.

This thing wouldn't sell any books, and Sunrise Books was a Transformationalist company. Why were they screwing themselves this way? Just to put a testimonial to Narcon on the air? But they were already shooting an up-front Narcon commercial. It didn't make sense.

" . . . to find out how a junkie like . . . I was . . . could be standing here holding a book . . . he was able to write himself . . . and how *anyone* can find . . . his own *Land of Milk and Honey.*"

"Cut!" said Georgie Prinz. "Okay, I think we've used up whatever positive forces we had in us today, so we'll call it a wrap."

Weller turned off the camera, got it ready for storage, and slunk toward the exit, hoping to escape without having to talk to anyone. What was there to say?

But Prinz caught up to him before he made it to the door. "Hey, how about it?" he said enthusiastically. "You could really feel the energy, couldn't you?" He was a thin, slightly round-shouldered guy in his late twenties, with stringy hair, intense eyes, and a frantic conversational tone; yet somehow there was also something of the puppy dog in him which aroused in Weller a certain gentle hypocrisy.

"Yeah, there's really . . . uh . . . spirit here," Weller said, and kept walking.

"Bet you don't see so many eptified consciousnesses working together on network shows, huh?"

"Different kind of scene . . ."

Prinz grinned at him. "And you haven't really synced in yet," he said. "Wait till you really get behind the second-level stuff. We're not just making commercials, we're really transforming, we're really getting into it."

"Uh-huh," Weller said wearily. "It seems that way to me already."

He reached the sound-stage door and stepped through, with Prinz still yipping at his heels like an earnest puppy. The balding man in the black turtleneck was waiting outside, eyes like ball bearings in a bloodless face.

"A word with Mr. Weller, Georgie," he said in a firm, flat voice.

"Sure Owen," Prinz said, his voice instantly subdued, and without another word he loped off toward the front of the building, disappearing into the warren of plywood partitions.

"I'm Owen Karel," the creepy character said, staring at Weller as if that were supposed to mean something to him. Weller cocked an inquisitive eyebrow.

"I'm the Monitor representative."

"Oh." So this was one of the Monitors. What did he want? It didn't figure to be anything pleasant.

"I've made an appointment for you to begin life analysis," Karel said. "Saturday at the Center."

"Is that an order?"

Karel grimaced slightly. "You may consider it a life directive, yes," he said. "I hope it will go smoothly. We've been requested to expedite matters by Harry Lazlo's office, but that doesn't mean we'll be any less thorough."

"Of course not," Weller said. There was something positively reptilian about this guy, and he had the kind of face you instinctively wanted to punch.

"I'm glad we understand each other," Karel said. "Lazlo is very enthusiastic about you, but I want it understood that the Monitors have the last word on permanent appointments. There are some rather questionable items in your dossier, so rest assured, we'll be monitoring you closely."

"I'm sure you're just doing your job," Weller said, inching away from him.

"That's the correct attitude," Karel said. "But then, you'd know that, wouldn't you?"

"If you say so," Weller said. "Ah, is there anything else? I've had a tiring day . . ."

"That will be all for now," Karel said solemnly.

"Well then, see you around . . ."

"You will," Karel said, then turned and walked off, leaving Weller standing there in the cold wake of his passage. Bro— *ther*! If this character were typical of the Monitors, he could see why they made even Benson Allen nervous. It was going to be *some* pleasure working around here. For a mad moment he felt a twinge of nostalgia for the good old days of *Monkey Business*.

"It's a screwed-up mess, really, it's incredible," Weller said, pacing around Garry Bailor's tacky living room, feeling tiredly superior, an emotion which gave him little satisfaction. "I've worked four different shoots now, and nobody seems to really know what they're doing. But they think they do. Oh brother, do they think they do!"

Bailor looked up at him from the couch, over the top of a can of beer. "Why does that surprise you?" he said. "You just told me that only Sara English has any real experience, and that was porn."

Jesus, Weller thought, is this guy really that dense? "But they keep getting *assignments*," he snapped. "They're booked solid for the next month. How can they keep getting work off the crap they turn out?"

"You told me that Transformationalism owns at least a dozen companies through fronts, including an advertising agency which funnels assignments to Changes," Bailor said. He shrugged. "One hand feeds the other. . . ."

Weller collapsed onto the couch beside Bailor. "Obviously," he said. "But it's not all in-house work. They're doing stuff for all kinds of companies that don't seem to have anything to do with Transformationalism. Hell, they're even going to do some political spots for a mayoral candidate upstate. And it's all the same—technically horrible and loaded down with not-very-subtle Transformationalist propaganda. How the fuck do they get away with it?"

The more he learned, the less sense it made. Every script seemed to be written on two levels. If it were a vegetable-chopper commercial, the machine "transformed kitchen chores into creative cooking art." Ticky-tacky houses in a crummy development were "at the leading edge of Los Angeles's expansion into the twenty-first century." Lawrence Savings and Loan "transformed your money into the instrument of a better tommorrow." You could "eptify your bodily functions and cleanse your mind of metabolic blockages" with Walden Health Foods. If they were selling a laxative, they'd probably say that you could "ride the changes out your asshole."

What were they doing with all this? Bombarding the public with a few key Transformationalist terms over and over again so that when old John Q. came across Transformationalism itself, it would seem familiar and have positive connotations? It reminded Weller of the "subliminal advertising" paranoia of the 1950s, when people were convinced that their television sets were sneaking secret messages into their subconscious minds. Was Transformationalism actually *doing* that?

For that matter where did the scripts come from? He had yet to see a writer, and a few times he *had* seen Owen Karel handing bound scripts to Sara. Were the *Monitors* making this stuff up?

If this game were only being played with companies owned by Transformationalism, he could understand it. But banks? Political candidates? Restaurants? Why were they continuing to shell out good money for bad commercials loaded with subliminal Transformationalist crap?

Bailor took a sip of beer. "Maybe they have their hooks into *everyone* they're making commercials for," he suggested.

Weller snorted. "Banks?" he said. "Used-car lots? Kitchenware companies? An aerospace outfit? Man, if they own everything that they're making commercials for. . . ."

"They wouldn't have to own all their clients," Bailor said. "All they'd need would be Transformationalists in key places.

An account executive . . . a vice-president . . . a sales manager . . ."

"A *political candidate?*"

Bailor looked at him peculiarly and shrugged.

"You're making me paranoid," Weller said. "Do you know something I don't?"

Bailor grimaced. "That kind of stuff I don't *want* to know," he said. "In my line of work it's very unhealthy. As long as I just take a few followers away from these outfits, I'm merely an annoyance. They tolerate my existence. But if I start getting into their corporate involvements, if they think I'm becoming a threat to them on an organizational level. . . ." He shuddered. "Jack, if you find out anything like that, be sure not to tell me. Let's keep this strictly on a one-to-one deprogramming level, okay?"

"*Thanks a lot,*" Weller grunted. Bailor's see-no-evil attitude frightened him more than anything else had. The son of a bitch knows more about Transformationalism than I do, and he doesn't want to know any more. What should that tell *me?* And with "Monitor life analysis" starting tommorrow, too, whatever that is. . . .

"Do you mind if we talk about the Monitors, Garry?" he said sardonically. "Or is that subject taboo too?"

"I'll tell you what I know," Bailor said. "But I'll be honest with you. I've never worked with anyone that's been this far in before, not someone who's working for them and dealing with the inner organization."

"*Inner organization?*"

"That's what the Monitors seem to be," Bailor said. "A kind of Transformationalist secret police, under Steinhardt's direct control. It's a big, complicated organization with lots of fronts, and it would seem that Steinhardt uses the Monitors to make sure the accounting stays honest, to make sure everyone who works for the movement toes the line. As I understand it, a directive from Fred Torrez, who runs the Monitors for Steinhardt, can even overrule the heavies like Allen and Lazlo. That's about all I know."

"And all you want to know," Weller said bitterly.

"You got it. I don't mess around with people like that because I don't want them messing around with me."

"*Marvelous,*" Weller snapped. "Fucking marvelous!"

Bailor looked at him coldly. "You didn't ask my advice when you decided to go to work for them, now did you?" he said.

"And what would you have told me?" Weller snapped. "To stay unemployed? That you'd put my bill on the cuff?"

Bailor shrugged. "Maybe that you should rethink the question of whether or not all this is worth it to you," he said.

"It's a little late for that, isn't it?" Weller said. "Now what about this damned life analysis thing?"

Bailor took a long pull of beer. He squirmed on the couch. He looked really uncomfortable. "I don't think it's another process," he said. "More like a security check. I suppose what you can expect is some pretty heavy but straightforward interrogation."

"Bright lights and rubber hoses?" Weller said. Jesus, all this was getting positively unreal. What have I gotten myself into? Bailor doesn't even want to know. Do I? Can I really handle this?

He looked at Bailor and tried very hard to suppress the hostility he felt toward the cowardly bastard. Bailor was beginning to look sleazy, weak, and not exactly a man to lean on should the going get rough. Yet there was no one else he could ask, no one else to talk to about it.

"Do you really think I'm in too deep?" he asked. "Are you saying I should pull out of this thing now, while I can?"

Bailor leaned back and spoke softly and slowly. "You're about through with meditative deconditioning, and we seem to have pulled that much off," he said. "If you keep playing the same part, you'll probably get through life analysis too. And after that we should be home free to Annie. . . . Of course, it *is* your decision . . ."

"Yeah, but what would you do in my place?"

Bailor laughed humorlessly. "I wouldn't get my ass into your position in the first place," he said. "But there is another factor. You're working for them. The Monitors have already ordered a life analysis. You know things about their operation that are not exactly public knowledge. . . ."

A chill went through Weller. "What are you saying?"

"I guess I'm saying that it wouldn't be so easy for you to pull out now," Bailor said. "Probably nothing earthshaking, but they wouldn't like it. So if you're going to have to go through that shit anyway, you might as well go ahead for a few more weeks till you get to Annie so at least what you'll have to go through will be worth it."

"What are you talking about?" Weller hissed. "What's going to happen to me?"

"Probably just some pressure," Bailor said cavalierly. "Phone calls at all hours. Ominous letters from the Monitors. Threats. Stuff like that. Why do you think I rent this dump and make it impossible for anyone to get my home phone number?"

"*Now you tell me?*" Weller said. His stomach felt as if it were filled with ice. Suddenly he felt small and powerless and Bailor seemed to be talking to him across an immense and isolating distance.

"Hey, don't freak out," Bailor said. "It's not as if they were going to plant bombs in your car or send hit men after you." He frowned. "A least I've never *heard* of them going that far. . . ."

"That's comforting," Weller said wanly. "That's very comforting."

Bailor seemed to be thinking some private thoughts, and from the look on his face they weren't too reassuring.

"Are you thinking of bugging out on me, Garry?" Weller asked sharply.

Bailor snapped out of his reverie. He smiled a horrid plastic smile. "Take it easy, Jack," he said. "We'll come through it okay."

"Sure *we* will," Weller said sourly. It's us against them, he thought, regarding Bailor narrowly. Only *them* keeps getting bigger and *us* keeps getting smaller. He remembered the old joke about the Lone Ranger and Tonto surrounded by a horde of hostile Indians. The Lone Ranger turns to Tonto, and he says, "Well, it looks like we've had it, Tonto." And Tonto looks at the Lone Ranger, and *he* says: "What do you mean *we*, white man?"

Weller took the elevator up to the seventh floor of the Transformation Center in the grip of a strange psychic flatness compounded of ennui, boredom, and a growing sense of superiority to the Transformationalist milieu in which he had become immersed. He couldn't even work up much of a healthy sense of paranoia about the imminent opening round of Monitor life analysis.

Working as a cameraman for Changes Productions was even more tedious and creatively noninvolving than directing *Monkey Business*. Being a cameraman meant standing around waiting interminably for the next shot to be set up under the best of circumstances, whereas directing even the worst schlock meant attention to business at all times. Indeed the director was the guy who kept the cameraman standing around waiting for him to get his shit together, as Weller soon rediscovered when the roles were reversed.

And when the directors were as incompetent as the amateurs he was being forced to work under, the cameraman spent his whole day in a state of impatient, contemptuous boredom. Further, when the mind behind the viewfinder was that of a director, it took to second-guessing every take of every shot in advance, setting it up, instructing the actors, and shooting it over and over again mentally before the actual director on the set did it his way. And of course, nine times out of ten, the Changes Productions directors did it wrong, extracting footage far inferior to what Weller was shooting inside his own head. So even the advance second-guessing soon became a tedious mental ritual, a mind game that ran automatically in his head, programmed by boredom, edged by contempt.

What gave the tedium a lunatic piano-wire tension was that Weller knew he was the only person in the building who felt that way; he was surrounded by enthusiasm and dedication and people who were ecstatically convinced they were doing work of cosmic significance.

Georgie Prinz turned out to be a former dope dealer who had been in processing for two years and who lived and breathed Transformationalism twenty-four hours a day. The other two directors he had worked with were an aging pornographer filled with guilt for what he had been and a one-time New Left media freak who was now convinced that Transformationalism was the true Revolution and that the commercials he was shooting were the highest form of media guerilla warfare. Between them, Georgie Prinz, Max Silver, and Shano Moore put out enough rhetoric and useless energy to light Pasadena, but without the skill and talent to focus it, it just kept the actors and crew in a perpetual state of ideological fervor and working confusion.

When he saw Sara English, he felt that he could cut the sexual vibes with a knife, but if it were anything beyond his own horniness and her background as a one-time porno starlet, she had yet to acknowledge it with a word or gesture. So far it was just one more turn of the screw.

Weller found himself locked inside his own skull, bored, angered, confronted with his own horniness, and alienated on his mountaintop of professional disdain.

Even the meditative deconditioning sessions were losing

126

their bite as Weller sensed the process drawing to a conclusion. Now that he was locked inside his own mind all day, double thinking his way through the life scenarios became just another automatic mind game. He knew exactly what Sylvia was looking for, and feeding it to her was as easy and mechanical as giving the directors the stupid shots they were calling for.

From the speed with which the scenarios were coming and Sylvia's attitude, he could tell that he was giving her optimized readings on the brainwave monitor almost as fast as the words came out of her mouth. Worship and trust for the Great Man? Just adjust the focus a hair. Self-sacrificing dedication to the Cause? Zoom in for a medium close-up, please. His mind was becoming as precise a mechanical instrument as his camera. It couldn't be long before he was officially declared an "optimized consciousness." The process was almost over, and that was all that kept him going. Even Annie was no more than a faceless abstraction shimmering in the distance across a desert of dull gray boredom.

So now it was time to confront Monitor life analysis, the last barrier. Satisfy *these* bastards, he told himself as he entered the room, and the whole horrible game would be over.

Once again he was in a small cubicle like the meditative-deconditioning room, but this time the man behind the desk didn't even have a brainwave monitor in front of him, just a fat manila envelope and a ball-point pen. The Monitor himself was a wiry, streetwise-looking Chicano in his late twenties, with short black hair and hard, uncompromising eyes.

"I'm Gomez, I'll be doing your life analysis," he said in a thick emotionless voice. "Sit down, Mr. Weller."

Automatically Weller sat down. That voice sounded as if it were used to giving orders and just as used to having them obeyed.

"Understand what this is up front, so we won't get locked into personalities," Gomez said, scanning some material in the folder as he spoke. "My job is to evaluate your life—not just your consciousness, but how you live, what you're likely to do, where you're really at, the whole picture. Processing is for you, but this for the movement. If you're going to be one of the people presenting Transformationalism to the world, Transformationalism has to be sure of you. Dead sure. And the movement has to come first, not your personal feelings. Got that?"

"I understand," Weller said.

"Good." Gomez looked up and his heavy lips creased in a faint smile. "Because you're gonna think I'm a pretty mean hombre before this is over. You may hate my guts. You may think I've got it in for you personally. None of that is true. I'm serving the movement as I've been directed to, and *your* directive is to cooperate totally. We're both working for the same thing, even if it doesn't always seem that way. Got that?"

Weller nodded, somewhat stunned by this belligerant assault, this seemingly deliberate provocation to paranoia. He hated Gomez already, and he wondered whether that was not precisely what he was being programmed to feel.

"Okay," Gomez said, "let's get moving." He paused and fingered the folder. "I hope you're not surprised to hear that this is your dossier, and that we have pretty complete data on the obvious stuff. So we won't waste time on a lot of trivial things we already know. Up front, Weller, what kind of lames do you think we are? Who do you think you're kidding?"

"*What?*"

"Okay, let's get rid of *that* one right now. Your wife gets a life directive to split because of your hostility to the movement, and you run in here and do an apeshit act, and then suddenly you join Transformationalism and bullshit your way into working for Changes. You think the *Monitors* are that stupid? You think we've never seen this number run before? You're here to con us into letting you see your wife. Don't call me an asshole by denying it, man!"

Weller reeled, totally unprepared for Gomez's instant, contemptuous, and sure insight into the true nature of the game. Watch it! he told himself. This is a new ball game, and this guy is *sharp*. But it seemed to him that if they had let him come this far, the game was still on, and this must be a tactic. He wants me to react. What kind of reaction would the convert Jack Weller have? Anger is too obvious. . . .

Instead Weller slumped in his chair and issued a mournful sigh. "How can I deny that that's what brought me to Transformationalism?" he said. "But don't *you* have enough faith in the movement to believe that it could've Transformed me, even against my will? Don't insult *my* intelligence. The movement wouldn't have had anything to do with me if you didn't think that were possible."

Gomez's face became neutrally blank. "Explain," he said evenly. It seemed like an encouraging sign.

"Explain what?" Weller said. "That meditative deconditioning showed me where I was coming from? That the guy who came in here to get his wife back had his face rubbed in his own smallness? That Transformationalism gave me the balls to quit a lousy job that was turning me into a zombie? That I finally want to do something meaningful with my life?"

"Yeah," Gomez said. "You've got to convince me that what you just said is true. That's what your life analysis is all about. It ends when I'm convinced you're telling the truth or when I'm convinced you're lying. So convince me."

"How am I supposed to do that?"

"Don't worry about that," Gomez said with a feral smile. "It's my job to get it out of you. You just answer the questions. Now, what do you think of Changes Productions?"

"Uh . . . it's a pretty impressive outfit . . ." Weller said cautiously "Pretty high-energy people . . . and it seems to have a lot of potential. . . ."

"Don't hand me that bullshit, Weller!" Gomez roared. "I'm a *Monitor*, not one of your dingbat co-workers! We don't wear rose-colored shades! The truth, Weller, not patronizing crap!"

Once again Weller was stunned and disoriented by Gomez's blunt and contemptuous honesty. None of his previous experiences with Transformationalism had prepared him for *this*. He couldn't game it through, he couldn't come up with the correct response to program. He was left with only an edited version of the truth.

"Okay, so professionally speaking, it's a mess. A lot of rank amateurs who have no idea of what they're doing." Weller paused, made his voice soft and plaintive. "But I meant what I said about potential. The work you've got lined up, the facilities, the capital. . . ."

"We'd really have something if we had the right people in the creative end?"

"Yes."

"*Such as yourself?*" Gomez said sardonically.

"Such as myself," Weller shot back automatically. Then, backing it up softly: "Harry Lazlo knows where it's at."

"*Harry Lazlo* . . ." Gomez muttered peculiarly under his breath. Then, louder: "Harry Lazlo knows where Harry Lazlo is at. *John* knows where Transformationalism is at. Never forget that, Weller. You talk about you being the right kind of person for the creative end—but what do you conceive the creative end to be?"

"Huh?"

"*Huh?*" Gomez mimicked. "Not whatever Lazlo told you. What do you think the movement really wants to do with Changes Productions? Why are we into something like that? And no superficial bullshit, please!"

Once more Weller couldn't guess what the right response was supposed to be; once more he chose a guarded version of what he imagined was the truth. "Aside from making money, it would seem that the idea is to get the Transformational message on the tube, to plant the terminology and some of the feeling in the public consciousness when people think they're watching something else. 'Subliminal advertising,' they used to call it."

Gomez smiled faintly; for once he seemed to be pleased. "Very good, Weller. The true goal is to promote Transformationalism, and everything else is a means to that end. Thank God you didn't try to hand me any bullshit about *Art*. So the question is, if you were in a creative position, could you really optimize yourself behind those parameters?"

"I think so," Weller said. For once the right answer seemed obvious.

But not to Gomez. "Come on Weller, don't jive me," he said. "You're an ambitious professional director. You expect me to believe that you'd be functioning at optimum churning out Transformationalist propaganda?"

Lord, but this guy is disorienting! Weller thought. I've got to steer this into an area he knows nothing about. "But it's not overt propaganda," he said. "It's subliminal stuff sneaked into commercials for other things, eventually fiction films and TV episodes. Just underlying ideology, right?"

"So?"

"So what do you think doing episodic TV is like?"

Gomez looked at him perplexedly. I've finally got this guy out of his league, Weller thought. Time for a highfalutin' snow job!

"You think there isn't an underlying ideology in network TV?" he said cynically. "You think a rash of cop shows, for example, doesn't have anything to do with subtle government pressure? Creative artists *always* have to work within ideological parameters. Look at the paintings that were produced during the Middle Ages and tell me they had nothing to do with Catholic ideology. Look at Socialist Realism. As long as you're free to do the best work you can within the parameters

130

you're given, you really can't expect anything more."

Gomez leaned back. He fingered the dossier. "Now that is a nice fancy answer," he said. "I'm not sure whether it's bullshit or not, but it sure is nice and fancy." He hunched forward and glared at Weller. "If I were a commissar, I'd want to know whether you were really a dedicated Communist, though, now wouldn't I? If I were a Jesuit, I'd have to know whether you were a sincere Catholic, or just a heretic determined to get along."

"Would you?" Weller said. "Or from your point of view, wouldn't it be the end product that counted?"

"It depends, doesn't it?" Gomez said. "The Communist Party might be satisfied with your work, but the Church wants your soul."

"And which way do you see Transformationalism?" Weller asked.

Gomez laughed. "What a question to ask a poor simple boy from the barrio," he said. He got up. "We'll have another session in two days. Same time, same room." Clutching the dossier, he walked toward the door. He paused, extracted a white envelope from the folder, came back, handed it to Weller.

"Oh yeah," he said, "this is for you." Then he was gone.

Knowing what it was going to be, Weller tore open the envelope. Inside, perfectly typed on Transformationalist letterhead, was another letter from Annie. Or her ghost-writer.

Dear Jack:

So you're working for Transformationalism! I can't tell you how much that means to me. I can't tell you how happy it's made me. But you must know. I know you do.

Now that you're working for the movement, and now that you're in life analysis, I'm allowed to tell you that I'm working for the movement too, and in a very important project. God, how different it is from the old days! Every moment has meaning. I feel like a different person. No, not like a different person, like the real me, the me I always wanted to be. I'm dying to tell you all about it, and once you've passed your life analysis, I'll be able to tell you, not in a letter, but in the flesh. In a few short weeks we'll be together again, they've promised me. And what we'll have to share!

131

Until then, work well, love, think of me, and eptify yourself behind this brief period of waiting. Remember that we'll be together again before you know it.

Love,
Annie

Mechanically Weller folded the letter, put it back in the envelope, and stuffed it in a pocket. Only then was he brought up short by his own lack of any really deep reaction.

Is it because it really told me nothing? he wondered. Because of the jargon? Because he wasn't even sure that Annie had actually written it? Because it seemed so impersonal, so abstract, so . . . so *Transformational?*

Why did the words on paper conjure up neither an image of her face nor the sound of her voice nor the aura of her presence . . . ? Why did the letter remain an abstraction? Can it be that it's *Annie* that's becoming an abstraction to me? he asked himself. Like an old soldier, is the Annie I remember just fading away?

Or is it that this room just seems so empty without Gomez in it? Now that he thought about it, Weller realized that there had been so much electricity sparking between himself and Gomez during the life-analysis session that the letter from Annie had been like an afterthought. Face it, Weller, a bring-down.

For he had definitely contacted a whole new level here, a hint of vast, unplumbed depths within the Transformationalist scam. There had been more brutal honesty, more gut-level intellectual depth, more sheer psychic power in those few minutes with Gomez than in his entire previous experience with the movement. The Monitor had been really impressive, somewhat infuriating, and slightly terrifying. And he had definitely gotten off on the confrontation. There was dread here, but there was also a fascination twisted around it.

Whatever it had been, Weller found that it still held the focus of his attention, even in the face of this letter from Annie. Annie seemed so long ago and far away now, and the life-analysis session, even in retrospect, seemed so hyperreal, so immediate.

Jesus, Weller thought, I kind of enjoyed that. I'm almost looking forward to the next one! Somehow Gomez had fed a hunger he hadn't even known he'd had. A hunger he still couldn't name.

Nine

Owen Karel had been on the set for at least half an hour now, and although Weller knew that the Monitor had other things to watch on this shoot, he felt the continual pressure of those cold hard eyes on the back of his neck. For he knew they were extensions of Gomez; in their last session Gomez had made it clear that the verbal fencing was only half of the life-analysis process.

"Not to make you paranoid, Weller," he had said, "but you *do* realize that trying to con me would be futile? I get actual life-situation reports on you from Karel, and by the time this is over, I'll have integrated what you do with what you say. What's significant is not absolute consistency—no one expects that—but what the patterns of inconsistency reveal. Patterns of patterns, and you have to be really Transformed to read that, so there's no point in you trying to figure out what I'm looking for and putting on a little act."

So Weller knew that he was being watched like a bug under a microscope, and every time he saw Karel, he pictured the Monitor representative writing mental notes on him in a phantom dossier. But he couldn't figure out how Karel could learn anything significant from watching him stand quietly behind a camera. He wondered if the paranoia cut both ways—if the Monitor's cold eyes read significance into the way he stood, the expression on his face, the clothes he wore.

This commercial, now, seemed to be a straightforward pitch for Transformationalism itself. The set was a typical suburban living room, and four actors played a typical suburban family. Dad in a dark business suit. Mom in women's-lib fatigues. Sonny in long-haired hippie gear. Sis in a Jesus Freak persona with an unsubtle wooden cross around her neck. According to the shooting script they preached their respective ideologies at each other in the first twenty seconds. Then a voice-over made a twenty-second pitch for Transformationalism as the bridge which transcended conflicting life-styles. Cut to the same family, now discoursing sweetly together, all harmony and light. In Transformationalist jargon, of course.

Georgie Prinz had shot the final sequence yesterday, and except for the inevitable technical foul-ups, it had gone pretty smcothly, since the actors were all dedicated to the cause and therefore had little trouble spouting Transformationalism at each other with total conviction. But this morning Georgie was trying to get the opening sequence on tape, and in take after take he just couldn't find the handle.

The problem was partly technical. Shooting a scene in which four characters gibber at each other all at once at cross-purposes was very hard to do realistically under the best of circumstances. The director had to get the actors to cross-interrupt each other in a way that sounded realistic. It helped if the actors were professionally competent, which these were not, and it helped if the director knew enough to keep them from reacting to each other's lines as cues. Neither being the case, poor Georgie just kept trying the same thing over and over again and kept getting stuff that even he could see was totally stilted and dead.

Weller wondered if the presence of Karel was exacerbating the situation; Georgie kept glancing surreptitiously at the Monitor, as if he realized he was fucking up and believed that Karel knew it too. Weller also wondered if Karel was knowledgeable enough to recognize incompetent directing when he saw it, or whether he just liked to make people nervous.

"Okay, let's try it one more time, and then we'll break for lunch," Gerogie said, returning to his position beside the camera. "Please, people, ah . . . try to be spontaneous . . . er . . . stay inside your own heads, let me hear you all at once." He paused, cocked an inquisitive eyebrow at Weller. Weller nodded back, indicating that he was ready. Oh boy, was he ready!

"Lights . . . roll 'em . . ."

"Transformationalism is the Bridge, scene two, take twelve."

"Speed."

Georgie hesitated, and Weller, peering through his viewfinder, could imagine him nibbling his lower lip and sneaking a look at Owen Karel. "Action!"

"—grow up and think about a real job—"

"—getting fed up with your chauvinist attitude—"

"—don't know why I stay around this uptight house—"

"—accept the love of Christ as the answer to—"

Pure blind awful! Weller thought. They were still spouting bits of dialogue sequentially, straight from the script, politely cuing each other. Instead of sounding like a babbling argument, it sounded like the silliest sort of chopped-up stage dialogue.

"Cut!" Georgie shouted. Weller turned off the camera and stared at him. Georgie gave a nervous little shrug and finally seemed about to ask Weller something when he was stopped short by something he saw across the sound stage.

Weller turned to look. Karel had quietly disappeared, which he had a habit of doing, and Sara English, enticing in a short red dress, was walking across the sound stage toward them, accompanied by Shano Moore, dressed in his inevitable jeans and army shirt. How much had she seen? Was Georgie going to get a chewing out? Might there soon be a crying need for a new director on this turkey . . . ?

But Georgie didn't seem worried. "Take an hour for lunch," he called out, and sure enough Sara didn't even mention what was going on on the set.

"Come have lunch with us, Georgie," she said. She turned to Weller and gave him a long, hot smile. "Why don't you come along too, Jack?" she said casually. But she was looking straight into his eyes, pouring out the vibes, and Weller imagined he had heard something *carefully* casual in her voice. Did she want to get to know him personally, was he reading the vibes right? On the other hand, she *was* inviting him to lunch with two directors. Was there something significant in that? A signal of some subtle alteration in his status, foreshadowing an imminent change?

Or is it just wishful thinking and horniness? Weller wondered nervously. Am I starting to read significance into everything?

That was as good a definition of paranoia as any.

The significant lunch with Sara English and the two directors turned out to be nothing more ceremonious than hamburgers at a nearby coffee shop. Weller sat on one side of the booth with Shano Moore, Georgie and Sara on the other. Sara still hadn't said anything to Georgie about this morning's futile work by the time they had ordered, and Weller toyed with the idea of saying something himself.

But he damn well knew how *he* would have reacted to some friendly little tips on directing from his cameraman, and he didn't know how Sara would react to his pulling rank and credits, so he held his peace. He had the uneasy conviction that not even Sara had any idea of how lousy the whole operation was, and that she would take any negative criticism

135

as an attack on Transformationalism and report it to Gomez through Karel. Gomez seemed to have no illusions about what was going on, but he was judging Weller according to unknown parameters, and *anything* might be some kind of hidden life-analysis test.

"Georgie tells me you've done a lot of directing, Jack," Shano said as their orders arrived. "How come you're just doing camera work?"

Weller nodded at Sara, tossing the question to her. "Jack has to wait for Monitor clearance," she said. "He hasn't reached a high enough level yet."

Shano nodded. "I can dig it," he said. "A guy needs a lot of processing to get his talent behind serving the movement, especially when his trip is as authoritarian as directing."

A lobotomy would help, Weller thought sourly. "What do you mean by that?" he said instead.

"Man, I come from the same place," Shano said. "I mean, a director is like a general, right, and the crew and actors are his army, and he gives like *orders*. He gets to feeling like whatever he's shooting is *his* thing."

"Ah, a believer in the *auteur* theory," Weller said lightly.

Shano looked at him blankly. Apparently he had never heard of the *auteur* theory, and neither had Sara or Georgie.

"That's not where I'm coming from," Georgie said. "We're all soldiers of Transformationalism, like, doing our optimum thing for the movement."

"For sure," Shano said. "That's the transformation you've got to go through. Same thing in the old Revolution. Guys who were into creating their own stuff had to get a lot of bullshit about art out of their heads before they could get behind the idea that they were serving the cause, not their own egos, before they could get behind taking political direction. You wouldn't believe the shit that went on! That's what I dig about Transformationalism—we transform consciousness first, before we put someone in that position. Otherwise you get all kinds of crap from creative people whose egos keep them from really serving the movement."

"You sound like Mao Tse-tung," Weller said dryly.

"You dig Mao?" Shano asked brightly.

"I haven't read the book, but I've seen the movie," Weller drawled.

There was a moment of silence during which Sara leaned forward on her elbows and seemed to be studying Weller intently over her cheeseburger. Have I put my foot in my mouth? he wondered. Do I lose brownie points for being a smartass? But it was Shano who seemed to have said the wrong thing.

"You've still got some of that political programming in your head, Shano," Sara said, all the while looking at Weller as if this was for *his* benefit. "We don't want people suppressing their creativity for the sake of the movement; we want our people in a state of eptified creative consciousness *while* they're working on getting the message across. Otherwise the product is low-level stuff with no life to it." She gave Weller a stunning smile that went straight to his crotch, and, under the table her foot brushed accidentally against his calf. "What do you think, Jack?" she said.

I think this is an awful lot of highfalutin' bullshit over a bunch of crummy commercials, Weller thought. But he smiled back at her, and said, "Transformationalism optimizes consciousness, so you can hardly expect the product to get the message across if the people making it aren't turned on creatively." How's that for party-line bullshit? But he couldn't help throwing in a zinger. "Of course, just as talent is no substitute for dedication, dedication is no substitute for talent."

"But processing releases the talent in everyone," Georgie insisted.

"It can't release what isn't there."

"That sounds like an elitist remark," Shano said self-righteously.

"Aren't we an elite?" Weller replied, looking straight at Sara. "Can you set out to transform the world and not consider yourself an elite?"

Sara's eyes flashed something at him. "I never thought of it that way," she said.

"That's bullshit," Shano said. "Transformationalism is open to everyone. The whole idea is to transform the total consciousness of all the people."

But Sara wasn't paying any attention to Shano. Something was vibrating in the air between her and Weller. An instant later he felt her calf against his and knew it was real. Was this a game, or was she really attracted to him? With her flesh touching his, at the moment he didn't give a damn. She was sucking up what he was saying, and she was giving him an unambiguous sexual signal, and it gave him a heightened sense of his own being much like what he felt when he was directing well, and he would bloody well ride it and let *them* cope with him for a change.

"Transformationalism is no democracy," he said. "Any more than a shooting set is. If we believe we can improve the consciousness of the public, and we're trying to sell that to them, *and* being Machiavellian about it in the bargain, then we're *functioning* as an elite, whether we have the balls to admit it to ourselves or not."

"I never thought of it that way before," Sara said, rubbing her leg against Weller's.

"Maybe you should be a Monitor . . . ," Shano muttered.

"What did you mean by that?" Sara snapped, suddenly removing her leg from contact with Weller's flesh.

"I dunno," Shano mumbled. "It just came out."

Abruptly Weller felt angered, frustrated, yet above it all. Perhaps it was the withdrawl of Sara's sexual attention, but now they all seemed like characters in a film he was directing. He knew their motivations and where their reactions were coming from, but he himself was the unmoved mover. Some perverse and perhaps cruel impulse made him want to push them just a wee bit further. He had been manipulated and evaluated for so long that it gave him a long-lost sense of power to play director, to keep things stirred up.

"I can see where Shano's coming from" he said. "I mean, that *is* where the Monitors are at, isn't it? They *do* function as an elite, and they're not exactly shy about it. And they're functioning as an elite in relation to *us*, now aren't they?"

Sara flushed. "The Monitors perform a necessary function," she said tightly. But her eyes did not exactly portray total conviction. Of course not! Weller thought. She's supposed to be the head honcho, and there's old Karel peering constantly over her shoulder and overruling her whenever he feels like it.

"Exactly, Sara," Weller said evenly. "And their necessary function is to guide *us* with superior insight. They're *Transformationalism's* elite, the level above us."

"I never thought of the Monitors as superior beings," Sara said indignantly.

"*Really?*" Weller oozed. "They're closer to John. He chooses them, trains them, and puts them in the position they're in. If you don't regard them as higher consciousnesses, why obey them? Just because you're afraid of them?"

"I'm not afraid of Owen Karel," Sara insisted, with zero conviction.

They were all looking at Weller very peculiarly now, and

138

he wasn't quite sure just what it was he was doing. But whatever it was, it had sure hit a nerve!

"Hey, man," Shano said nervously, "What kind of game are you playing? Why are you running this number?"

"I'm not running any number," Weller said sweetly. "I'm just being sincere. I respect the superior consciousness of the Monitors." He paused, lowered his voice an octave. "What's the matter? Don't you?"

"Maybe you *should* be a Monitor," Georgie said, and in his eyes was the clearly written thought: *maybe you are*. So that's it! Weller thought, laughing inwardly. They're seeing Monitors under their beds. I've really succeeded in making them paranoid!

He gave a throaty, ambiguous chuckle. "Should I be called upon to serve . . . ," he said slyly.

Sara looked sideways at Weller. What was that look in her eyes? Admiration? Lust? A new kind of respect? Or was it fear? Weller had a flash of insight into what it must be like to be a dedicated Transformationalist, an insider like Sara, wielding power over those below you but always looking over your shoulder and wondering. Fearing the Monitors, resenting them, but prevented by your very belief from even admitting it to yourself.

"I think it's time to get back to work," Sara said uneasily. Weller wondered if she would dare report this little conversation to the Monitors.

He wondered if she dared not to.

Ceremoniously Sylvia unplugged the headband jack from the brainwave monitor, slowly took the electrode band off Weller's head, and placed it on the table between them. Weller could anticipate her words before she said them, for Garry Bailor had called the shot two days ago. "Congratulations, Jack, you've completed your meditative deconditioning."

It had been the only positive thing about his last meeting with Bailor. "They're not making any money off you now," Bailor had said, "so they have no reason to prolong it. And from what you tell me about this life-analysis thing, it seems to be mainly a matter of trying to determine whether or not the programming has really taken hold."

"So now what?"

"Now you've got to get past this Gomez character," Bailor said.

"How am I supposed to do that?" Weller asked. "He's ten times sharper than any of the other bozos I've had to deal with. He's getting reports on me from Karel, from Sara English, from God-knows-who-else, and I can't even figure out what the right answers are supposed to be."

Bailor seemed to shrink backward across the couch away from him, coolly distancing himself from the whole damn situation.

"I told you, I don't know a damn thing about what goes on at this level," he said. "You're in deeper than anyone I've ever worked with."

"That's a big fucking help!" Weller said angrily.

Bailor shrugged. "Seems to me *you're* the expert at this point, not me. The number you ran on them in the restaurant, giving them a little paranoia about maybe you being a Monitor, was something I never would've thought of, and professionally speaking, I think it was probably brilliant. It should make whatever reports they turn in on you as bland and nonforthcoming as they can get away with. But dealing with Monitor interrogation techniques. . . ."

He seemed to cringe, and inch even further away from Weller, as if Weller had some loathsome disease. "I don't know anything about it, and I don't *want* to know anything about it. To tell you the truth, this is getting a little heavy for me."

"*Really?*" Weller snarled. "And what about *me?*"

"You're the guy with the motivation, I'm just a hired gun," Bailor said coldly. "This is your life, but to me it's just another job. I can't afford to get in too deep. I walk a thin line as it is."

A cold fear insinuated itself into Weller's anger. "Are you saying you're going to bug out on me, Bailor?" he said. "You want to give me my fifteen hundred dollars back?"

"I didn't say that," Bailor said quietly. "I just mean there's a line I won't cross. I'm not going to do anything to get the Monitors interested in *me*." He smiled falsely. "Look, this stage of the game is *your* trip, not mine. It's an acting problem. Gomez is your audience, and you know what part you have to play for him. *You're* the film director, you know this stuff. Maybe what you've got to use is, what do they call it, Method Acting. If you don't know enough to fool this guy by presenting the surfaces you think he wants to see, then internalize the part; don't act, *be*."

"Thank you Lee Strasberg," Weller had muttered, and he had left soon thereafter; disappointed, pissed off, a little worried about the depth of Bailor's commitment and the real extent of his expertise.

But now he had to admit that Bailor, for all his deficiencies and apparent cowardice, was basically right. What else was there to do? Hadn't that been what he had been doing since he went to work for Changes Productions? Hadn't his performance reached a certain peak in the coffee shop?

He had played Jack-Weller-the-convert so well that he had gotten *real* converts to wondering if he might be a Monitor. And it hadn't been a piece of calculated surface acting; it had come bubbling up out of him unbidden. He had really synced into the part, operating at optimum consciousness. And somehow, at least temporarily, it had given *him* the power.

Maybe I should ride with it, he thought, looking across the brainwave monitor at the smiling Sylvia. I seem to have convinced her and her damned machine.

"Well, how about that," Weller said genially. "I've made it."

"Well, of course, there are further levels, further processes," Sylvia said. "But now that you're in Monitor life analysis, they'll decide what you go on to next, when you're ready for it."

"Tell me," Weller said with crafted spontaneity, "have you ever processed a Monitor?"

"A *Monitor?*" Sylvia said, her face screwing up into an expression of uneasy surprise, almost of outraged propriety.

"Sure. I mean, someone has to give the Monitors their meditative deconditioning, right?"

Sylvia seemed to relax slightly. "Oh," she said, "you mean have I ever processed someone who later *became* a Monitor? Yes, a few times. But you surely don't suppose that actual *Monitors* receive processing on *my* level!"

"Well, who *does* give Monitors the processing that makes them Monitors?"

"Er . . . ah . . . the Monitors themselves, I suppose . . . maybe even John . . . I don't really know. . . ." She seemed really shook. "Why are you asking me all these questions about the Monitors?" she said more sharply.

Weller shrugged diffidently. "I guess because I think they're fascinating people," he said. He rose, suddenly took her hand, and shook it. Sylvia's hand was limp and unresponsive,

141

and she was eyeing him most peculiarly. "Don't *you* think they're fascinating people?" he said, with smarmy sincerity. "Don't you admire their heightened awareness?"

Sylvia could find nothing to say to that.

"Well, I've got to go to my life-analysis session now," Weller said breezily. "It's been nice working with you."

And he left her standing there, wooden-faced, having suddenly been dismissed by *him*, thinking God-knows-what. I've really found something that keeps these nerds off-balance, Weller thought buoyantly, as he took the elevator to the seventh floor of the Center.

If only it could work on Gomez. But why *couldn't* it? Somehow fascination with the Monitors had become a piece of the part he was playing, one of those little schticks that appear from nowhere and give a performance unexpected depth. Why not keep it? Maybe even Gomez isn't immune to flattery.

When he entered room 703, Gomez tracked him with his eyes as he walked to his chair with a very strange expression on his face, as if Weller were some exotic and rarely seen animal. He sat there studying Weller silently for long moments while Weller gave him the old Transformationalist Stare back.

"You're full of surprises, aren't you, Weller?" he finally said.

"Am I?"

"Come off it, Weller. What was that number you ran on Sara English and her flunkies?"

"What number?" Weller asked innocently.

Gomez shook his head sourly. "*What number?* You've got them half convinced you're a Monitor, and you ask me what number?"

Weller shrugged. "I'm not responsible for what goes on in other people's heads," he said.

"Cut this shit out!" Gomez snarled. "Stop jacking me off! I've got the reports. What was all that crap about the Monitors?"

Weller shrugged. In for a dime, in for a dollar, he decided. "All I remember saying is that I thought the Monitors were an elite because they had a higher level of Transformational consciousness," he said blandly.

Gomez pursed his lips and rolled his eyes briefly toward the ceiling. "You expressed an awful lot of enthusiasm for Monitor discipline," he said.

"What's wrong with that?"

"Motherfucker!" Gomez hissed under his breath. Then, in clipped, controlled tones: "You know damn well what the general attitude is toward the Monitors inside the movement. They're afraid of us. They resent us. Nobody accepts Monitor discipline with *enthusiasm."*

"I do," Weller insisted.

Gomez groaned. "All right," he said, "we'll play your little game. Suppose you explain your loving devotion to the Monitors."

It seemed to Weller that Gomez really was off-balance, that he had never heard anything like this before, that he couldn't have gamed this one out beforehand. It seemed that he had at least temporarily gained the initiative, that he was finally confronting his interrogator on a more or less equal footing. You're sharp, he thought, but you're no superman, Gomez.

"I'll be honest with you," Weller said, at least half truthfully. "Until I ran into you, there wasn't anyone in the movement who impressed me as a superior type, someone with as much or more on the ball as me. But I can't outthink you, and I can't figure out what you're thinking, and I've got to respect that. It fascinates me. It proves to me that my consciousness really *can* be improved by processing because frankly, I don't think you were born with a better brain than mine."

"That's a fancy brand of *manteca* you've got there," Gomez said sardonically. But his voice had no real edge to it, and Weller sensed a certain fascination with what he was saying behind those hard eyes. How could Gomez *not* be intrigued? In his own mind he had to believe that what Weller was saying was true, yet it was also the grossest form of fawning flattery. Gomez knew both aspects, and the personal paradox had to make him feel pretty damn ambivalent.

"I'm a hard case," Weller said, boring in. "You've as much as admitted it yourself. When I lock horns with a harder case, I've got to be impressed. Or don't you think you're as good as I do?"

"Cute, Weller, very cute," Gomez leaned back and drummed his fingers on the dossier in front of him. "As long as we're whispering sweet nothings to each other, I've got to admit that you're a hard one to figure out too. Your motivations for joining Transformationalism were transparently hostile. Yet all the reports come out clean. A competent processor says you've successfully completed meditative deconditioning. You feed me all the right responses. . . ." He shook his head ruefully.

"But . . . ?" Weller said.

"But I don't trust you, Weller, I don't trust you at all. I can't find any reason to declare you a regressive, but I can't certify you either."

"Sounds like you don't have enough faith in what you're working for," Weller said. "Sounds like maybe you're not sure that Transformational processing works."

"Oh, bullshit!" Gomez snapped irritably. Then suddenly he became more reflective; his eyes became more inward-directed, his voice softer.

"I'll level with you," he said. "There's no question that in general, Transformational processing does work. *In general*. But you're a so-called creative type, and we've found that most people like you have a very strong resistance to the idea of being processed. People who work with their minds are afraid of losing their talent if they let someone play with their heads.

"Besides," he said more sharply, "you're a director. You know acting. You're into creating fictions. In short, you're a professional bullshitter. And I get the feeling you're playing some kind of game with me right now."

Jesus, have I outsmarted myself? Weller wondered. Have I gone too far? Or would he have the same suspicions about me no matter what I did? At least this way it's out in the open. . . .

"But if I am sincere, I'd be saying the same things, wouldn't I?" he said. "The reports would read the same."

"So they would," Gomez said slowly.

"And you *do* have to reach a decision. . . . And Harry Lazlo *is* anxious for me to start directing. . . ."

"I don't have to answer to no Harry Lazlo!" Gomez snapped.

"But you *do* have to answer to someone, you do have to decide," Weller said. "In a court of law I'd be innocent unless proven guilty. . . ."

"This isn't a court of law, Weller," Gomez said. "No one passes a Monitor life analysis until we're certain. Period."

My God, what have I done? Weller thought. He had a vision of being trapped in this room forever, chewing over the same material with Gomez again and again, locked in a permanent stalemated life analysis. "We've reached an impasse?" he said dully.

Gomez laughed. His demeanor brightened, and once again he seemed impenetrable and on top of things. "Well, well, well," he said mockingly, "it's still possible for our little Monitor lover to underestimate us, is it? No, Weller, we haven't reached an impasse. We have our ways. We'll get at the truth, never fear."

"I'm glad to hear that," Weller said, putting as much sincerity in his voice as the sudden sinking sensation in his stomach would allow.

"Are you, Weller? Are you really?"

"I know where I'm coming from, and I want to convince you. What do I have to be afraid of?"

Gomez laughed again. "What indeed?" he said. "Well, we'll soon see."

"What's going to happen now?"

Gomez gave him the Transformationalist Stare, and this time Weller had neither the energy nor the will to resist. He found himself looking across the desk into those hard, unwavering eyes—transfixed, and more than a little frightened.

"We have several interesting alternatives," Gomez said. "The choice will have to be made on a higher policy level. You can consider that a compliment."

"If you say so," Weller said. What have I gotten myself into now? he wondered nervously. How have I outsmarted myself this time?

Weller had been waiting for the Monitors to drop the other shoe for three days, so when a gofer told him that Sara English wanted to see him in her office, he leaped immediately to the nonspecific paranoid conclusion.

It was a pretext, Karel would be there, and he would . . . what? As he made his way through the maze of plywood partitions toward Sara's office, Weller tried to imagine what the Monitors were going to spring on him and came up totally dry. Rubber hoses? Sodium pentathol? He couldn't even come up with a paranoid fantasy that would hold up as an image in his mind long enough to even focus his dread on a specific fear.

And when he reached the office, Karel wasn't there and neither was Sara—only Arlene Harris, Sara's pudgy assistant, shuffling some papers on the untidy desk and hanging up the phone. I must be really going nuts, Weller thought. I've got to stop jumping at shadows.

"Where's Sara?" he asked. "I was told she wanted to see me."

"Oh yes," Arlene said. "She said something about that. I

145

think she's on Shano's set. I'll go get her; you wait here."

She left, and Weller found himself sitting alone on a folding chair beside the desk, idly scrutinizing the office. It wasn't much—just the desk, the two chairs, a small Xerox machine, and some plywood filing cabinets. On the desk were a phone, some reels of video tape, an old styrofoam coffee cup, assorted scripts, clipboards, and piles of paper. Nervously Weller found his fingers sorting randomly through the papers on the desk.

Then something on one of the documents he was fingering happened to catch his eye. There were three sheets of paper held together with a paper clip, and what had caught his eye was the word "CONFIDENTIAL" stamped in red on the top of the first sheet. Naturally he couldn't resist picking it up and reading it.

Below the red "CONFIDENTIAL" the words "MASTER CONTACT SHEET" were typed in black capital letters. The rest of the sheets were covered with company names, phone numbers, and the names of people, arranged in corresponding columns.

There must have been a hundred or more entries. Weller recognized the names of some of the companies Changes Productions was doing commercials for; in fact it looked like they were all there. But there were scores of other companies listed too—two major studios, a very large bank, a supermarket chain, a local TV station, a chain of restaurants, a network office, two magazine publishers; dozens of really major companies, and dozens more entries that Weller didn't recognize.

It looked like a random listing of important and not-so-important businesses with no discernible pattern. Companies, phone numbers, and, apparently, a key contact at each.

Contact? Wait a minute! *Master contact sheet? Confidential?* Good God, Weller thought, can this be what I think it is? It had to be! A master list of Transformationalist contacts at over a hundred companies! Hadn't Sara or someone *said* that they had their people planted all over the place? Wasn't that how Changes Productions was able to get so many assignments despite the lousy product they churned out? Sure, someone would have to have a list of the Transformationalists at the companies the movement didn't control, and this had to be it. . . .

But this. . . . *This!* This list was enormous! A network of over a hundred key people that the movement could call on in Los Angeles alone. Secret Transformationalist agents every-

146

where, throwing work to Changes Productions—and what else? *What else?*

Was this just a compilation of the movement's wishful thinking, or were all these people really under life directives to follow Transformationalist orders? Did Transformationalism *really* have this kind of power?

A bubble of fear was beginning to form in Weller's gut. This was Mafia-level stuff, this was really major, this—

His heart skipped a beat as he heard footsteps approaching. Quickly he picked up a pile of scripts and slid the Master Contact Sheet under them. If they caught me looking at that thing. . . , he shuddered. That list was potential dynamite. If the information got out, all those people would lose their jobs, the movement would stand to lose millions, and there would be a major public scandal. He didn't want to think about how far they would go to protect its confidentiality. It might just be *all the way*. He wished he had never seen the damned thing, he wished he didn't even know about it. . . .

Sara walked into the office, smiled at him warmly, and sat down behind the desk. "Congratulations," she said, positively beaming.

"Huh?"

"Haven't you been told yet?"

"Told what?"

"Starting next Monday, I'm allowed to let you direct."

"*What?*" Weller goggled at her, dumbfounded. After the last session with Gomez how the hell was that possible? No way I could've passed life analysis, he thought. What's going on here? What number are they running now?

"The word just came down from Owen Karel," Sara said, looking at Weller peculiarly. "What's the matter, Jack, aren't you pleased? You look really strange."

"Uh . . . yeah, well, I'm really surprised. I mean no one's told me that I've been passed by the Monitors, and in fact I don't see how I could have been. . . ."

Sara frowned. "Come to think of it, Karel didn't mention anything about that. That's weird. That's really weird."

"It sure is," Weller said. "I mean, just between you and me, I've been led to believe that my Monitor is having a lot of trouble making up his mind about me. He even told me he was going to consult at higher policy levels. Do you think . . . ?" Could this have been the doing of Harry Lazlo?

"*Higher policy levels?*" Sara said, eyeing Weller very

147

narrowly. Was that fear in her eyes, or what? "That must mean *Torrez*," she said, almost hissing the name. "Only Torrez himself could overrule the policy against letting someone who hasn't passed life analysis direct."

She leaned forward across the desk, and now she looked not only confused but . . . turned on. "Look, Jack," she said uncertainly, "maybe this is as good a time as any . . . I mean" . . . She paused, seemed to be gathering resolution. "I'm attracted to you," she said. "I mean I'd really like to ball you. And now maybe there isn't any life directive against it . . . do you know?"

"What? WHAT?"

Sara ran a point of pink tongue over her lips. "Does it really surprise you that much?" she said.

"Yes . . . no. . . ." Weller felt a surge of heat in his loins, but at the same time there was a twinge of loathing in his gut. "What are you talking about, a life directive against it?"

"I've passed life analysis and you haven't," Sara said matter-of-factly. "So, of course, I'm under life directive not to go to bed with you. But I'm not sure whether this changes things or not. Can't you tell me?"

"Can't I tell you?" Weller said weakly. Pow! Bam! Zam! It was all coming so quickly. They're letting me direct. Sara wants to ball me. There's a fucking life directive against it! And *she* wants *me* to tell her what's coming off?

Sara looked at him with naked sexual hunger, but at the same time there was an edge of paranoia to it, a nervous look that gave Weller the feeling he had some kind of power over her. But for the life of him, he couldn't figure out how or why. "Look, Jack, I know I shouldn't be asking this," she said, "and I know you probably won't answer, but. . . . Oh hell, are you or aren't you?"

Weller could not help coming out with the line. "Only my hairdresser knows for sure."

"You're toying with me," Sara pouted.

"*I'm* toying with *you*? Jesus Christ, what are you talking about?"

"All right, if you want to be *that* way about it. . . . They give me a real director, but they tell me I can't use him to direct because he hasn't passed life analysis. He turns me on, but I'm under life directives not to go to bed with him. Now they tell me you *can* direct, but they don't tell me whether you've passed life analysis, so I don't know whether we can get it on or not. They leave it deliberately vague."

148

Sara sighed. "What am I supposed to think? You've already got me talking about things I shouldn't be talking about. I've put myself in your hands. Can't you tell me? Are you one or not?"

Finally Weller realized what she was asking. Am I or am I not a Monitor? Good God! Part of him wanted to go on with the charade, part of him reveled in the sense of sinister power that her paranoia was giving him, and he understood all too well what kind of pleasure you got from really being a Monitor.

His body told him that, yes, he wanted to go to bed with her, he had been without a woman too long, without sexual release or even desire, without the warmth of a body against his in the night. And beyond that, what she was saying now took courage, at least in her own head. It was a risk she was taking, and she was taking it for him. It was a moment of human honesty in an endless miasma of mind games.

But yet another part of him was totally repelled by the thought of touching someone who would *wait for permission* from the Monitors before acting out her own feelings. He knew now that he would never ball Sara, not even with someone else's dick. There was too much pity in the way, and too much contempt.

"No," he said, "I'm not a Monitor."

Sara studied him quietly for a long moment. Then she got up, bent over him, and then kissed him on the mouth, long, lingering, and tongue deep. Weller found his body responding like a man dying of thirst, but his heart was a solid block of ice, and his stomach writhed with disgust.

They parted and looked at each other, eyeball to eyeball. "I believe you," she said. "I'm going to ask Karel if it's all right. . . . If that's okay with you."

Weller was torn, and he felt trapped. He was horny as hell, and she was massively attractive. But the thought of balling her now, after asking the permission of the Monitors, was totally loathsome to him. At the same time part of him wanted to grudge-fuck her brains out; he wanted to fuck her silly *because* they wouldn't let him, because he wasn't about to put up with *that* kind of shit. And beyond all that, there was the part he was supposed to be playing: *that* Jack Weller would ask permission like a good little boy.

Weller could only nod foolishly. "Ask the bastards for their blessing," he muttered under his breath.

"What?"

He sensed that the moment of honest reality had long since passed. There was a part to play, and he had to do it. "I said I'd ask Gomez too," he said. "I'm seeing him tonight." Boy, will I ask the son of a bitch!

She smiled at him, and once again he felt a small flash of human contact, sad and forlorn. "Doesn't this get to you, Sara?" he said. "Don't you feel a little silly having to ask permission?" He started to rise from his chair. "What do you say we just do it right here right now across this desk and to hell with life directives?"

Sara jumped back about two feet. "I've got to get back to the set now," she said, making for the door. "Be patient, Jack, they know what they're doing. . . ."

Then she was gone, leaving him sitting limply on the chair, his body twanging with ultraviolet rage.

Too fucking much! he thought, drumming his fingers nervously on the stack of scripts piled on the desk. What's going on? Why are they going to let me direct? A bright flash of paranoid poison went through his mind—could Sara be part of it too? Could this whole number have been some test dreamed up by Gomez? The coincidence of the timing smelled awfully fishy. Could *anything* be mere coincidence around here?

"Shit!" he snarled, picking up the stack of scripts and slamming them back down on the desk.

Then his eyes fell on the Master Contact Sheet which he had accidentally uncovered.

Oh really? he thought slowly. *Oh really?* He picked up the sheaf of papers, fingered them speculatively. He got up and peered out the doorway. No one in sight.

Well, why the hell not? he thought. I've seen this damned thing. Whatever danger that puts me in, I'm in already. He went over to the Xerox machine, turned it on, then paused and thought again. This list was potential dynamite to the movement, it could be one hell of a weapon. What do I have to lose? he decided. If I don't have to use it, no one will ever know. But if I *do* have to use it, then for a change I'll have *them* by the balls!

Quickly he copied the Master Contact Sheet, slipped the original back under the pile of scripts, folded the copies, and stuffed them into his pants pockets. They want to play Gestapo games, I'll give them Gestapo games! he thought.

Push me too far, you motherfuckers, and you'll find out I can play the game like a Monitor too.

Ten

Gomez seemed to have recovered his impenetrable veneer of enigmatic toughness since their last session. He sat behind his desk steepling his fingers and smiling a tight, sardonic smile that set Weller's teeth on edge. "Sit down, Weller," he said coldly. "This won't take long."

Weller perched on the edge of his chair, gladder than ever that he had a copy of the Master Contact Sheet locked in his house. If worse came to worse, this bastard was going to find out who held a high card in the hole!

"I've discussed your case with Torrez, and we've charted a scenario," Gomez said. "You've already been informed of part of it."

"I have?"

"You think that the directive to let you begin directing could have come from anywhere short of Monitor headquarters?"

"I see," Weller said. But do I? Throwing goodies my way hardly seems to be what this business is about. Is Sara part of the deal too?

Gomez leaned back in his chair. "We've decided that we've carried life analysis as far as it could go in your case," he said. "And that turned out not to be far enough. So now we're giving you a chance to *show* us where you're really at. What you do as a director will be part of it." He gave Weller a false grin that told him that the other side of the coin was going to be something nasty indeed.

"I'm sure I can satisfy you as a director," Weller said fatuously.

"I'm sure you can too," Gomez said. "If you could ream out a monkey show every week, I'm sure you can produce anything we tell you to to our satisfaction without having your head behind it. A hired gun is a hired gun. As far as I'm concerned, that will prove nothing."

Weller flushed with anger, or with a flash of something that he tried to convince himself was anger. It must have shown on his face, for Gomez gave a short, brittle laugh.

151

"Well, we do have some insight into ourselves, don't we?" he said. "Whether we can stomach it or not."

Weller said nothing, determined not to give the son of a bitch the satisfaction of an answer.

"Well, down to business," Gomez said coldly. "The purpose of this session is to issue two life directives. You've already gotten the first: you are directed to devote your full creative energies to to producing material for the movement, starting Monday." He paused and flashed a feral grin. "You understand that the outcome of your life analysis now depends on how well and faithfully you fulfill your life directives. . . ."

"I can handle it," Weller said evenly.

"Good," Gomez said slyly. "And I hope you can eptify your consciousness behind the second life directive too. Because also starting on Monday, you are hereby directed to report to the Transformation Center for a room assignment."

"What?"

"You've been placed under total Monitor life programming," Gomez said, seeming to taste and relish every word. "You're going to have an opportunity to live Transformationalism full-time. During the day you'll direct for Changes Productions. You'll sleep in your room at the Transformation Center every night. There will be a midnight curfew. You'll be assigned certain housekeeping tasks. And of course, you'll be closely monitored at all times, and the spirit with which you fulfill these life directives will determine the outcome of your life analysis."

"How often am I allowed to take a piss?" Weller snarled. He couldn't believe what he was hearing, he couldn't believe they would go this far. And yet, wasn't this precisely what had happened to Annie?

"You can piss whenever you want to, Weller," Gomez said. "You'll even have commissary privileges, though eating at the Center is optional."

"You're really serious about this?" Weller said. "You really expect me to—"

"Quite the contrary," Gomez snapped. "I really expect you to tell me to go fuck myself. Because I think you're a phony, Weller. I think your so-called dedication to Transformationalism is a scam. This is your opportunity to prove it, one way or the other. Understand the situation. You've been given a life directive, not an order. You can choose to obey it or not."

"And if I don't?"

Gomez shrugged. "If you don't, you'll be declared a regressive. You'll be fired from your job. You'll be permanently barred from all Transformation Centers. All members of Transformationalism will be under permanent life directive to ostracize you. There will be no second chance."

"That's all?" Weller said dubiously.

Gomez laughed. "Oh, we might be able to think up a few more things," he said, deliberately making it sound totally sinister.

"What about sex?" Weller asked, probing for how far this really went, for whether or not Sara was involved.

"Ah yes, Sara English," Gomez said smugly. "A tasty piece of ass."

Weller's jaw went slack. "You know that too?" he said softly.

"It surprises you? Why? Sara requested a clarification from Owen Karel like a good little girl. And she told you she was going to do it, didn't she? She's a good Transformationalist; she accepts Monitor discipline."

"Jesus Christ!"

"Now to answer your horny little question," Gomez said. "Sara English falls into the same category as your wife: a full-time Transformationalist who has passed life analysis. You haven't made that level yet. You are forbidden to have sex with anyone who has, and they're forbidden to have sex with you. You can ball anyone you want to outside the movement unless they've been declared a regressive. But not in the Center."

"And I've got to be back in my own bed by midnight, or I turn into a pumpkin?"

"You got it," Gomez said. He laughed. He leered at Weller. "Sticks in your craw, doesn't it, Weller?" he said. "Some Transformationalist you are! Go ahead, tell me to get stuffed; that's what you're going to do, isn't it?"

Weller forced his mind into a state of logical, detached clarity. He didn't need Bailor to tell him that this was the acid test. If he refused to accept the life directive, it would be open warfare with Transformationalism. He didn't feel as fearful about that as he would have yesterday, not with the Master Contact Sheet as ammunition. If they started really harassing him, all he had to do was send copies of the Contact Sheet to the media, to the presidents of all the non-Transformationalist companies on the list, to the district attorney, the IRS, and any other interested agencies he could think of, and Transformationalism would be in worse shit than anything they could lay on him.

But all that could get him would be revenge. Sweet as that might be, it wouldn't bring Annie back. It wouldn't help him find her. It would only make it more impossible.

However, if he did the unexpected and played along, that would be a critical step toward finally convincing even Gomez of his sincerity. Provided he could endure the situation with a smile and maintain the act full-time under constant paranoid pressure.

But what would it be like to place himself so totally in their hands? *Could* he maintain the act long enough to pass life analysis and get to Annie? How long would that take? Would he crack? What would happen to him if he did? There were too many imponderables—he *had* to see Bailor before he made the decision.

"Do I have to tell you my decision now?" he asked.

"You do if you want a final chance to tell me what you think of me," Gomez said. "After tonight, you won't be seeing me again."

Temporize, Weller told himself. You don't have anything to lose by that. "You've got me all wrong," he said. "I don't want to tell you off. This is a heavy life decision for me, but I understand why you're doing it, and I don't resent it." He smiled ingenuously. "You're trying to find out where I really stand, and you're confronting me with the same question. And you're forcing me to answer it. I can't say I like it, but I can't help admiring the process."

Gomez shook his head unbelievingly. "You really *can* surprise me, Weller," he said. "You're telling me you're accepting the life directive?"

"I'm telling you I really have to think about it," Weller said. "Do I have to give you my decision now?"

Gomez shrugged. "We're beyond bullshit," he said. "From here on in, it's what you do that counts. You either show up Monday or you don't. You don't have to say another word."

Weller gave Gomez the old Transformationalist Stare. "Then let's leave it at that," he said. Gomez stared back at him. Their eyes locked for a long moment, a contest of wills, without communication.

It was Gomez who broke it off with a little laugh. "You're something, Weller," he said. "I'd really be glad to be wrong about you. If you turned out to be the real thing, you'd be quite an addition to the movement. You might even have the head to be a Monitor." He reached across the desk and shook Weller's hand. "I can't say it hasn't been interesting," he said. "Though I can't say it's been nice knowing you, either."

"Likewise," Weller said, and he meant it. If Gomez had not been an agent of Transformationalism, if that sharp, superior mind had not been programmed by John B. Steinhardt, if he wasn't a Monitor, they might have been friends. There were not many men he respected the way he respected Gomez, despite everything, in the face of every reason not to. Ironically he was pretty sure that Gomez felt the same way about him. In a strange way they were going to miss each other.

Weller poured himself a shot of straight bourbon and gulped it down. Pouring himself another, he found his attention caught by the condition of his living room, something he had managed to avoid noticing for weeks.

Dirty glasses, pizza cartons, beer cans, and old Kentucky Fried Chicken buckets covered every available inch of table space. Dust was everywhere, like a carpet of filthy snow. The kitchen, he realized, was even worse—mounded with cruddy dishes and pots, the stove larded with grease, the refrigerator filled with rotting unnameables. The bedroom was a pit of dirty clothes and grimy sheets, and the towels in the bathroom looked and smelled like something in an old gas-station men's room. I'm really becoming a slob, he thought. As if I were refusing to adjust to Annie's absence, as if I were taking it out on the house, as if cleaning up the place would be admitting something I won't let myself admit. Maybe living at the Center is the right idea. At least I'd *enjoy* crapping *that* up.

He shuddered, swilled down his second drink, went to the telephone and dialed the number of Bailor's exchange. He had a scheduled meeting with Bailor on Saturday, but that was too long to wait. He had to have it out now, tonight. He had to get the decision made immediately; living with the uncertainty was unbearable.

The operator answered on the third ring.

"Hello, this is Jack Weller. I want to get in touch with Garry Bailor immediately."

"I'm sorry, Mr. Weller. Mr. Bailor is no longer with us."

"*What?*" A bubble of acid liquor burst in Weller's gut.

"He's canceled the service."

"Well, then give me his home number. This is an emergency."

"I can't do that, Mr. Weller."

"Well, then for Chrissakes, call his home number and tell him that I'm trying to reach him. You can bend the rules that far, can't you?"

There was a pause at the other end of the line. Then the operator's voice said, "Well, if it's really that important to you. . . ."

"Believe me, it is!"

"I'll give it a try. Give me your number and I'll call you back."

Weller gave her the number and hung up his phone. Not more than thirty seconds later, it rang. He snatched it up on the first ring. "*Yes?*"

"I'm sorry, Mr. Weller. Mr. Bailor's home phone has been disconnected."

"Oh my God . . ."

"I'm sorry . . ."

"Yeah, well, thank you," Weller muttered, hanging up the receiver. A cold gray fear crept over him. The dust, the dim yellow light of the single lamp, the dirty glasses and old food containers, the heavy weight of the empty house, it all seemed to be closing in on him. His last link to the outside world had been severed. He was finally, totally, frighteningly alone.

What the fuck has happened to Bailor? Where is the son of a bitch? What's he doing to me?

He stood up. "Shit!" he screamed, kicking the coffee table. "Motherfucker!" He felt his control of himself slipping away, and he didn't know what was on the other side. And he didn't want to know, either.

Maybe Bailor's at his apartment. Yeah, maybe he's got some other poor schmuck in there. Well, screw that! For a hundred bucks a week, he can damn well be there when I need him.

Weller drove to Bailor's Hollywood apartment like a maniac; leadfooting the accelerator, slamming through the gears, winding the engine out raggedly, cutting off cars, daring a cop to stop him. He drove as if he were in a Grand Prix race, keeping the car constantly on the thin edge of danger, so that his entire consciousness would have to be occupied with the task, so that there would be no room for anything else.

156

At the entrance of the building he rang the bell to apartment 3C. No answer. He rang again. Still no answer.

Then he noticed that the doorbell was no longer marked by Bailor's cover name, "Larry Jonas." A sliver of paper with the name "Rademacher" hand-lettered on it had been slipped into the nameplate slot. He checked the mailboxes. "Rademacher" had replaced "Jonas" there, too.

"Goddamn motherfucker!" he screamed, and he smashed the heel of his hand against a whole row of doorbell buttons, pressing three or four of them at random.

A moment later the entrance buzzer sounded. He slammed the lobby door open and ran up the three flights to apartment 3C, his shoes clanging harshly on the steel stairs.

There was a dim light in the curtained picture window. The son of a bitch was there after all! Weller pounded angrily on the door with his fist. "Open up, Bailor, you son of a bitch! Open this goddamn door!"

The door opened, and a young man with long blond hair, naked to the waist, stood in the doorway zipping his fly. A blast of pot smoke hit Weller in the face.

"What the fuck do you want, man? Let's see your warrant."

"I'm not a cop," Weller snapped. "Where the hell is Garry Bailor?"

"Who?"

"Garry Bailor. The guy who lives here. Larry Jonas."

The longhair studied him with red-rimmed eyes. "Are you tripping, man?" he said.

"Look, what happened to Bailor? The guy who rented this apartment?"

"I don't know, man. I just rented this place yesterday."

"Are you a Transformationalist?"

"No, man," the longhair said. "I'm a Scorpio. You're really stoned." He looked past Weller nervously, and following his gaze, Weller saw that people were looking out their doorways across the courtyard. "I wish you'd cool it," the longhair said. "We don't need any cops here, man. You want to come in and get your head together, that's okay, we've got some downs."

All the raging energy went out of Weller like air from a balloon. I'm standing here gibbering, he realized. I'm off my nut. "Sorry," he said quietly. "I didn't mean to hassle you."

"That's okay, brother. You want to sit down? You want a couple of reds?"

"No. Thanks," Weller said, turning away and heading for the stairs.

"You're sure you're okay, man?"

"Yeah," Weller said over his shoulder, "I'll survive."

But by the time he had reached his car, he wondered about that. Bailor had disappeared and pulled the hole in after him. Or someone had *made* him disappear and wiped out all traces of his existence. Were the Monitors even now interrogating him? Had they simply snuffed him?

Or had Bailor been a phony all along? A Monitor agent that they used to establish a dependency so they could yank the rug out from under him at this strategic moment? Weller shuddered—that was *real* paranoia, delusions of reference, they called it. The paranoiac believes that the whole world is a conspiracy organized against him.

He got into the car, started the engine, and began driving home. He drove slowly and carefully now, letting the driving become a mindless task, lost in his own thoughts.

All that really mattered now was that Bailor was gone. The decision was now Weller's alone; there was no one left to help him make it. There were only two alternatives and both seemed totally unacceptable. If he gave up, if he let himself be scared off, he would have nothing—no Annie, no job, no prospects, no hope. Transformationalism had become the totality of his existence; they had swallowed him whole already. But if he went on, he would be sucked in even deeper. Along that path might lay something even worse than becoming a total cipher—he might end up really being programmed, truly converted. He might end up becoming the enemy he was fighting. Both alternatives were unacceptable, but he was *forced* to choose between them.

He parked the car in the garage and went into the house. The miasmic depression of the filthy living room was unbearable. The emptiness of the bedroom was unendurable. The foul kitchen filled his mind with memories of Annie cooking there, the room all spotless and shiny. Even the toilet seemed like the Black Hole of Calcutta. He wandered from room to room aimlessly, like a ghost, unable to stand being anywhere in the house. It was dead, it was a moldering tomb, and his life was a corpse, rotting inside it.

He felt the decision unfolding its inevitability within him. A line from an old Dylan song cycled through his brain over and over again. "You're invisible now, you've got no secrets to conceal."

Finally he realized that some deeper level of his psyche was trying to tell him something, because the line was only half-true. He had nothing left in his life, but he *did* have a secret to conceal. Or reveal.

The Master Contact Sheet. There was enough ammunition there to make the movement pay dearly for what it had done to him. At the very least it represented a kind of insurance...

I'll Xerox up a lot of copies, he decided. I'll put them in sealed envelopes with cover letters, stamp them, and address them to the district attorney, the *Times*, a couple of TV stations, and the IRS. I'll make up four packets of duplicated lists to be sent to the media and the authorities. And I'll mail them tonight—to my agent, to Wally Bruner, to Bob Shumway, and to Uncle Bill—with instructions to mail out the envelopes if they don't get word from me to the contrary every thirty days.

I've really got something on them, he realized. And this is fail-safe. And this can do more than assure my own safety. I can use it to blackmail them into letting Annie go once I find her! One member more or less certainly isn't going to be worth having that Master Contact Sheet made public to them!

And if I go on, if I live at the Center, maybe I can dig up more dirt, maybe I can build up a dossier that will destroy them once and for all. Maybe I can somehow get Annie back and torpedo Transformationalism too.

He found that now that the decision had been made, he could stop pacing and sit down on the edge of the couch. He had nothing left to lose, but he now had plenty to gain. The risk was great and the odds imponderable, but his commitment to the battle had been total for a long time. He only had to look around the house to realize that. The war was on already, all he could do was dare everything and go in for the kill.

Eleven

Weller found an overnight parking space only two blocks away, trudged wearily into the Los Angeles Transformation Center, showed his pass to the gatekeeper, took the elevator to the fourth floor, entered his unlockable room, and flopped down on the bed to wait till six-thirty, when dinner, such as it was, would be served.

Like a good little Transformationalist he had been taking his meals at the Center during the four days he had been there. The idea of eating alone in tacky downtown Hollywood grease parlors was monumentally depressing, and he never seemed to have the energy to do anything else. Besides, they had him down for dishwashing, and he'd have to be back at the Center by seven-thirty to do his assigned shit work anyway.

The room itself was as featureless as such a tiny cubicle could be: a Salvation Army bureau, a closet, a night table with a single lamp, a cheap motel desk and chair set, and a bed. The carpet was a dingy beige, and the lime-green walls were not even adorned with a framed photograph of John B. Steinhardt.

A monk's cell, or not even that, since a monk spent a lot of time in his cell contemplating, whereas this room was a place to sleep and nothing more; deliberately designed, no doubt, to be so obnoxious that the occupant would be forced to spend most of his waking hours in the communal areas of the Center, soaking up the Transformationalist group-think. If the Center had not once been a hotel, the toilets probably would've been communal too, with the privacy doors taken off the crappers.

Weller checked his watch: five minutes after six. He could start drifting down to the dining room soon. Not that he looked forward to dinner with any enthusiasm, but being awake in this room for any length of time made anything else seem relatively attractive. Well, *almost* anything else. He could go to the library and browse through Transformationalist

160

textbooks and pamphlets or the complete science-fiction novels of John B. Steinhardt. He could go watch some inspirational tapes in the video room. He could take part in a rap session on some fine point of Transformationalist dogma. He could sign up for some role-reversal games. He could masturbate, if the lockless door didn't make him too paranoid.

Or he could go down into the private lobby and chew the fat with some of his fellow inmates and amuse himself by trying to figure out who was a Monitor or who would be reporting what he said to whom.

He had done that his first night at the Center, after stowing his clothing in his room, eating a solitary meal, and giving himself his first case of housemaid's hands washing dishes in the kitchen. Might as well find out what I've gotten myself into, he had thought, as he dried his hands. He left the big restaurant-style kitchen, walked down the hall past the dining room, and entered the private lobby, which had probably been a meeting room in the days when the Center was a hotel.

It was a big barn of a room, with a high ceiling, and scars on the asphalt-tile floor where a stage had obviously once stood. Mismatched old couches, chairs, and low tables were scattered around the room in no particular pattern. One lemon-colored wall was graced by the biggest standard photo of Steinhardt that he had yet seen. There was an urn of coffee on a table in one corner, and in another an ancient black-and-white television console was muttering to itself with no one watching.

About thirty people drifted around the room in small groups. Most of them were younger than Weller, and most of them, male and female, wore jeans, T-shirts, army-surplus gear, or finery snatched off the racks at the May Company. Weller immediately felt like an alien, as if he had wandered onto the wrong set.

He drifted around the room quietly and invisibly, like the Flying Dutchman, absorbing random bits of dialogue.

"—said she had gotten an appointment to the Institute—"

"—one of John's early novels, but you can tell the seeds are there—"

"—is a better mediatative deconditioner than Carson, if you ask me—"

"—that's right, the Monitors! At least they're going to give me a preliminary screening—"

161

"—really a bitch eptifying my consciousness behind that one. It's my major block—"

No one seemed to be talking about the Dodgers, politics, dope, sex, career, movies, or anything else that didn't relate to Transformationalism. Could it really be that these people had no private inner lives, nothing beyond the Transformationalist programs they were running on?

He glided to the periphery of a group of four: a dark-haired woman in her late twenties seated on a couch with an intense-eyed young man with a strange 1950s crew cut, two other men standing in front of the couch talking to them, one with longish blond hair, the other a burly type in T-shirt and jeans.

"—of course, it's just a rumor—"

"—sounds possible, and everyone knows they're doing things at the Institute years ahead of anywhere else—"

"—assuming thoughts *do* have a one-to-one relationship with brain waves, I don't see why you *couldn't* produce a given state of consciousness by reversing the polarity of a brainwave monitor—"

"—but *John* doesn't make that assumption anywhere—"

"—doesn't say no, either—"

The woman on the couch looked up at Weller; she was thin, plain-looking, and something about her face made her eyes seem as if they were set too close together. "Hi," she said, "You're new here, aren't you?"

Weller nodded noncommittally.

"Have *you* heard anything about the brainwave inducer?"

"Not much," Weller said ambiguously.

"Are you into mind-matter interface theory?" the woman asked. "None of us really are. Do you know if it's even possible to produce a state of consciousness electronically?"

Weller shrugged. "I'm in the media end myself," he said.

The blond longhair looked at him strangely. "You work for Changes?"

Weller nodded.

"What do you do?"

"I direct."

There was an intake of breath; they were suitably impressed, but there seemed to be something more, a certain tension seemed to have descended on the little group. "Then what are you doing *here?*" the woman asked.

"Just following a life directive."

"That's weird," the crew cut said. "That's really weird. There's no one else on that level living here."

162

The four of them studied Weller guardedly. I'm older, I'm in a position way above them, and there's no one else here like me, Weller thought. It must be more Monitor paranoia. He resisted the impulse to play to it; this was definitely a time to maintain a low profile, and for all he knew, one of *them* could be a Monitor.

"So it goes," he said, shrugging, and drifted off, leaving what he was pretty sure would be an altered conversation behind him.

Weller glided in and out of a few more conversations—a discussion about a young man's problems with getting his parents to accept his commitment to the movement, a disputation about the significance of a minor character in *Transformational Man*, a rehash of last night's role-reversal game—all of which served only to increase his sense of alienation.

This really *was* a roomful of people who ate, slept, and drank Transformationalism. More than that, the people living at the Center seemed to be the very bottom end of the movement—shiftless, confused kids without a pot to piss in or a dime to contribute to Transformationalism's coffers. Scooped up as Steinhardt's slavies as they might have been by the Hare Krishna movement or the Jesus Freaks, had they happened to be caught by those wavelengths first. The psychic *lumpenproletariat* of the seventies.

One night of trying to relate to *that* had been enough for Weller. Better to stay in his room twiddling his thumbs than put himself in a situation where he would be bound to shoot his mouth off sooner or later. There was no way he could keep talking about Transformationalism with these kids without finally telling them a thing or two or being tempted to play Monitor, and they didn't seem to talk about anything else. And he *knew* that the Monitors would be getting reports on anything he said to anyone.

Six-twenty. Time to drift down to the dining room, he thought. If I'm in luck, they'll let me keep to myself. Though he had a hunch that if he seemed to be making an effort to keep to himself, it would be a black mark in a dossier somewhere too.

The dining room was set up like a high-school lunchroom, or, Weller thought darkly, like something in a prison. There was a line of steam tables behind a counter that ran the length of one wall, and the rest of the room was filled with rows of long tables and cheap plastic chairs. Privacy was a hit-or-miss proposition, a matter of picking an empty stretch of table and hoping it didn't fill up after you sat down. About a dozen people were already eating, and the line by the counter was already fifteen people long, so the chances of being left alone didn't look too good.

Weller took a tray and dinnerware, waited dully on line for a few minutes, and finally got his turn at the steam tables. The choice, as it had been every night, was pretty grim. Poisonous-looking tamale pie. Spaghetti with lumpy meat sauce. Knockwurst and sauerkraut. Macaroni salad. Some kind of ghastly bile-green vegetarian stew with brown rice. The food was as cheap and crummy as it could get without inciting a revolution, even among these dedicated servants of the movement. Reluctantly, Weller settled for the knockwurst and kraut, macaroni salad, and coffee and scouted around for an unobtrusive corner where he might have a chance to be left alone.

People were scattered pretty evenly around the room, but there was a stretch of about a dozen empty seats at the end of a table near a big garbage bin. Weller went over and took an end seat right by the garbage, hoping that would be unattractive enough to keep away his fellow inmates.

But he hadn't managed to get down more than a few forkfuls of macaroni salad and a single bite of knockwurst when a pimply young man and a guy about his own age sat right down across the table and introduced themselves with friendly enthusiasm.

"Hi," said the kid. "I'm Tod and this is Harry."

"You're new here," said Harry, "and we noticed you weren't mixing much, so we thought we'd help you get acquainted."

"I remember what it was like *my* first few days here," Tod said sympathetically. "I didn't know anyone, and I figured everyone else had had much more processing than I did and wouldn't be very much interested in a lower consciousness like mine."

Despite his better judgment Weller found himself warming to them a bit—it *had* been a lonely four days, and they *were* apparently just trying to be friendly. "I'm Jack," he said, but he still didn't feel like saying more.

"How much processing have you had?" Tod asked conversationally.

"Block-auditing and meditative deconditioning," Weller muttered.

"You've completed meditative deconditioning?" Harry asked.

164

Weller nodded.

"How long did it take?"

"About a month."

Both of them looked quite impressed, even amazed. "I took the crash course," Weller explained.

Harry turned green with envy. "You must have a lot of money. I'd love to be able to do that, but I'm broke, and I'm working my way through processing doing the usual shit work, and that only gets me two sessions a week. I want to be a processor, but you've got to go all the way through meditative deconditioning before they'll even consider you, and at this rate it's going to take me at least another two months."

Very interesting, Weller thought. Apparently the amount of free processing you get depends on how much they value the work you're doing for them. There ain't no such thing as a free lunch here! "I'm not rich," he said. "I'm working my way through too." He was trying to be just one of the boys, but he was beginning to realize that people who got sucked in through the Celebrity Center got much different treatment than the peons all the way down the line.

"What kind of work are you doing for the movement?" Tod asked.

"I'm working for Changes Productions. As a director."

"Wow."

Now they were *really* impressed. Shit. No doubt everyone in the center would know about it by tomorrow. He was being trapped into becoming a local celebrity, and he didn't like it at all.

"Then you must've passed life analysis," Harry said. "Was it rough?"

Uh-oh. It was a delicate moment. If he told them the truth, they would think something very strange was going on, but if he lied and told them he *had* passed life analysis, it would get right back to the Monitors, and that would probably be a heavy black mark. "Pretty rough," he said. "In fact, I'm not quite through."

They both looked at him narrowly. "And they're letting you *direct*?" Harry said suspiciously. "I've never heard anything like that before."

Weller tried a different shrug. "I'm a pro," he said. "I've done network directing. Changes Productions has an awful lot of work. I guess they just figured they needed me to help out right away."

"Far out," Tod said. "Maybe I've seen something you've

165

done?" But the older man's gaze was still lidded; either he sniffed the odor of the Monitors, or he was jealous, or both.

"I hope not," Weller said dryly. "It's all been Saturday-morning garbage kiddie shows."

"Wow, it must be a big change doing *real* work for the movement then," Tod said. "I hope I'll find something that important to do."

"They seem to be able to eptify your contribution," Weller said. "I'm sure they'll find you the maximized slot." Jargon, anyone?

"You must've met some of the real high-consciousness people," Harry said with open envy. "What are they really like?"

"I've met Benson Allen and Harry Lazlo," Weller said, glancing at his watch. It was getting time to end this little chit chat before it got into dangerous areas. The way these guys were forcing the conversation, *they* could be Monitors. "They're about what you'd expect—high-powered, together people."

"Hey, maybe you'd like to come to our rap session tonight," Tod said. "We're going to have a block auditor talking about cultural correlations of block patterns."

"Sounds interesting," Weller muttered. "But I've got to be on the set early tomorrow, and I'm down for dishwashing." He checked his watch again, this time conspicuously. "In fact, I'd better get going. Been nice talking to you."

"We'll see you around," Harry said. "Maybe we can really talk sometime. I'd really like to know what life analysis is all about."

"Yeah, sure," Weller said, getting up and shoveling his scraps into the garbage bin. He sighed as he moved off toward the dish-stacking area. Who would've thought I'd ever be glad to go spend an hour washing slimy dishes and cruddy pots? he thought. Well, it looks like I'm going to be forced to interact with these people whether I like it or not. As a local point of interest, yet. He had to admire the way Gomez had set up this test situation—there wasn't going to be any place to hide.

"Roll 'em!"
"*Brainwave Monitor,* scene five, take two."
"Speed."
Weller surveyed the set for a moment. The meditative deconditioner was the real thing, so he had no trouble getting a credible performance out of her. The actor playing the client was a real client too, but he was also just enough of a professional to be having difficulty playing the client he really

was without overacting. Weller had finally gotten around that by running through each take half a dozen times before he rolled any film, so that he was dulled enough to simply respond mechanically to the processor as he would in the real situation.

The lighting was good—a whole order of magnitude better than anything Georgie or Shano had been able to do— a medium bright spot on the processor, soft backlighting for the client, establishing the relationship with a subtle visual image. The off-center and slightly low camera angle would give the whole scene an almost imperceptible larger-than-life icono-graphic quality. He was getting solid professional commercial footage, and he was getting it superfast by Changes Productions standards. Sara had to be pleased. . . .

"Okay," he shouted. "Action!"

"You are walking along the beach, and far away over the surf you see an arm waving and hear a cry for help," the processor said. "You're not a good swimmer, but you dive into the water, going into the center of your fear to rescue the person in distress . . ."

Then ten seconds of silent concentration on the part of the actor playing the client, which would seem like subjective minutes on film . . .

Weller wasn't even sure what they were going to do with this mini documentary on the brainwave monitor. The stuff they had given him to shoot would run about three minutes, but the script was full of interpolations like "narration to be added" and "insert stock footage," so he didn't even know how long the finished product would run, or even what it would be like.

He cued the next line of dialogue.

The client looked up, smiled gently, and said: "I felt physi-cally afraid, but I did it. I really felt I was there, and I was able to conquer my physical fear. . . ."

They're really playing it close to the vest, Weller thought. Shoot these scenes like a good little boy, and we'll slap some narration around them. Not only didn't he have any creative control over content, the damn script didn't even tell him what the eventual content would really be. It was almost a laboratory experiment designed to test his purely technical skills without letting him come within a mile of creative control. *Almost* a laboratory experiment?

The processor nodded sagely. "The monitor showed that you really eptified your consciousness behind that scenario,

Mr. Carson," she said. "I think you'll now find that you deal with physical fear much better in real time. We're ready to go on to another block."

Good stuff, such as it is, Weller thought. They've got to be pleased with what I'm turning out. Unless some Monitor somewhere in analyzing my goddamn lighting and camera angles for subliminal regressiveness and disloyalty to the movement. That seemed like total paranoia, but around here total paranoia had a nasty way of coinciding with reality.

"Cut!" Weller shouted. "Okay, very good folks, that's a take. We'll take a ten-minute break, and then go on to scene six."

Weller mopped his brow and walked over to the back of the sound stage where Georgie had been watching. He saw that Sara had walked in at some point and was standing beside him, looking pretty pleased.

"That was very good, Jack," she said. "You're doing good work, and you're really keeping ahead of the shooting schedule."

Ever since they had both been officially told that it was a no-no for them to go to bed together, she had been all business; she acted as if that little scene in her office had never been played. Which was all right as far as Weller was concerned; what physical attraction he had felt for her had been dissolved away by a distant contempt.

"If you ask me," Weller said, "the shooting schedules could stand to be tightened up around here. I mean, I don't really feel I'm rushing anything."

"You're really sharp," Georgie said somewhat ruefully. "I don't think the rest of us could work that fast; we just don't have your experience."

Weller felt like a bit of a shit; he really hadn't meant to point out Georgie's deficiencies as a director. "It takes time," he said. "But you'll learn, don't worry about it."

"Well, anyway," Sara said, "I just came here to tell you we're all invited to a party Saturday night at the Steinhardt house."

"The Steinhardt house?" Weller said. "We're going to meet John?"

Georgie laughed. "No way," he said. "John's hardly ever there, and he *never* comes to his wife's parties."

Weller cocked an inquistive eyebrow at Sara.

"The Steinhardts have a big house in Bel Air," she said. "You could call it a mansion. John's not there very often, but

168

his wife Maria lives there, and she throws these really huge parties."

"I've been to a couple," Georgie said. "They're really something. Film people, movie stars, real jet set. *You* should love it."

"It sounds charming," Weller said sardonically. Just what I need, a phony Hollywood party! He looked deliberately at Sara; some random impulse made him want to rub things in. "Will you be my date?" he asked.

Sara frowned, but there wasn't any real emotion in it. "You know I can't do that," she said. "We have our life directives."

"Not even a lousy date at a giant Hollywood party?" Weller teased. "Even if I swear not to make a pass at you?"

Sara began fidgeting. "Please . . ." she said plaintively.

"Well, then screw it!" Weller snapped petulantly. "I don't want to go to some crummy Hollywood party anyway."

"You *have* to go," Sara said.

"Have to go? What the hell do you mean, I *have* to go?"

"An invitation to one of Maria's parties is like a life directive."

"What? What the hell kind of shit is that?"

"That's the way John wants it," Georgie said reasonably, as if that were a logical explanation for anything.

"John and Maria have a very complex relationship," Sara said. "They don't see each other very often, but they're very close. Maria doesn't have any official position in the movement, but she's, well, *John's* wife."

"Sounds like the ideal marriage," Weller said sourly. "But why does she want us there?"

Sara shrugged. "Maria likes crowds. She likes show-business people." She smiled forlornly. "She'll probably really like you," she said.

"Do you mean that the way I think you mean that?" Weller said.

"It could happen," Sara said quietly. "You can pick up your invitation in my office."

"And I really have to do this?"

Sara nodded.

Part of Weller was mightily pissed off at the *chutzpah* of Steinhardt's damn wife actually ordering him to go to her bloody party. But another part of him was curious to meet her. Steinhardt's wife. As close to the center of Transformationalism as you could get. Be honest with yourself, Weller, if

169

you weren't being ordered to go to this thing, you'd damn well want to go. There was a certain fascination to the idea of actually meeting someone who slept with the Great Man.

"Okay," he said. "I guess I'll see you there." He had to admit that he felt a certain excitement at the notion of penetrating to the very eye of the storm.

His hands soaking in a galvanized iron sink full of hot, greasy suds, pulling out plates, giving them a lick with a sponge, dipping them in the rinse tub, stacking them on the rack, Weller had his nose rubbed in the incongruities of his position and the kind of total power over his life that they implied.

In the hermetically sealed little world of the Transformation Center, he had had a certain notoriety and status thrust upon him, virtually against his will. By now everyone knew he was a director at Changes, and he could become a center of attention whenever he so chose and all too many times when he didn't. Tomorrow night he would be a guest at Maria Steinhardt's party, and the poor nerds at the center would go crazy with envy if he let them know about *that*.

Yet at the same time, here he was, forced to do the lowest scut work as if they were carefully reminding him that the movement giveth and the movement taketh away; all power to the movement. *As if?* What else was it but a deliberate demonstration of their total power over his life? You *vill* go to Maria Steinhardt's party. You *vill* wash dishes. You *vill* demonstrate the proper enthusiasm. Jawohl, and you *vill* like it!

It was also an object lesson in the dichotomy at the heart of Transformationalism. The penniless people who lived at the center, dedicating their lives and free labor to the movement, were no less suckers than the millions paying through the nose for processing. Whatever the marks had to give—money or labor—Transformationalism took. The slavies and the taxpayers were just two aspects of the same undermass that supported an elite which began with the processors, and narrowed up into the Monitors, the Allens and the Lazlos, and peaked into a Steinhardt mansion in Bel Air.

And they had set it up so that Weller was both a member of the elite and one of the lowliest peons simultaneously—parties at the Steinhardt mansion and dishwashing at the Transformation Center. Perhaps that's what they're trying to do, he thought, force me to identify with the elite by rubbing my nose in the alternative. Or maybe what they're telling me is that there is only one real elite and its name is John B. Steinhardt.

Weller finished the last dish in the sink, wiped his hands, and walked out of the kitchen into the hallway, paying no attention to his fellow scullions. I'm not one of these suckers, he told himself, but I'll be damned if I'll become one of the suckees, either.

"Hi, Jack, why don't you come along to our rap session?" Tina Davies had accosted him again—a tall, gangling blond in her mid-twenties, who had been trying to latch onto him for about two days now. There didn't seem to be anything sexual in it—in fact, come to think of it, there was a vast lack of sexual energy at the Center, considering that there were so many young people jammed together in a communal situation —rather it seemed to be a kind of evangelical fervor, the desire to be the one to lead this enigmatic figure fully into the fold. "We're going to discuss the roads to Transformationalism."

"The roads to Transformationalism?"

"You know, what brought us as individuals to the movement."

Weller studied her intense, angular face. What *did* bring these people to Transformationalism? He had to admit that the question intrigued him, and he also realized that if he stayed away from all the optional activities much longer, he would risk blowing the whole thing. So—what the hell . . . ?

"Okay," he said, "why not?" He only hoped he could walk the right line when he was forced to tell them why the hell *he* was there.

The rap session was being held in a fair-sized room on the fifth floor. Couches along three walls formed a kind of rude conversation pit. Four people were already there: Harry the would-be processor, a young kid named Bill whom Weller had met briefly once before, and a couple sitting thigh-to-thigh on one couch whom he hadn't yet seen. Tina and Weller sat down on the empty couch, and she did the honors.

"This is Jack Weller, Jack, you already know Bill and Harry, and this is Ted and Lori Brenner." She paused while everyone nodded foolishly to each other.

"Well, I guess I might as well start things off," Tina said. She took a deep breath and began to recite, as if the whole rap were rehearsed.

"I was one of the last of the college radicals, just old enough to become a political activist as the movement was dying out. So I found myself with a degree in nothing-in-particular and a life commitment to working for social change, with nothing dynamic to work through. I couldn't get behind the religious trips everyone was getting into, not after being so heavy into scientific socialism.

"And then a friend of mine dragged me to the Transformation Center. I tried a couple of processing sessions, and then I found myself reading in the space of a couple of weeks everything John had ever written. I found that Transformationalism was something I could get behind. The old New Left didn't reach into the mind, and the religious cults and consciousness-raising groups weren't into changing society, but Transformationalism had it all together—historical perspective, a plan for transforming society, the organization to carry it out, and scientific methods for transforming individual consciousness. Transform society as you transform your own life, John says, and for me that says it all."

There was a long and somewhat embarrassing silence; the others seemed to feel almost as uncomfortable as Weller after listening to this little set speech. Finally Bill spoke up hesitantly.

"Man, I wasn't into anything like revolution. What *I* was into was smack. I won't go into that whole bummer. But I finally did manage to get off the shit through Synanon. And then who was I? I could identify with being an ex-junkie, or I could be nothing. So I left Synanon, and of course it wasn't long before I was shooting smack again. Well, I knew enough about where that was at to get really freaked out, so I got myself into the Narcon program, not even knowing it had anything to do with Transformationalism, I mean, I hadn't even *heard* of Transformationalism.

"Well, they got me off smack again, but the processing didn't stop there. They got my head into the emptiness that got me into shooting smack in the first place. They showed me how it was the frozen reality we live in that fucked me up, and they showed me how we could change it. They gave me something to live for besides the next fix, a way to keep changing and be a something instead of an ex-something. Why am I into Transformationalism? Man, because it's my life; it's made me something more than a nothing."

This time there was no silence afterward; old Harry started rapping immediately.

"Same thing with me, only I didn't even have anything like heroin, I was such a zero. I could've gone to college, but I didn't give a shit. I started working shit jobs right out of high school, and then I got drafted, did two years in Texas, never even got to Nam, out of the army and into more shit jobs. Fucked a lot of women, never lived with one for longer than three months in my life, and then one morning I woke up and I was over thirty, and I had no one, and I was nobody going nowhere. I went through a year or so of bumming around, doing stupid cheap burglaries, getting sauced all the time, and I was such an invisible nobody, I couldn't even get myself busted.

"One day I just wandered into this Center pissed out of my mind, and instead of calling the cops, the people here took me in, dried me out, and started processing me. It was like coming in out of a fog I'd been in all my life. Now I have a purpose. I want to be a processor. I'm in Transformationalism because it told me what I want to be when I grow up."

Weller stared across the room at the Brenners. They stared back at him with what seemed like the same reluctance to speak. A would-be revolutionary, an ex-junkie, and a nobody wanting to be somebody, Weller thought. Empty people waiting for something to fill them with itself. He wondered what the Brenners' story was, and he wondered what they thought *his* story was. He gave them the old Transformationalist Stare, forcing them to speak first. Finally they relented, speaking in turns with a single voice like some musical-comedy team.

"It was our marriage," Ted Brenner said. "I had a good job as a computer programmer, and Lori was teaching school. We had bread, we had things to do, and we loved each other, but somehow it was adding up to nothing."

"We started swinging," Lori Brenner said. "Ted started fucking everything in sight, and so did I."

"But it was boring," Ted said. "Just a stupid game of cocks and cunts. All we were doing was punishing each other for punishing each other, and we weren't really even getting off behind *that* trip."

"We quit our jobs, took our savings, bought a VW bus, and drove around playing hippies for a year. But it all seemed dead inside."

"We couldn't even get into hating each other," Ted said. "And we couldn't even find anything else to hate. So we got new jobs and started going heavy into all the consciousness trips."

"You name it, we tried it. Esalon, Arica, Scientology, the whole number. Finally we tried Transformationalism because we had tried just about everything else."

"And Transformationalism finally showed us what was wrong,"

173

Ted Brenner said with sudden fervor. "All the personas we tried on didn't fit because we were looking for roles to wear like new suits of clothes, final forms for our consciousness, when the only thing that's really real is change."

"We must have known that on some level because we kept putting ourselves through changes, but the mistake we made was trying to find a permanent fit."

"But now we've got something to be committed to together that keeps changing and keeps growing and isn't trying to find a place to stop," Ted Brenner said. "We're in Transformationalism so that we can keep evolving together through the movement."

Weller cringed inwardly as all eyes inevitably turned toward him. The Brenners were a little too close to home. Maybe he and Annie had never gone in for guru trips or done hippie escape acts—their careers had sucked up all that bored thirst for growth and change—but hadn't they also been perpetually reaching for personas that were always out of reach, model lives that were never fullfilled, wet-dream fantasies of the future that allowed them to hide from the boredom and emptiness of the everlasting now?

Maybe that's why Annie got sucked into this thing in the first place, he realized. And me? Isn't that really why I'm following her into Transformationalism? Because without this dumb quest, without Transformationalism, without these mind games, what would I really be but a lonely nobody going nowhere?

He had to say something, and he could hardly get away with an outright lie, so he let it bubble up from his guts, editing out only the worst of it at his lips.

"I was directing a lot of shit, and my wife was an actress who was going nowhere, and we were trying to live in a dream world where I was forever about to do my first feature and she was going to be a star next week. And then my wife got involved in Transformationalism and left me. . . ."

He paused, sighed, spit it out. "Okay, so I joined strictly to get her back," he said. "Well, I haven't gotten her back, and here I still am. Why? I don't know. Because I've got nowhere else to be? Because I have to find out what the fuck happened to Annie?"

He laughed bitterly. "Sometimes I think I'm here just because I have to find out why I *am* here. Because I know I'm not who I was, and I don't know who the fuck I am now. Transformationalism is always talking about riding the changes;

well, I guess that's what I'm doing. Transformationalism started putting me through changes when my wife left; I didn't like it then, I'm not sure I like it now. But it hasn't stopped, and as of now, I've got no direction home. I'm here because I'm here because I'm here. It may not be as inspirational as all your little stories, but it happens to be true."

Weller collapsed against the back of the couch, feeling purged, as if after a thoroughly necessary puke. That really *is* the truth, he thought. I don't even know these goddamn nerds, and now I've spilled my guts to them. How about that? What does it all mean?

They were all eyeing him uneasily now, as if he had somehow violated the sanctity of the process, as if his lack of inspirational bullshit to match their own were some kind of personal insult. As if they were all a cabal of goddamn Monitors, weighing him, and finding him wanting.

Well, fuck you! he thought. You wanted to hear about my road to Transformationalism, and that's what you got, with no bullshit. I said it, it's the truth, and I'm glad. If you don't like it, go stick it up John B. Steinhardt!

Twelve

The Steinhardt house turned out to be a walled compound within the private community of Bel Air. Only the parking lot, close by the main gate, was outside the perimeter, and the gate itself was a massive steel affair overlooked by a closed-circuit television camera.

It was open as Weller arrived, but it was guarded by two big bozos in incongruous red carhop uniforms with pistols holstered to their waists. Nine thirty and there were already twenty or thirty cars in the lot and a minor jam on the street outside. Weller gratefully gave the Triumph to a real carhop and walked up to the gate fingering his printed invitation somewhat uneasily. There were half a dozen people at the gate ahead of him—no one whom he recognized personally or famewise—and the guards were collecting their invitations and passing them inside with a cold and intense scrutiny that gave Weller the impression that they were really Monitors.

Weller gave his invitation to one of the guards, endured a professionally suspicious eyeballing, and entered the grounds of the estate. The house itself was a big two-story pseudo-Spanish job, all white stucco and red tile, set back from the wall across a wide expanse of well-manicured lawn studded with an eclectic selection of palms, oaks, and evergreens, and hedged with bright red and overpoweringly fragrant bougainvillea. Everyone was walking straight down the flagstone path to the entrance; a "Keep-Off-The-Grass" sign would have been superfluous.

Inside, the ground floor was a series of large, airy parlors opening onto a central Spanish-style courtyard, with a low central fountain, short shade trees, bright beds of flowers, a maze of marble pathways, and a sprinkling of pseudo-Greek statuary. A second-story balcony ran all the way around the courtyard, dripping ivy. There were about a dozen people in the courtyard, and two or three dozen more scattered throughout the ground-floor rooms. These were all furnished as sitting rooms, with plush couches and chairs, brocaded or lavishly papered walls, nondescript representational paintings of landscapes, still lives, and figures, and endless little tables and wall shelves all stuffed with figurines, floral arrangements, and assorted bric-a-brac. The upper story of the house seemed to be off limits.

There was a buffet set up in each room, with a single waiter serving the usual conspicuous-consumption items: caviar, assorted hot hors d'oevres, smoked salmon, sliced beef, turkey, ham, endless salads, and pickles. There were six parlors, and in the largest two, which took up entire sides of the first floor, full bars had been set up. Quiet, indeed almost subliminal, Muzak murmured everywhere.

Weller got a Wild Turkey and water at one of the bars and wandered aimlessly from room to room, feeling at once alienated from his surroundings and peculiarly at home. He had certainly been to parties like this before, if never quite in a place on this scale or reeking quite this much of money. The sort of Hollywood party that was usually put on by a hot shot new director or producer rolling in bread but short of connections. Every celebrity in town would be invited, but if half a dozen real heavies showed up, it would be a smashing success. So the house was papered with invitations off every PR, freebie, and agent list in town, filled with unknown people who usually didn't even know each other, extras to create a crowd scene.

Here, however, celebrity spotting seemed a futile game. There were a few faces that Weller recognized from TV commercials or long strings of bit parts, but nothing that he could even connect a name to. There were some striking-looking Plasticine women in gold lamé, silk pants suits, plunging necklines, and bare backs, but they seemed to be window dressing for older men who might be minor-league producers, or just as easily successful Beverly Hills realtors. There were some lavishly dressed older women with clean-cut beachboy-type consorts in tow, but there were no rich hippie types, no conspicuous displays of tailored denim, beads, or feathers, and what few younger men he saw were, with the exception of the gigolos of the rich bitches, random loners like himself.

As far as Weller was concerned, it was instant boredom, so much so that after about half an hour, he found himself actually longing for the Changes Productions people to show up already and at least give him someone to talk to.

He was getting his third drink when he finally spotted a familiar face. It was Harry Lazlo, resplendent in a royal blue suit, white shirt, and red ascot, elbowing his way to the bar with a honey-blond young starlet type on his arm, luscious dark eyes, and a totally vacuous expression on her face.

As Lazlo ordered drinks, Weller maneuvered himself into position so that they would come face-to-face, hoping that Lazlo would recognize him; much more couth under the circumstances than forthrightly reintroducing himself. Lazlo's gaze intersected his; there was a flicker of recognition, and that would have to do.

"Jack Weller, Mr. Lazlo."

Lazlo smiled a broad Hollywood smile. "Oh yeah, our pro TV director," he said. "How's it going? What do you think of this little bash?"

Weller let a little grimace flicker across his face. Lazlo laughed, held up a palm. "Don't answer that," he said. Then, sotto voce, "Have you ever seen such a collection of phonies?"

"Upon occassion," Weller said dryly.

Lazlo laughed again, and then began walking away from the bar as he spoke, indicating that for the moment Weller was invited to join his little entourage. "Maria is quite a little star collector, *would-be* star collector, right? Every few months she throws one of these things and invites everyone from Charlton Heston to Jackie Kennedy, and what she gets is what you see—a few TV producers, high-priced hair dressers, the old girls from Palm Springs, the bottom end of the freebie lists, tired old agents and PR men, and like that. Plus all the Transformationalist heavies in town." He shook his head ruefully. "Some people never learn. Hope springs eternal, right?"

"I've met the type," Weller said, as they reached breathing space in the middle of the room. He was somewhat surprised that Lazlo would betray such open disdain for Steinhardt's wife to someone like him, but he was pleased to go along with it.

"Have you met Maria?" Lazlo asked.

Weller shook his head.

"Well then, come on, let me do the honors, such as they are," Lazlo said, grabbing Weller's elbow and tugging him toward the courtyard. "I'm sure the old buzzard wants to meet you."

"Huh? I'm sure she doesn't even know my name."

Lazlo laughed. "Who said she knew your name? You underestimate yourself, kid. Or you overestimate Maria. You've actually directed network TV, and that's more than you can

178

say for ninety-nine percent of the people here. As far as Maria's concerned, there's no business like show business. Why do you think she invited everyone from Changes Productions in the first place?"

"I don't know—why did she invite everyone from Changes Productions in the first place?"

Lazlo grimaced wryly. "Because Changes is owned by Transformationalism, and Transformationalism is owned by John, and she's John's wife, and that's the closest sniffing distance she can get to show-biz people. And you're something special right, because you've actually worked in the major leagues."

"Huh?" Weller grunted dubiously, with a certain queasy feeling developing in his stomach.

"Don't worry about it," Lazlo said, dragging him out into the courtyard. "Maria will make it perfectly clear, like the man says. Now lessee. . . ."

By now the courtyard was quite crowded; the benches were mostly filled and a couple of dozen people were milling around with drinks in their hands and platters of food. Lazlo scouted around; finally a look of recognition dawned on his face, and he led Weller and the silent girl toward a small group of people gathered around a woman seated alone in queenly state on a marble bench just in front of the gurgling fountain.

The woman on the bench was in her middle forties or so, with a smooth, once-stunning face that was just starting to sag slightly, and big dark eyes that still flashed fire and brimstone. Her dark brown hair was lightly streaked with gray, and she wore a reasonably tight green silk pants suit. The total effect said that she knew her age, and also knew that she still looked good enough not to have to hide it.

The court gathered around her included a gray-haired woman in a flowing caftan festooned with astrological signs, two older men in dark suits, a hard-looking tough who seemed to be a bodyguard, a good-looking younger woman in a midnight-blue dress, and a balding old weirdie in a white yoga suit. They fell back as Lazlo approached as if they knew that they were extras.

"Hello, Harry," Maria Steinhardt said, in a deep throaty voice that seemed edged with habitual sardonicism. She looked at Weller appraisingly, without meeting his eyes. "Who's your friend?"

Lazlo brought forth the blond on his arm. "This is Bridget," he said, also with a sarcastic twist.

179

"Not her, *him*," Maria Steinhardt snapped.

Lazlo laughed, and it really seemed to bug her. "This is Jack Weller," he said. "One of our directors at Changes."

"*Really?*" Maria said, looking at Weller again, but this time staring straight into his eyes for a long moment. "And what were you before Harry scooped you up into his clutches, Mr. Weller?"

"Jack's one of my prize acquisitions," Lazlo said. "About the only director we've got with network TV credits."

"Don't be so rude, Harry, I was talking to Jack," Maria said. She smiled at Weller, cocking her head to one side and leaning it on her hand. "Do you like being a prize acquisition?" she asked.

"Depends on who's doing the acquiring," Weller said instantly. The vibes she was putting out toward him seemed rather obvious; indeed, they seemed intended to be obvious. Well, if that were the game, he might as well go along with it for a bit.

Maria laughed, mugging at him with an exaggerated lecherous smirk. "The obvious question," she said, "is what's a nice boy like you doing in a place like that?" Sycophant laughter gurgled briefly in the background.

"Serving the movement," Weller said uncertainly, realizing immediately how fatuous that sounded as Maria made a moue of distaste.

"How tiresome," she said.

"We all serve John in our own ways, don't we?" Weller said, putting an edge on his voice. He nodded briefly over his shoulder. "And we all reap our own rewards."

There was a subliminal ooh, and Lazlo did not look especially pleased. Maria Steinhardt glared at him with what seemed like a sudden flash of anger. Weller glared back—not the old Transformationalist Stare, but a challenging dose of masculine libido. Maria's intensity didn't fade, but it seemed to transform itself from anger to something else.

"Touché," she said toothily. "Very interesting. Perhaps we can have a little chat later on, when things mellow out a bit." She turned to regard her entourage, a gesture of dismissal.

"*Perhaps,*" Weller said bitchily, determined to have the last word. Then Lazlo eased him out of the little group and took him to one side.

"Beginning to get the idea, kid?" he said.

"It seems fairly obvious," Weller said. "A bit *too* obvious. I mean, *John's* wife. . . ."

180

Lazlo laughed. "There once was a woman from Thames, who was found of unusual games," he recited enigmatically. "Don't worry about the Great Man, kid. Maria has carte blanche, and John is too smart to try screwing around with her. Whereas Maria. . . ."

He laughed again. "Whereas Maria does little else," he said. "Well, I've gotta go see a man about a dog." And he moved off with the blond on his arm, leaving Weller wondering what the hell was going on between him and Maria, between Maria and Steinhardt, wondering what kind of game he was getting involved in, and what the percentages might be.

Weller drifted aimlessly around the party for another hour or so. Lazlo seemed to have disappeared, and by now the house was choked with guests, to the point where there were dozens of people balancing plates of food and looking fruitlessly for a place to sit down, to the point where the noise level began to make extended conversation almost impossible, to the point where Weller was beginning to consider gettting the hell out of this boring mob scene. He had made his obligatory appearance, he had met Maria Steinhardt, and surely no one would notice anyone's early departure in this mess.

But an idea taking from in the back of his mind kept him from leaving. *Maria Steinhardt*. Had she just been flirting, playing a little game that she would play with a dozen young men tonight, or was there something more to it? If she really *does* have the hots for me, Weller thought, I should play it for all it's worth. Because it *could* be worth a lot. Maria was John's wife, and as such, she was a pipeline directly to the heart of Transformationalism. If she wanted to—if he could make her want to—she could easily find out where Annie was, and maybe even more. From what he had seen, from what he sensed, there was little that Maria could not have her way within the world of Transformationalism. Only Steinhardt himself could say no to her, and he had a feeling that even Steinhardt couldn't exactly defy her will with impunity. Screwing around with John Steinhardt's wife was about the most dangerous game he could conceive of, but the potential rewards—

"Jack! There you are!"

Sara English had appeared at his side, flanked by Shano Moore and Georgie Prinz. She was wearing a stunning low-cut red dress, but the way the three of them were huddling

181

together, like white faces in a ghetto (or black faces at a country club), made her seem quite pathetic to Weller, a sad contrast to the powerful and charismatic Maria.

"Quite a show, isn't it?" Georgie said, looking around like a little kid allowed to attend an adult party.

"Yeah," Weller grunted. "A real mob scene." He felt himself being swept up into their little group for want of anything else to do, but he immediately wanted to ditch them. They weren't where this was at, and he certainly wasn't where *they* were at.

"See anyone you know?" Sara asked, meaning, no doubt, anyone from the great world of Hollywood out there, a connection that he could make for them.

"Just Harry Lazlo," Weller said, irked both at her, and at the fraudulent show-biz aura that the three of them were trying to suck up. At the same time it amused him to think that Maria Steinhardt was essentially coming from the same silly place.

"Shall we move around and see what's happening?" Shano suggested.

So the four of them wandered around the house for what seemed to Weller like forever. It was painfully obvious to him that he was expected to point out the non-existent luminaries, as if he were one of those characters standing on Sunset Boulevard hawking maps to the Homes of the Stars.

Instead Sara, Shano, and Georgie ended up somewhat forlornly pointing out some of the Transformationalist heavies to Weller. Benson Allen's second-in-command. Allen himself. The head of the San Francisco Transformation Center. Someone or other from Narcon. Executives from various Transformationalist companies. Apparently anyone who was anyone in the local chapters of the movement was constrained to appear at Maria Steinhardt's parties. Except for the insight it gave him into just how powerful Maria really was within the movement, Weller found the whole thing stupifyingly boring and somewhat pathetic. All this, and Maria still couldn't corral even a minor name off a theater marquee; the whole thing must be an exercise in total frustration for her.

They were drifting out into the courtyard for the fourth or fifth time when Weller's eye was caught by a man sitting alone on one of the benches, sipping a drink, and leering quite unpleasantly at the passing throngs. He was wearing a black suit with a black turtleneck; his slick black hair was cut short in an almost military style, his swarthy face was hard and rather brutal-looking, but his dark eyes gleamed with an intense, sardonic intelligence. Although many people were obviously looking for a place to sit down, no one approached the bench where this isolated figure sat. The whole effect was quite sinister and disquieting.

"Who the hell is *that*?" Weller asked, nodding his head toward the man in black as they passed close by his bench.

Sara, Georgie, and Shano all seemed quite disturbed by his question, and they hustled Weller far out of earshot before anyone answered. Even then, Sara spoke in a surreptitious half whisper.

"That's Fred Torrez."

"The Director of the Monitors," Georgie added.

Weller laughed. "I thought he was some kind of Mafia hit man," he said.

"That's not funny, man," Shano said, looking uneasily over his shoulder. "Shit, the way he *looks* at people. . . ."

"What's the matter?" Weller insinuated. "Does he scare you?"

"He's just not a dude you want to have notice you . . ."

"Ah, *there* you are!" Maria Steinhardt suddenly appeared from around a bend in the path and grabbed Weller ever so lightly by the elbow.

"Come, let's have our little talk," she said, looking deep into his eyes and touching the rim of her upper teeth casually with the tip of her tongue. "If you'll excuse us," she said to Sara, Georgie, and Shano in a negligently commanding tone. And she whisked Weller off to a relatively secluded corner of the courtyard where a small tree cordoned off a little private alcove.

Still holding onto Weller's elbow, Maria leaned up against the bole of the tree, arching her breasts against the green silk of her suit, as if daring him to notice by stepping back. Or by moving forward.

She nodded toward the crowd but kept her eyes fixed on his. "Well, do you like what you see?" She said.

Weller half laughed. "Some of it," he said. "Do you like what *you* see?"

Maria slowly and deliberately lowered her gaze to stare forthrightingly at Weller's crotch. "Some of it," she said. "I could like some of it. To tell you the truth, I find most of the people I invite to these parties pretty boring myself. Lord, Transformationalism and Transformationalists bore my ass off!"

"Then why do you throw these parties?"

183

Maria slowly swayed upright, away from the tree trunk, so that her body was now only inches from Weller's, so that he could all but feel the heat of her. She looked up into his eyes.

"For some of it," she said. "Sometimes I do meet someone who interests me." She shifted her weight back and forth from foot to foot, left, right, left, right, moving her pelvis subtly closer to his. "You, for instance," she said. "You don't seem like one of John's usual little patsies." She smiled. "Yes, I do believe I would really like some of it."

Still looking directly into Weller's eyes, she suddenly reached out her hand and unexpectedly grabbed his cock. Electricity shot through Weller's body, and he twitched involuntarily backward. She looked at him as if nothing were happening and began to knead his loins with her palm and fingers. Weller suppressed a groan, and then arched his pelvis toward her, moving into it, offering himself.

"You can have as much as you can take," he said.

"You'd be surprised what this old lady can take," Maria said, removing her hand and grinding her pelvis slowly against the front of his pants, once, twice, thrice. Weller groaned, reached out his arms toward her—

And she glided away nimbly to the side. "Now that we understand each other," she said conversationally, "I must be getting back to my guests."

Weller stood there, his flesh inflamed, feeling like a perfect ass.

Maria laughed. "Don't pout," she said. "In a couple of hours people will start leaving, and then we can continue our little chat in private. Upstairs. See you later." And then she danced away from him, back toward the crowd.

Weller stood there for long moments, trying to collect himself. I'm going to fuck Maria Steinhardt tonight, he thought. It's what I wanted, isn't it? But what he hadn't expected was that he really *did* want it. It was supposed to be just his way to Annie, but that old lady had really turned him on. He felt his body throbbing for her. And that was something he hadn't counted on at all. There was something treasonous about it. Somehow he had counted on more control. God, it's been such a long time. . . .

He sighed, readjusted his pants, and headed back in the general direction of where he had left Sara, Shano, and Georgie.

But he hadn't taken half a dozen steps before Fred Torrez crossed his trajectory. Without stopping or pausing, Torrez stared at him for a long hard moment, pinning him like a rabbit with those bright reptilian eyes. Then he was gone, leaving Weller quivering with a flash of unreasoning, paranoid dread, as if the Director of the Monitors really were omniscient, as if Torrez had heard and seen all and was even now plotting something sinister and unfathomable.

The party dragged on and on. Georgie, Shano, and particularly Sara grilled Weller incessantly about his little scene with Maria Steinhardt, and Weller found himself making up a long intermittent cock-and-bull story, the gist of which was that Maria had been hungry for some show-biz patter and he had simply supplied her with same. As they wandered through the now-diminishing crowds, talking to no one but each other and getting more and more bored, Weller found himself making up imaginary details of the show-biz rap he had supposedly fed Maria—every silly story that had floated around Hollywood for the past two years.

At least it succeeded in deflecting their attention from the subject of Maria Steinhardt. Already, before anything had even really happened, Weller felt the need to draw a veil of secrecy over any connection between Maria and himself. From time to time Fred Torrez moved across his line of vision, sometimes chancing to look his way, sometimes not. But the mere sight of Torrez was enough to flash him into total paranoia about what he was going to do. According to Sara, Torrez had to be involved in issuing the life directive ordering him to live at the Transformation Center; therefore he was definitely not beneath the man's notice. If the Monitors found out that he had balled Maria Steinhardt. . . .

What? Did Maria really have carte blanche to ball anyone she wanted to, as Lazlo had intimated, or would the long arm of John B. Steinhardt reach out through the Monitors and . . . and what? How far would they go? *All the way*?

Soon the party began to wane, people started to leave, the rooms became less crowded, and the detritus—the empty glasses, the overflowing ashtrays, the dirty plates, the bits of food scattered on the floor—began to move into the visual foreground. The pseudogala atmosphere swiftly evaporated as the place began to look like the morning after the night before. Once the exodus had begun, it proceeded rapidly, as if by signal or command, and within the hour there were only a couple of dozen people left in the whole house, standing around in isolated little groups, saying their good-byes and making their departures.

"Well, I think we're going to take off now," Sara said as they ambled into the room nearest the main entrance. "You want to come along, Jack? Maybe we can get some coffee or something?"

"*Or something?*" Weller said archly, giving her a little deliberate significant eye contact, more out of pique than any expectation of a positive response.

"Maybe a hamburger," Sara said sullenly, pointedly looking away.

"No, I think I'll hang around here a little longer," Weller said casually.

"I see," Sara said.

"Do you?"

"I think so," she said quietly. Then the three of them left together, and Weller went out into the empty courtyard and sat down on a bench. He sensed that he was about to cross another divide. The Transformationalism that he had known thus far was the world of the believers, the soldiers, the suckers. Even the processors and strong-arm boys, even Monitors like Gomez and Karel, belonged to the loyal legions. But the world he was about to penetrate dick first, the world of Lazlo, Maria Steinhardt, and maybe even Fred Torrez, was something else again. Here the denizens weren't the captives of illusion but the captors. He was moving into the center of Transformationalist power, where the dangers were greatest, but where the secrets were known, and where the levers of power that could get him to Annie could be manipulated at whim. By Maria. He was entering the bottom half of the ninth inning one run behind, and it was time to swing for the fences.

"There you are . . . ," Maria Steinhardt appeared, looking slightly drunk, her hair disarrayed, a slattern wildness in her eyes. She put her hands on Weller's shoulders, leaned down somewhat woozily, and kissed him open mouthed and deeply, her breath tasting of alcohol, her tongue reaching hungrily down his throat, a hand fumbling in his pants. It only lasted a few moments, and then she was tugging him off the bench by the hands.

"Come on upstairs, my tasty little morsel," she said, and she led him up a flight of outside stairs to the balcony, down a second-story hallway and into the bedroom.

The walls of Maria Steinhardt's bedroom were a deep maroon, the ceiling was a somewhat lighter shade of the same color, the carpet was black, and the dresser, tables, chests, moldings, and bed frame were of heavily oiled wine-dark mahogany. The bed was covered in leopard skin, and the only light was a bloody reddish glow from a frosted overhead fixture. The total effect was of sinister, somber, feral power, reeking of murky S-M scenes. "You wait here for a moment, and I'll be right back," Maria said, disappearing into a dressing room.

A tremor of uneasiness went through Weller; this was, after all, a woman drenched in power, and her sexual preference might very well turn out to be some ugly domination number. So far, he thought, she's been treating me like pliant raw meat off the rack. Well, to hell with that! he decided, taking off his clothes. You may be the boss lady of Transformationalism, baby, but not in bed with this good old boy. You want to play games, games you'll get, lady!

A few minutes later Maria emerged from the dressing room. She was naked; nipples erect on slightly drooping breasts, hair down around her shoulders, all in all a surprising turn-on. Except for the high black boots she wore and the little golden dagger hung on a chain around her neck. She stood across the room, legs akimbo, hands on hips, arching her body toward him. "Well?" she said challengingly.

Oh really? Weller thought. He felt himself hardening, but in mind no less than body. Meat for the monster? Is that what you think you're getting?

Slowly, silently, he walked across the room toward her, stopping with his chest inches from her breasts, looking down into her eyes with a cold, emotionless expression painted across his face. They stared at each other for a long moment, engaged in some ambiguous psychic contest, the outlines of which were but a dim perception of sexual warfare in Weller's mind. I'm here to put this bitch in my power, not the other way around, Weller thought. So I had better be the director whether she likes it or not. *Especially* if she doesn't like it.

Silently he took her hands in his, prized them off her hips against sudden resistance, and placed them on his own shoulders. Then he cupped her chin in his hands and pulled her head against his chest. Slowly he forced her face downward pushing her to her knees.

As soon as her knees touched the floor, she moaned, and began kissing and nibbling the flesh of his stomach, moving her mouth teasingly, almost imperceptibly downward, feeling him respond, feeling him anticipating what was to come in her own sweet time. And regaining, so it seemed to Weller, a dominant position, at least in the recesses of her own mind.

Not good enough! he thought coldly. He gripped her around the jaw with his right hand, pulled her head abruptly down, and with his right hand guided his cock between her lips. Then he put both hands behind the nape of her neck and pulled her toward him as he thrust forward from the hips.

She grunted throatily and seemed to give in entirely, sucking at him in a hungry frenzy, grabbing him by the buttocks and stuffing him into her as she began to use her mouth like a willing vagina.

Part of Weller was lost in animal lust and exquisite sensation, but another part was watching the whole thing with grim detachment, viewing it as a political act, a nasty power game that had to be played out to its dialectical conclusion.

When he came, it was in stony, tightly controlled silence, and without missing a beat, he kept her there for a long time afterward, lost in her private frenzy, until he had regained his ability to go on. On and on and on, he thought. I'm going to fuck you till your teeth ache.

He dragged her to the bed, threw her down on it, and entered her. Propping himself up above her on his elbows, touching her only from the waist down, he closed his eyes, and, light-years detatched from her reality, began to fuck her.

On and on and on he went, eyes closed, moving in an inexorable mechanical rhythm, fire in his body, ice in his mind. She moaned and she groaned and she clawed at him and she screamed and her writhing body spasmed again and again, but it was all taking place over an immense psychic distance. He was sticking it to John Steinhardt's wife. He was fucking Transformationalism itself, and it was the archetypal grudge-fuck. He felt like a medieval battering ram, pounding away at his enemy, as if he could fuck the whole movement into submission, as if by mastering Maria with his cock, he could master Transformationalism with his will.

On and on, until he could hear her breath coming in tired, ragged gasps, and then faster and harder, like a soldier sensing victory, like a shark sniffing blood. He felt as if he could go on all night, until she screamed for him to stop, until she begged for mercy, and then awhile longer. His body was the cold hard instrument of his will, and it felt neither fatigue nor, really, anything like normal sexual lust.

After a long time she began moaning, "Please . . . please . . . please . . . ," over and over again.

"More?" he asked harshly. "You want more, bitch?"

"No . . . no . . . enough . . . Jesus . . . I want you to come inside me . . . please . . ."

"Your wish is my command," Weller said sardonically, and he moved harder and harder and faster and faster, listening to her scream in what by now might be genuine raw pain, and finally exploded in a shower of cold metal sparks.

He rolled off her and lay on his back beside her. Maria was breathing hard and deep, her body heavily filmed with sweat. It took her several minutes to fully catch her breath, and when she did, she rolled half over and looked at him with wide eyes and a catlike smile.

"It's been a long time since I've been fucked like that," she said. "What got up your ass, baby?"

"Up my ass?" Weller said archly. "What are you talking about?"

Maria sat up against the nest of pillows at the head of the bed. "Oh, don't be juvenile," she said. "On you, it doesn't look very convincing. You're not one of John's little slavies. I can just imagine one of them having the balls to do what you did. Who the hell are you? What are you doing here?"

"I suppose you're going to report this to the Monitors," Weller said sardonically, all caution to the wind. "I'm sure it violates some life directive or other, and if it doesn't, you can always make one up."

Maria laughed. "On the contrary," she said, "if you've violated any life directive, I'll have it canceled retroactively. Fred Torrez isn't going to get his greasy paws on you; I want you around for more."

"You could really do that?" Weller said, wanting to believe it but finding it a bit difficult.

Maria laughed again. "Fred takes orders only from John," she said, running a fingernail up the length of Weller's stomach. "And John takes orders only from me."

"Oh, really?" Weller said archly, sitting up against the pillows beside her. "Just like that?"

"You *do* ask a lot of questions, don't you? I'll bet you're not a television director at all. Let me guess . . . The FBI? The Los Angeles Police? The Treasury Department?"

"I really am a director," Weller said. "Want to see my credits?"

Maria fondled his crotch. "I've already seen your credits," she said. "But none of that precludes the possibility of your working for some agency or other, now does it?"

"Paranoia strikes deep," Weller sang. *"Into your heart it*

will creep. . . ." He grinned at her. "Would you believe the KGB?" he said.

"Around here, I'd believe anything," Maria said. She put her arm around his shoulder. "Not that it would matter if you really were a spook. Believe me, no agency is going to be able to hurt Transformationalism. Certainly not with anything you can get from me."

"Hey, are you really serious?" Weller said. "Do you really think I'm working for some agency?"

"There is definitely *something* strange about you, Jack Weller," she said. "Or not strange enough. Remember, I've been with John since he was grinding out space opera for a penny a word. The three of us—John, Harry, and I—built the movement from the ground up, so I know exactly what kind of wimp gets roped in and what kind of loser ends up working for the movement for peon wages. I know it intimately, since I've balled maybe twenty or thirty of the creatures down through the years. And *you* are not that kind of creature. You do not talk like one. And you most certainly do not make love like one, my pretty."

"That's the nicest thing anyone has said to me in months," Weller said sarcastically. This is a sharp lady, he thought. Maybe I should just lay my cards on the table. "I'll level with you," he said.

"Oh, will you now?" Maria said archly.

"Up to a point," Weller said. "I'll admit that I'm not a one hundred-percent-convinced Transformationalist. . . ."

"Thank God!" Maria said huskily. "What bores they are! What assholes!"

Weller looked at her somewhat incredulously.

"You're shocked?" Maria said. "My God, surely you realize that the world is divided up between the suckers and the suckees. Surely you can tell which is which without a libretto."

"It just sounds kind of strange coming from John's wife."

Maria's expression darkened. She leaned over, grabbed the tip of his cock with two fingers, and ran the little golden dagger she wore lightly across the root of it. "If you call me that again, I'll cut if off," she said. Point made, she laughed, and sat back again. "You can't imagine what a loathsome bore it is to be *John's wife.*"

"And that's why you don't live with him?"

"John sits in the Transformational Research Institute in New York, playing wise man to all the scientists, sycophants, and flunkies he's hired," Maria said. "And it's gotten to the

190

point where he half believes it himself. He doesn't want to leave, and I can't stand it there. It's like being sealed in a bottle with the Great I Am."

"So why don't you leave him?" Weller asked. "You probably wouldn't have any trouble getting a huge divorce settlement."

Maria patted his cheek softly. "You *are* young, aren't you?" she said. "John and I have been together for over twenty years. I met him when he was a lousy science-fiction writer—and believe me, *lousy* was the word—struggling to pay the rent. He didn't invent Transformationalism, he didn't even want to take it over, Harry Lazlo and I had to bludgeon him into it. Even today, John has no head for business—"

"That's exactly what Harry Lazlo said."

Maria's expression darkened. "That son of a bitch!" she said. "But the money-grubbing bastard is right. The three of us have always been a stable triangle. John wrote the book, John spins out the crazy theories and invents the product, John plays god, but Harry marketed Transformationalism, Harry built our financial empire, and only Harry knows enough to run it. In a way it's no different from the days when John was writing science fiction and Harry was peddling the crap he wrote as his agent."

"And you?"

"Me?" Maria shook her head ruefully. "I'm the only person in the world who really understands John, and I'm the only one who understands that puffed-up *schlockmeister* Harry Lazlo well enough to keep tabs on what he's doing and keep him from getting any smart ideas about taking over the movement himself. I'm the only person in the world who can ever tell John when he's being an ass and get him to listen. Without me, John would be a full-time messiah drifting further and further away from reality while Harry took over the actual power like some kind of cancer."

"So it's not really a marriage anymore, it's a business relationship?"

Maria sighed. "You really don't understand, do you?" she said much more softly. "In our crazy ways John and I really love each other. These days, we can't stand being around each other for very long, but that doesn't change what's in our hearts. None of it really makes sense if you don't know John, and the horrible thing is that now no one really knows John except me—including John himself. You can't imagine what it's like . . ."

She tilted her head back and stared at the ceiling. "I'm not sure why I'm telling you all this," she said. "Maybe I need a shrink—and I certainly can't talk to a damn processor! But I might as well spill my guts; it may be good for what's left of my soul."

She smiled softly at Weller. "Understand that John is a tremendous man—full of life, full of ideas, spinning off sparks like a pinwheel. But he's also always been totally unfocused, and as full of bullshit as it's possible to be. As a science-fiction writer he was full of ideas that he was never able to take seriously, and he never gave enough of a damn about writing to do anything really good. What he loved was being an *author*. Going to every loathsome science fiction convention there was and blathering for days on end in a drunken stupor, absolutely mesmerizing people. What he was a genius at was bullshitting, which never really paid the rent."

She laughed sardonically. "When he discovered Benson Allen's little fan club, he had been in a total writer's block for a year and we were stone broke. Harry, who had been collecting ten percent of nothing for a year, smelled money, and so did I, but not John. To him the whole thing was a joke. 'I'm living out one of my dumb novels,' he used to say."

Her voice grew harder, more distant, almost wistful in a strangely bitter way. "But as the years passed and the money came pouring in, as hundreds of thousands of people began looking at John as the god of their personal worlds, as he came more and more to live in a closed universe where everyone he came in contact with agreed with his own half-serious image of himself as the Great I Am, John started to half believe it himself. Who wouldn't, love? 'Maybe I really know what I'm talking about,' he started to say. 'Maybe I'm transforming myself into the man of destiny.' "

She shrugged. "After all, he was now living in the fantasy situation he wanted for himself when he was an unsuccessful science-fiction writer. He was famous without having to write—John always loathed actual *work*—he could be a full-time bullshit artist, and he was a messiah, just like the heroes of all his crummy science-fiction novels."

She looked into Weller's eyes and grinned faintly. "Wouldn't you, Jack Weller?" she said. "If people made you rich and powerful and treated you like a god, wouldn't you start believing it yourself, even if you knew it was your own con that got you there?"

"I've never thought about it . . . ," Weller muttered inanely.

"Well, think about one more thing," Maria said. "Think

about how lonely it would be. Think about getting nothing back from anyone around you but reflections of your own bullshit. Think about living out your life inside a house of magnifying mirrors. That's where John would be without me. Think about loving a man like that, think about not really being able to help loving him and not really wanting to."

She leaned her head up against Weller's shoulder. "So we have our little arrangements," she said. "John lives out his fantasy without my confronting him with reality except when he wants me to, or when I think he needs it. And I have my Jack Wellers, my parties, my role as grand dame of Transformationalism when I need it. But strange to say, my sweet, our marriage is as solid as a rock, and it's for keeps."

She sat up again and regarded Weller narrowly. "Now that I've told you the story of my life," she said, "I bloody well expect to hear some truth from you in return. What are you doing here, Jack Weller?"

Weller had been listening passively, soaking it all up like a sponge, knowing that this moment was coming; fearing it on one level, but anticipating it with hope on another. This moment, after all, was what he was here for. And there really wasn't anything he had to tell her that wasn't in his Monitor dossier anyway.

"To make a long story short, my wife became one of the suckers, as you call them" he said. "Me, I wasn't buying, and she finally got a life directive to leave me. Now she's disappeared into the bowels of the movement, and I'm trying to find her. That's my ulterior motive, it's as simple as that. I'm not with any agency, I'm on my own." He shuddered. "Boy, am I on my own!"

"So you sold your nubile young body to this old lady to try and find your wife?" Maria said, shaking her head.

Weller remained silent, realizing that he had put himself in her hands and insulted her in the bargain.

Maria laughed. She placed her hand on the inside of his thigh. "You think I'm insulted, is that it?" she said. "Quite the contrary. I find it rather charming. You're taking a big risk with me, and you know it. It's all rather romantic, really, isn't it? I have a thing for younger men, and I've dragooned a lot of them into my bed, but seldom have they been motivated by anything as chivalrous as all that."

"For what it's worth," Weller said quietly, "you did really turn me on. I mean it wasn't exactly a chore . . ."

Maria kissed him gently on the lips. "You think I couldn't

193

tell that, poor baby? Look, let's be honest with each other. You love your wife. I love my husband. I don't want a real relationship with you, and you don't want a real relationship with me. What I want from you is sex, and I'm more than satisfied that you can please me. Can we make a deal?"

"Can you locate my wife Annie for me?" Weller asked.

"With ease," Maria said.

"Will you do it?"

Maria moved her hand into his crotch, teasing his flesh. "That depends," she said. "Are you willing to be my sex slave? At least part of the time?"

"Are you serious?"

"Indeed I am, love. I enjoyed the way you used me, but a poor old lady has to feel she's on top sometimes too."

"If you'll find Annie for me, I'm yours to command," Weller said. *Within reason,* he thought.

"We have a deal, my pet," Maria said. She kissed him again, this time long and deep, twining the fingers of both her hands in the hair above his ears. Still clutching him by the hair, she rolled over onto her back, leaned up against the pillows, and pulled his face to her breasts. "Now *you* will do *my* bidding, my sweet," she said, half laughing.

And she dragged his head slowly down the length of her body and into the soft lowlands of her inner thighs, while Weller, at first reluctantly, but then with a growing passion, licked, kissed, and nibbled at her skin.

When she clamped her legs tightly around his head and began rolling the hardness of her pelvis against the softness of his mouth, Weller found himself inflamed by the very abnegation of his position, perhaps even overcome by a certain affection for this strange and powerful woman, and her sighs and groans of pleasure were not entirely unpleasant music to his ears.

Thirteen

There were still guards at the gate to the Steinhardt mansion compound when Weller drove up in response to Maria's summons, and they still wouldn't let him take the Triumph inside the walls. He had to park outside in the empty parking lot and walk all the way to the front entrance to the house, where a young woman in a blue smock led him inside, through the eerily empty parlors of the ground floor, and up an interior staircase to the living quarters.

Now, in the early evening, with the ground floor and courtyard empty and in immaculate order, Weller found the house sterile and depressing, like an immense, plush prison cell, or a scaled-down version of Xanadu in *Citizen Kane*. He wondered how Maria could bear living alone in such a huge place, with only servants, guards, and flunkies for company. He began to think of her as quite a vulnerable person, and for some reason that thought deeply disturbed him.

Maria was waiting for him in a kind of small sitting room overlooking the courtyard, with a skylight ceiling, white wicker furniture, and a jungle of potted palms, ferns, and hanging plants. She was sitting in a big peacock chair in front of a small table, and she was wearing a white sleeveless dress. The whole effect was that of an antebellum mistress-of-the-manor in some depressing Tennessee Williams play.

Somehow Weller got the feeling that he was supposed to kiss her hand and call her "ma'am." Instead he gave her a quick kiss on the lips and sat down across the table. A young man dressed in blue appeared with a flagon of white wine and two goblets on a silver tray, served, and departed.

"Well, love," Maria said, "I've got good news and bad news. The good news is that I've located your wife."

Weller sipped at the cold wine. "And the bad news?" he asked.

"The bad news is that Anne Weller has been assigned to the Transformational Research Institute in New York," Maria said. "She's working on one of John's mysterious and boring research projects." She touched Weller's hand and smiled ruefully. "I'm sorry."

"What for?" Weller said. "That's exactly what I wanted to find out. That's great. I'm really grateful to you." I'm nearing the end-game now, he thought. All I have to do is get into this Institute thing and get her out. There must be other Garry Bailors I can hire if I have to.

"I thought the whole idea was that you wanted to see your wife again," Maria said.

"Of course."

Maria sighed. "I don't think you understand what I'm telling you," she said. "The Institute is under incredible security. A flea couldn't get in or out without a life directive directly from John. There's no way you can get in, there's no way she can get out, and no way you can even get a message through."

From somewhere—perhaps the way Maria was looking at him, desirously, nervously, apologetically—Weller found himself drawing upon a cold and almost bitchy cruelty. "Then what I need is a life directive from John to get me in, isn't it, Maria?" he said, regarding her coolly.

"You think I can—?"

"Can't you, Maria?" Weller said evenly.

"Look, I may have given you the wrong impression about John," Maria said, almost plaintively. "Most of the time I can pretty much have my own way, but the Tranformational Research Institute. . . . Nobody gets in there without a reason, *John's* reason."

"Well then, we have to give him a reason, don't we?" Weller said relentlessly.

Maria laughed. "You can be a ruthless, implacable bastard, can't you?" she said. "But in a way, I find that rather attractive."

Weller reached under the table and put his hand under Maria's dress, smoothing the soft flesh of her inner thigh. Maria ran her tongue slowly around the edges of her teeth.

"Let's go into the bedroom," she said. "Afterward, maybe we can discuss your little problem."

"You can be pretty implacable yourself," Weller said. But he let her lead him by the hand across the hall into the bedroom. I know where Annie is, he thought. *I know where she is.*

But the fact seemed only a distant anesthetized reality as Maria slowly undressed him and then flipped her dress over her head, revealing her total nakedness beneath.

196

Yet the things they then proceeded to do to each other, the kissings and lickings, the movements of body on body, also seemed to Weller to be taking place at some great distance from the locus of his consciousness.

He performed well, but he performed mechanically. Even as he thrust against Maria, he was thinking about Annie, about knowing where she was, about how to get to see her again. But he did not fantasize about making love to Annie while he was fucking Maria Steinhardt, nor did he feel guilty about the dichotomy between what he was thinking and what his body was doing. The only guilt he felt was over the fact that he had difficulty even forming a mental image of Annie's face.

Time passed, Maria had several orgasms, and finally appeared satiated, and Weller's mind returned to where it had been in the sitting room as if nothing had happened. Indeed, psychically, nothing had.

"Will you help me again?" he asked Maria as they sat side by side against the headboard.

"I told you," she said, "I just can't tell John to let you into the Institute. It won't work."

"The only way for me to get in there is for John to want me there . . . ?"

"That's right, love. I can't even get in when John doesn't want me around."

"Well, what goes on in this damned place?" Weller asked.

Maria shrugged. "Some psychiatrist named Bernstein talked John into setting it up at a ridiculous cost. Supposedly it's a kind of mental Manhattan Project, at least that's what John thinks he's doing. On the other hand, Bernstein may actually be taking John to the cleaners. Who knows? According to John they're experimenting with everything from new-model brainwave monitors to psychedelic drugs. Whenever I ask John what he thinks he's spending all that money to accomplish, I get Transformationalist gibberish. I think he's convinced that the Institute is going to be his monument to history or something."

"And what the hell is Annie doing in this place?"

"I don't know," Maria said quietly.

"You mean there are some things John keeps even from you?"

"Yes. I mean no. I mean he'd tell me if I asked, but he'd want to know why. . . ." Maria seemed uncharacteristically nervous, even furtive, as if they had drifted into an area where her relationship with John B. Steinhardt was not quite what she liked to pretend it was.

"Okay," Weller said more sympathetically. "I understand the problem. But will you do what you can to help me? If I come up with a reason for John to want me at the Institute, will you help me sell it to him as best you can?"

Maria eyed him narrowly. "You know," she said, "I'm beginning to get the feeling that you're some kind of agent again, that all this business about your wife is just a cover story."

"You can check out my dossier with the Monitors . . ."

"Oh, I already have," Maria said quite earnestly. "Still, if an agency *were* trying to penetrate the Institute, they might go to considerable lengths, even your wife. . . ."

Weller forced a laugh. "Are you really serious?"

"*Quien sabe?*" Maria said more lightly. "On the other hand, the thought does add a certain spice to things. All right, whoever you are, you figure it out, and I'll front for you. Up to a point."

"Marvelous," Weller said, giving her a kiss. "My superiors will be very pleased.

Pacing in his tiny room at the Transformation Center, Weller was unwilling to even go downstairs for dinner, though he knew that in two hours he would have to drag his ass to the kitchen to wash dishes. For days now the disjunctions in his life, the splits in his mind, were driving him up walls, and every additional input—at work, in the Center, in Maria Steinhardt's bed—just seemed to wind the spring a little tighter.

So near and yet so far. All these months of scheming, of loneliness, of turning himself into someone he no longer knew, had come down to a single point: get inside the Transformational Research Institute. Do that, and it would all be over, the unbearable psychic tension would finally be resolved. No more balling Maria, no more playing the cold demon lover. No more mind games. No more living at the Center. No more washing dishes. No more grinding out commercials for something he hated.

But how? How can I make Steinhardt *want* me to come to the Institute? What can I give to Maria to get to him with? How can I sell myself—?

Weller sat down heavily on the edge of the bed. Sell

myself? Or sell Steinhardt . . . ? Something was percolating up from the lower reaches of his mind. Eptify yourself behind the scenario, he told himself. It's there, I can feel it, I've got to reach for it.

Sell Steinhardt. . . . *Sell Steinhardt*. . . . What was it about those two words . . . ? Weller's mind ached, straining for an illusive thought that hovered just beyond his grasp, like the name of an old friend caught on the tip of his tongue, like a word in a foreign language he had studied in high school. *Sell Steinhardt*. . . .

Of course! he suddenly realized. Those two words have a double meaning! Sell myself to Steinhardt, or literally *sell Steinhardt* like so much corn flakes.

Or both.

It finally clicked, like a crystal suddenly forming in a supersaturated solution. I'm making commercials for Transformationalism, he thought, and they stink. Not because *I* stink, but because the scripts and actors stink. But *Steinhardt* on tape. . . . Steinhardt could sell a Corvair to Ralph Nader. I could make such Transformationalism commercials if I had John B. Steinhardt to use in them!

And with *his* ego, how could he not rise to the bait? How could he not at least want to talk about it?

That's it, that is fucking *it*!

But not immediately through Maria, he thought. Have to be more subtle about it. Plant the idea at Changes, let Karel know that I want to do it, and *then* use Maria to end-run around the Monitors when they come down on it. As no doubt they will.

He got up off the bed and began pacing again. He could hardly wait till tomorrow. Tomorrow, Sara and the whole crew at Changes were going to start getting a dose of how he *really* felt about what they were doing, and it was going to be a double pleasure dishing it out!

At the lunch break Weller casually wandered into Sara English's office, where Sara was sitting alone behind her desk going through some scripts. Since Maria's party there had been a lot of frost in the air between them, and Sara didn't deign to look up until after he had planted himself heavily in a chair beside the desk with a tired, depressed look painted deliberately across his face.

When she did look up at him, it was with a somewhat owlish expression, and when she spoke, her voice was diffident and distant. "What's the matter with you? Having trouble on the set?"

"No worse than usual," Weller grunted.

Now he seemed to have her full, alert, and surprised attention. "No worse than usual? What are you talking about? You've been consistently ahead of schedule since you started directing. There haven't been any complaints."

"*Marvelous*," Weller grunted sarcastically, leading her into it.

Sara sat up on the edge of her chair and studied Weller as if he had metamorphosed into some mythical monster. "What the hell's gotten into you, Jack?" she said.

"Don't you know? Can't you see it?"

"What *are* you talking about?"

"Oh, come on, Sara," Weller said in a carefully crafted tone of tired vehemence. "You *know* that what we're doing is shit."

Sara's eyes went wide, then narrowed. She sat stiff-backed upright in her chair and her tone of voice became defensive and clipped. "I realize we're not all up to your technical level—"

"Oh, can it, Sara!" Weller snapped. "Technical ability has nothing to do with it. What I'm turning out is shit too. A little faster, a little slicker, but just as shitty. It's really starting to get to me."

"What is?" Sara said uncertainly, but also somewhat belligerently. "You still haven't told me what you're talking about."

"It's the basic stuff," Weller said. "The scripts, and even more basic than the scripts, the very concepts of the commercials."

Sara's expression became rigid and her voice became almost mechanical. "You know where the scripts come from," she said nervously. "What's wrong with them?"

"What's wrong with them?" Weller said. "They're stupid, amateurish, and counterproductive. No matter how well made they might be, they'd still just be well-made garbage." He found himself taking gleeful sadistic satisfaction in finally venting the truth, even if it were for his own Machiavellian ends.

But Sara apparently didn't believe her ears or didn't want to believe them. "You know I'm going to have to report this to Karel . . . ," she stammered.

Weller deliberately ignored her and continued his diatribe. "The actors are impossible too, and the end product is something that couldn't sell thermal underwear to Eskimos.

It's really depressing, knowing you're doing your best and nothing but crud is coming about because the concepts, scripts, and actors you're stuck with guarantee a hopeless product. . . ."

Now Sara seemed really frightened. "Please stop it," she said shrilly. "Don't you realize what you're saying? Don't you know I have to report this? Don't you know that the scripts have the force of Monitor policy and the casting has the force of life directives?"

Weller shifted to a mode of tired resignation. "Of course, I know all that. But I tell you, I've reached the point where I finally don't give a damn. I care too much about what I'm doing to just sit back and let the Monitors fuck it up."

"*Jack!*"

Weller bled some wistful longing energy back into his voice. "When we have the potential to make a series of commercials that could double Transformationalism's national membership in a year."

"What?" Sara seemed to perk up a bit.

"I mean *John* himself," Weller said. "You've seen him on tape—now *that's* star quality! Boy, could I make commercials for Transformationalism if I could use John B. Steinhardt! Why *hasn't* Changes made commercials using John?"

"I don't know. . . . You know that kind of policy isn't made on our level."

"Well, why not? It damn well should be." Weller paused, as if slowly coming to an impromptu decision. "In fact, I think I'm going to make the request myself. In fact, you can consider it formally made as of now. I hereby propose a series of commercials using John to be shot by me. What are you going to do about it?"

"*Me?*" Sara squealed. "I'm not going to do a damn thing. If you think you're going to involve me in—"

"Well, then what do I do about it, propose it to Owen Karel?"

"Jack, there's nothing you can do. You can't issue a life directive to *John*. You can't go over the Monitors' heads. You can't—"

"Why not? What's wrong with this organization that it can't accept some professional advice?"

"Jack, good Lord. You haven't even passed life analysis. Do you know what they'll—"

"Fuck it!" Weller snapped, standing up. "I'm going to go find a typewriter, write a proposal, and give it to Karel."

"*Please—*"

"All right, if it makes you so nervous, *you* hand the proposal to Karel. With a complete report on this conversation. That should cover you with the Monitors."

"You're really serious about this, aren't you?" Sara said quietly. "You won't listen to reason?"

"I'm going to do it, Sara. Through you, or over your head to Karel. Your choice."

Sara sighed resignedly. "All right," she said. "You type up the proposal, and I'll hand it to Karel. But that's all I'm going to do. No recommendation, and I *am* going to report this conversation. I'm going to completely disassociate myself from this insanity."

"You do that," Weller snapped over his shoulder on the way out. "I'll have it on your desk in half an hour." The die was cast. Whether the Monitors passed the proposal along to Steinhardt or not, it was going to get there. He'd give channels two or three days, and then play his hole card—Maria, the Queen of Steinhardts.

For nearly two days Weller had been waiting for something to happen, for some Monitor ax to fall. He hadn't spoken to Owen Karel since Sara had transmitted his proposal and Karel hadn't spoken to him. But their paths had crossed several times, and each time the Monitor representative had given him a cold, withering, lingering stare. Apparently whatever was going to happen wasn't going to be decided at Karel's level. Was it possible that they would really buck it up directly to Steinhardt? Could it end up being as easy as all that? Sara had been avoiding speaking to him too, as if she feared contamination, as if she were determined to put as much distance between her and whatever was going to come down as possible, so it didn't seem very likely.

When the other shoe was finally dropped, Weller was in the kitchen at the Transformation Center washing dishes. A hand tapped him on the shoulder from behind. "Jack Weller?"

Weller turned and saw a big, gross bozo in T-shirt and jeans. "Yes . . . ?"

"Come with me."

"I've still got a lot of dishes to finish. . . ."

"You're to come with me right now. It's a life directive."

Weller shrugged, dried his hands, and let himself be led to the fourth floor, to the very same room where he had had his life-analysis sessions with Gomez. And when the door was closed behind him, it was Gomez himself who sat behind the desk, scowling and somewhat harried-looking.

"Sit your goddamn ass down, Weller." As Weller sat down in front of the desk, Gomez slid a piece of paper across it at him. "What the fuck is this?" he demanded.

"Just what it says," Weller said coldly.

Gomez snorted. "Just because you're screwing Maria Steinhardt, you think you can get away with this shit. Is that it?"

Weller blanched. "You know about that?"

"That's a pretty stupid question, isn't it, Weller?" Gomez said. "Not up to your usual standard. Now what the hell is all this about?"

Weller forced himself to be calm. "You tell me," he said.

Gomez leaned forward on his elbows and glared at Weller. "Stop jiving me," he snarled.

"I'm not jiving you," Weller said. "I made a suggestion in my professional capacity, and here I am hauled in front of you. Why?"

"Your professional capacity is to do as you're told," Gomez snapped. "Not to tell the Monitors their business."

Studying Gomez, Weller sensed that the Monitor was not entirely on top of this situation; something was rattling him, and Gomez didn't like it. He decided to probe deeper. "Is that what John said?"

Gomez laughed harshly. "You think that thing got to John?" he said contemptuously. "Karel passed it up the chain to Torrez, and Torrez kicked it down to me, and none too gently either."

"What are you trying to tell me?" Weller asked ingenuously.

Gomez reached across the desk, snatched up the proposal, balled it up in his fist, and tossed it over his shoulder onto the floor. "*That's* what I'm telling you, Weller," he said. "If it were up to me, I'd declare you a regressive right now and be done with you. You've gone too far."

Weller realized that Gomez had given himself away. He leered across the desk at the Monitor. "But it's not up to you, is it, Gomez?" he said. "Someone has ordered you not to give me a negative life analysis. Torrez? Or—"

"Cut it out, Weller," Gomez snapped. "You know damn well who protected you."

Weller laughed. "Sticks in your craw, doesn't it?" he said.

Gomez flushed. He ground his hands into fists. "You'd

better be a great lay, Weller," he said. "Because as soon as Maria Steinhardt gets tired of you, your ass is grass. And that doesn't just come from me, it comes from Torrez."

"But in the meantime . . . ," Weller insinuated, feeling a marvelous sense of his own power.

"In the meantime you'd better keep your nose clean," Gomez said. "We're under orders not to declare you a regressive, but that's as far as it goes. Any more of this crap, and we can still find ways of making it mighty uncomfortable for you around here."

It seemed to Weller that Gomez's threat was essentially hollow; in any event he had gone much too far to turn back now. The only way out was to press on. "What about my proposal?" he said.

"What about it?"

"I want it to go to John."

Gomez slammed his fist on the desk. "I told you. Torrez himself vetoed it. That's the end of it."

"Not good enough," Weller said quietly.

"*Not good enough?*" Gomez shouted. "What the hell do you mean, *not good enough?*"

"I mean I don't accept it," Weller said evenly.

"I don't give a shit if you accept it or not; that's the way it is."

"Is it?" Weller said softly. "Is it really? You've got a choice, Gomez. You can transmit my proposal to John through the regular Monitor channels . . . or I go the alternate route. You and Torrez won't look so good if John overrules you personally, now will you?"

Gomez gaped. "You wouldn't dare."

"Oh, wouldn't I? You've just told me that my ass is grass if Maria stops protecting me. That's my hole card. What do I have to lose by betting my whole stake on it?"

Gomez half leaped out of his chair, raging. "I'm warning you, Weller!" he screamed. "You lay off or—"

"Or *what?*" Weller sneered contemptuously.

Gomez subsided back into his chair. "Don't underestimate us," he said. "If you push this thing any further, it's Coventry for you."

"Coventry?"

"One step from being declared a regressive," Gomez said. "And not such a large step at that. You've been warned. You can take it as being official."

Weller stood up. "Do you have anything more to say?" he asked.

Gomez sat there silently, as if disbelieving his own senses.

"Then I'll be going if it's okay with you," Weller said. Holding his breath, he walked to the door. Gomez was silent. Weller opened the door, glanced back at the immobile Gomez, and stepped through into the hallway.

"Motherfucker!" he heard Gomez whisper to empty air as he closed the door behind him.

"Hot shit!" Weller exclaimed to himself. You played that beautifully, kid, he told himself. From here on in, the name of the game is escalation.

Maria Steinhardt lay naked on her bed, her head propped up on one elbow, staring at Weller, who sat up against the headboard looking down at her like the Great Sphinx. "You realize, love," she said, "that you are in my power. Fred Torrez was ready to declare you a regressive, and I don't think you fully realize what that means. Trying to communicate directly with John was pushing it too far; Torrez is an awful enemy for anyone to make. And now you want me to get this proposal to John in direct defiance of the Monitors! Don't you recognize *any* limits?"

"You said you'd do it," Weller said distantly. "You said if I came up with a reason for John to want me there that you'd get it through to him. Isn't this idea something that will appeal to him?"

Maria laughed. "*Appeal to him?* It's just the sort of egoboo that he loves to get drunk on. But how am I supposed to put it to him?"

"Tell him the truth," Weller said. "Tell him that the Monitors blocked the proposal and that I appealed directly to you."

Maria scowled. "Don't you realize that telling him that would be telling him that you're directly defying a Monitor life directive?"

"So what?" Weller said.

"So what? So if John doesn't like it, there's no way I can protect you from *him*."

"You think that's going to happen?"

Maria sat up beside him. She shrugged. "With John, even I don't always know," she said. "Don't forget, he'll read your Monitor dossier, maybe even talk it over with Torrez. Anything the movement knows about you, John will know."

Weller reached out a hand and flicked at her nipple. "In-

205

cluding what's going on here?" he asked. "Is that what you're afraid of?"

"You really think he doesn't know about us already? You think I could go to bed with anyone without John knowing? You think when I stopped Torrez from declaring you a regressive, he didn't report it to John?"

"So when you present my proposal to John, he'll know exactly where it's coming from and why?" Weller said. "You think that'll make him turn it down and ax me without ever talking to me?"

"On the contrary, pet," Maria said. "He'll want to meet you. It'll probably get you into the Institute. But have you given any thought to getting *out*?"

Weller felt a slight twinge of dread. He *hadn't* given too much thought to how he would get Annie and himself out. . . . But the Master Contact Sheet, was damned good blackmail material, and the fail-safe copies had already been mailed.

And ever since he had begun this course of action, ever since his first night with Maria, his sense of his own power had been growing. There wasn't anything logical about it. It was a psychic thing, a sense of more fully inhabiting his own skin, perhaps something as simple and irrational as a slow and gradual rediscovery of the possibilities of his own courage. The way he had gotten away with defying Gomez had been the capper. Now he was beginning to feel that there was nothing he would not try, nothing he would not dare.

"You let *me* worry about that," he said, surprised at the ominous strength he heard himself putting into his own voice.

Maria must have heard it too, for she seemed to shrink back from him slightly. "What if I decide I just don't want to do it?" she said.

Weller ran a hand teasingly through her pubic hair. "Then you lose my lovely young bod," he said. On impulse he added, "As well as my goodwill."

"What's that supposed to mean?" Maria asked uneasily.

Weller felt a streak of cold cruelty leaping from his core to his mouth, like a sudden dagger drawn from a hidden scabbard. "You're always kidding me about working for some agency," he said lightly. "What if it isn't a joke?"

Maria's eyes widened. "You're not serious?" she whispered.

"Did I say I was?" Weller answered ambiguously. "But what if I was? What if something bigger and stronger than Transformationalism were closing in?"

206

"What could that be?" Maria said scornfully. But there was the slightest edge of nervousness in her voice.

Weller laughed. "The federal government," he said. "Maybe even the Mafia . . ."

"The Mafia . . . ? Oh really!"

Weller shrugged. "Transformationalism is a large business with a lot of useful contacts," he said. "Might make an attractive-looking meal to an even bigger fish. Someone might want to make you a merger offer you couldn't refuse."

"You're not serious . . ."

"Did I say I was?" Weller repeated archly. "But *if* I was, who ended up protecting whom might turn out to be a horse of a different color . . ."

Maria studied him narrowly. "You're just playing a game with me, right?" she said.

"Right." Weller said fatuously. "I'm just playing a game with you."

They stared into each other's eyes for a long, silent moment. "And you're just playing the same game with me," Weller said evenly. "You're going to speak to John as you promised to." He arched an eyebrow at her. "Aren't you?"

Maria smiled at him, somewhat nervously, somewhat wantonly. "If you want to play that game, I'll go along with you," she said. She laughed. "I wish I really believed you. I find something feral about it. I think it's turning me on. Grrr!"

She leaned over and sunk her teeth into Weller's earlobe, a really hard bite that sent a flash of pain to his brain. He tried to pull away, but she hung on, gnawing and growling. She rolled over onto him, reaching between his thighs.

Something snapped inside Weller—perhaps it was the sharp pain, perhaps it was the persona he had assumed, perhaps it was the need to ram the lesson home, perhaps all three. He threw his arms around Maria and wrestled her off of him. He slapped her lightly across the cheek; she gasped, more in surprise than pain, and released his ear.

Weller flipped her over onto her stomach, pinioning her to the bed at the waist with his hands, raised his torso above her, spread her legs, and thrust between them.

"No! No!" Maria screamed in shock and outrage.

"*No?*" Weller snarled. "You're telling me you don't want it?" He laughed wildly and drove deeper.

Maria screamed in pain, but began to move her body

207

against his, and soon the tone of her screams lowered, became a mewling of pain mixed with pleasure as she thrashed and ground slowly against him, impaled like a vassal, hating it and loving it at the same time.

Weller found himself stunned at what he was doing, astonished at his own sadism, and even more astonished at how much it pleased him to have Maria Steinhardt writhing in pain and pleasure beneath him. He snarled gutturally and found himself going with it completely—the savagery, the feral animal pleasure, the sophisticated mental power trip—with a demonic energy he had never felt before. He was a stranger to himself. The Jack Weller that had been would not be capable of something like this.

But that was in another country, and besides the lad was dead.

Weller entered the lobby of the Transformation Center at six fifteen, after an unusually long shooting day, feeling bone weary and piano-wire tense. Two days now and he had heard nothing from Maria Steinhardt. He had no idea how long it might take for her to speak to Steinhardt, nor how long it would take Steinhardt to react, nor what form the reaction might take if it turned out to be negative.

But the tension of waiting was becoming unbearable. At the studio Sara was totally ignoring him, and even Georgie and Shano seemed reluctant to be seen in conversation with him, as if word of what he was doing had filtered down to their level. Even his own crew seemed rather taciturn and sullen, thought that might just be an extension of his own paranoia in an admittedly paranoid situation.

Weller paused at the gate desk, waiting to be recognized by the guard and passed through to the inner lobby. But instead of just nodding and passing him through, the guard pointed silently to a piece of paper taped to the front of the desk.

"What . . . ?"

Silently, insistently, the guard jabbed his finger at the notice. Grunting, Weller bent over slightly and read it:

NOTICE: GENERAL LIFE DIRECTIVE

Jack Weller has been placed in Coventry by directive of the Monitors until further notice. No member of this Transformation Center may speak to Jack Weller except in the necessary course of relaying official directives, instructions, or information authorized over the signature of Benson Allen. Failure to obey this directive will result in one week's Coventry. Second offenses will be considered regressive behavior.

Weller stared at the guard in disbelief. The guard pointedly looked away, then buzzed him through the gate. Woodenly Weller walked to the bank of elevators. Another copy of the same notice was taped to the wall between the two doors. There was another Coventry notice inside the elevator. And between the elevator doors on his floor. And further down the hall near his room. What *was* this juvenile horseshit? Did they expect anyone to take this boarding-school hazing tactic seriously? Did they expect *him* to take it seriously?

He took a quick piss, washed his hands, and went down to the dining room, where he spotted Coventry notices outside the entrance, at the head of the food line, and on the garbage bins. The silly fucking things were everywhere.

He got a plate of franks and beans and potato salad at the steam tables, where the servers wouldn't meet his eyes, and looked around for a place to sit. This time, perversely, he wanted to sit with people he knew, with some of the nerds who had been sucking up to him, to blast this stupid Coventry thing apart before it really got started. Tina Davies was sitting at the end of a table opposite Ted and Lori Brenner. There was an empty seat next to Tina, and Weller took it.

"Hi, Tina," he said. "How's it going?"

Tina stared down at her plate and continued to shovel spaghetti into her mouth.

"Ted? Lori?"

They wouldn't even meet his eyes.

"What the fuck is this?" Weller snapped. "Are you people actually going along with this juvenile nonsense?"

Tina gave him a furtive look; Ted and Lori ignored him completely. It was beginning to get to Weller. The whole thing was like some kind of stupid high-school joke, and it was getting on his nerves on exactly that sort of cretinous level.

"What's the matter with you assholes?" Weller said conversationally. "You have shit for brains?" Still no response. This was no longer funny. Weller was really getting pissed off, and now he was determined to get a rise out of these bastards.

"You stupid motherfuckers!" he shouted loudly. "You spineless dog-faced baboons! Don't you have any minds of your own?"

The noise level in the dining room suddenly dipped as

everyone looked to find the source of this unseemly disturbance. But when people saw who was doing the shouting, they immediately looked away again. Weller had the feeling he could have whipped out his cock and pissed in his plate and no one would dare to notice.

Tina, Ted, and Lori exchanged nervous looks. Then, without a word the three of them got up at once and moved to another table, far across the room.

"Son of a bitch," Weller muttered to himself. He was surprised at how quickly this silent treatment had gotten under his skin. It was not so much that he craved the conversation of any of these nerds as it was anger and amazement that people who had been pestering him for attention for weeks were actually obeying this asshole directive to the letter. As if they had no minds of their own at all. Was that what this was supposed to be too, in addition to everything else—a demonstration of total Monitor power?

Weller looked around the dining room. Two tables away, Harry, the aging nobody who wanted to be a processor, sat alone picking at his food. Weller decided to give old Harry a try; no one had been forcing his company on him more than Harry. Weller picked up his tray, walked over, and sat down across the table. Harry deigned to look up at him with a sad, somewhat wistful expression.

"Hi, Harry," Weller said gently, forcing himself to swallow his anger. "Are you playing along with this silent treatment too?"

Harry deliberately met his eyes for a moment, then looked down at his plate.

"I see," Weller said. "Because you're afraid not to?"

Harry looked up. His expression hardened. He glared at Weller. The meaning of it seemed totally incomprehensible.

"Do you even know *why* this is happening?"

Harry looked down at his plate.

Weller found that the anger was quickly leaching out of him, replaced by a certain sadness, not for himself, but for the poor zombies who were willing to eat this kind of shit, play this stupid game, without even knowing why. But as he thought of the games he had successfully run on Maria Steinhardt and the way he had faced down Gomez, that sadness became less sympathetic, became overlaid with contempt. The suckers and the suckees . . . he thought.

"You know, Harry, I feel sorry for you," he said. "You've got to feel like a fool doing this. They've made you into a gutless coward. You want to be a processor, but don't you also want to be a man?"

Harry looked up angrily. His lips began to move as if he were about to break the silence. Then he caught himself, gave Weller a hang-dog look, and got up and walked away.

Weller sat there, isolated, but taking a certain comfort in it now. After all, he thought, I never really wanted to have anything to do with these people anyway, and this doesn't exactly make them more attractive. Now, at least, they'll really leave me alone.

He cut off a piece of frankfurter and forked it into his mouth with some baked beans. Yech! The food was greasy and tasteless as usual, but by now it was also as cold and limp as a wet washcloth.

Fourteen

Weller took a sip of his honest-to-God mint julep. Across the courtyard the fountain gurgled, and the sweet smell of blossoms filled the cooling evening air. Maria Steinhardt sat on the bench beside him, dressed in a brocaded kimono, her hair wild around her shoulders, her eyes smoky with satiation. Money, sex, and languor perfumed the atmosphere. It all seemed light-years away from the grinding, sullen tension of the set, the vicious, nerve-shattering silence of the Transformation Center.

"At first it really didn't get to me," Weller said. "But now. . . . I come back from work, and I eat by myself. They point and grunt at me in the kitchen while I'm washing the goddamn dishes. I walk into a room, and conversation stops as soon as I get within earshot. Even at work no one talks to me unless it's in the line of duty. It's beginning to drive me a little nuts. I mean, I know I'm becoming a bastard on the set. If it keeps up much longer, I'm afraid I'm going to start talking to myself."

Maria shrugged, not very sympathetically. "You knew what you were getting into, Jack," she said. "I can't do anything about it."

Weller took another cooling sip of his drink. "I didn't ask you to," he said. "Frankly I don't give much of a damn about improving my present situation. I want to get to the Institute. If that ends up being impossible, or if I'm kept waiting much longer, I'm just going to pack it all in."

"*All* of it?" Maria said, arching an eyebrow and moving closer.

"All of it," Weller said evenly. And I'm beginning to mean it, he thought. I'm pressuring her, but I'm not *just* pressuring her. If I can't get to the Institute, there's no further point in torturing myself. I'll release my own copies of the damned Master Contact Sheet and let the fur fly where it may.

"Well I've spoken to John," Maria said. "Twice . . ."

"And?"

"And he's amused."

"*Amused?*"

"John loves to think in twelve directions at once," Maria said. "I could tell that the idea of starring in commercials tickled him. But, of course, he knows about you and your wife and why you're doing what you're doing. And that amuses him too, on a different level. I have the feeling that this Coventry directive was his idea. He's playing with you. He's toying with you. He's running one of his silly experiments."

She put a hand on Weller's thigh. "And of course, he knows all about us," she said. "That amuses him too."

"I don't think I follow that one," Weller said sourly.

Maria placed her hands on her knees, leaned back, and stared up at the darkening sky as she spoke.

"It's hard to explain, and it's not very pretty," she said. "Our arrangement permits me my little affairs, but John doesn't exactly like it. It's more of a quid pro quo. If he forced me to stay at the Institute, or if he expected me to be totally faithful to him while he was off playing the Great I Am, it *would* be divorce-court time, ducks. Aside from the fact that my divorcing him would drive John crazy, it would be one holy horror for Transformationalism, because this is a community-property state, love, and I have enough on John and his whole movement to drag it through the gossip columns for months."

She looked at Weller and smiled rather sadly. "So John permits me my little affairs," she said. " 'Your little ego-booster shots,' he calls them. Not that there isn't truth in that, not that there isn't a certain amount of love in it too. I mean, he understands me, he knows what a beating my ego has to take as the wife of the God-Of-All-He-Surveys. But John is a man too—even though he likes to pretend he's transcended all that—and it does give him a perverse satisfaction to be able to view what I'm doing in as tacky a light as possible."

She patted Weller's knee. "And the idea that you're . . . *servicing me* for the most obvious of ulterior motives amuses him on that level."

"Pardon me while I puke," Weller grunted. What she had told him made him feel small and toadlike indeed. *I think I'm running numbers on them,* and all the while I'm a spear carrier in their loathsome little porno movie. Blech!

"Takes one to know one," Maria said. "In the Biblical sense of course."

"Well, where does your charming little psychodrama leave me?" Weller asked.

"Leave us not be crude, my pet," Maria said gaily.

Weller was beginning to steam. He had a fantasy impulse to smash his fist into her face.

"I mean what do you think John is going to do," Weller said, through grinding teeth. "Is he going to turn me down, or do I eventually get to the Institute?"

"Always an eye for the main chance, hey?" Maria said teasingly. She laughed. "Oh, I believe John will eventually want to see you," she said blithely. "After he's extracted the maximum amusement from this little situation. You just have to hang on, love." She gave him a cold, hard look. "And make sure that I don't tire of you before then," she said.

"What's that supposed to mean?" Weller said belligerently.

Maria stared into his eyes. "I don't think you like me very much now," she said. "Well, I can tolerate that. I can even be amused by it. Because like me or not, you have to please me, don't you, lover?"

Weller glared back at her, seething with rage and loathing.

Maria laughed cruelly. "It does something for this old lady's poor battered ego to have a young man like yourself in her power. And at the moment the way you feel about me just makes it all the tastier."

She stood up, reached down, picked up the hem of her kimono, and lifted it, exposing her bare fur of dark pubic beard.

Weller jumped to his feet, grossed out by this unlikely act.

Maria laughed. "Right now I want you to eat me," she said. "Right here, just like that. On your knees."

Weller's hands convulsed into fists. He took a half step forward, violence pounding through his arteries. "You lousy—"

"Of course, you don't *have* to do it," Maria said. "We can just call it quits right now. In which case. . . ." She let the sentence dangle around a smug, amused smile.

Weller stood there frozen, his mind unable to function, while his treasonous body found itself being turned on by the very vileness of the situation, the pure brutal animalism of her domineering command.

Maria put a hand atop his head. He did not resist. "Eat my tired old cunt, lover," she said hoarsely. "Be my little slave, you dirty mind-fucker, you. Down on your knees!"

Trembling, resignedly, but not without a surge of perverse and twisted passion, Weller sank slowly to his knees. The worst of it was that a part of him knew that he was going to enjoy it, that in a moment he would be lost in her triumphant moans, that somehow the self-loathing he felt was being transformed into the demon desire to master her with pleasure. And she knew this and was getting off on it, and that, most vile of all, was making his body throb with a sickening lust.

Weller plodded numbly down the hallway to his room, passing one of the fading Coventry notices taped to the wall. He had to admit that the silent treatment had finally gotten to him.

His life had become a dreary tunnel of isolation—from meaningful human contact, from anything that gave even a dim and feeble pleasure. He felt like a rat in a totally deterministic maze. A tasteless silent breakfast in the commissary, eight hours at Changes Productions shunned by his fellow workers and communicating only on a technical level, a grim lonely dinner at the Center, an hour of dishwashing, then walking around the Center like an invisible ghost or reading nothing in particular in his room until he was sleepy enough to blot out the world and begin the cycle again in the morning.

Now he understood what the Monitors were doing. Gomez, and beyond him, Torrez wanted him out, but thus far Maria was preventing them from simply declaring him a regressive, so the only way they could get him out was to make him leave of his own volition. So they were making his life a torture to be endured. All that kept him going was waiting for a summons from Steinhardt to go to the Institute. That was the contest he was locked into with the Monitors: could he endure the silent treatment until word came down, or could they drive him into giving up?

Even his hours with Maria were now part of it. Sex with her had become a contest of wills in which he held a losing hand. If he didn't please her, he would be at the nonexistent mercy of the Monitors. Maybe she had even lied to him. Maybe she had never spoken to Steinhardt about his proposal at all. Maybe that was part of a cruel mind game too: something to make him endure the agony of Coventry forever, to lock him in perpetual stasis which would eventually break him to their will.

Weller reached his room, went inside, took a piss, and sat down on the edge of the bed to wait until the dining room opened so that he could pass another hour shoveling bad food into his face in stony silence. I've got to get out of this, he thought. I'm starting to feel like the walls are closing in on me.

Well, why not? he thought. I've got two hours till I have to show up to wash dishes, I could go out to eat. Most of the restaurants in the area were greasy joints, and he really didn't have the time to drive somewhere else, but there was a pretty good Chinese restaurant on Cahuenga, and he'd have time to get there, eat, and walk back. Why not?

He bounded off the bed, combed his hair, took the elevator to the lobby, and walked defiantly out of the Transformation Center, past the deliberately unseeing eyes of the guards and inmates, and out into the non-Transformationalist reality of the streets.

During the short walk to the restaurant, Weller found himself enjoying the anonymity of the streets, the tackiness of the porno shops, the bars, the sleazy massage parlors, the very scurviness of the denizens of downtown Hollywood. Although this had never been his world, it was very much like the world he had lost in a basic human sense: chaotic, plotless, random; uncontrolled by Monitors, life directives, or Transformationalist mind games. Like his lost world it was full of frustrations, boredom, desperation, and thwarted dreams, but at least it was a world of natural human evolution and natural human conflicts, not a hermetically sealed universe proceeding according to the plans, scenarios, and whims of one man and the power structure he had built to contain it.

That thought gave Weller some comfort, but it also made him feel somewhat alien out here in the free air, less than human, a creature of the psychic catacombs, a halfling.

The Chinese restaurant was a rather plain storefront with an extensive menu posted on the window. Inside, dim lighting, square tables with white clothes, Chinese paintings and instruments on the walls, and a kind of gilt-and-red pagoda facade across the entrance made a pass at atmosphere. At this early hour the place was almost empty. But as a waiter led him toward an isolated table-for-two, Weller spotted Johnny Blaisdell, his sometime press agent, eating at a table in a corner with his wife Madge. A moment later Johnny spotted him.

"Jack! For Chrissakes! Are you alone? Come over and eat with us." Johnny waved at him, very Beverly Hills with his silvery hair, air force shades, and mint-green leisure suit, with his honey-blond wife in a tightly tailored denim dress festooned with turquoise and silver.

216

Uneasily Weller went over to their table. The Blaisdells were an apparition out of his old life, the world he had lost. Once he had inhabited their reality and been one of them. Seeing them now and feeling his own sense of alienation, he had a sickening floating feeling of not knowing who he was or whether he still had a reality.

"What are you doing here, Johnny?" he asked as he sat down. "This isn't exactly your usual turf."

"We're going to an early sneak preview up on Hollywood Boulevard," Madge said.

"Yeah. Hey, you want to tag along? I can probably bullshit you in."

"No thanks," Weller said automatically. "I've got to be back at the Transformation Center by a quarter after seven." He could've bitten his tongue off after he said it, the way both of them looked at him as if he were the carrier of some loathsome disease.

"Yeah, I heard you had gotten really involved with Transformationalism," Johnny said. "How's your head, boy? You still just chasing Annie, or have they got you hooked?"

"How did you find out?" Weller blurted, and then realized how paranoid he sounded.

Johnny shrugged. "Word gets around," he said. Then the waiter appeared and sidetracked the conversation while Weller ordered a Martini, hot-and-sour soup, and chicken with peanuts and hot chilies.

But after the waiter left, Johnny returned relentlessly to the subject. "Look, Jack, I know where you're coming from, but don't you think you might be getting in over your head?"

"What are you talking about?" Weller said guardedly.

Johnny laughed rather humorlessly. "Hey, don't get paranoid," he said. "I only mean you haven't worked for a long time and—"

"I'm making commercials for Changes Productions," Weller said defensively.

"Who the hell is Changes Productions?"

Weller sighed. "A Transformationalist company," he admitted in a very small voice.

"Oh shit, you're *working* for them?" Johnny said. "Jesus, if you're *that* hard up, I ought to be able to—"

"Not, it's not like that, Johnny," Weller said. "I have to keep working for them; it's the only chance I have of finding Annie."

"So they've still got her somewhere . . . ," Madge said.

217

Weller nodded glumly. For some reason he found that he was very reluctant to discuss the whole thing. He recognized that as paranoia in himself, which made the conversation doubly distressing.

At this point the waiter arrived with Weller's food and drink. There was another break in the coversation during which Weller gulped down half his Martini and began to feel a little looser. After all, these were friends of his, sort of, and they cared about him, they were worried about him. They surely weren't agents of the Monitors or anything like that.

"Just how deep into Transformationalism *are* you, Jack?" Johnny asked. "I mean you're *working* for them. . . ." He studied Weller more narrowly for a moment. "I mean, you're not, you know, *converted*, are you?"

"Shit, no!" Weller exclaimed. He gulped down the rest of his drink and began picking at his food with chopsticks. "No fucking way!" he said vehemently. "You have no idea what it's like. I mean, they've got me living at the goddamn Transformation Center! It's a loathsome, Fascist organization, and all I want to do is find Annie and get us both out."

"Sounds like a tall order from what I hear," Johnny said.

"I can handle it," Weller told him. "Worse comes to worse, I've got some inside information I can—"

"Jesus, he's beginning to sound like Rich Golden," Madge muttered.

"Who?"

Johnny Blaisdell groaned and shot his wife a warning look.

"Who's Rich Golden?" Weller insisted.

"Just some nut," Johnny said, with obviously forced casualness.

"I think maybe Jack should talk to him," Madge said.

"Oh, for Chrissakes, Madge," Johnny snapped. "What will Golden do but make him more paranoid?"

"That's the point," Madge insisted. "If Jack's really so involved with Transformationalism, it might do him some good."

Johnny fingered his chin thoughtfully. "You might have a point," he mused.

"Will someone please tell me what this is all about before *you* drive me crazy?" Weller demanded.

Johnny shrugged. "Well, what the hell . . . ," he said. He looked at Weller with as serious an expression as Weller had ever seen on his face.

"Richard Golden is . . . or was . . . a hotshot journalist a few

218

years ago," he said. "Mostly film stuff, but a pretty good muckraker now and again too. The girl he was living with— I forget her name—got gobbled up by Transformationalism, just like Annie. Well, Golden was a tough, hot-blooded son of a bitch with an exaggerated idea of the power of the press, and instead of playing whatever game you're playing, he went after their asses. Nosed around and started writing magazine pieces about Transformationalism, even had a contract to do a book about it at one point, I think."

Johnny paused dramatically and forked some food into his mouth. "Well, Transformationalism proceeded to go after *his* ass," he said. "They sued him about a million times, and they sued the magazine that printed the pieces, and finally they started suing anyone who tried to publish anything he wrote. Never won anything in court, but they made him a very undesirable boy to publish, and they bankrupted him with lawyer bills."

Johnny shrugged. "I don't know much more," he said. "All I know is that these days Golden bombards every column and press agent in town with totally libelous stuff about Transformationalism. I mean, genuine lunacy. You know, they own GAC and MGM and Howard Hughes, and they control your phones and have half of Washington in their pocket, and they're sending out secret control rays from the Capital Records Tower, and generally polluting everyone's vital bodily fluids. He's gone all the way round the bend."

"But apparently he does know a lot about Transformationalism," Madge said.

"Yeah, I mean, he's spent the last couple of years totally obsessed with the subject," Johnny said. He grinned wanly. "I suppose he must know a lot of real dirt too. Even paranoiacs have enemies."

"How can I get in touch with this guy?" Weller asked. Rays from the Capital Tower seemed a bit much, but there was little else that he didn't believe possible when it came to the powers and tentacles of Transformationalism. If nothing else, this guy Golden might have some stuff that would go nicely with the Master Contact Sheet in his blackmail file. And something else made him want to meet the man; here, after all, was someone he could really talk to, crazy or not.

"I could call him and set up an appointment," Johnny said uncertainly. "If you really want to get involved in that insanity . . ."

219

"You think I'm not involved already?" Weller said dryly.

"Yeah, but you're not down on your knees chewing the rug yet," Johnny said. "I mean this guy is cray—zee!"

"Please do it, Johnny," Weller said. "I think I owe it to myself to look into it."

"Okay," Johnny said, "I'll give it a try. But I don't guarantee anything. I mean, Golden sees Transformationalist agents under every bed. It'll take some convincing."

"That's the name of your game, isn't it?" Weller said.

Johnny laughed. "So it is," he said. "Give me a call about noon tomorrow, and I'll let you know how it goes." He glanced at his watch. "Hey, it's getting late. We'd better get the check or we won't make it. Sure you won't come along, Jack?"

"No," Weller said. "I really can't. But thanks. Thanks for everything."

"*De nada*," Johnny said. "Anything I can do to help." He looked at Weller narrowly. "I mean, *almost* anything. Don't *you* start hitting me with daily paranoia stories about Transformationalism, okay?"

"Even if they're true?" Weller asked.

Johnny grimaced. "*Especially* if they're true," he said. "If there's really a conspiracy out there controlling my vital bodily fluids from the Capital Tower with secret rays, this old boy doesn't want to know about it. As far as I'm concerned, my clients already give me all the paranoia I can handle."

The address that Johnny Blaisdell had given Weller turned out to be a crumbling and sinister-looking apartment house on a slimy back street in Venice a couple of blocks from the beach; an area haunted by spectral hippies left over from the sixties, ghostly old beatniks left over from the fifties, and wasted junkies living very much in the perpetual now. Parking spaces at the beach were at a premium, so Weller had to park four blocks away and walk nervously down the dark streets, tensing every time he passed a shadowed alleyway.

This is really the pits, he thought, as he climbed the crumbling flight of concrete stairs to the building entrance. He checked Golden's apartment number on the mailbox—3C —and entered the building through the unlocked inner door, for there were no working buzzers.

Up three flights of stairs smelling of old cooking grease and piss and into a dim hallway with peeling yellow paint and a series of doors, each one painted a different fading color.

Three-C was painted battleship gray, and the door had a peephole and three locks in it.

Weller banged sharply on the door, and a moment later there was an eye at the peephole. "Jack Weller," he said, as per Johnny's instructions, "the man from Changes."

Click! Slok! Blang! The sounds of locks being turned and bolts being thrown, and then the door opened. A gaunt figure wearing T-shirt and jeans stood there outlined in the dim light, with matted brown hair that looked as if it hadn't been combed in a week, big sunken eyes, an etched beak of a nose, and a heavy five o'clock shadow.

"I'm Rich Golden," the man said. "Inside."

Weller stepped directly into a dark kitchen. He could make out the rough shapes of mounds of dirty dishes and pots heaped in the sink and more on the drainboard. His nostrils were assailed by the odors of old food scraps, garbage, and pot. Golden threw a bolt, turned three locks, and led him through a beaded archway into a kind of living-room-cum-office.

There was a musty old couch heaped high with papers, files, newspapers, reels and cassettes of tape. There were two chairs, also heaped with paper and crud. There was a big fancy desk with a typewriter, a telephone, a complex tape-recorder rig, and a metal gooseneck lamp which cast a harsh cone of white light on more papers, files, newspapers, pictures, and tapes. Two walls were lined with filing cabinets, and the tops of the cabinets were piled nearly to the ceiling with more files and papers. The room was lighted by a naked bulb covered by a pink Japanese lantern. The air was blue with pot smoke. And the only two windows were completely covered with tinfoil.

Golden casually cleared sitting space on the couch by dumping some heaps of papers, files, and tapes on the dusty floor. He sat down, lighted a half-smoked joint that had been sitting in an ashtray on the arm of the couch, exhaled smoke as Weller gingerly sat down, and said, "Let's get on with the briefing."

"Briefing?" Weller said uncertainly.

"Blaisdell told me your situation," Golden said, "and he told me you wanted a briefing on Transformationalism. I've checked him out, and I don't think he's in on it, though of course you never can tell. If you're paranoid, I could play back our conversation for you. Naturally I tape all my phone calls."

"Uh . . . I don't think that's necessary," Weller said.

Golden giggled nervously. "Right," he said. "Tapes can be doctored anyway, so what would it prove? You wouldn't believe what *they* can do with tapes."

Weller was having difficulty following the logic of Golden's conversation, if indeed there were any. "Tapes? *They?*"

Golden looked at him strangely. "Transformationalism," he said. "The conspiracy. They can even synthesize your voice with a computer. They've got me making threatening crank calls all over town. Destroys the credibility of the real thing." He pushed the burning joint at Weller. "Take a hit."

"No thanks," Weller said. He was having enough trouble understanding what Golden was saying without getting stoned!

"You really should," Golden said. "It randomizes your synapses and keeps the programming from taking hold in your brain. Blocks the control waves too. I've been doing a lid a week since I got into this. It's the only thing that keeps me autonomous. That's why *they* are against legalization, you know. No? Yeah, well you don't know what I know. But that's why you're here, right?"

"Right," Weller said. But he was beginning to wonder. So far, Richard Golden seemed crazy as a bedbug. He didn't even know where to begin, what to ask. He felt totally disoriented.

"Well, where do you want to start?" Golden asked. "The heaviest stuff? The snuffs?"

"*Snuffs?*"

"Wait a minute," Golden said. "I'll go get the snuff file file." He got up, rummaged in his filing cabinets for a few minutes, and came back with two fat folders. He handed them to Weller. "Snuffs," he said. "The first file is the certains. Second is the probables."

Weller leafed through the first file. There were newspaper clippings of murder stories, neatly typewritten lists of names and dates cross-indexed to the clippings, and pages of typed notes that seemed to be in some kind of code. The second file was more of the same, but there was a lot of weird stuff about the assassinations of JFK and Bobby Kennedy.

"Surprises you, doesn't it?" Golden said. "You can hardly believe it. But it's all there in black and white. I estimate that they've done maybe a hundred snuffs. Including both Kennedys. Possibly King, too."

"*What?*"

Golden laughed. "Right, you think I'm crazy, and I don't

blame you. But I've got evidence that both Sirhan and Oswald received Transformationalist processing. And how do you think Jack Ruby contracted cancer in prison? They can do it to you with rays. They've got all kinds of things at that Institute of theirs. Why do you think I've got tinfoil on my windows, huh?"

"Are you serious?"

"Everyone thinks I'm crazy," Golden said. "Even *I* think I'm crazy. That's part of the technique. They don't just discredit everyone who's onto them, they try to turn you into a mental wreck so you stop believing it yourself. You want proof? Take a look at this!"

He rummaged through his files again, muttering and cursing to himself, and came back with another folder. "This is hard investigative reporting," he said. "I got myself a book contract on the basis of this material. It's a file on the companies they control, though I certainly don't guarantee that it's complete yet. Some of them they own through fronts, some of them they control through key personnel. Take a look."

Weller looked through the neat compilation of lists, corporate letterheads, newspaper and magazine clippings, and carefully typed interview transcriptions with ever-growing unease. He recognized companies from the Utopia Industries listings in the lobby of their office building. He recognized companies and names from the Master Contact Sheet. There was no doubt that some of this stuff was true, and only a really top investigative reporter could have ferreted much of it out.

But there was more, much more. Studios. General Motors subsidiaries. Names of local phone-company executives scattered throughout the country. Oil companies. Radio stations, TV stations, publishers, newspapers, and national magazines.

Much of it he knew to be true. Some of it was so clearly fantastic that it had to be pure paranoia. But in between were dozens or even hundreds of companies and executives who might or might not be really under Transformationalist control. And all of it seemed to be the product of the same brand of very professional investigative reporting. Where could you draw the line between paranoia and horrible reality?

"Well, what do you think about *that*?" Golden finally said.

"Very impressive. Very scary," Weller admitted. "And I've got confirmation of some of it. How in hell did you dig all this out?"

"Professional secrets," Golden said, taking a long drag off his joint. "I was one hell of an investigative reporter, I know

223

how to dig out a story. And I've been at this full time for years. I wrote two dozen articles about it, and three of them were published, and people knew I was doing a book before they came down on me. People talked for a while. Before they started disappearing. Before they killed my book and kept my articles from being published. Whatever they do, they can't keep me from doing what I know best. And someday . . . someday. . . ." Golden began to tremble. He balled his hands into fists, released them, did it again, four times in quick succession.

He took a quick drag off his joint, bounded off the couch, and snatched four huge files off the top of one of the cabinets. He sat down and dropped them heavily on the floor in front of him.

"Look at this shit!" he said shrilly. "Know what it is? My media files! Records of all the lawsuits they threw at me. Letters from magazines telling me they won't publish what I write. Think I'm just being paranoid? I've also got records on three dozen writers, reporters, and TV newspeople that Transformationalism has beaten into the ground for daring to say anything about them. Lawsuits. People getting fired for no apparent reason and then never getting rehired. Reporters just *disappearing*, man! Getting cancer. Being committed to mental institutions. Bankruptcies. Phony dope raps."

Golden bounced off the couch and went to his desk. "Think I'm crazy, huh?" he said, touching his phone. "Well, maybe I am. They sure try hard enough. Phone calls in the middle of the night every night for months. Now they're tapping it, and I think they're sending subsonic vibrations—fourteen cycles a second, the panic frequency, look it up—through the dial tone. I may be crazy, but I'm not full of shit."

Golden abruptly seemed to calm himself somewhat. He sat back down on the couch. "Look," he said, "Blaisdell told me what your situation was, otherwise I wouldn't have taken this chance, not unless I knew you were really in danger, I mean, how do I know you're not a Monitor, right? For that matter how do you know I'm not a Monitor? How do either of us know *Blaisdell* isn't a Monitor . . . ?" Golden blinked, as if realizing that he was wandering.

"Shit," he said, sucking on his joint, "what I'm trying to tell you is that I come from the same place you do, is why I'm taking this chance. They sucked up Carla, my old lady, just like they did your wife. Only instead of being nuts enough to try and infiltrate them—and *you* think *I'm* crazy!—I went

224

after them head on, power of the press, and all that bullshit."

Golden got up, went to the desk, took a plastic bag of grass and some rolling papers out of a drawer, and began to roll a fresh joint. "But that's what it was, bullshit," he said. "Man, the so-called power of the press is like pissing into a hurricane up against something like Transformationalism."

He lighted the joint and began pacing in small circles, puffing on it as he spoke. "Shit, they destroyed my career. I mean, I'm *good*, I've sold articles everywhere, magazines came after *me*, and now I couldn't get an assignment to cover a cat show for the *Valley Green Sheet*. You know why I'm still alive? Because the fuckers figure I'd be more trouble to them dead than alive. I've got information that should send them all to jail for a thousand years, and I can't *do* anything with it. No one will touch it, no one dares listen to me. But I'm a well-known crank on the subject of Transformationalism; if I were murdered, *then* maybe there'd have to be an investigation. If I hadn't understood that early on and gone totally public, I wouldn't be talking to you now."

"Why don't you turn over this stuff to the police?" Weller asked. "Or the FBI? Or even a congressional committee?"

Golden laughed maniacally. He went over to a row of filing cabinets and leaned against them. "The police? The government?" he said scornfully. "In here I've got records of how many congressional campaigns have been financed with Transformationalist money. How many state legislators they control. How many cops they own." He shook his head and sat down on the couch beside Weller.

"What I'm trying to tell you," he said in a strangely subdued voice, "is give it up, man. Don't you yet understand what you're up against? Transformationalism controls over a billion dollars in capital. They snuff people. They control dozens of politicians. They can stop anyone from writing anything about them. They know more about brainwashing and mind control then anyone. And at that Institute of theirs, they've got whole platoons of Dr. Frankensteins inventing subsonics that can control your mind through your phone, rays that give you cancer, drugs they can put in the water to turn people into zombies, machines that can read your thoughts, and other machines that can put thoughts into your head. Give it up, man! You can't beat the bastards."

"What about you?" Weller said. "You're still fighting them. . . ."

"*Me?*" Golden said bitterly. "What the hell else can I do?

225

They took my love away from me, they took my career away from me, and they're trying to take my mind away from me. I've got no choice. What am I supposed to do? It's keep going or become a junkie or commit myself to a nut house or kill myself. Fighting Transformationalism is all I have left. There isn't any other me."

Weller stared into Golden's red-rimmed eyes, and what he saw shook him to the core. With his cancer rays and Kennedy assassinations and hypnotic dial tones, there was no doubt that Golden was far around the bend. Yet it was also certain that some of his material was the real thing—the Master Contact Sheet proved that. If some of it were true, how could Weller be sure that any specific part of it *wasn't* true, except for the rays and the phone paranoia and the Kennedys? If most of the material on companies controlled by Transformationalism were true, if the media file were the real thing, if the political files weren't pure paranoia, then he was up against something that made the Mafia look like the Knights of Columbus. The Master Contact Sheet might be worthless as blackmail material if Golden, with all his files, was so totally impotent.

But even more frightening was what he saw in the man himself. This broken, raving creature had been a top journalist; Johnny Blaisdell had said so, and Johnny knew who was whom. And whatever else was or wasn't true, it was an indisputable fact that it was Golden's involvement with Transformationalism which, one way or another, had reduced him to this state. An involvement that had begun just as his involvement had begun. "Fighting Transformationalism is all that I have left," Golden had said. "There isn't any other me."

And you, Weller? he thought. What other you is there now? Are you looking at your future? Are you looking at what you're becoming?

"Can't you get yourself out of it, Golden?" Weller said. "Can't you move to New York or somewhere, get your head straight, and start all over?"

Golden sighed. "You still don't have the big picture," he said. "I've been declared a regressive. They're all over the country, and they watch me all the time. Wherever I'd go, they'd know. Wherever I try to get published, they'll stop me. Their rays reach everywhere. They're keyed into the national phone system. There's no way I can escape them. All I can do is keep on fighting until they stop me." He took a long hit on his joint. "Which, some day, they surely will," he said.

Weller sighed. There was a long, long silence. Finally Weller stood up. "I think I'd better go now," he said. "I've got a midnight curfew at the center and it's getting late."

"Yeah," Golden said. "I've told you what I can, and you sure don't want them looking into where you disappeared to tonight." He smiled softly. "Good luck, Weller," he said. "I hope you make it. I know you won't, but I hope you do."

Golden extended his hand. Weller took it, making it, for some atavistic reason, an old-fashioned fists-upraised sixties handshake. "You too, brother," he said.

For the first time in months, he had met a kind of kindred spirit, someone with whom he felt a strange sense of solidarity.

You poor bastard, he thought, as Golden closed his locks and bolts behind him. You poor, brave bastard.

Fifteen

Weller walked slowly and reluctantly down the stairs from Golden's floor; even the inside of this ominous and reeking building seemed a reality preferable to what he was returning to. Maybe Golden is right, he thought. Maybe I should just get into my car and keep driving. Maybe I really can't fight Transformationalism or get into the Institute. Maybe this waiting is the final mind game, one that will go on and on until they reduce me to a basket case like him. Maybe if I get out of their reality, they'll stay out of mine, and maybe that's the best thing I can hope for. . . .

He reached the ground-floor landing, opened the inner door to the vestibule, and stepped inside. He was about to open the outer door when a big man dressed in black suddenly stepped out of the shadows outside to block him.

He whirled and saw that another man in black had materialized inside the building behind him, blocking the inner door as well. He was caught like a rat in a trap.

The man outside the building stepped into the vestibule. He was blond, with thin, angular features and burning blue eyes. He didn't look like any crazed junkie mugger. "Mr. Weller," he said, with grim Los Angeles cop politeness, "you are to come with us." But this was no cop either.

The man inside the building came up beside him. "Relax, Weller," he said in a rough voice tinged with irony. "This isn't a stick up. We're Monitors." This bimbo was dark and swarthy and looked like an ex-boxer gone slightly to fat.

Before Weller could react at all, each of them took him gently by an elbow, and they propelled him numbly outside where a third Monitor was waiting, this one in his forties with a steel-gray crew cut.

"No trouble?" asked the crew cut.

"No trouble, Irv," said the swarthy one. "You're not going to give us any trouble, are you, Weller?"

It had all been done so quickly and smoothly that Weller was only now beginning to experience his own reactions—

fear, anger, but also a numbed acceptance of the *fait accompli*. "What the fuck is this?" he snarled without very much conviction.

"You know what it is, Weller," Irv said. "Fred Torrez wants to have a little talk with you. You have not been behaving in a very highly evolved manner."

"Relax, Weller," said the swarthy one. "We're not going to drop you in the Pacific. Our directive is to deliver you to Torrez, healthy, and more or less in one piece."

"And if I don't want to see Torrez?"

"Then," said the blond, "we're authorized to coldcock you and drag you there."

"Let's move it along," said Irv, who seemed to be the leader. He stepped in front of Weller and began walking rapidly as the other two, still holding Weller by the elbows, brought him along.

Weller found himself moving with them in a state of almost relaxed resignation. The only other alternative was to get himself a beating, and in a weird way he found that surrendering his will to the inevitable produced a certain release of tension, an incongruously calm floating feeling. Part of him still felt that it was unmanly not to resist, but there was no energy behind it except a certain bloodless guilt at going along so meekly.

They took him around the corner to a big, black, late-model Buick. Irv got in behind the wheel and the other two shoved him into the backseat between them. Inanely Weller remembered that his Triumph was parked in a zone that would get him a ticket or even a tow away tomorrow morning.

"What about my car?" he said. "It's in a morning no-parking zone." It sounded asinine under the circumstances, but it also intruded a homey note of mudane reality into this dreamlike situation which was oddly comforting.

"Give me the keys, and we'll send a man around for it later," the blond said. He laughed. "We wouldn't want you to get towed."

Numbly Weller handed over the keys. He even found himself muttering, "Thanks," as if it were the most natural thing in the world. His mind simply couldn't connect with what was happening; it was all like some dumb gangster movie. He wondered if this were what a prisoner felt like on his way to the electric chair; was that why they never seemed to struggle?

"Uh, my car is—"

"We know where it is," Irv said. "You've been closely monitored for a long time. Did you think you could see a regressive like Golden without us knowing about it?"

Weller sighed. He wondered if on some level he hadn't known this was going to happen, if some part of him hadn't deliberately provoked it. Certainly he was reacting strangely enough, as if this were a fate he had long since accepted.

Irv started the car and eased it out of its parking space. "Oh yeah," he said, "don't forget the mask."

The blond Monitor reached behind him and snatched a while cloth bag off the rear window shelf. "Put it on, Mr. Weller," he said, handing him the bag.

This was finally just a bit too much for Weller's sense of reality; this was B-movieland. "You're not serious," he said.

"Put the fucking thing on!" the swarthy Monitor snarled. "You're going to Monitor Central, and no one gets to know where that is but us."

"Up yours, Charlie!" Weller said angrily. "Enough is enough!"

Instantly the blond Monitor clamped his forearm under Weller's chin and began choking off his air. The other Monitor cocked his fist inches from Weller's jaw. "You can wear the mask, or I can knock you into the middle of next week," he said. "Your choice."

"Put it on," said the blond, and he tightened his pressure against Weller's windpipe. Choking, and really scared by now, Weller numbly pulled the mask on over his head.

Immediately the pressure on his throat was released. "That's better," a rough voice said. "You'll be much better off if you get it through your head that we mean business and do what you're told."

Trapped in the blind white universe of the mask, Weller found himself sinking back into a floating resigned state of consciousness, lulled by the continuing silence, the swaying and rolling motion of the car, the sense of total discontinuity with the outside world.

How far or where they had driven, Weller found impossible to guess. At times the car seemed to be climbing—up into the Hollywood Hills? At other times he seemed to hear the sounds of the ocean—along the beach? They had been driving maybe twenty or thirty minutes when the car stopped, the engine was turned off, and a voice said: "All right, Weller, we get out here."

Hands guided him by the elbows along what felt like a

gravel path, up a short flight of stairs, through a door, down a hall, up more stairs, down another hall, and through yet another door. Then a brisk deep voice said, "Sit him down, take off the mask, and leave us alone."

Hands pushed him down into a chair and then removed the mask.

Weller found himself blinking in another world of white. As his eyes adjusted, he saw that he was sitting in a tiny room whose walls, ceiling and even floor were painted a shiny, pure white. A harsh overhead fixture bounced right off all the gleaming white surfaces, cruelly punishing his eyes. In front of him was a white Formica desk. Even the intercom and the folder on the desk were white.

Behind the desk, the only visual relief from the white glare, was Fred Torrez. His black hair, black suit, black turtleneck, and hard black eyes seemed cleverly chosen to force him into the center of visual attention.

"The truth, Weller," Torrez snapped in a rough yet somehow cultivated voice. "Now. What were you doing consorting with an extreme regressive like Richard Golden?"

Torrez's dark eyes, cunningly amplified by the glaring white stage set, bored into him like lasers of pure void. Understanding the trick was little help. Torrez had knocked him completely off-balance, and Weller had no idea of how to respond, none at all.

"Uh, well, you know about my idea to do some new commercials—"

"Please spare me the insult of low-level evasions," Torrez said silkily, favoring Weller with the smile of a very intelligent shark. "Assume that I understand you better than you do yourself, and we'll get along." He patted the folder on the desk. "You're all in here for one who has the eyes to read it. We know you think you're our dangerous enemy. You've been congratulating yourself on fooling us into partially accepting your phony conversion with a few stupid acting tricks and the help of Garry Bailor."

"*You know about Bailor?*"

Torrez waved a finger at him like an approving schoolteacher. "We begin to get the picture, eh?" he said. "I told you, didn't I? Assume the Monitors know everything. Assume we know about Maria Steinhardt. Assume we know *why*. Assume we know why you want so badly to get to the Institute. Assume we're smarter than you are, and we'll both save ourselves a lot of tedium."

231

"Is Bailor—?"

"A Monitor? Dead? Programmed? I'm sure you'd like to know," Torrez said sweetly. His face abruptly hardened and his voice dropped an octave. "But I'm here to ask questions, Weller, not to answer them!" he snarled. "Now why did you do such an obviously stupid thing as have a chat with Richard Golden?"

Reeling, clutching psychically for purchase, Weller sat there like a dummy, unable to concoct a mode of response. *What kind of people are these?*

"I'll help you, Weller," Torrez said coldly. "I'll lay all your cards faceup on the table for you. You joined the movement to get your wife back. You went to bed with Maria in order to locate her, and in that you have succeeded. Congratulations, Weller."

Torrez cocked his head and grimaced sardonically in response to Weller's surprised reaction. "What do I have to say to convince you that you're not on our level?" he said. "That you concocted this little scheme to use John in commercials in order to penetrate the Institute and recapture your wife, and you used Maria to bypass me in order to reach him with your bait? Face it, Weller, we read you like a psychomap."

"You seem to know all the answers, so why bother asking questions?" Weller managed to grunt silently.

"Because a visit to Richard Golden was definitely not in your program," Torrez said. "A piece of moronic counter-productivity. Too self-destructive to be credible. The only possible explanation within your life scenario is that you went to Golden for blackmail material with which to pry your wife out of the Institute. And all I want to know from you is what you imagined that blackmail material could be?"

He doesn't know! Weller's mind suddenly snapped into sharp focus. Torrez doesn't know about my having a copy of the Master Contact Sheet and he doesn't know about the fail-safe mail drops. That's what he's looking for, but for once he doesn't know what it is. It's my only edge. I've got to keep it from him.

"What makes you assume an unevolved schmuck like me was thinking that far ahead?" he said.

Torrez glared at him. "Are you going to tell me that you're just riding the changes? Or that this stupid commerical business is sincere?"

"You wouldn't believe me if I told you."

"Try me, Weller," Torrez said harshly. "You might be pleasantly surprised."

Oh God, what I need now is a super piece of misdirection! Weller thought desperately. I need space to think. I don't know what the hell I'm doing. I've got to get him off onto something else.

"It's John," he said off the top of his head.

"John? *What's* John?" Torrez was authentically puzzled. Definitely derailed for an instant. Weller reached deep within himself, let a half-recognized truth pop into his consciousness, and molded the ultimate piece of acting of his career around it—craft informed by a certain spontaneous authenticity.

"Okay, I admit it all," he said with convincing lameness. "Everything you said is true except for one item. I really *am* sincere about wanting to make those commercials . . . or at least I'm sincere about using them as an excuse to meet John."

"Why do you want to meet John?" Torrez asked, with what seemed for the first time like a flicker of human interest.

"Because Transformationalism *is* John Steinhardt. Look at all that's happened to me. I'm not the same person anymore. I don't know exactly who I am. Is Tranformationalism making me a zombie or eptifying my mind? What is John? That's the answer I'm looking for, that decides everything. John *is* Transformationalism, and without knowing him, I know nothing."

Weller stared into Torrez's eyes with flashing sincerity. "You know the man," he crooned enviously. "You know the true reality. You must understand what I'm saying."

A veil of dreamy wistfulness seemed to fog Torrez's hard, logical eyes. "So you are driven to comprehend the fullness of John B. Steinhardt," he said softly. "Yes, I think I can believe that. But you're a fool to think that's possible, that your consciousness can contain a complete image of John's reality. Madre Mia, I tried for years, and what I finally learned was I've been very lucky to find the favor of a greater man than I."

"You expect me to swallow that? A man like you, in your position? That's the official line, Torrez, what you tell the suckers. That kind of bullshit is why I have to meet John myself. I just don't buy you as a worshiper of the Great I Am."

Torrez laughed with unexpected sincerity. "You think you know me because you've talked to me a few minutes? Maybe

233

you do. But how much of me is John's creation? How much really is left of the dumb little punk he found leading a street gang all those years ago . . . ? I look back on what that kid was and I look at me now . . ." He shrugged. "And you *still* don't believe that John is something neither of us will ever fully understand?" he said sarcastically.

Weller saw that the mask had slipped, if only for a moment, revealing a flash of Torrez's human reality; whether Torrez had crafted this or not, Weller was convinced. Fred Torrez worships Steinhardt. I believe it. One step from the top, and he sincerely worships the man. It mesmerized Weller with a kind of secondhand awe.

"A nice piece of misdirection, Weller!" Torrez cracked, snapping back into his previous mode, back behind the mask.

"You don't believe I'm sincere?"

"Do you?" Torrez said with a thin smile. "Think about it. Of course, I believe you. Who could've gone through what you've gone through and not be obsessed with the question of John's ultimate personality? You just realized that yourself, didn't you? You started out misdirecting me with a piece of stage business, but as you spoke, you were realizing that it was the truth."

Weller broke out into a cold sweat. Is this guy fucking *telepathic?* Or am I really as transparent as all that?"

"And now I've raised your consciousness another level by pointing it out to you, haven't I?" Torrez said, with the first slight hint of smugness. "But that doesn't mean that the old programs don't persist. You're still running one that says penetrate the Institute, reprogram your wife, and blackmail your way out with something from Golden. And I hope all this has convinced you that you're not leaving here until you tell me what that something is."

As Torrez glared darkly at him out of the white glare, it seemed to Weller he was really nervous about something, that he was under some kind of pressure, that he was projecting certain vibrations of frustration. He knows about everything but the fact that I've got copies of the Master Contact Sheet in mail drops, that maybe I *do* have a way out of the Institute if I get there. But he thinks it's something I was trying to get from Golden, not something I've already got secured! *And this whole interrogation is based on that error!* All I've got to do is convince him that he's right . . .

Which means that this is some kind of security check. . . .

Which means that word has already come down from Steinhardt! Weller suddenly realized. And the word is yes! I'm going to the Institute—if I can convince this guy that I'll be powerless once I get there. All I have to do is feed him something credible along the lines he wants to hear. He's on the spot as much as I am.

"All right, you win," Weller sighed. "I thought it would be better to take a little insurance with me, and I had been told that Golden was the world's expert on Transformationalism. But when I got there. . . . Well, I guess you know, don't you? The guy is crazy. Hypnotic telephones. Kennedy assassinations—"

"And cancer rays from the Capital Records Tower," Torrez said. "So you're going to tell me that Golden's files were such a rat's nest of paranoia, credible data, and whatever lies between that none of it seemed useable."

Weller's face fell, for that was exactly the line he was going to take.

"Let's not waste time here while I browbeat you into admitting that there was *something* there you thought you could use against us," Torrez snapped. "Let's be civilized adults and agree to consider that process completed, shall we? So what was it?"

Stick as close to the truth as you can and still lie, Weller told himself. It's the only possible way to get anything past this guy. "All right, all right," he whined, with a petulant show of resignation. "So he had this big file on Transformationalism's corporate connections . . . from his investigative-reporting days, sound stuff that seemed credible . . . but . . ."

"But what?" Torrez's attention seemed to have narrowed to a tight point of focus.

He believes that, Weller thought. All I have to do now is convince him I don't have it, that I'd have no leverage over them when I get to the Institute.

"But he wouldn't let it out of his hands long enough for me to copy it," Weller said. "Your boys grabbed me as I came out the door, so I couldn't have it hidden anywhere. So all you have to do to prove I'm telling the truth is search me."

Torrez leaned back in his chair and studied Weller for a long moment while Weller held his breath. It would work, I *am* clean. I've turned his own logic in on him.

"Very well, Weller," Torrez finally said. "We'll search you all right, and I'm sure we'll come up with nothing. I'm sure

235

you still have some strong regressive programs running, but it really doesn't matter any more. From here on in, you're under total Monitor control."

He smiled his shark smile at Weller. "Because you're getting what you wanted. Tomorrow morning we're flying you to the Institute." He pressed a button on his intercom. "Send Irv in for Mr. Weller," he said. "Standard Institute security procedure."

Weller had only a short moment to savor his triumph. Then the three men who had snatched him entered the interrogation room. "Good luck, Weller," Torrez said. "But then, you've already had it." He nodded to the guards.

"This way," said Irv. The other two pulled Weller to his feet by the elbows, hustled him down a featureless white hallway, up two flights of stairs, and into a small green cell containing only a john and a Spartan cot.

"Strip," said Irv.

"*What?*"

"Take your clothes off, Weller. Standard security procedure. We'll go through them and return them to you in the morning."

Woodenly Weller took off his shoes, socks, trousers, and shirt and handed them to the blond Monitor.

"The shorts too," said Irv. "Don't be bashful."

"What's the matter? You think I've got a gun in my shorts?"

"Just do it!" snarled Irv.

Weller sighed, then stepped out of his shorts, handed them over, and stood there naked; vulnerable, depersonalized.

"Now lean your hands against the wall and spread your legs."

"What the fuck—"

"Help him!" snapped Irv.

The other two Monitors each grabbed one of Weller's wrists and slammed his palms up against the wall, while Irv spread his legs by kicking his left foot to the side. Then he bent down and examined Weller's rectum. "Okay, he's clean. You can release him."

Weller came off the wall boiling with fury and outraged dignity. But the three Monitors standing shoulder to shoulder in front of him instantly brought home the total powerlessness of his position, the futility of even making some smartass remark, which he couldn't come up with anyway.

"Okay," said Irv. "Sweet dreams."

Suddenly, as if on cue, each of the other two grabbed one

236

of his arms and whipped them behind his back in a double half nelson. Irv pulled a hypodermic out of his jacket pocket and jabbed it painfully into the pit of Weller's right elbow.

Weller felt the sharp needle pain, then a pins-and-needles pressure traveling up his arm, then a rubbery feeling in his knees, a soft fuzziness intruding upon his sensorium.

Irv withdrew the needle, and the other two released his arms. Weller stood there for a long moment, boiling with fury, shaking with fear. He took two hesitant steps forward. His head began to whirl, his vision doubling, then tripling, and then his knees began to turn to Jell-O.

"Onto the bed," said a distant voice.

Arms eased him backward onto the cot just as his legs went out from under him. Everything seemed to be moving in slow motion through a clear but viscous fluid. "Son . . . of . . . a . . . bitch . . . ," he heard his own voice mutter thickly as his leadened eyelids drooped toward unconsciousness.

The last thing he heard before the blackness closed in was the heavy click of the door lock.

Weller drifted up from inky dreamless sleep along a line of sparks that seemed to be traveling slowly down his right arm across his shoulder up his neck and into his head, where it expanded into a dull ballooning throb. He opened gummy eyelids to see vague towering black shapes against a sea of green. He rubbed his eyes, trying to gather his scattered thoughts as his vision slowly came back into focus.

He was lying naked on a cot in a small green room. His body felt strangely detached from his mind, heavy with a luxuriant lassitude. His thoughts seemed to be coming very slowly and somehow no cerebral event seemed to have any real import. He was somewhere in something called Monitor Central. He had been drugged. He was going to the Institute. He had met Fred Torrez. He dimly realized that wild emotions should be coursing through him, but nothing seemed important. No thought was more than a random image flitting across the surface of his mind, nothing seemed to associate itself with anything else.

The three Monitors who had brought him here were standing over his cot. One of them held a pile of clothes. Another held two empty hypodermics. All three of them were studying him. Why did they bother? He was an inert pile of putty. What possible interest could he have for anyone?

"He's awake," said one of the figures in black. "Let's get him up and dressed."

Hands gripped Weller's arms and lifted. He seemed to float effortlessly up off the cot like a big helium-filled balloon. Nothing seemed to take any effort at all. How warm and peaceful it all was!

"Come on, Weller. Let's get dressed."

Clothes seemed to slip onto his body of their own accord, like live slithering things. No effort was required of him. All he had to do was float in the warm viscous air and everything would be taken care of. Wasn't that nice? Wasn't that better than . . . than . . . whatever . . . ?

Something was fitted over his head and now he was in the middle of a fluffy white cloud, just drifting along peacefully. It was much nicer than the green room and the black figures, much more soothing, far more relaxing. He was abstractly aware that hands were gripping his arms, holding him up, guiding him along through the cloud. Or rather holding him down to keep him from drifting away into the stratosphere, for his feet seemed to be skipping featherlight over some level surface. And if they weren't holding him down, why then he would probably bounce slowly away like a big, silly beach ball.

Bounce, bounce, bounce, slowly down some stairs, losing altitude, though his head remained in the nice white cloud. Across another surface, down more stairs, another level. . . . He lost count. It began to seem as if he had been doing this for a very long time—years, maybe—as if it might continue forever. Forever? What was that? The concept seemed illusive. It had something to do with watches and hourglasses, but there were neither watches nor hourglasses up here in the clouds. . . .

Then he found himself sitting on a soft bench, with the presence of a body on either side of him. A roar and a whir, and the bench started to move. It must be a car. I must be sitting in a car. We're going for a ride. Isn't that nice?

For a long time or for a short time, at any rate definitely for *some* period of time, the car floated along, speeding up, leaning around curves, slowing down, stopping now and again, while Weller drifted peacefully in fluffy whiteness. The various motions of the car made him feel a little strange, as if there were a heavy balloon inside him, filled, perhaps, with water instead of air, so that it moved around more sluggishly with

238

the motion of the car than the rest of him, wallowing and surging.

Finally the car stopped, and the engine sound died away. Hands guided Weller out of the car and onto his feet. Then the mask was taken off his head, and he was momentarily blinded by painful bright lights.

Still half-blinded he was guided across another level surface, and by the time his eyes cleared, he was standing at the entrance ramp to a small, sleek jet aircraft with two engines at the tail, all silvery and shining in the bright smoggy sunlight.

"An airplane ride?" he said, his mouth all cottony. "Where are we going?"

The three black figures ignored the sounds that were coming out of his mouth, and they guided him up the ramp. The inside of the airplane was like a nice little living room: brown leather armchairs, some of them beside little airplane windows, others arranged around a small wooden table; wooden paneling, and a navy-blue carpet.

The three black figures guided him to one of the chairs around the table. But Weller couldn't see out a window.

"Could I have a window seat?" Weller asked politely. "They're not all taken, so could I have one, please."

"Oh, for crying out—"

"Let the man have his window seat," said the one with the steel-colored hair. "Maybe it'll keep him quiet. They told us not to give him another shot unless we really had to."

The nice man helped Weller to his feet and guided him to a soft window seat in the middle of the cabin. His body melted into the buttery cushions and seemed to fade away, so that only his eyes were left, looking out the window across a concrete runway and a field of parched grass at a tiny control tower shimmering through the gray-blue smog, far, far in the distance. Hands fastened his seat belt to keep his body from floating up out of the seat, which would make it hard for him to look out the window. They were taking good care of him. They thought of everything.

Then he heard a sudden loud roar which went on and on and on. And then the plane began to move along the ground, so slowly you could hardly tell it was happening if you weren't looking out your window, if you didn't see the control tower disappearing as the plane swung around.

The plane moved along the taxiway just like a car driving down the freeway, only much slower, as if it were creeping through rush-hour traffic, though there didn't seem to be anything else in sight. There were even white lines and symbols painted on the concrete, just like a highway.

Then the plane stopped. It pivoted like a cannon being aimed. The sound got much louder and it started to vibrate like some great beast straining at its leash. Suddenly the plane was moving again, faster and faster and faster, and then Weller felt something kick the back of his seat even as he melted further into it; there was a sudden, sharp, floating feeling that made the water balloon inside his body slosh and gurgle sending strange and not-very-pleasant waves through the clear Jell-O of his flesh.

He looked out the window and saw the ground dropping away, then tilting crazily to the right, becoming smaller and smaller and smaller. Far below he could see thousands of little toy buildings, and even little tiny toy cars moving along a toy highway. Then the world outside the window became a soft white fog for a time, just as it had been when the black figures were leading him along into the car.

When the fog cleared, Weller saw nothing but bright blue sky above and a carpet of white wool below stretching from horizon to horizon as far as he could see. It was very beautiful, and it was so incredibly peaceful, just like the white hazy feeling in his mind, just like the fluffy softness of his body melting into the seat, as featureless and undisturbed as his clear blue empty consciousness. I could drift here forever, he thought. Maybe I will. Wouldn't that be nice? His eyelids grew sensuously heavy. After awhile he couldn't tell whether his eyes were open or closed. Not that it mattered.

Sixteen

White clouds and blue sky, and sometimes, far below like a huge and beautifully made full-color map but without all the lettering and lines, visions of sere dun-colored desert, shoulders of furry green mountains, checkerboards of brown and green, moving past ever so slowly like time itself, like thick clear molasses.

Sometimes the colors would melt into warmy curvy shapes that floated and engulfed each other like amoebas. Sometimes the amoebas would devour each other, leaving only warm blue or velvety soft blackness. Sometimes he would see the dark figures seated around a table doing something with cards and stacks of money. Once in a while a face would peer into his and then become an amoeboid shape or a fluffy white cloud or just infinite blueness.

It lasted forever, or it lasted no time at all. How could he tell? Why would he want to bother? It was so pleasant just to float along through the softly moving shapes, riding the gentle swell of the infinite river of time, totally peaceful, totally calm, no ticking of watches or rapsing of sharp-edged thoughts to spoil the perfect peace of being a soft white cloud, of being nothing at all.

But then something happened to spoil it. He could feel a painful pressure where someone might have had ears, and the water balloon inside him seemed to rise unpleasantly upward.

Looking out his very own window, Weller saw the ground rushing up at him; low, wooded, rolling hills, incredibly lush and green. Then the world outside tilted and spiraled, and he saw tiny toy houses, open green fields, and a long gray line scribed on the ground, whirling up at him like a pinwheel.

The world straightened out and whooshed up at him. The model-railroad trees became real woods blossoming up just below the window, and the gray line on the ground became a concrete runway rolling arrow straight beneath the plane.

There was a hurricane sound which made him momentarily shut his eyes in confused terror and then a huge bump and more hurricane.

When he opened his eyes again, he saw that the plane was rolling to a stop in front of a low white building with a forest-green roof. Behind the building were the waving dark-green crowns of tightly packed trees. The forest extended around both edges of the building completely enclosing a large open area of thick green grass. They had landed in a huge grassy clearing in an endless wood. Wasn't that nice? The trees were full of deeply green foliage tossing gently in the wind, and the grass was like a picture postcard of an English park. It was so much greener and richer than the vegetation of Southern California that it didn't seem quite real. It was like a movie set of some African jungle, like a fairyland.

"End of the line, Weller," a voice said. Then hands were unbuckling his seat belt and guiding him down an aisle, through a door, and out into open air, incredibly fragrant with the green smells of growing things and the rich brown odor of loamy forest floor.

They guided him down a ramp, his legs very rubbery, his head reeling with the fragrant forest smells on the sudden free breezes, the expansion of the visual universe from the cramped reality of the jet to a disorienting infinity of green.

At the bottom of the ramp a bald older man dressed in white shirt and pants as if ready for a tennis match was waiting in a green golf cart. The Monitors sat Weller down beside him. The bald man smiled at him. "Welcome to the Transformational Research Institute," he said.

Weller smiled back at him but his mouth refused to form any words. The bald man scowled at the Monitors. "Fried to the eyeballs?" he said.

"Standard security procedure," said the gray-haired Monitor. "He's all yours now."

The bald man shook his head. "That will be all," he said to the Monitors, in what Weller thought was not a very friendly tone of voice. Then with a sudden lurch and a soft gentle hum, the golf cart drove off across the bright-green field toward the line of woods.

"I'm Dr. Irving Carson," the bald man said with exaggerated slowness. "I suppose it's up to me to apologize for the state you're in. Rest assured, we don't go in for such crudities here at the Institute."

Weller smiled at Dr. Carson. He wondered what Dr. Carson was apologizing for. But it all seemed much too complicated to bother with. It seemed much nicer just to enjoy the ride

242

and smell the trees than to try to figure out what all that meant.

They drove into the woods and along a complex network of concrete paths, past a series of rough wooden bungalows, a low windowless white building, and a big four-story brick structure which looked like a small, posh hotel. Through the trees, Weller glimpsed more bungalows, a swimming pool, what might have been a barn, and another low white building. The Institute seemed like a very nice place, a very private country resort for very rich people. They've sent me on a vacation to the country, Weller thought. Isn't that considerate?

The golf cart pulled up beside the entrance to a small one-story building built of rough-cut gray stone. Dr. Carson checked his watch. "Dr. Bernstein has squeezed in an hour for you in thirty minutes," he said. "But we'd better clear the cobwebs out of your mind first."

Very gently Dr. Carson led Weller out of the golf cart, took his arm, and guided him inside the stone building. The halls were painted a soothing deep yellow with rich natural-wood moldings. There were women in crisp white nurses' uniforms bustling about and men in doctor's smocks. It seemed to be some kind of small hospital, though it didn't have that awful hospital odor or that sterile hospital decor. Weller was sure he was going to like the Institute if even the hospital was so nice and cozy.

Dr. Carson led him into a small examining room filled with medical cabinets, instruments, and strange lamps. But it was painted a bright royal blue and had pretty pictures on the walls, so Weller was not at all uneasy as Dr. Carson sat him down on the edge of the examining table. This was such a nice place that he was sure the people would be very understanding and friendly and that no one would hurt him.

Dr. Carson took a hypodermic out of an autoclave, went to one of the cabinets, and came back with a vial and a cotton swab. He stuck the needle through the rubber top of the vial and filled it with clear fluid. He swabbed the pit of Weller's right arm. "This won't hurt at all," he said, and stuck the needle into a vein.

As Dr. Carson slowly depressed the plunger of the hypodermic, a hard cold sensation moved up Weller's arm, across his shoulder, and into his head. Something like cotton candy began to melt away in his mind, slowly replacing itself with a dull, throbbing ache. His consciousness seemed to sink back into his body, and he became aware that all his muscles were aching and trembling. A terrible feeling of weariness came over him.

By the time Carson had withdrawn the hypodermic, Weller was shaking with fatigue, his eyeballs burned, his brain seemed to be trying to beat its way out of his skull, his mouth tasted like a toilet bowl, and a black rage was boiling through him. I've been drugged! he thought. I've been fried out of my mind for hours! How long has it been? Where the hell is this place . . . ? New York! Jesus, I've been stoned out of my mind clear across the country! Son of a bitch!

"How do you feel now?" Carson asked.

"*How do I feel?*" Weller snarled. "You bastards pump me full of downers and you ask me how I feel? I feel like I've swallowed a quart of Lysol, you son of a bitch! My head is killing me!" A sudden wave of nausea passed through him and his head swam with vertigo. "Jesus . . . ," he groaned.

Carson smiled fatuously. "Well, at least you're obviously no longer sedated," he said. "Please understand that we at the Institute don't approve of these crude Monitor tactics."

"Fuck you," Weller moaned. I think I'm going to puke, he decided. I wish I could cut my fucking head off.

Nothing fazed Dr. Carson. "You're going to be surprised at all the advances we've made here," he said, going to one of the cabinets, taking out a bottle of green liquid, and pouring two inches of it into a water glass.

"You might as well begin your education with this," he said, handing the glass to Weller. "Go ahead, drink it. You'll feel much better."

Weller eyed the poisonous-looking stuff suspiciously. "What is it?" he said. "Rat poison?"

"Something for your head," Carson replied. "A massive dose of megavitamins. Plus a mixture of amino acids, MAO inhibitors, alkaloids, L-dopa, and central-nervous-system stimulators. Replaces depleted enzymes. Tones up the synapses. Raises the biochemistry of the brain to optimum function. We call it eptifier. Go ahead, drink it. Satisfaction guaranteed."

Weller sighed. Even a dose of cyanide would improve how he felt at this point. Resignedly he gulped down the green liquid. It tasted like cod-liver oil mixed with hair tonic.

"I don't feel any different," he said belligerently.

"You will," Carson said. "It takes a few minutes to metabolize." He checked his watch. "We've got to meet Dr. Bernstein

244

now," he said. "You'll be a new man before we reach his office."

By the time they had reached the golf cart, Weller was beginning to feel almost human; at least he could walk without vertigo, was no longer in imminent danger of barfing, and his pounding headache had receded to a vague broken-glass feeling in his brain.

Carson drove off in the general direction of the big brick main buildings, past bungalows, two low white buildings, the swimming pool, tennis courts.

"This place used to be a private resort for the idle rich," he said. "Institute Central was the main hotel. Most of the buildings you see were here when we bought the place. All we've had to build are a few lab buildings and the computer complex. There was even an airstrip, though the runway had to be lengthened and resurfaced to take John's Learjet. Still, it was an ideal purchase. As far as the outside world knows, it's still a private resort, and even most of the security set up was already in place."

Carson smiled at Weller confidentially. "I believe the original owners were Mafia connected," he said. "Who else would've had the estate already enclosed by electrified barbed-wire fencing and had guard-dog kennels already set up? As I understand it, even our Dobermans and Shepherds were bred from stock they threw into the deal."

Perhaps it was the fresh air, or perhaps the Institute really *had* developed a magic hangover cure, for Weller found that his mind was becoming crystal clear. It was obvious to him that Carson's chatty little talk was coldly calculated to casually inform him that this place was under very tight security, that he could forget about just walking out whenever he pleased.

Realizing that, and realizing how alertly he had perceived it, he also realized that his headache was now gone, along with his vertigo, his nausea, his muscular tremors, and even his fatigue. Even the cruddy taste in his mouth was fading away. He could feel and enjoy the intermittent warm sunlight dappling his skin through the trees and smell the heady wet perfume of an eastern forest, so unlike the dry chapparal of Southern California. Birds chirped music in the treetops, and his eyes caught them flitting from branch to branch. Goddamn it, he was beginning to feel not merely recovered, but physically great and mentally alive.

245

"You ought to package that stuff as Instant Hangover Cure," he told Carson. "You could make millions."

"Oh, it's much more than that," Carson said. "For now we don't want to call public attention to the Institute. But Dr. Bernstein will brief you. Arthur's not only the director, he set the place up. It's as much his baby as John's."

They had reached the main building: a rambling four-story brick structure with a big glassed-in portico, and a main entrance facade done up with pseudo-Georgian white columns. Carson drove around to the side of the building where another golf cart was parked beside a round redwood table. Sitting at the table was a slightly built man in his sixties in tan chinos and matching bush shirt, with thin birdlike features and long, unruly white hair, looking for all the world like a mad scientist from central casting.

The old man got up as they pulled up beside him and got out of the golf cart. "Ah, Mr. Weller," he said, extending a bony hand. "I'm Arthur Bernstein. I trust you've recovered from your trip well enough to take the ten-penny tour. John wants to get you oriented as quickly as possible for some mysterious reason, and this is my only free time for two days."

Weller shook Bernstein's hand perfunctorily, studying the old man's face. Though Bernstein spoke in a high, rapid voice and seemed to tremble with nervous energy or perhaps merely the frailness of age, there was something calm and oceanic about his cool green eyes, as if some vaster and entirely different being inhabited this ancient fleshly envelope.

"No thanks to the Monitors," Weller said. "But I've got to admit that the stuff Dr. Carson gave me is something else again."

Bernstein cocked an eyebrow at Carson.

"Formula three," Carson said.

Bernstein nodded. "Good enough for a start," he said. "Monitor security measures aren't exactly designed to insure mental clarity," he told Weller. "But then, that's their business and enhancing consciousness is ours, hmmm? It all balances out. Well, we'd better get started. As usual, my schedule is terribly tight."

With a dismissive nod to Carson he led Weller to the other golf cart and drove around to the main drive at the front of the building. "John tells me you're highly motivated, Mr. Weller," he said. "Excellent. You won't be disappointed. We're at the cutting edge of human knowledge here. The

246

Institute is the essence of Transformationalism—our goal is nothing less than the total understanding of human consciousness on a rigorous scientific level, and no expense has been spared to give us the means of achieving it. You're a lucky man to be here, Mr. Weller."

It had all come out rapid-fire and flawlessly like an often-repeated guidebook spiel, but Weller sensed that Bernstein was sincere; that he could not even entertain the notion that anyone else did not share his dedication to his work. The movies' traditional mad scientist—except there was no disheveled aura of crankiness about him.

Bernstein abruptly stopped the golf cart in front of a low windowless white building. "This is our computer complex," he said. "The logical place to begin."

He led Weller into the building through a double-doored, airtight vestibule, down a gleaming white hallway, and into a huge room. Reels of tape spun on memory units. Card-punch machines and automatic typewriters clattered. Numbers, curves, and shapes flickered on dozens of assorted cathode-ray tubes. A dozen white-smocked technicians scampered around busily like the machine tenders of *Metropolis*. The exciting electric odor of ozone hummed in the air. Whatever this place actually *did*, Weller had to admit, it certainly would make the ideal set for a movie about itself.

"The sum total of the most advanced human knowledge about the mind and its workings is stored and correlated here," Bernstein said, with the ardor of a doting grandfather. "The memory banks are updated daily, so we can call up a realtime picture of where we stand at any moment. It all comes through here."

Bernstein sat down in front of a typewriter with a screen display. "I'll show you," he said. He typed a few lines. "Brainwave change correlations with eptifier formula twelve," he said, as columns of figures appeared on the screen. "The molecular structure of RNA." A helical chemical diagram replaced the numbers. "Yesterday's creativity curve of Frederick Conners." A spiky curve replaced the chemical diagram.

"And so forth," Bernstein said, looking back and up at Weller.

"I'm afraid all this is Greek to me," Weller said.

"Oh?" Bernstein said, surprised for some reason. "I thought you were going to be filming some of our activities for the archives," he said. "I had assumed John sent for a man with the technical background."

Is *that* what I'm supposed to be here for? Weller wondered. Or is Steinhardt not above even telling *this* character some cover story? Something told him he should keep his mouth as shut as possible.

"My technical background is in film making," he said. "I guess John felt it would be easier to brief a professional film maker on the technicalities than to make a director out of some scientist."

Bernstein looked at him most peculiarly. "I see," he said. Suddenly, for no discernible reason, he was nervous.

He stood up and seemed to distance himself inside a professorial persona. "I'll try to keep it in layman's terms then," he said, waving his arms for emphasis, almost as if he were on a lectern. "Here at the Institute we are experimenting in many areas. We're trying to obtain as total a description of human consciousness as possible. The structure of the brain. The biochemistry of the mind. The electronic nature of thought and mental states themselves. We are quite close to our first-stage goal, a rigorous scientific model of total human consciousness, a biophysics of the mind."

He leaned against the typewriter console, more for emphasis than for support. "In this computer everything we have learned is stored and constantly updated as we learn more. This computer also does the necessary calculations for all of our various projects." He thumped the console affectionately.

"But this computer contains much more than even that," he said, a far away look coming into his oceanic green eyes. "It contains a complete systems model of what we now know of human consciousness. A subprogram simulates the biochemistry of the brain, another simulates brainwave patterns, yet others simulate sight, vision, smell, all the human sensory imput. And so forth. Everything that interacts to form human consciousness can be made to interact electronically here in patterns and combinations of our choosing. Are you following me so far, Mr. Weller?"

"I'm not sure," Weller said. "Sounds to me like you're playing with one of those intelligent computers that get temperamental and take over the world. I may not be a scientist, but I've sure seen the movie."

"*Artificial intelligence?*" Bernstein snorted. "Pointless rubbish! We're not trying to imitate the human mind with some clumsy simulacrum. We're using a computer simulation of how the human mind works so that we can learn how to make it work better. We test our experimental results against our computer model of consciousness to see whether our inputs make its outputs simulate the known human patterns. If they do, we know we have learned something, and if they don't, we know we have to update our model."

He smiled a fatuous, reassuring smile at Weller. "Rest assured, Mr. Weller," he said. "We're not replicating Dr. Frankenstein's monster in electronic software. We're simply using the latest computer technology to maximize the efficiency of our research and development programs. If those fools at the Pentagon did the same, they'd save the taxpayers ten times over the cost of financing this work."

From the vehemence of the sudden shift Weller got the feeling that Bernstein had had some frustrating experience with the military-industrial complex at some point in his past.

"I gather you've worked for the Pentagon then?" Weller asked.

Bernstein did a short take and hurriedly ignored the question. "And now I think you'd like to see some of what we are actually doing in concrete terms, wouldn't you, Mr. Weller?" he said. "There's really nothing here to actually see, is there, after all? Nothing that would make for dramatic film. And that's what you're here to do—isn't it, Mr. Weller?"

"Yeah," Weller said, unable to fathom why Bernstein had become almost fearful of him. Could it be more Monitor paranoia, even at this level? Even the director of the Institute has to watch over his shoulder for secret Monitor agents?

"Shall we continue the ten-penny tour?" Weller said, amusing himself with a slightly authoritative tone that did indeed seem to keep Bernstein guessing. "I'm sure your time is valuable."

Bernstein whisked Weller around to about a dozen assorted laboratories within the next hour, exactly like a plant manager showing what he imagined were choice locations to the commercial director sent down to him from the home office to film his premises. Long on scenes where people were doing outré things with exotic equipment, but short on specific information as to what was really going on.

There were three or four chemical laboratories full of glass tubing, electronic instruments, and foul smells. According to Bernstein they were experimenting with brain biochemistry.

What did that mean?

They were experimenting with chemical enhancement of consciousness.

"Why, Dr. Bernstein," Weller chided, as they stood in one of the bubbling alchemist laboratories surrounded by tables of incredibly complex glassworks, "you mean you're inventing new kinds of psychedelic drugs?"

Bernstein almost physically flinched. "Psychedelic drugs are to what we are doing here as a witch doctor is to a brain surgeon," he said indignantly. "You're not alone, Mr. Weller. Most people have difficulty distinguishing science from witchcraft in this area. As witness the impossibility of getting research grants from the government or from industry. Only John Steinhardt has had the vision to support this work. Everyone else has assumed that I'd be concocting mind poisons for rebellious youth."

"You've got to admit that seems like a fine distinction to a layman like me," Weller said. "Are you saying you're *not* inventing new ways to get stoned?"

"Get stoned?" Bernstein snapped. "What an archaic, useless concept! Is that what you felt today when you drank the eptifier, Mr. Weller? Stoned? High? Disoriented? Hallucinative? I think not!"

"Was that stuff developed here?" Weller said, suitably impressed.

"Of course it was," Bernstein said. "We're not interested in strange new alkaloids that produces random disorientation. All human consciousness exists in a biochemical matrix. Therefore there must be chemical differences in the brains of ordinary men, morons, and geniuses, for example. Our goal here is nothing less than to develop the chemical means of giving every human being on the Earth the brain metabolism of a charismatic, creative, visionary genius."

"Like John?" Weller said half humorously. How Faustian could you get?

"Like John," Bernstein answered, in utter dead earnest. "Beyond John. There is no reason why we cannot go beyond the raising of the mass consciousness to the level of the best of us. Someday we will know enough to go beyond eptifying what we evolved with and create the biochemical base for a whole new level of human consciousness that has never existed before. True Transformational Man."

"Are you really serious?" Weller asked.

"Of course, I'm serious," Bernstein said. "Don't you find that your mind is working as well now as it ever has? Isn't that proof that we have at least begun the process?"

250

Considering that he had had the mind of a carrot not too long ago, Weller had to admit that his head seemed to be rolling along in high gear. He had been able to grasp most of what Bernstein was talking about once the technical jargon had been left behind. He had picked up the man's Monitor paranoia and even played with it. He had sussed out that Bernstein had worked for the Pentagon, had been unable to get research grants for this kind of work from the usual sources, and thus was grateful to Steinhardt for backing him. But not grateful enough, apparently, to trust him entirely. Not bad, Weller, not bad.

"I guess you have a point, Doctor," he said.

From there, Bernstein had grown a little less hostile, a little less contemptuous, though his nervousness remained. At least he stopped assuming that Weller was skeptical of everything he saw. And for his part, Weller was beginning to question his own skepticism too.

There were dissecting laboratories filled with bottled brains and sensory-deprivation tanks and huge human-sized mazes with moving walls and strange optical effects controlled from a central console and so many other things that he had seen so fast that it all became a blur. It was clear that Transformationalism had spent tens of millions of dollars setting up this place. It was not clear at all how they could possibly expect to return a profit on the investment, which certainly could not be said of any other of John B. Steinhardt's manifold enterprises.

Bernstein himself might be a little weird, a little defensively self-righteous, a little afraid of phantom Monitors, maybe even a little nuts in spots, but he did seem to be sincere about what he was doing. If anything, a little *too* sincere. And the wonders he was predicting seemed more and more possible as Weller got a fuller and fuller picture of how many people were working here, how many projects they were running, and how much this must be setting Steinhardt back. One thing Transformationalism didn't seem to be into was expenditure without results.

Was this what really lay at the heart of Transformationalism? A dedicated effort to advance the level of human consciousness with Steinhardt's own psychic Manhattan Project? Was it possible? But how could something really worthwhile come out of the cynical scams, the broken lives, the power trips, the mind-control numbers, the fascist secret-police methods of the Monitors? How could you make gold out of shit? How could you advance human consciousness by screwing up human minds?

The tour was almost over, and they were about to enter the building where the biofeedback labs that had developed the brainwave monitor were located. Bernstein and Weller were getting along at least to the point where Bernstein had started to notice Weller's mood.

He paused, touched Weller on the arm, studied his face for a moment, and said, "You seem a bit confused, Mr. Weller. Are you having trouble understanding what you're seeing?"

"In a way."

"Well, is there anything you'd like me to clarify for you before we wind things up? This will be our last stop, and I can only give you about another seven minutes of my time."

Weller laughed. "There's plenty I'd like you to clarify for me," he snapped, "but I doubt if you can."

"Try me," Bernstein said, giving him a grandfatherly look with those big eyes.

Well, here I am at the Institute, Weller thought. If I'm not going to be me now, I don't know when else I will. Try me, the man says . . . ?

"All right, Dr. Bernstein, I'll try you. Don't you ever think about justifying what you're doing to yourself? While you're playing with your fancy scientific toys, don't you ever think about what pays for them?"

Bernstein slammed the inquiry shut like an angry clam. "I would think that the justification for our work would be self-evident to anyone with a modicum of intelligence."

"I'm not talking about what you're trying to accomplish, Dr. Bernstein," Weller said. "For the sake of argument, let's say I'm sold on that." He paused, pondered for a moment. Bernstein was obviously sincerely dedicated to what he was doing, perhaps too dedicated, judging from his little dig at the Pentagon. But he also had expressed distaste for Monitor methods and seemed to have a certain fear of them. If nothing else, it would be interesting, perhaps ultimately useful, to find out where he really stood.

"I'm talking about Transformationalism," Weller said.

"*Transformationalism?*" Bernstein's expression became distant again, guarded.

Leave us not be too obvious, Weller thought. "Look, you apparently worked for the Pentagon," he said, "and I doubt somehow that you were truly dedicated to the military aspect of the work. You probably didn't give much thought to that; all you were interested in was the funding. Now you're being funded by Transformationalism. How about leveling with me? Do you give a damn about the people whose money is supporting your work now?"

Now Bernstein was obviously furious at something, but he kept his rage under tight control. "I get the feeling you're a Monitor, Mr. Weller," he said, biting off his words.

"Oh, come on, Doctor. Would John send someone to spy on *you*?"

Bernstein just snorted.

"So you yourself feel that your dedication to Transformationalism might be questioned?" Weller said devilishly.

"All right, whoever you are," Bernstein said, "if this is going to get back to John, then let it. John knows that he and I have a working relationship, a quid pro quo, that I am not a worshiper of his and never will be. That was made clear and agreed to at the outset. We both know that, don't we, so shall we stop playing games? I'm doing exactly what I said I would. John has no reason to question my loyalty, and I resent being grilled like this."

"You just told me you'll never been a worshiper of John, and in the next breath you tell me he has no reason to question your loyalty?" Weller said.

"Don't play your little Monitor games with me!" Bernstein said shrilly. "I know more about the mind than your kind will ever dream of knowing."

"But Dr. Bernstein, I never said I was a Monitor," Weller said. "I'm not a Monitor. I'm making a film. I'm just trying to get some depth in my material. Honest. Really."

"Just as you say," Bernstein said coldly. "Shall we conclude our innocent little tour then?"

So saying, Bernstein turned and trotted into the biofeedback building, forcing Weller to tag along at his heels and terminate the conversation. I'm not sure why I'm doing this, Weller mused, but it's beginning to get a little interesting.

Bernstein whisked him in and out of a series of electronic workshops and laboratories, where brainwave monitors were being assembled from crated parts, where lab technicians were working on scratch-built experimental models, where other electronic esoterica were being fiddled with.

"Our earlier work with biofeedback led to the brainwave monitor," Bernstein told him. "Or rather we went to biofeedback principles to invent what John was looking for."

"The brainwave monitor was John's idea, not yours, then?" Weller asked, as Bernstein led him down a long blue hallway.

"I've never claimed otherwise," Bernstein said defensively, but also with a strange tinge of contempt. "John wanted an impressive-looking device that would scientifically measure mental states. He told me forthrightly that the processee's belief in the credibility of the brainwave monitor was what counted. As he put it, 'It would also be nice if it kind of worked. But whether it does or not, I need it in three months.' "

Bernstein shook his head, and now he seemed to be talking half to himself. "Those were the parameters. It then became a simple matter of turning biofeedback machines into a kind of lie detector. After all, a lie detector is a crude attempt to measure mental states indirectly. It measures skin resistance and breathing rate and so forth, which measures physical stress, and if you assume that physical stress correlates with mental stress, you at least have a machine that tells you when a question is making someone nervous."

"That seems pretty crude to me," Weller said. "And it's not admissable evidence in court in many places."

Bernstein didn't look at Weller, but his voice sharpened, as if he were talking to a bright student who had just made an intelligent point. "Of course. It doesn't at all get at what's going on in the brain. The electroencephalograph does that, gives you a picture of the brainwaves, and biofeedback work proves that brainwave patterns have some correlation with mental states because it shows that people can learn to change their brainwave patterns on a screen by meditating, or deliberately thinking hostile thoughts, for example."

Bernstein paused outside a heavy steel door. He looked up at Weller, and for the moment at least seemed to forget that he thought Weller was a Monitor. "So you see, it was really a rather simple matter to turn a standard multichannel biofeedback machine into the brainwave monitor. About all I had to do was turn the screen around so that the processor was watching it rather than the subject whose brain was wired into it. In fact, as you've seen, we put the things together out of standard biofeedback components, for the most part. John's idea was the main thing, what I did was rather an obvious solution to the technical problem."

"But does the thing really work?"

Bernstein shrugged. "At least it does *something*," he said.

"After all, thought is an electronic phenomenon in the brain, so in theory such a device should be possible."

"*In theory?* You mean the brainwave monitor is a phony?"

Strangely Bernstein didn't slip back into his Monitor paranoia. Somehow Weller had gotten him onto his professional program. "The brainwave monitor does give us data on what's going on inside the brain," he said. "Interpreting it coherently is the problem. We don't yet know enough to judge whether the thing does what we say it does or not."

"You mean not even *you* know whether it's real or a phony?"

"Precisely, my dear Mr. Weller," Bernstein said, putting his hand on the knob of the heavy steel door. "That's why we're running many of our projects here on determining relationships between brainwaves and mental states. On John's direct orders. We don't know what we have ourselves."

Something ironic came into his attitude. "Now in here," he said, "we have something else that's eating up a lot of time and money *at John's direct order*." Was Bernstein trying to say something to Steinhardt through what he supposed was a Monitor overseer? That he himself thought that Steinhardt was wasting his time on crackpot schemes? That Steinhardt should realize that it was after all *his own* money he was wasting, along with the time of busy scientists?

Bernstein led him into a small, stark cubicle like a projectionist's booth. One whole wall of the room was a heavy window overlooking a larger room where, of all things, some kind of unreal concert was going on. A piano player, a saxophonist, a drummer, and a guitarist were jamming silently behind the soundproof glass. Each of them wore a brainwave monitor headband, trailing a long wire which was plugged into a bank of electronic consoles lined up behind them like monster amps. The consoles had four oscilloscopes wired into them. Four white-smocked technicians were studying them intently, fiddling with controls. A fifth technician was supervising the group—not the musicians but the control technicians.

"What on God's green Earth is *that*?" Weller exclaimed.

"*That*," Bernstein said, "is our latest project. "An attempt to reverse the brainwave monitor. If specific brainwave patterns correlate with specific mental states, why can't you induce specific mental states by transmitting their electronic patterns *into* the brain? So here we have a group of jazz musicians improvising. Each one is receiving controlled electronic input into his brain, and the patterns of various mental state models

255

are tried. Can we make the saxophone player more creative? Can we give the piano a depressive chord structure? Can we make the drummer pound out an angry beat?"

"Push-button brainwashing," Weller whispered. "A goddamn mind-fucking machine!"

"I suppose it might be," Bernstein said dryly. "If it worked."

"It doesn't work? Then why are you doing it?"

"This project is being pushed forward on John's *direct orders*," Bernstein said, making the last two words a disclaimer of any responsibility of his own. "He thought of the idea, and he believes in it. This isn't all of it either; we're doing the same thing with other areas of creative work, among other things. It's quite an extensive series of projects."

"Which you, I gather, think are a wasted effort."

Bernstein snapped back into his official shell, as if he were addressing Steinhardt through a supposed Monitor but was determined to get his displeasure through without crossing some invisible line. "The idea has merit and possibilities, but it's about twenty years premature. We don't even know to what extent the brainwave monitor works, and here we are trying to program thought processes through electronic wave patterns. It's like trying to do chemistry before you've figured out the nature of the atom.

"But then, John was a science-fiction writer, *not* a scientist. He could brilliantly visualize an inevitable scientific development long before the state of knowledge necessary to bring it about. Ten or twenty years from now this kind of thing will be possible here at the Institute, and then this work will have to all be done over again anyway. Right now. . . ."

He shrugged. "John is as entitled to his obsessions as I am to mine," he said. "After all, he's paying for both."

With that he opened the door and ushered Weller back into the hallway. "And that concludes the time I have to spare, Mr. Weller," he said. "I'll drive you to Institute Central, where, I understand, there is a temporary room waiting for you. I hope I've been informative."

"Oh, you have, Dr. Bernstein, you have," Weller said. Bernstein gave him another nervous look, and they walked back to the golf cart in uneasy silence.

"There's just one thing," Weller said, as he climbed into the cart beside Bernstein. "A while back you told me John had no reason to question your loyalty. Yet apparently you think his pet project here is wasting your time. I mean, what kind of loyalty is that?"

Bernstein stared at Weller. His eyes flashed through anger and then seemed to glide upward onto some plane of oceanic calm, beyond Monitor paranoia. "The only kind of loyalty that's worth anything," he said. "Honest loyalty.

"Mr. Weller," he said, starting the golf cart, "awhile back you also asked me about my moral position on where my funding came from. Well, now I'll tell you. Before I met John Steinhardt, I had a vision of transforming human consciousness, and no hope of bringing it about."

They drove past the computer complex and out onto a main pathway, past labs and bungalows and guard-dog kennels and who knew what else. "I dreamed of a facility like this and the freedom to use it," Bernstein said. "But what I was actually doing was pitiful and frustrating. I spent years working in inadequate laboratories niggardly financed by poverty-stricken universities. I spent years working for military psychological-warfare units. For a time I was even reduced to doing motivational research for an advertising agency."

He waved an arm as if to embrace the entire Institute. "And then John came along," he said. "A man who also had a vision of the further evolution of human consciousness, maybe not the same vision, but at least a vision. But John wasn't like me. Somehow he knew how to apply his vision to the real world. He knew how to make money. He already had vast financial resources. And he was willing to use them."

Around a gentle bend in the path the brick main building became visible behind a low copse of trees. "Mr. Weller, have you ever heard of a government or a corporation spending millions of dollars to advance scientific development purely out of a desire to advance the course of knowledge and better the human condition? I haven't. Only John B. Steinhardt is doing that without any foreseeable hope of turning a profit."

They reached the front of Institute Central. Bernstein stopped the golf cart and turned to Weller. "And you can doubt my real loyalty to John?" he said contemptuously. "I don't have to agree with all his methods to be loyal to him, I don't have to believe that he always knows what he's talking about, and I don't even have to understand his motives. Because I don't care if he's doing it to feed his ego or leave a monument to posterity or achieve scientific respectability by validating his own pet crackpot theories or make himself more powerful or all of them. My loyalty to John is based entirely on the fact that we share a common goal which both of us believe is of transcendent importance."

He looked Weller full in the face but seemed to speak through him to someone else, to Steinhardt. "As far as I'm concerned, that makes any other differences irrelevant. And I trust John still feels the same way."

"Oh, I'm sure he does," Weller said, climbing down from the golf cart. "I don't think you have anything to worry about."

"I'm glad to hear that," Bernstein said. He turned on the golf cart's electric engine. "I hope I've helped you with your film," he said. "I will see you again when you're ready to shoot this film, won't I, Mr. Weller? You will be shooting a film, won't you?"

"You'll have to ask John that," Weller said. "He's the boss."

"I understand the message," Bernstein said peculiarly, and he drove off leaving Weller to wonder what message he had just transmitted from the ectoplasmic Steinhardt.

Seventeen

After having dropped out of an airplane in a drugged stupor directly into a guided tour by the director of the Institute himself, Weller was abruptly left dangling in limbo for a night and day and a night again. Perhaps it was some kind of Transformational lesson or perhaps a bureaucratic screw-up or perhaps just sheer indifference.

His room here was a far cry from his crummy hole at the Los Angeles Transformation Center. Pine paneling, thick green carpeting, a comfortable bed, even a color television set which not only brought in all the New York stations, but gave call-up access to a library of Transformationalist tapes. The closet and chest had even been filled with new clothing, and what was more, the stuff fitted him. If he were a prisoner, this was the Alcatraz Hilton.

That night Weller ate Beef Wellington and Peach Melba in the Institute Central commissary, laid out much like the grim dining room at the center, but with white tablecloths, softer lighting, a gourmet menu, and a small choice of wines.

This was definitely a more clannish crowd, the favored few at the Institute. Nobody tried to force themselves on Weller here. Far from it. There were tables of middle-aged people in white smocks, a blue-jean crowd, hard-noses who might be Monitors or security guards, and they didn't even seem to mix much with each other.

Eating in isolation, Weller had the feeling that he was totally cut off from the internal lines of communication of the Institute and would be until some word came down from the Man. People weren't going to talk to strangers here unless they were officially introduced.

And when he went back to his room, he realized that he was totally cut off from the world outside as well. There was no phone in the room. He hadn't noticed that before. In fact, when he thought about it, he realized that he hadn't seen a phone anywhere in Institute Central. Well, that figured. With barbed-wire fences, guard dogs, body searches, and security guards, the Institute could hardly be expected to have pay phones to the rest of the world for its inmates. The Alcatraz Hilton was exactly what it was.

Enough was enough for one day, and he fell asleep almost before he hit the pillow. He would face tomorrow when it came.

But the next morning, after a late breakfast in the nearly empty commissary, what he found he had to face was nothing and lots of it. There was something called the "Directive Desk" in what had been the lobby of the hotel and behind it was an earnest young girl in white, with bright young eyes and a slightly ravaged complexion.

"Is this where someone might leave a message for me?" Weller asked her.

"A message?"

"Yeah. I just got here and I don't have the faintest idea of where I'm supposed to go or what I'm supposed to do or if I'm to report to someone. No one bothered to tell me."

"Well, let's see if we have any updated directives for you, Mr. . . . ?"

"Weller, Jack Weller."

She checked a grid work of cubbyholes with nameplates above them. "If there is one, it's here," she said.

She came back with a single sheet of paper that she had taken from one of the cubbies. "Here it is, Mr. Weller!" she said brightly. She read from the paper. "Operant directive, Jack Weller, until further updating. Await next directive. Provisional Q-level privileges. There you are!"

"Where is that?" Weller said. "What does it mean?"

"Oh, it's quite simple. You're free to do whatever you want until you get a new directive, which will probably come through here. Within Q-level restrictions, of course."

"*Q-level restrictions?*"

"Full commissary privileges," the girl recited. "No phone privileges. No admission to restricted areas without a specific directive to the contrary. No unauthorized communication with permanent personnel." She smiled at Weller. "It's like being on vacation," she said. "We have a pool and a tennis court and lots of woods to walk in. Relax and enjoy yourself."

"Swell," Weller grumbled. Don't call us, we'll call you. I didn't exactly come here to go swimming and walk in the woods, he thought. Well, maybe it might be worthwhile to take a look around.

Without a golf cart the Institute suddenly became a much

bigger place, a small town spread out thin over many acres of woodland. Weller found that on foot it was very difficult to gather an overall image of its totality. Wandering up the main path that Bernstein had driven him down the day before, the buildings and facilities no longer seemed so crowded together, there was no sense of a "Main Street" or even a university quad. The hilly landscape had been left more or less intact, and the woods that covered it had only been sheared away where a building or a path needed the empty space. Everything was half concealed by the hills and hollows of the landscape and heavily shrouded by thick copses of trees.

And for the population that this place must have, there were precious few people to be seen wandering the grounds. Most of the buildings that Weller passed had signs out front that said, "Admittance Under Directive Only." He got the feeling that that applied to just about every individual part of the whole. Computer people couldn't get into chemical laboratories. The biofeedback labs would be closed to biochemists. There was probably a whole volunteer army of Transformationalist slavies doing the necessary dirty work who couldn't get into anything but the facilities set aside specifically for them.

"Q-level restrictions" seemed to mean that he was limited to Institute Central, the old resort facilities, and the open paths and woodlands. Look, but don't try to touch.

Hardly in the mood for swimming or tennis, Weller decided that the most useful way to kill time would be to walk through as much of the Institute as he could. He might run into Annie. And if nothing else, it would tire him out, which might be an aid to turning his mind off, not a bad thing when all you can do at the moment is grind your mental gears.

So he wandered off the main path into the woods, trying to keep more or less in a straight line so that he could eventually come to an edge of the property, the first logical step of any foot survey. He followed a path going in his direction past a lab and some bungalows, then reentered the woods when it veered away to the right.

It took him about ten minutes of walking on the shaded brown earth of the woods to reach the fence.

It instantly flashed him an image of a prison camp. The woods abruptly ended in a defoliated zone ten yards wide. A rectilinear spider web of thin wires formed a ten foot high fence between where Weller stood at the edge of the woods and the clear zone. A similar fence ran along the other side of the zone where the woods began again. This triple barrier of electrified fence and cleared zone seemed to go all around the property line. Weller walked alongside it, up and down hills, around bends, until by the changing position of the sun, he could tell he had circled the whole grounds.

Twice he saw uniformed and conspicuously armed guards zipping along inside the fenced zone in golf carts. He instinctively melted back into the woods at their approach. Once he saw a pack of Dobermans patroling in the fenced-off zone, sniffing and reconnoitering as if it were their territory. They dashed snarling and yowling up to the fence as they got a whiff of him, and Weller ran off deep into the woods until the pack sounds died away.

Carson wasn't kidding about the security. Although the Institute was all woods and tennis courts, it was sealed off like a military outpost. The bucolic setting only cleverly masked the fact from inquiring outside eyes.

Weller went back to Institute Central for lunch after completing an entire circuit of the barrier without finding a break. Even the airstrip was inside of it.

After lunch he followed paths at random to see how much of the network he could cover on foot, since, presumably these paths went everywhere.

He came upon several areas within the Institute grounds that were sealed off from the rest of the place by their own fenced perimeter, though here the barrier was a simple, high barbed-wire fence, and no prowling dogs were in evidence. These sealed compounds included a colony of small bungalows surrounding a low white building in a shaded hollow, a motor pool and security area, and a low house of gray stone capped with a huge, shimmering geodesic dome.

Each of these compounds had a single gate and the guards looked like standard-model Monitors without visible armament. Within the Institute grounds, apparently, it was assumed that fences would be respected.

Weller spent a long afternoon wandering about in this methodical fashion, but what struck him was how little he was actually able to see: the outsides of buildings, the fences around other buildings, occasional people in golf carts humming by like lords of the manor, and one or two peculiar looks as they passed.

It was eerie. A velvet-lined prison camp through which he was allowed to wander at will as long as he didn't try to get into anything. He was totally cut off from contact with the outside world and any realistic hope of physical escape, and at least at the moment he was cut off from any real contact with what was going on within the world of the Institute too. They could keep him in this state forever if they wanted to—cut off from the outside world, unable to find Annie, unable to see Steinhardt, eating three fine meals a day, and haunting the Institute grounds like a ghost.

After a heavy solitary dinner of tournedos of beef and a full bottle of Burgundy, Weller took an after-dinner walk, feeling more like a ghost than ever in the clear dark night full of towering trees and intermittent bright starlight.

Maybe this is Transformationalism's final solution to the Jack Weller problem, he thought. Maybe all I've succeeded into doing is talking my way into John Steinhardt's version of jail.

That thought was just a little too scary out there in the lonely darkness, and it drove him indoors, into the light, into his room, where he further removed himself from any more paranoid contemplation of his real situation by gorking himself out in front of the tube until he felt tired enough to fall into what he earnestly hoped would be dreamless sleep.

Weller was abruptly jolted into wakefulness by an insistent pounding at the door to his room. Blinking sleep from his eyes, he staggered out of bed and pulled on a pair of shorts, noticing blearily that the sun was just rising over the tree line outside his window, filling the world with a grim, gray early morning light.

Furry-mouthed and evil-tempered, he opened the door and grunted, "Yeah?"

A burly man in a black T-shirt and jeans stood there looking horribly awake and impatient. What the hell did he want at this ungodly hour?

"*John* has invited you to have breakfast with him at his house," the man said with infuriating politeness. "Within the half hour," he added more authoritatively. "Get shaved and dressed. I'll wait for you out here."

"Urrr . . . ," Weller grunted and closed the door. Christ, he thought, dragging himself into the bathroom, and I'm half-asleep. No doubt the son of a bitch planned it that way!

He took a quick shower, shaved, brushed his teeth, combed his hair, pissed, and put on white ducks and a blue short-sleeved shirt. By the time he had finished, his mind was more or less awake, though he found himself wishing for a belt of that magic brain stimulant Carson had given him. He felt alert enough to face an ordinary day's work with equanimity, but confronting John B. Steinhardt over breakfast seemed to call for an eptified state of mind of which he still didn't feel capable.

The Monitor was still waiting in the hall. He took Weller to a waiting golf cart and drove over to the fenced-off compound that enclosed the gray stone house capped with the geodesic dome. The morning chill and the heatless rising sun began to shock Weller's brain into fuller wakefulness as a guard passed them through the gate and the golf cart pulled up beside the building's entrance.

The Monitor led Weller into the house through a quite ordinary doorway and into a large vestibule faced with living rock. Beyond he could see a short hall that opened into a living room with an enormous Henry-Moore-looking sculpture as a centerpiece. On the wall of the vestibule, hanging slightly off-center, was a single, small Cubist oil painting; the signature was that of Pablo Picasso. A spiral staircase, all hand-rubbed brass, led upward into a blaze of sunlight.

"John's waiting for you up there," the Monitor said, pointing to the spiral staircase. "I stay here."

Nervously Weller ascended the staircase into a confusion of plants, sunlight, and chaos.

From the inside the dome was entirely transparent; the sun was a great ball of pale orange fire illuminating the eastern half of the world, and the woods and buildings of the Institute encircled the chamber like a great living landscape painting. A forest canopy of potted plants hung across the top of the dome, casting long, confusing dappled shadows. More plants —small palms, bonsai and palmettos—were scattered around the circular room, seemingly at random.

And there were all sorts of clutter crowding the big room as if it were the playpen of some enormously wealthy adult child. A big reflector telescope set high on a steel platform equiped with its own ladder. A huge video recording and playback console. Free-standing bookcases seemingly set up at random. An antique globe of the world four feet in diameter. Dozens of clocks, ranging from antique grandfathers to a Spilhaus Space Clock. A rosewood bar. A tremendous globular tropical fish tank. Untidy heaps of nameless electronic equipment. A Van de Graaff generator. Cases, tables, and shelves overflowing with maps, small statues, chess sets, models of airplanes, ships, and spacecraft. A pinball machine. As many as twenty lamps, no two in a matching style.

The furniture was equally weird. A huge macrame hammock on a steel frame in the middle of the room. A large oak desk with an immense old carved chair behind it. A watercouch covered in black velvet. Camel saddles. Nests of large paisley floor pillows. Leather director's chairs scattered all over the place. And in the eastern quadrant of the room a big, round butcherblock table with a director's chair in front of it, and a complicated-looking black leather recliner behind it.

Leaning back in the recliner, wearing only a pair of white Bermuda shorts with rolls of fat hanging out over the waistband, was John B. Steinhardt. His thinning gray hair was longer than in his official pictures, his moustache was slightly bushier, his naked chest was grizzled with thick gray hair, his complexion was pink fading into red, his watery blue eyes were somewhat bloodshot, though far more lively than any photograph could portray, and he had a long cigar stuck in the corner of his wide, heavy-lipped mouth.

Somehow it was not exactly Weller's fantasy image of the Great Guru in his throne room.

"Ah, so we meet at last!" Steinhardt called in a gravelly barroom voice, as he brought his recliner to an upright position. "Sit yer ass down!"

Shakily Weller planted himself in the director's chair opposite Steinhardt. There was a big pot of coffee on the table between them, two place settings with cups, a bottle of green fluid, and a half-empty fifth of Jack Daniels. Up close, Weller saw that Steinhardt's face was deeply lined and blotched here and there with spider webs of red capillaries.

"Have a little pick-me-up," Steinhardt said, pouring two inches of the green fluid into each of two glasses. "You look like shit." He paused, hesitated, then poured an inch of bourbon into his own glass. "Shot of booze in your eptifier?" he asked genially. "Kills the taste. No matter how much tinkering they do with the formula, it still tastes like piss."

"A little early for me," Weller said, picking up his glass.

"Low level, Jack, low level," Steinhardt said. "If you take enough eptifier, you can drink like a fish from sunrise to sunset and still feel like Adonis. Why do you think I had my boys invent the stuff?" With that, he downed the contents of his glass in two quick gulps. Weller choked down his eptifier glumly. So far, the Great Man seemed like an old rummy.

"Breakfast!" Steinhardt suddenly bellowed. "We're ready for *breakfast!*"

A moment later a young blond girl wearing skintight white short-shorts and a tiny halter that barely contained her trim high-pointed breasts came up the spiral staircase bearing a silver tray with cream, sugar, and two covered dishes.

She put the tray down on the table, served them coffee, and uncovered the dishes, revealing what appeared to be eggs Benedict. "My own recipe," Steinhardt said. "Westphalian ham, and béarnaise instead of hollandaise, with bialys instead of muffins. Eclecticism, my motto."

He smiled a rubber smile and put his arm around the girl's waist. Abruptly he pulled off her halter, revealing perfect pink-tipped breasts. "Now ain't that a pair of knockers?" he said, as the girl stood there with a sincere smile plastered across her face. Weller's mouth fell open.

Steinhardt laughed uproariously. "Okay, Sally, you can go now," he said, slapping her on the behind.

When she had gone, Steinhardt stared across the table at the shaken Weller, eyes twinkling with inner amusement. "I'm a disgusting old fart, right?" he said. "You're appalled. You expected the Maharishi and you got King Farouk. You can't figure me out. You sure you don't want some booze?" He poured a dollop of Jack Daniels into his coffee and took a sip. Suddenly his face became deadly serious, his eyes like sapphire lasers.

"Of course, it's all a con," he said slyly. "Just wanted to see how you'd react. Who knows, within the next thirty seconds, I may whip out a bowie knife and cut your prick off for balling my wife." Again Steinhardt broke himself up into rumbling laughter.

Weller sat there transfixed, not knowing how to react. Everything about Steinhardt seemed so totally unexpected, so totally unpredictable. For want of anything else to do, he took a bite of his eggs Steinhardt. They were delicious.

Steinhardt took another sip of his spiked coffee. "Now then, m'boy," he said in a W. C. Fields voice, "about this off-the-wall idea of yours about me making commercials. . . ."

Shakily Weller eyed the bottle of eptifier. If the stuff really worked—and it did seem to—he could use all the eptifying he get. "May I?" he said, picking up the bottle.

"By all means," Steinhardt said. "The crazed magnificence of my total being must be scaring the shit out of you."

Weller poured himself another shot of the green fluid.

Immediately Steinhardt topped it off with a slug of bourbon. As Weller started to protest, he held up his palm. "My wish is your command," he said. "I kid you not."

Resignedly Weller gulped down the whole mess. The whiskey sent fire to his stomach and heat to his brain. For a moment his eyes watered. When they cleared, he felt a surge of psychic energy; his synapses seemed faster, his mind was racing, and Steinhardt didn't seem quite so intimidating.

"Look, I don't have to tell you what hot shit you are, obviously," he said. "But maybe I do have to tell you that the commercials we're turning out now stink."

Steinhardt nodded. "Recruiting creative people and keeping them creative while keeping them recruited is one of our central, unresolved paradoxes," he said. "So far, old Heisenberg has been laughing up his sleeve at us."

Not knowing what to make of that, Weller pressed doggedly on. "I'm the only real pro you've got," he said. "And you'd be the knid of video personality who could sell Communism to Barry Goldwater—under my direction."

"No doubt, no doubt," Steinhardt said around a mouthful of food. He paused, gulped down a slug of coffee. "But if you think I'm going to waste my time making used Transformationalism commercials, you have the consciousness of an earthworm."

Poleaxed, Weller could only mutter, "Why?"

"*Why?*" Steinhardt roared. "Did Jesus Christ make TV commercials? Did Buddha? Did Greta Garbo? What happens to my shadowy, enigmatic mystique if I start peddling Transformationalism myself like so much snake oil? Down the willy-hole it goes, and you can't run a movement like this without an authentic enigmatic mystique. To make commercials I'd have to assume an image, a frozen instantaneous persona. Aside from what it would do to this glorious movement, it would bore the piss out of me. So forget that cockamamie idea, Jack. It's shit for the birds."

"Then . . . why did you bring me here at all?" Weller stammered, his mind reeling. Steinhardt was proving impossible to figure out, too confusing to even think straight around, as if his brain projected an enormously powerful magnetic field which screwed up any mental compass within its sphere of influence.

Steinhardt leaned back, poured himself half a glass of straight whiskey, and sat there toying with it, staring up at the canopy of hanging plants. "I once read a science-fiction story," he said. "Or maybe I wrote it, I cranked out so much crud in the old days it's hard to remember which. Anyway, there was this all-powerful ruler of an alien planet who wanted to perpetuate his rule 'beyond the grave,' as we used to say in the old pulp days. So he built himself a giant computer, and he programmed his own personality into it. Then he programmed the thing to pick succeeding programmers according to how closely they matched his own personality, and he programmed it to breed the whole race into an ever-closer mass approximation of this ideal personality, namely his own. A thousand years later *they* were *him*."

Steinhardt lowered his gaze to stare at Weller, and suddenly there seemed to be something crazed and monstrously monomaniacal leering at him across the breakfast table. "How do you like *that* little wet dream?" Steinhardt said. "The entire human race graven in the image of yours truly!"

Weller reacted from the gut. "It makes me want to puke," he said.

Steinhardt broke up into rumbling laughter. He reached across the table and thumped Weller on the shoulder. "Ah, I think my instincts were right about you," he said. "My own fantastic processing techniques have put a head on your shoulders."

"Huh?"

"*Huh?*" Steinhardt mimicked. "You're right, of course. It's a stupid, disgusting, regressive idea, the exact opposite of what I'm determined to leave behind when I shuffle off to Buffalo."

"I think you left me around the last bend," Weller muttered.

"Don't worry," Steinhardt said, "you'll get used to it." He steepled his hands and seemed to become more serious.

"The story I've just told you is the history of all previous religions, social movements, and attempts to create higher levels of human consciousness," he said. "A hotshot like me comes along, shatters generations of fixed consciousness, reignites ongoing change, and sets up a movement to perpetuate the situation. If he doesn't end up swallowing his own hype—a long assumption in this racket, let me tell you—it works as advertised as long as he's alive to keep throwing off changes. But once a Buddha, Jesus, or Steinhardt croaks, he becomes a graven image at the service of the surviving organization."

Steinhardt paused, took a sip of whiskey, shook his head sadly. "You see, we shaved apes are entropy junkies. People get tired of free consciousness, they get a sick craving for a new, stable mind freeze. And what do they do? When the psychic liberator is no longer around to kick them in the ass, the organization he's left behind turns him into a new object of worship, iconized and Madisonavenuized for all time. In his name they turn his historical image into an instrument of the very kind of brain-freeze he's busted his balls to destroy. The legacy of Jesus is Billy Graham. In the name of revolutionaries like Marx and Lenin we have a bureaucratic state. The party of Lincoln ends up as the party of old Tricky Dick. You're dead right, m'boy. It is to puke!"

Weller sat there transfixed while this monologue went on. This weird old drunk was apparently also an authentic visionary thinker. It didn't add up to a coherent whole; Weller couldn't reconcile these two Steinhardt personas no matter how much he tried. And he had no idea of what the man was getting at.

"But what does all this have to do with why I'm here?"

Steinhardt leaned forward and stared at Weller with cold, penetrating energy. "When I'm dead, I don't want my assorted disciples and ten-percenters to own my image," he said. "I don't want them turning the memory of John B. Steinhardt into a billboard behind which the usual religion-money-power-mind-control shell game does business as usual. I want my memory to keep generating changes *despite* the legacy of Transformationalism, to be a continued source of creative chaos. And *that's* why you're here, Jack, *that's* why I need a director."

Suddenly Steinhardt went through another change, took a sip of coffee, and went back to eating his eggs. "And that's also why I don't want to make commercials," he said. "They'll have me making too many commercials when I'm dead as it is. What I want to make while I'm still around sniffing the flowers is a kind of anticommercial. A video-taped last testament to be released far and wide when I croak. A half hour? An hour? Six hours? I dunno. We'll have to figure that out."

He waved his fork in the general direction of Weller's face. "But I'll tell what I want it to be like," he said. "I want it to be full of internal self-contradictions. I want to contradict all the bullshit Transformationalism is inevitably going to say about me for the next thousand years, and then I want to contradict my own contradictions. I want to reveal myself as a drunken teenybopper-fucking pathological liar as well as a saintly liberator of human consciousness. I want to tell dirty jokes and frame timeless epigrams. I want to live on on tape *completely independent* of Transformationalism, and I want a testament that will make it absolutely impossible for anyone to ever write the bottom line on John B. Steinhardt."

"I'm not sure I understand," Weller said uncertainly.

"Old Mao Tze Tung *almost* got the idea with his notion of permanent revolution," Steinhardt said. "But he got too caught up in his own ego trip and ended up with a society forever consulting his Little Red Book of epigrams. It's fun to be a god when you're alive, but when I'm dead, I want to revert to the public domain, as it were."

Perhaps it was the double dose of eptifier, or perhaps the sheer force of Steinhardt's personality, but Weller felt his mind opening up to encompass this weird concept. A tape of Steinhardt supporting and debunking Transformationalism at the same time would indeed counterbalance the power of Transformationalism in the only way possible, with a dialectic between the ghost of Steinhardt and the inheritors of the movement he had founded. The Steinhardt testament would by definition always have to be the last word on the subject, but if it were properly made, no one would be able to be sure what it said: Even in death Steinhardt would remain the center of the movement, and the center would be void. The idea had style.

"Well, what do you think?" Steinhardt asked. "Could you help me put together something like that?"

"I gather you would write the script?" Weller said dryly.

"*Script?*" Steinhardt bellowed. "*Write?* Are you nuts? I'll get gibbering drunk and babble at the camera for about thirty hours. Then you'll go shoot a lot of footage here and at the centers and put together something vaguely coherent out of the whole mess."

"Uh . . . I'd be willing to give it a try," Weller said. "When do you want to start?"

His head felt as if it were flying off in all directions at once. He was overwhelmed by Steinhardt, appalled by the arduous task that was being proposed, challenged by the concept and by the prospect of working with this incomprehensible creature. And he suddenly realized that no thought of Annie had crossed his mind during the whole conversation. His reason for being here in the first place had been driven from his mind by the force of Steinhardt's personality. How in the world can I manipulate this conversation for two seconds? he wondered. How can I dare to bring up what I came here for in the first place? Somehow, at this moment, before Steinhardt,

270

his own petty personal problems seemed gnatlike, picayune, beneath cosmic notice.

"Not so fast," Steinhardt said. "I didn't say you had the job yet. I was just asking whether you wanted to try out for it. I mean, how can I be completely sold on a character like you, who wormed his way in here by fucking my wife, who's played games with nerds like Garry Bailor, who's driven some of my best Monitors screaming up the walls, who's got poor old Doc Bernstein shitting in his pants?"

But Steinhardt spoke in such a genial—indeed almost affectionate—tone that Weller could hardly work up even a healthy twinge of paranoia.

Steinhardt took a final sip of coffee and stuck his cigar back in the corner of his mouth. "So I'm assigning you a guide who will also be a commissar," he said. "Someone who will stick close to you and give me a better bottom line on where your consciousness is really at. You'll spend some time getting the feel of the operation here and shooting the shit with me from time to time. You'll be trying to sell yourself to me just as you would any other producer—while your guide reports back. *Then* we'll see what's what. It's your big break, Jack, make the most of it. If you don't blow it, you'll be a big man in the movement. Not only that, you'll share a little piece of my ineffable immortality. But there's plenty of time, I ain't about to kick off by next Tuesday."

Steinhardt rose somewhat ponderously from his recliner. "Now then," he said impishly, "shall we go downstairs and meet your comrade commissar?"

He led Weller down the spiral staircase, into the vestibule, along the hall, and into a huge living room whose major feature was a giant sunken conversation pit with the huge flowing abstract sculpture growing in its center like some science-fiction tree. Seated alone at the far side of the pit and partially hidden by the sculpture from the angle at which they had entered was a woman wearing a white blouse and tennis skirt.

As they rounded the sculpture and she came into full view, Weller's heart skipped a beat and a big hollow balloon exploded in his stomach, sagging him at the knees, sending blood rushing in waves to his head.

The woman in white was Annie.

But a changed Annie. Her long blond hair had been cut short into a severe pageboy. Something was subtly different about her mouth. And her eyes. . . . They were preternaturally

271

bright, but it was a cold vitality; younger, older, timeless as glacial ice.

She rose to meet them, staring evenly at Weller with an absolutely unreadable expression. For his part, Weller could not find a word to say; his whole being vibrated with an immense silence, an echoing emptiness filled with half-formed memories, with anticipated expectations of this moment that had nothing to do with the reality itself. The whole world seemed to funnel down to a point centered between her eyes.

It was Steinhardt who broke the silence with a great booming laugh. "Jack, meet your guide and comrade commissar," he said. "And let this be a lesson to you, kiddo. You were promised you'd be reunited with your wife when you were sufficiently transformed. Well, how do you like your ultimate processor, Charlie?"

He laughed again, took Annie's hand, placed it in Weller's, and drew them together by throwing his arms wide around both of their shoulders. "For the moment, at least, you have my blessings upon your union, chilluns," he said. He withdrew his arms, walked away, waved his hand, shook his head, and left the room rumbling with laughter.

They stood there alone staring at each other like long-lost lovers, like blind dates, like strangers. "God," Weller finally said, "I just don't know what to say."

Annie smiled, a thin ghost of smiles remembered. "Neither do I."

Then abruptly they were in each other's arms, bodies pressed together, shapes fitting into well-remembered shapes, lips tasting well-remembered lips, and for a while it seemed to Weller that months of time had been annihilated, as if this were only one more in an endless series of embraces down through the years, as if the space between this time and the last had never existed.

Yet as their tongues touched and their bodies moved on each other, he came to feel a subtle alienness, the feeling of the first touch of a new lover; not so much the thrill of fresh flesh, but rather an indefinable psychic distance, a subliminal newness.

They parted and sank down onto the upholstered lip of the conversation pit.

"It's over," Weller sighed. "It's really over."

Annie laughed. "That's funny," she said. "I was about to say it was just beginning."

A nervous tremor went through Weller's body. This moment was nothing like anything he had anticipated. Words, even coherent feelings, were coming so hard. No time had passed since she left. A thousand years had gone by. He couldn't get it together. "Well, how the hell are you?" he asked inanely.

"Great," she said. "Fulfilled. Whole. And you, Jack? They haven't told me much. Just enough to write those two letters, and then a lot of Monitor security silence . . ."

"I've gotten here," Weller said.

"So you have." Annie broke out a great big old-time smile that began to warm the strange ice around Weller's heart. "So you have!"

She hugged him fiercely. "I *have* missed you!" she said. "It's been fantastic, but it hasn't been easy. It's been a long lonely time. . . ."

She rubbed her cheek against his. "If I hadn't *known* it was the right thing for both of us, I don't know whether I would've been able to go through it just for myself. But all that's over now. You've come back to me transformed. And you're going to be working directly with *John*. If I didn't love you so much, I'd be green with envy."

The cold, distant feeling that had begun to dissipate began to close in on Weller again. For even now, in what should have been a personal moment, a joyous moment of reunited love, the massive shadow of John B. Steinhardt still hung over them, a gigantic afterimage that would not fade, a presence that intruded upon their intimacy by the very force of the man's absence. Weller had the urge to grab Annie's hand and run—out of the house, through the woods, over the fences, past the dogs, three thousand miles back in space and time to their house in long-lost, long-ago California.

"Hey, can we get out of here?" he said. "Is there someplace we can be alone?"

Annie kissed him lightly on the lips. "Sure," she said. "I've got my own cabin in the Colony. But it's going to be *our* place now. You're authorized to move in with me. It's a new beginning for us. Ah, it's so wonderful the way things fall into place when you have the courage to ride the changes!"

She hugged him again, took his hand, and pulled him to his feet. "Come on!" she said. "Let me show you our new home."

Weller forced a happy smile and a bouncy walk as she led him out of Steinhardt's house. Why, he wondered, do I feel

273

like this? I should feel happy, I should feel I've come home, I should feel I've won. Why can't I let joy into my heart? What's wrong with me? Why do I feel this dread? Why do I feel I'm holding hands with a stranger?

Eighteen

Birds sang, sunlight poured through the treetops, and Annie was babbling excitedly as they walked along the pathways of the Institute to God-knows-where. The air, the effort of his own body, the presence of Annie beside him, the rap that he was simply letting wash over him, all combined to relieve Weller of the pressure of his own thoughts. *We'll just walk through the woods and then make love, and we won't have to think of anything for a while. . . .*

". . . such high-energy people at the Colony. Maybe we can even rig up a mobile unit for you while you're working with John. We should really get some meaningful results out of *that*!"

As Annie paused at the crest of a gentle slope crowned with trees, Weller realized that he had lost all track of whatever it was she had been talking about. And she *was*, apparently, talking about something that meant a lot to her. "The Colony?" he said. "What's that? You keep talking about it, but I'm afraid I've been too happy to pay much attention."

Annie led him through the line of trees. In the hollow beyond Weller saw perhaps two dozen bungalows shaded by trees and clustered around a low white building. He thought he recognized the scene from yesterday's walking tour. And sure enough, when he took a closer look, there was the fence surrounding the area and the guarded gate.

"The Colony," Annie said, nodding in the direction of the cluster of bungalows.

"Yeah, but what is it? What goes on?"

Annie looked at him peculiarly. "Don't you know?" she said. "It's one of the few projects under John's personal directive; it's got top priority. We've got about twenty residents now—writers, painters, sculptors, even a photographer."

"You mean Transformationalism is running some kind of *artist's colony*?" Weller said with some surprise. "What on earth for? As a reward for creative people in the movement?"

"Oh no," Annie said, "it's not for movement people. Everyone has to be a working professional with real credits. They get three months free room and board and unlimited free processing while they work on their approved projects."

"In return for which?" Weller asked. There *had* to be a *quid pro quo*. Selflessly bankrolling a playpen for indigent *artistes* seemed way out of character for Steinhardt.

"In return for which they serve as subjects for our experiments with creativity," Annie said.

"What sort of experiments?" Weller asked, with a picture of some diabolical Frankenstein laboratory in his head.

"They're circuited into brainwave monitors while they're actually doing their creative work," Annie said. "We're recording creative consciousness so we can monitor the changes different Transformational processes make in their creativity. So we can try out different eptifier formulas."

"What for?"

"*What for?*" Annie said, dumbfounded. "So there'll be no more writer's blocks. No more down days on the set with you dragging yourself home in a black funk. We're going to be able to optimize creative consciousness with eptifiers and new processes. Some day doing creative work is going to be a conscious function that you can turn on like a faucet. We're going to take all the agony and frustration out of it. We're going to turn creative consciousness into a permanent state of mind."

The notion had to be seductive to anyone who had ground his way through day after day of deadening hackwork, but Weller's mind didn't get caught up in that for very long. His consciousness was focused on Annie. He had never seen her so totally into what she was doing, not for what she might get out of it, but for the thing itself. But what the hell *was* she doing?

"You didn't say anything about actors," he said. "What are you doing to optimize your creativity, Annie?"

"Oh, I'm beyond all that," she said breezily. "You have no idea what a relief it is. There was never anything creative about my so-called career. I was just trying to become a movie star; rich, famous, a wet-dream fantasy for guys sitting there in the dark watching me on the screen. It was all just a super ego trip. I was empty inside, and all I was doing was trying to fill that empty space with fame and adulation."

"And that's it?" Weller said sullenly. "All those years of trying, and you walk away from it just like that?"

Annie smiled at him, and the tranquil radiance of it nearly

276

drove him crazy. "Can't you understand how wonderful it is to stop trying to feed your own starving ego and be totally involved with what you're doing on a really meaningful, fully eptified level?"

"Well, what the hell *are* you doing?" Weller grunted.

"I'm a creativity monitor," she said.

"A *what*?"

"I work in the creativity program. I'm in charge of the brainwave tapes. I keep records of who's doing how much work on what. I help decide which process to run on who when."

Weller's growing anger broke through for a moment. "Sounds boring as hell," he said.

"It's vital work, Jack," she said somewhat testily. "It's important to the movement."

"Running a time clock is probably important at MGM," Weller said sourly. "That doesn't make the job less of a bummer."

"It's not just mechanical work," Annie insisted. "I'm working to create more creative consciousness. And I'm one of the people involved in project decisions. I'm the one who evaluates how well which programs are working on the subjects."

"So you're not just a clerk, you're a cultural commissar," Weller blurted.

"Commissar?" Annie said, laughing. "Where did you get a crazy idea like that?"

"From the highest authority," Weller said. "Steinhardt told me flat out that you'd be giving him evaluation reports on *me*."

Annie's expression finally darkened, as if she had just realized that they were having something like an argument. "You make it sound so awful," she said. "But it's not like that. I'm not spying on you, I'm helping you. Together we're going to convince John that you're the man for the job. I don't have any doubts. Do you?"

"No," Weller muttered, unable to express what he truly felt. Anger, sadness, a sense of loss. That it had gone this far! That Annie could trade her career for playing Comrade Commissar to a bunch of freeloading writers and painters! That she could even report back to Steinhardt on him and expect him to approve of it! That he couldn't feel free to say a damned true thing about it! Oh baby, baby, I've got to get us the fuck out of here—fast!

There was a long period of awkward silence. Then Annie

broke it with a warm smile that seemed like a forced act of will. "Let's not spoil today with an argument then, okay?" she said breezily.

"Yeah, sure, okay," Weller said, making himself smile back. She took his hand and led him down the far side of the hill. There was no trouble at the gate—the guard recognized Annie and had gotten an updated directive on Weller too.

Annie led him to a secluded cabin in a corner of the compound, heavily shaded by towering oaks, its rough wooden siding blending it into the landscape.

Inside were two rather small rooms and a full bath. The bedroom was paneled in knotty pine, with rich blue draperies and bedspread. The other room was a combination living room, kitchen, and dinette in the manner of a family style motel. There was a compact stove-sink-refrigerator-combo unit behind a Formica breakfast bar with yellow stools. There were two easy chairs, a leather couch, a low round walnut table, a desk, and a color television set. Plush green wall-to-wall carpeting, anonymous framed prints, a complete set of pots, dishes, and silverware. Everything but the checkout notice. And, of course, an extension phone. Apparently even a "creativity monitor" did not rate free contact with the outside world.

"Cozy, isn't it?" Annie said as they sat side by side on the couch after the ten-cent tour.

"Yeah, all the comforts of Las Vegas," Weller said. He found that he had made an unconscious decision not to bring up the matter of missing phones. Already he found himself being somewhat guarded with Annie, slipping easily into the persona he had crafted for himself during his stay in the movement, and hating himself a little for it. But both Steinhardt and Annie had made it quite clear that she would be reporting on him as if he were one of the Colony guinea pigs, and nothing that he had seen in her so far gave him any confidence that her loyalties were not still split. Transformed? he thought bitterly. Yeah, that's just about the measure of how we've both been transformed.

And here we sit, he thought, knowing its long since time to make love. I know it, you know it, but where's our reality? There are so many piled up changes in both of us that we're like two kids sitting in the backseat of a parked car with our strangenesses and desires forming an invisible wall of tension between us.

Later, after the long ice was broken, making love could just

278

be making love again, but now it was something that *had to be done*, which made Weller's first move a willfull act of determination.

Weller snaked his arm around Annie's shoulders. She moved hesitantly into the crook of his arm, but he could feel a holding back, a tension, in the pressure of her body against his. They turned to face each other, eye to eye, lips shimmering across a spark gap from lips, close enough for Weller to smell the perfume of her breath.

"Well . . ."

"Well . . . ?"

"Oh, this is ridiculous!" Weller said, trying to giggle it and failing, and he reached out, pulled her to him, and at last touched his lips to hers.

At that moment psychic tension alchemized itself to almost tearful lust, and the body's visceral memories and longing freed him from the paralysis of the mind. The kiss became deep and melting and endless, a dissolution of the tension interface between them.

Weller released his breath into her and tasted her answering sigh, and at last he was free from history and expectation, free from the games and torments of the mind, a human animal come home to his own.

They kissed and they touched, and they tasted each other anew. Clothes came away fumbling in haste, and in what seemed like one continuous bright moment, Weller was deep inside her.

But not deep enough. As he felt her body responding beneath him, he found himself wanting to concentrate his total life-force into the knightly lance of his cock. He had to thrust its purifying length into the ambivalent shrouded core of her and reconquer the lady of his heart from the dragons of the mind.

So what had begun as one thing became another. Tender homecoming became a demonic exercise in fancy fucking. Male ego lust combined with righteous wrath and messianic husbandhood to turn him on in darker and deeper ways than he had ever been before.

Once she began to cry out in orgasm, he threw himself into the center of her ecstasy with even more heightened fervor. He wanted to keep her there for a long, long time. Until she was reformed from the chaos of ecstasy around *him*, purified of that which had been put there by Transformationalism.

On and on he went, moving into the sound of her rising

and falling cries, determined to keep her changes coming until he had fucked her brains clean.

When he finally came himself, it was with blinding, uncontrollable force that shook him to his toes, but even that wasn't enough. Far from being a culmination or a release, it was a goad and a challenge. He wanted to pour himself through this instantaneous pipeline to her center, flow with his own seed, and fill her with himself.

He went on and on afterward until they were both far over the ragged edge of exhaustion, panting and heaving for air.

"My God, it's been a long time," Annie said huskily. "Ah, I've missed you!"

As soon as words returned, Weller felt himself returning from the cosmic battlefield. Now they were neither engaged in some Armageddon of lust and will, nor were they tension-ridden strangers. Now we're just Jack and Annie again.

Annie smiled impishly at him. "It was a lot better than I remembered," she said teasingly. "And as I remember, what I remember was pretty damn good."

"Pretty *fucking* good!" Weller said, and a laugh managed to bubble out of him. What had to be done, had been done, and from here on in, their lovemaking would become what it had always been—neither a thing of cosmic tension between them nor the golden path to the reclaimed Annie of his desires.

That battle was going to be decided on a psychic level, not in bed.

On balance he found he couldn't decide whether that was a blessing or a curse.

In a gesture of housewifely normalcy Annie stacked the last of the dinner dishes in the sink, wiped off her hands, and sat down beside Weller on the couch, which happened to be facing the television set.

But once again her words came not from his wife but from her Transformationalist persona. "I think it's time for you to get your first look at what we're doing here at the Colony."

They had lazed away the afternoon making love and talking, and their lovemaking had become more and more ordinary, even as Weller had known it would, for which he was warmly grateful. The more familiar it seemed, the more of a home-coming it was. There were times when the pleasure of making love to your own wife became the kinkiest sex trip of all.

But he also wondered if they hadn't done so much lovemaking partially because it kept them from talking. She was shining with the fulfilling light of Transformationalism—what had been a time of agony for him had been a golden age for her. He couldn't be honest with her about what he felt about the movement, nor could he react from the heart to what she told him.

So whenever words replaced touch, the walls were up, and their conversations swiftly degenerated into stylized fencing matches, half-sincere and half-political, in the most loathsome sense of the word.

The last one, mercifully terminated by steak and home fries, had come pretty close to the edge.

She couldn't get over how wonderful it was that he had left *Monkey Business* and become a director for the movement. "God, it's so good to see you out of there and doing something real. It's like seeing you get out of prison."

"If you consider shooting television commercials a step up from kiddie shows," Weller said.

"But they're *Transformational* commercials. They're doing something real to change the world, it's not just a meaningless Hollywood sausage factory."

"I seem to remember you had a pretty strong desire to become an Armor Star frankfurter yourself," Weller said testily. "And believe me, all I'm doing now is turning out a different brand of baloney."

Annie looked at him narrowly. "You're not happy to be working the movement?" she said. "You don't believe in what you're doing?" Suddenly he had the feeling that there was a tape recorder built into the nearest lamp. That was definitely a commissar-type question.

"They're wasting my talents," Weller said, backing off from the test. "I want to be doing the best I can, and churning out commercials is not it, I hope."

"But that's why you're here, Jack!" Annie said more brightly. "You've reached a level of consciousness where they'll *really* let you direct." She kissed him on the cheek. "You're even going to get to work with *John*! If that doesn't make you proud, it sure does me."

"Well, it's good to hear that," Weller said sullenly. "Seeing as how your little reports on me will help determine whether I get to do it or not."

"Oh Jack, don't be so paranoid about it. It's nothing, just a formality. Do you think you'd be here at the Institute with me if John had any real doubts?"

"That didn't seemed to be John's attitude," Weller said.

281

"Do you really think you can understand John's attitudes? We're *all* supposed to report any regressive tendencies we see in each other. It's for everyone's own good."

"That's charming," Weller snapped. "Does that mean I'm supposed to report any regressive tendencies *I* see in *you?*"

Annie actually got nervous for a moment. "Why? Have I said something wrong?"

The humorlessness of it was ridiculous. "Well, I'm not entirely convinced that some wee part of you isn't still interested in a regressive career as a movie star," Weller chided, trying to zing her into seeing the fatuousness of of such an extreme of Transformationalist zeal.

"Really?" she said earnestly. "I really think I've eliminated that block, but if that's what you're picking up, it may be what I'm putting out on some level, and maybe you should report it."

"Oh Annie, can't you tell when I'm putting you on any more?"

"I've forgotten all those tacky little Hollywood games," she had said, giving him a look of momentary contempt.

Fortunately at that point there had been a loud sizzle from the broiler as the steaks called angrily for attention, and the ideological tension that had been building up to a confrontation again had been aborted once more, this time by the dinner table instead of the bed.

But now the dishes were in the sink, and the fencing match would probably begin again, because now they were going on a tour of the Colony, according, no doubt, to his directive for the day. Well, there was no point in delaying the inevitable, and he did have a certain curiosity about what was going on here.

"Okay," he said. "I guess it's time I got the grand tour."

The first stop was in the low white building at the center of the cluster of cabins, where a big, loftlike room was divided up into a series of cubicles. What was going on looked like standard preliminary processing: a subject wired into a brainwave monitor and a processor reading off block-auditing sequences or life scenarios. Half a dozen people undergoing standard block auditing and meditative deconditioning? Here, at the Institute? It didn't make sense, not after what he had had to go through to get here.

Silently he motioned Annie into the access hall. "What's going on here?" he said. "How come you're running such low-level processes on these people? I was told that no one got into the Institute without going all the way through life analysis. What are these beginners doing here?" He found to his surprise that he somehow felt indignant about it.

"The people at the Colony are an exception," Annie said. She suddenly began to look uneasy, as if there were something going on that she didn't care to talk about.

"Why?"

"Well . . . ah . . . the Colony has a dual purpose. . . ."

"Dual purpose?"

"Shall we go meet some of the people at their work?" Annie said with forced brightness.

"You haven't answered my question."

"It's really pretty technical, and I don't think—"

"Come on, Annie, this is *me* you're jiving!" Weller snapped. "Besides, you're my official guide, and if I'm going to work with John, I have to know these things."

Annie fidgeted for a moment, caught up in some unguessable conflict of directives. "Well, okay. The truth is we have a problem attracting creative people into the movement and keeping them there," she finally admitted grudgingly. "They just don't come to the regular Transformation Centers—that's why John thought up the Celebrity Centers. And when we do get them into processing, they almost always drop out at low levels. Something about creative consciousness seems to block processing."

"So you lure them here with free room and board so you can play with their heads."

"You make it sound so tacky."

"Isn't it?"

"Not at all," Annie insisted righteously. "If something about Transformational processing turns off creative people, we've got to learn what it is and correct it. If we don't bring Transformational Consciousness to the very people who mold mass consciousness, how can we create a Transformational culture? We've got to make Transformationalism chic with the molders of public consciousness."

"A direct quote from John?" Weller said dryly.

"More or less. John is very concerned with this problem, having been a writer himself. But we are getting somewhere, thanks to the Colony. We can process a hundred people a year here. Processing may not be what they come for, but at least they get it, and some of it must stick."

"If creativity interferes with processing, I'd bet my bottom dollar that processing interferes with creativity," Weller said angrily. "How much creative work have *you* done lately?" For that matter how creative have *I* been since I got involved in this mess, he realized glumly. All these mind games sap up psychic energy like vampire bats. No wonder creative people instinctively avoid it! But these poor bastards here get it force fed to them like I did.

"How much work is really getting done in the Colony?" Weller said sharply. "I'll bet all your guinea pigs are sitting around on their asses or reaming out crud to justify their existences."

"That's not so," Annie said. "With modified processing and eptifiers, we're succeeding here. People are being processed and working creatively at the same time. I'll show you. I have to collect some brainwave recordings anyway."

"Sure, why not?" Weller said. "Let's see if the guinea pigs are spinning their exercise wheels."

Annie took him through a copse of trees to a nearby cabin where an emaciated man in cut-off jeans was working on a large abstract canvas in a midden of paints and brushes. But instead of the beret that seemed to go with the act, he wore a brainwave monitor band, but without a wire lead in evidence. As for the work in progress Weller might not have known much about art, but he knew enough about baloney.

"Hello, Jerry," Annie said. "This is my husband Jack. He makes commercials for the movement. He'll be staying with me now." There was something cold and guarded in the way Annie spoke. She had pointedly avoided mentioning that he was going to be working with John with an instant cover story, and that was something she had seemed womanly proud of, a boast about him that he would've thought she was dying to make.

"Jerry Winter," the thin man said. "So you're the latest inmate of Uncle John's Funny Farm?"

Annie shot Winter an absolutely poisonous look, and Winter seemed to fear it. "Oh come on, Annie," he said ingratiatingly, "it's just a little affectionate inside joke. Don't lose your sense of humor."

He succeeded in forcing a rueful little smile from her. "I'll just change your tapes, and we'll get out of your way," she said. Then, with painfully obvious emphasis, "I can see you're right in the middle of important work, and I'm sure your tape will confirm it."

She went over to a piece of equipment half obscured by some canvases which looked like a small brainwave monitor without a screen. Instead, reels of tape were spinning atop it at low speed. Annie shut it down and began rewinding the tape onto one reel.

"Is that really what this place is like, a booby hatch?" Weller asked Winter while Annie was absorbed in changing the tapes.

Winter laughed uneasily. "Come on, man," he said, "it was just a joke. We all love it here. This is the best place on the circuit. I've been living at artists' colonies for three continuous years now, so I ought to know. The food is great, the scenery is attractive, and the booze is free. What more could anyone ask?"

Annie started threading a new tape in the machine from a large pile behind it. Winter glanced in her direction, then said confidentially: "Of course, it *does* get a little weird. Being wired into these machines all day. The processing sessions. The strange potions they give us to drink."

Annie came back with a reel of tape in her hand, and Winter changed gears again. "As you can see," he continued much more loudly, "we're treated like pampered pets. So if our hosts ask us to contribute ourselves as subjects to their experiments, we'd be ingrates to complain. How sweet it is, compared to teaching Art One to snot-nose kids!"

"And you are working well here, aren't you?" Annie said.

Winter beamed at her, and presented his work in progress —an endless spaghetti bowl of random multicolored strands that looked as if he had doodled with it forever and as if he could jive it along for twice as long as that. "See for yourself," he said, with a grand paternal flourish of his arm.

Weller had trouble not breaking up, and he had a feeling that Winter was choking on his own laughter too.

Annie accepted that as an exit line, and they left for the next cabin. Weller didn't know whether to be embarrassed at the way Winter was putting on his own wife, or to be amused and pleased at the way he was professionally sponging off John Steinhardt.

"Don't take Jerry too seriously," Annie said as they walked across an expanse of shaded brown earth. "As you can see, he pretends not to take himself seriously either. It's a common mind block with creative people. But you can also see that he *is* doing creative work."

"Oh sure," Weller muttered, reluctant to pursue the subject further and start another argument. "Uh . . . by the way, I noticed there weren't any wires from the headband to the recorder," he said, in an effort to change the subject. "What do you use, a radio transmitter in the headband?"

"Uh-huh," Annie said, as they reached the door to the next cabin, "better mobility." Apparently however, she was not about to switch tracks. "Now *here* we have someone who is as creative and sincere as you could imagine," she said. "Magda Talbot Lawrence, author of ten published novels."

"Never heard of her," Weller said.

"Well . . . uh . . . they've all been gothics or sex novels up until now," Annie said in a smaller voice. "But that's why she's here," she said more brightly. "Now she's working on a meaningful novel about the Spanish conquest of Mexico. We're giving her the freedom and consciousness to do serious noncommercial work."

In the front room of the cabin a pudgy gray-haired woman in her fifties was typing furiously on an electric typewriter. A fat manuscript was piling up neatly on her desk with Prussian precision. She merely glanced up as they entered. Her face was lined and hard, and she had the eyes of a dedicated proofreader; bored, bleary, but punctiliously alert.

"Please, no conversation now, Annie," she said in a schoolteacher's voice. "I'm right in the middle of a critical scene, and I can't interrupt the flow."

"I'm only here to collect the tape," Annie said defensively. "I didn't mean to intrude on a creative moment."

"Well, you have, my dear, you have," said Magda Talbot Lawrence. "You don't want to create negative results in your experiments by intruding upon my creative consciousness, now do you? So please go about your business quietly, and let me continue to go about mine."

With that, she determinedly resumed typing, and Annie felt constrained to walk on tiptoe as she did her business and led Weller out of the cabin with a psychic finger to her lips.

"*Now* tell me people aren't creating here!" she said triumphantly, when they were outside in the free air.

"Well, she looks creative, anyway," Weller said. He wondered whether Magda Talbot Lawrence was the real thing, a tough old bird who was determined to get some work done no matter what went on, or whether her freeloading act was just more sophisticated. Either way, the manner in which she seemed to control the situation and Annie had to be impressive.

"Still the skeptic, Jack?" Annie said, fondling her precious reels of tape. "But these tapes go beyond personas and appearances. When we feed them through the computer, we *know* who was really in what state of consciousness when. Scientifically."

Then how come your top scientific brain Bernstein apparently thinks that's baloney? Weller wanted to say. "Uh-huh," he muttered, retreating into his own thoughts. Brainwave patterns characteristic of the creative parts of the mind at work, he could believe. But a machine that could tell whether crud or genius was coming out by reading brainwaves was probably another gizmo out of the science-fiction mind of John B. Steinhardt. An electronic shit detector was a little hard to swallow, especially in the light of how much bullshit there was here that didn't seem to register on their meters.

The final four cabins that they visited confirmed Weller's opinion that the *artistes* of the Colony were taking John B. Steinhardt and Annie for a ride. There was a young hippie poet who mumbled stoned aesthetic impenetrabilities. And a wood sculptress who wore a muumuu and seemed ready to serve them her special herbal tea. There was a science fiction writer, perhaps a pensioned old crony of Steinhardt's, churning out one more in a long line of potboilers, and ready to deliver an hour-long sermon on the sins of the New York literary establishment at the drop of his own wrongly ignored name. Finally there was a once-famous novelist who hadn't published a book in eight years, who was supposed to be working on some kind of screenplay about his own life, and who was maintaining very well considering that he seemed fried to the eyeballs.

They were a slick collection of ducks, and they knew they had a soft touch here. The con job they seemed to be doing on Transformationalism seemed at least as professional as anything Transformationalism was running on them.

It pleased him to think that know-it-all Steinhardt could still be sucker enough to be exploited by artsy-fartsy slickies even while he was running his programs on *them*. It restored some of his confidence in his own ability to cope with the Great Man.

"Well, do we have artists or don't we have artists?" Annie said smugly as they walked to their own cabin.

"They're artists, all right," Weller said. "The medium is the message."

The next morning Annie went to work somewhere right after breakfast, and Weller, left alone to sit and wait for nothing in particular, had a flash of what it must have been like for her to stay at home most days waiting for the phone to ring while he was at the studio. He began to understand the attraction of her new life for her. Here she had programmed activity all day that she was convinced was meaningful. She in effect was happier in a nine-to-five job than as a free-lance actress. Was that the thing she had found out about herself that made her happy to give up her career?

One thing you had to say for the Institute, thought seemed to develop complexities in this environment.

He hung around the cabin for an hour or so then took an aimless walk around the compound. When he got back, John B. Steinhardt was waiting for him perched on a golf cart and looking like Teddy Roosevelt as the Great White Hunter in a bush suit with a silver flask sticking out of a pocket.

"Climb aboard, kiddo," Steinhardt rumbled. "We're going to run a little program on old Doc Bernstein. It'll give you the feel of what I want to do with my testament, and we'll have a little fun with the pompous old fart."

"What did you have in mind?" Weller asked, climbing into the cart.

"Your Monitor act, bucko," Steinhardt said genially. "Don't be coy with me, cobber. Bernstein's half convinced you're a Monitor, and we both know it."

"So?"

"So," said Steinhardt, starting the car and heading off toward the compound gate. "So we'll help keep his thinking Transformational."

"I have no idea what you want me to do," Weller said.

"Just disagree with me all the time to the best of your ability," Steinhardt said. "I'll do the rest."

Steinhardt waved patricianly to the guard at the gate, and they buzzed off in the direction of the computer complex. Weller had no idea of what sort of test this was going to be and how he was supposed to pass it. He had a momentary urge to ask Steinhardt for a belt from his hip flask.

"By the way, that reminds me that Annie seems to feel you may have a regressive attitude toward the Colony," Steinhardt said.

Anger coursed suddenly through Weller, not without an admixture of fear. "What did she report I said?" he asked, barely containing his belligerent indignation.

"Why, the poor lass thinks that you believe that our resident intellectuals are a bunch of phonies," Steinhardt said, sur-pressing a grin that showed only in his eyes. "That their only creative area is that of the mooch artist."

"Uh . . . I don't remember saying. . . ."

"Come on, kiddo, don't try to out-insult me," Steinhardt said genially. "Neither of us is as stupid as we're both pretending. Or course our intellectual zoo here is full of blocked writers, artsy con men, and bullshit artists who can't make it in the marketplace. You think the heavyweights are going to be attracted by free food and flop?"

"But these people are ripping you off and you know it?" Weller said perplexedly.

"You're concerned for my well-being," Steinhardt exclaimed, breaking up into bellowing laughter. He took the flask out of his pocket and unscrewed the cap. "I'll drink to that!" he said, toasting Weller and taking a gulp. "But then, I'll drink to anything!"

"You think that's *funny*?" Weller said.

Steinhardt nodded, then waved his flask at three passing technicians. "I'm touched," he said. "To think that you're concerned for my well-being. I always said I was too easily taken advantage of." He broke up into laughter again.

"Would you mind letting me in on the joke?" Weller asked.

"M'boy, these clowns are perfect for my purposes," Steinhardt said. "When they leave here, they'll hang around in bars talking about themselves for hours on end, bullshit forever in endless seminars, and make ends meet by occasionally teaching our impressionable youth. They'll talk about their favorite subject, themselves, in as favorable a light as possible, and that will improve *our* image in media and publishing circles. Ten years of processing hype artists like these, and Transformationalism will be table talk where the intellectual and media elite meet to eat."

"So it's just a con to sell more Transformationalism!" Weller blurted.

"Everything Transformationalism does is a con to sell more Transformationalism," Steinhardt said matter-of-factly. "But everything is also something else. If I can develop processes and eptifiers that will make *these* characters creatively conscious, I'll have it."

"Have what?"

Steinhardt became more intense than Weller had ever seen him. "The philosopher's stone, kiddo," he said. "The ability to make men creative at will. The key to a Transformational world. The culmination of everything I'm trying to do. The new millennium."

"And, incidentally, a cure for writer's block," Weller couldn't help cracking. It made more sense now. All this must in some way be a grandiose attempt to break his own years'-long block.

Steinhardt took it with a smile. "Incidentally, my ass!" he said. "Being at the mercy of my own subconscious drove me nuts. Try waiting three years for nothing to come, and you'll see what success here can mean. My goddamn writer's block is the essence of the problem."

"The Great I Am," Weller muttered under his breath.

"What did you say?" Steinhardt said sharply.

"Nothing," Weller replied, for he realized that that was what Maria was always calling Steinhardt, and he certainly didn't want to sidetrack Steinhardt into *that.*

Steinhardt grinned at him strangely. "That was no lady, that was my wife," he said. "When will you learn how far I really am ahead of you, kiddo?"

At that moment they finally reached the computer complex. "And now for our next Transformational lesson of the day," Steinhardt said, parking by the entrance. "Remember, laddybuck, disagree with me as best you can. I'm sure that you'll do fine, now that we've gotten in a little practice."

Storming through the computer complex, Steinhardt accosted Bernstein in the main control room, typing on a keyboard below a display screen. "There you are, Arthur," he said. "We've been having a little discussion I'd like your expert opinion on."

Bernstein looked up, saw that it was Weller with Steinhardt, and seemed to retreat immediately into some psychic distance. "What is it now, John?" he said slowly. "As you can see, I'm busy right now."

"Well, this is a matter of cosmic importance," Steinhardt said. "Jack here thinks our creativity program is a waste of time and money, that we're chasing after the unattainable."

Bernstein looked sharply at Weller. "And what's more, he thinks that you seem to be of the same opinion." Now Weller looked at Steinhardt in surprise. What was this role that Steinhardt was casting him in?

"I've never made a secret of the fact that I believe a lot of this brainwave stuff is of questionable validity," Bernstein said indignantly. "You don't have to send Monitors around to find that out."

"Let's just say that Jack here has persuaded me to look at my obsessions with a more open mind," Steinhardt said, ignoring the innuendo. "So let's have some updated results."

"As you wish, John," Bernstein said coldly. "So far, we've verified that there are certain brainwave patterns that always seem present when a subject is doing creative work." He touched some keys. A series of four regular wavy lines appeared on the display scene. "Subject Jerry Winter in ordinary conversation." He played more keys. The top two lines flattened out while the bottom two seemed more agitated. "Same subject in the act of painting." He typed a long sequence. Five more brainwave patterns appeared on the screen, all closely approximating Winter's. "Five random Colony subjects in objectively verifiable creative states."

Bernstein looked up and back at Steinhardt. "Conclusion: creative states are always associated with characteristic brainwave patterns," he said.

"But we've known that for a long time, Arthur," Steinhardt said impatiently. "What about *inducing* creative consciousness electronically? That's what you're supposed to be inventing. That's the number-one priority under my personal directive." How long is it going to take?"

Bernstein spoke to Weller, or to Steinhardt through Weller. "John insists that I leap to the next conclusion and build him a creativity machine."

"That's right," Steinhardt said. "I don't see why you're having so much trouble with the piddling details. I gave you the whole idea myself. Reverse the polarity of a brainwave monitor so you can broadcast the creative wave pattern into the brain. Create the right electronic environment, and the creative juices should start to flow."

"You see, Mr. Weller," Bernstein said, "we've built such a device according to John's specifications, and we *have* been experimenting with it—"

"So where are my results?" Steinhardt roared. "I'm getting tired of all this dicking around."

"We're still not getting them, John," Bernstein said. "Fear panic, anger, and tranquility we seem to be able to induce electronically, because they're simple and powerful mental states that override the subtleties. But electronically induced creativity eludes us. Because although certain brainwave patterns are always associated with creativity, it does not necessarily follow that creative activity always arises from the presence of those patterns. It's obviously not a straight causal relationship."

291

"That's a lot of bullshit," Steinhardt said. "I'm not asking for perfection yet, I just want something that more or less works." He gave Weller a kick and a sidelong glance. "You just want to forget about electronically induced creativity so you can concentrate on the chemical stuff."

What am I supposed to do now? Weller wondered. Disagree with him? Disagree with *what*?

"*That chemical stuff*, as you call it, John," Bernstein said, "is what's getting the best results." He touched a few keys. The six closely approximating brainwave patterns on the screen coalesced into one average pattern. "Charactertistic creative pattern." Bernstein typed another sequence, and a second series of brain traces appeared, quite different from the first. "An ordinary subject in resting state," Bernstein said. "The same subject told to write a paragraph about himself." The second pattern moved into a somewhat closer approximation of the first. "Now with eptifier." Now the approximation of the second pattern to the first became much closer.

"Conclusion," Bernstein said, "eptifier elevates the creative consciousness of an ordinary subject doing something like a creative task. Further conclusion: this is the line of research we should give our number-one priority."

"You see what I mean?" Steinhardt said to Weller. "He's dragging his feet on *my* project so I'll forget about it and let him ride his own hobbyhorse." Again Steinhardt gave Weller a little kick. Disagree . . . ? How . . . ?

It suddenly dawned on Weller that maybe both of them were chasing rainbows. Steinhardt, with his idea of playing the brain like an electronic organ and Bernstein, with his genius drugs. They were both trying to create *talent* out of thin air. And all these damn brainwave patterns could possibly show was creative effort, not *results*. Disagree? It was easy enough to disagree with them both.

"Well, I can see Dr. Bernstein's point about electronically induced creative consciousness," he said, giving Steinhardt what he wanted first. "Seems to me if you recorded Michelangelo working on the Sistine Chapel and Joe Blow grinding his heart out on his fifteenth unpublishable novel, the screen would show the same damn thing."

"Exactly," Bernstein said, obviously pleasantly surprised. "All we can measure is a state of effort. Other states also seem to produce the same brainwave pattern—stress, for example, and even meditative deconditioning. We can produce the pattern at will electronically, but not the results."

Steinhardt winked at Weller. Weller decided to throw a curve and disagree with Bernstein too. "On the other hand," he said, "all you can do with the eptifiers is produce heightened effort in the same situation, not better product, right?"

"So far . . . ," Bernstein muttered. "But if we could concentrate more effort—"

"So what you're saying is that we're both equally full of shit," Steinhardt said.

"I didn't—"

"No, no!" Steinhardt said, holding up his palm. "That's exactly the kind of feedback I want to get. That's why I wanted you to look things over without preconceptions, Jack. Now what's your recommendation?"

"Recommendation . . . ?"

"We're at an impasse here," Steinhardt said. "I'm willing to listen to reason. That's why I asked you for a fresh opinion. Where do we put our number-one priority? With Arthur's vast scientific background or my vast instinctual vision? Make your recommendation."

By now Weller couldn't figure out what would be taking which side against whom, nor whose side Steinhardt really wanted him to take. Bernstein looked at him very nervously. Sure, as far as he thinks, I'm about to deliver some kind of official Monitor opinion. But what the hell is going on in Steinhardt's head? Well. . . .

"Well, if it were up to me, I guess I'd say go both ways," Weller said. He looked at Bernstein slyly, then exchanged his end of a confidential glance with Steinhardt. "Trouble is," he said, "the good doctor here is motivated to make the eptifier experiment succeed at the expense of the electronic stuff." He smiled sweetly at Steinhardt. "And you're biased in the opposite direction."

"I'm biased only toward getting results," Bernstein said angrily.

"Oh come on, Arthur, he's right," Steinhardt said. "If I can admit it, so can you. Question is, what do we do about it, Jack?"

Weller shrugged, having reached the end of his line of bullshit.

Steinhardt clapped his hands together. "I've got it," he said brightly, but with a certain falseness, even sarcasm, to his tone that gave Weller the idea he had been working around to this for a long time. "We'll make it a contest."

"A contest?" Bernstein muttered uneasily.

"I'll free you to work full-time on the eptifier experiments, Arthur," Steinhardt said. "That's what you want, isn't it?"

Bernstein looked at him suspiciously. "Yes," he admitted grudgingly.

"Great. Then it's settled. Hayakawa will take over supervision of the brainwave-induction experiments. You'll both go full bore. At the end of three months we'll see who's produced more results, and the losing project will be canceled."

"Science isn't a contest!" Bernstein said angrily. "This isn't fair. It's blackmail."

"Oh, come on, Arthur," Steinhardt said soothingly. "I'm putting my own pet project in the same jeopardy as yours, and I'm the boss of *everything*. Fair is fair. Wouldn't you say so, Jack?"

I guess I'm still supposed to disagree with him, Weller thought. "Well, to tell you the truth, it does sound a little unscientific, John," he said.

"You're not here to tell me what's scientific or not, bucko," Steinhardt said angrily. "What the hell do you know about it? There's too much Monitor interference in scientific affairs around here anyway. Wouldn't you say so, Arthur?"

Suddenly he was directing his confidential looks at Bernstein. What the hell did I do wrong? Weller wondered.

"For once I agree with you, John," Bernstein said with some emotion.

"Then that's that," Steinhardt said. "I've listened to enough advice, and now I've decided. Turn over the induction experiments to Hayakawa. So it is written, so it shall be."

"But John—"

Steinhardt held up his hand. "I hear no more," he said. "Come on, Weller, I want a word with you."

He led Weller out to the golf cart without a word, but with an attitude that glowered at him like a thundercloud about to burst. But once outside Steinhardt leaned up against the golf cart and broke into laughter. "Perfect, kiddo," he said. "Now do you see what I'm getting at?"

"*Huh?*"

"Come on," Steinhardt said, climbing into the golf cart. "It's really quite simple. I'd hoped you'd get it for yourself." Weller got into the cart beside Steinhardt, and they began driving back in the general direction of the Colony.

"Observe what we've done to old Bernstein's head," Steinhardt said. "Now he'll bust his balls to prove his own theories while Hayakawa gives his all to prove mine. And he's not sure whether I just saved his baby from cancellation at the recommendation of the Monitors. You took his side against me and my side against him, so he doesn't know what to think about you. Whose influence am I under? And how much?"

"But what's the purpose of that, except to create paranoia?" Weller said.

Steinhardt laughed. "That's *exactly* the purpose," he said. "Paranoia is the great motivator of subordinates. Creative chaos, m'boy. The operant characteristic of great leadership such as mine. That's exactly the effect I want my taped testament to have. The kind of ongoing chaos that maintains a true Transformational Consciousness. I mean you've certainly got to admit that we put Bernstein through *changes*."

He looked at Weller speculatively. "And in regard to you, I wanted to see if we could work together in the production of such Transformational mischief," he said. "And I think we could. But the trouble is, the more you convince me that you're the man I need, the less you convince me that I can trust you. Once more I find myself caught in our central paradox."

"Which is?" Weller said, lost in Steinhardt's maze of machinations.

"Which is that talented people don't seem to trust Transformationalism, and Transformationalism doesn't seem to be able to trust creative talent," Steinhardt said. He took his hands off the wheel to wave his arms momentarily, as if to embrace the Institute. "You think I don't know that all this is my pigheaded Faustian determination to manufacture creative talent out of the general run of mediocrities we attract? To synthesize what I can't extract. My God, I was a creative type myself, and I would've avoided anything like Transformationalism like the plague if I couldn't get to be guru. You think I don't understand where people like you are coming from?"

"Then why not forget the power trips and mind games?" Weller said. "Why not surround yourself with independent equals like Bernstein?"

"*Bernstein? Equals?*" Steinhardt roared. "I don't have any equals! Creative talent is one thing; being what I am is quite another. I need creative people to *serve* me, not to tell me what to do."

"You're really serious?" Weller said. "You really think you can surround yourself with talented slaves?"

"Slaves?" Steinhardt said. "Why are you people all so dense?

I've got slaves coming out of my asshole! I need wide-awake *servants.*"

"There's a difference?"

"Of course, there's a difference," Steinhardt said, calming down a little. "I know more about making people do what I want them to than any man in history. I can manipulate their minds like a maestro. But what I need is people who are self-motivated to serve the cause, with their talent intact and their minds unprogrammed."

"Sincere, dedicated, self-motivated, creative talent that does what it's told?" Weller said. "You don't ask for very much, do you?"

"No, I don't," Steinhardt said seriously. "I don't want you worshiping me because I'm such a charismatic son of a bitch. I have enough of that to make me puke. I want you to be dedicated to what I'm doing because you believe in it, because you know it works, because you see that I'm right—of your own free will. Think about it."

They had reached the gate to the Colony compound, and Steinhardt was silent as they passed through it and drove back to the cabin where Weller was staying with Annie, no doubt trying to give Weller the time to see the clear, pure light.

He stopped the golf cart in front of the cabin, leaned back, took a slug of whiskey, and regarded Weller as if he were a father pleading for the love of his errant son. "Look, the way I've handled you is a kind of experiment, Jack," Steinhardt said. "By the time Maria brought you to my attention, every little thing about you was in your dossier. I knew exactly what you were doing and why from the beginning. Torrez wanted you dealt with in the usual way, but I said: no, Fred, this guy's got style, let's give him his run. Let him follow his own star to me, but let's throw the book at him. If he makes it on his own hook, playing his own game, and we transform him from a regressive to a believer in the process, he'll have gotten there *creatively*, and we'll have solved one of our central problems."

He put his hand on Weller's shoulder. "So here you are, kiddo," he said, "and I still don't know if my little experiment worked. Are you sincere, Weller? You've got everything to gain. Work with me, and you'll be rich and powerful, and your talent will be optimized. All you've got to be able to say to yourself is, 'I was wrong, and John Steinhardt is right,' and a whole new world opens up. I kid you not."

Weller stared silently at Steinhardt. For a moment he felt

296

the force of a bond of sincerity between them, the impact of a powerful and perhaps even genuinely great man asking for his willing allegiance. He's right, Weller thought. He's offering me the world. Money, power, Annie, a chance to do really creative work. Why can't I just give in and accept it? Why does it repel me?

Why, said the other side of his head, can't you learn to love Big Brother?

So when he finally answered, his words were those of his carefully crafted persona, the character which had brought him this far, and which he could not abandon for the sake of John B. Steinhardt. "I'm ready to go to work for you right now, John," he said.

"Jesus, I know that, laddy-buck," Steinhardt said. "But are you sincere about it, or are you still just a good con man?"

Weller laughed. "I'd probably give you the same answer you'd give me to that one," he said.

Steinhardt laughed with him. "I'll drink to that answer," he said, toasting Weller with his flask and gulping down a slug of whiskey.

His eyes narrowed, he shook his head speculatively, and seemed to suddenly withdraw into some private, murky head space. "But as I've said before," Steinhardt said darkly, "I'll drink to anything."

Nineteen

Weller sat watching Annie wash the dinner dishes in the little sink from an unsettling cinematic distance. Close-up of her hands moving the sponge across the plates, pull back for a low-angle full shot on her body bent over the sink, emphasizing her silent psychic distance from his camera-eye.

He had to physically blink himself out of this distancing mode, this cinematic paranoia. Either I'm really going nuts, he thought, or this really is a totally paranoid situation.

From the Great Man he heard nothing, but every casual conversation with Annie got immediately steered into the deep waters of Transformationalism, as if Steinhardt were pressuring her to accumulate data. The line of questioning was rather obvious.

What had Steinhardt said to him? What was it like really working with *John*? What did he think Steinhardt thought of him? What did it feel like to have your consciousness enhanced with prolonged contact with the Font of All Wisdom?

It *could* all have been covered by the reverent curiosity of a true believer, if it weren't transparently designed to uncover his true feelings about the Great I Am. He sensed that Annie was constantly watching and recording his reactions—these past two days—*monitoring him*, to coin an odious phrase.

It would have been classical paranoia if Steinhardt hadn't openly told him that was exactly what she was going to be doing. I'm not paranoid, he thought. It's really happening. My wife is willing to spy on me for Transformationalism, and there's no doubt about it.

And what are *you* loyal to, Weller? he thought. To a wife who doesn't want your loyalty on your terms and won't return it? To a dead-end career that maybe you can never go back to? What the hell *is* there in your life besides Transformationalism?

He knew that he really only had two alternatives. He could try to blackmail his way out of the Institute with the Master Contact Sheet and hope that he would make it. And hope against everything he knew that she would choose to come with him when push came to shove.

Or he could accept John B. Steinhardt as his personal savior. And keep Annie. And become rich and powerful. And become a different person.

Obviously there was only one logical, Transformational conclusion. Steinhardt had set it up so that a rational man had only one self-interested choice. Gain everything or lose everything was reasonably clear-cut. But he rebelled against that logic. There was no way he could find it in his heart to love Big Brother. At this point he was beginning to wonder whether that made him a hero or a masochist. Perhaps they amounted to much the same thing.

Annie finished the dishes, dried her hands, and walked slowly over to him, thighs rubbing lightly together, blouse undone to the third button, and a come-hither look in her eyes. "I've got plenty of time before I have to go to tonight's staff meeting," she said, sitting down beside him with a little toss of her hair and a wiggle of her ass.

But Weller was finding it hard to relate to her sexually since she had started interrogating him on the sly. Making love to her was becoming more and more difficult and less and less satisfying. Whenever he made love to her, he felt that a world of eyes was looking on over their shoulders, and two of them were *hers*.

So once again he pretended to ignore the obvious, and for once did a little sly interrogating of his own. He leaned forward and said, "What happens if I do end up directing John's little project? What happens then?"

Annie angled her body away from him and looked at him in confusion. "What happens then? What do you mean?"

"I mean us," Weller said. "Once it's over, where do we go from there?"

"*Over?*" Annie said shrilly. "Once *what's* over?" Her voice suddenly hardened into the commissar's tone he had been hearing for days, and he had neither the heart nor the stomach to confront it.

"I've got to admit this has been good for us," he began cautiously. "But this place is like a hothouse. Sooner or later we've got to return to the real world and pick up the threads of our lives."

Her eyes became distant and impenetrable. "Our old lives are dead," she said. "Old instantaneous personas. We're not

299

those people any more. We can't go back, we can only go on. Can't you see that, Jack?"

"Sure," Weller said sadly, and he really could. "But what we are now are instantaneous personas too. Riding the changes got us here, but some day we're going to have to ride the changes out, or we'll end up becoming dead shells again. There aren't any final destinations. John would say so himself."

"I don't like what I'm hearing, Jack," Annie said in an almost threatening tone. "You're telling me you want us to leave the movement. Isn't that really it?"

Even now, especially now, when a single "yes" would finally bring them to the inevitable confrontation, Weller's courage failed him, and he found himself drawing back from the brink. "No," he said. "Not leave the movement, just have some lives of our own, too. Not turn our backs on Transformationalism, but not let it swallow us whole, either. Some kind of compromise between serving the movement and serving ourselves."

"As far as I'm concerned, serving the movement *is* serving myself," Annie said coldly. "I don't want to go back to Hollywood ego tripping. I won't. I can't."

"*Can't?*" Weller snapped. "Don't you think you'd better take a hard second look if leaving here is something you think you *can't* do? Whatever happened to freedom? Don't you ever miss it?"

"You're just running a cheap word game," Annie said angrily. "I can't leave because I don't *want* to leave. Freedom is what I've finally found in Transformationalism. Freedom is working for something that transcends your own petty ego, something that takes you outside the limits of your self, that makes you a part of a greater destiny."

Her voice had become that strident commissar speech he had come to know all too well. But suddenly it became soft, personal, and immediate as she touched a palm to his cheek.

"Poor baby," she said, "I don't think you've ever found anything like that for yourself, have you? Not even here, not yet. Oh Jack, wasn't I the same way? We blamed it on the Hollywood system, but even our dreams and ambitions were confined by our own egos. If only *we* were free to do *our* things, we'd find what we were looking for, we'd really be creative people, we'd be all right. A movie star and a hotshot feature-film director, right? All we ever thought of was moving up in the Hollywood machine that was grinding us down."

Her eyes brightened, and she began to radiate energy, peace, genuine contentment. "You can't see that till you get out of it," she said. "Not till you find what was missing all along. And I've found that in Transformationalism. I feel whole now. I feel home. This is my life, this is what I was meant to do. I feel it completely. All I need to be totally happy is to have you share it with me."

Weller finally felt the full force of the vast gulf that had opened up between them. He could no longer hold back the knowledge that had been building in him since that very first reunion in Steinhardt's house. He was losing her. Winning her back from Transformationalism had turned into another dead dream. And beyond this terrible pang of impending loss was something that was almost envy. Though the cause might be delusion and Transformationalist programming, she genuinely felt the kind of fulfillment he had always longed for. Where he was empty, she was filled. What she had was something he both loathed and envied, a state of consciousness that might be Steinhardt's conjuring trick, but one that he craved to experience.

I wish I could, he found himself thinking without fully understanding it. If only I could!

"I want to share what you feel too," he said. "But I'm not sure that Transformationalism is something that can get me there."

"It can be, Jack," Annie said, snuggling against him. "All you have to do is let it."

"That's what John says too," Weller said wearily.

"Well, there you are . . ."

"And where is that?" Weller sighed.

"Let me show you," she said. "Let me take you home." She put her arms around his neck and kissed him, with as much love and sincerity as he had ever felt.

He kissed her back with the same depth of feeling in his heart, made more poignant by a foreshadow of doom. But their realities didn't seem to connect, it was as if rubber gloves sheathed his whole body, like making love through a condom.

After awhile he let her lead him into the bedroom, and she clutched him fiercely as they made love, as if she wanted to absorb him into herself, into that which filled her. He longed to let himself go, to merge with the woman of his heart, and let that surrender take him where it would.

But something held him separate. He could no more bear

to lose himself than he could to lose her. He could not follow her this final mile any more than she could follow him. Their trajectories had diverged. He felt that he had entered the twilight of their life together, that from here on in any time they made love might be the last.

And yet, he thought, as she sighed into his ear, it doesn't have to happen. All I have to do is not make it happen. What is it that I'm clinging to that makes me throw everything else away? I don't even know.

Yet whatever it was, it seemed too precious to let go of. Even if it cost him the death of their love. For surrendering himself to Transformationalism for her sake, sweet though the rewards would be, seemed also like a kind of death.

That night, while Annie was attending some staff meeting, there was an unexpected knock on the door. When Weller opened it, John B. Steinhardt was standing in the doorway.

He wore black pants and a white shirt open almost to the navel. With his gut hanging out and his eyes quite bloodshot, he looked like a beery truck driver, and the unopened bottle of Jack Daniels he held by the neck completed the image. By the look and smell of him, he was half shit-faced already.

"Come on outside, bucko. We're going to get drunk together in the moonlight," he said. Weller stared goggle-eyed at this apparition, not knowing what to say to such a proposal.

Steinhardt took hold of him by the bicep and pulled him outside into the clear, fragrant night air. "Kiddo, I've talked with you, I've gone over Annie's reports fifty times, I've watched you in action, and I still can't make up my mind about you," he said. "It has finally occurred to me that maybe the reason is that you're having the same trouble with *me*. So I said to myself, let's have this out man-to-man, let's share the old sacrament and get pie-eyed together."

He paused, reached into a pocket, and took out a pint of green fluid. "Better chugalug this eptifier first," he said, handing the bottle to Weller. "I'm talking about *serious* drinking."

Automatically Weller found himself choking down the vile stuff as they walked away from the cabin toward the margin of the woods. The idea of getting drunk with Steinhardt held its terrors, but it also intrigued him. In some absolute way he found himself agreeing with Steinhardt that it was the right and manly thing to do, and that made him feel something like affection for the son of a bitch.

"Good a place as any," Steinhardt said, picking out the trunk of a big tree and lowering himself to the ground against it. He uncapped the bottle of bourbon. "Have a slug," he said, handing the bottle up to Weller. "Take a good big one and wash that crummy taste out of your mouth."

Weller took a long swallow of whiskey and sat down beside Steinhardt. From where they sat halfway up a gentle slope, the bungalows of the Colony were half-hidden in the trees, the guards and fences were invisible, and a bright half-moon cast silvery shadows down into the hollow. The cool night breeze carried no scent of the things of men. They might be anywhere. They might be anyone.

"Have some more," Steinhardt rumbled. "You've got a lot of catching up to do."

Weller shrugged and took another long drink, feeling the warmth of it filling his belly and radiating out toward his fingers and toes. He handed the bottle over to Steinhardt, who took a big gulp, then handed it back with a drink-up motion of his forearm.

Weller took another drink. The moonlight seemed to flow and glow like a river of water. Crickets hummed in his ears.

"What do you really think I am?" Steinhardt said. "A drunken old phony who lucked into something good, right?"

Weller felt a direct circuit opening up between the top of his head and his mouth, bypassing caution and logic. Well, what the fuck? he thought, taking another belt of Dutch courage.

"You got to admit, John, you're not exactly the ideal vision of an ascetic guru," he said.

Steinhardt took the bottle and gulped down a drink. "Fuckin'-A," he said. "I'm a complex son of a bitch."

"Why are you doing this?" Weller asked.

Steinhardt laughed. "To save the world," he said. "To make an easy buck. Because it's there. You think I know?"

"I mean why are you getting me drunk?"

Steinhardt handed back the bottle. "Because you've got a bad case of psychic constipation," Steinhardt said. "Think of it as Ex-Lax for the mind."

Weller took another drink. "Yeah?" he said. "Seems to me *some* people I could mention have verbal diarrhea."

"For sure, laddy-buck," Steinhardt said, snatching away the bottle. He took another drink. "I got onto the booze in the old days. When you have to crank out twenty thousand words a week just to survive, verbal diarrhea is a survival value. And

303

it hasn't done me wrong, now has it? Y'know, I believe I was half shit-faced all the way through *Transformational Man*. When I discovered Benson Allen's little fan club, I had to read my own damned book just to find out what the hell I had written."

"Did ya like it?" Weller giggled, recovering the bottle.

Steinhardt laughed. He shrugged. "It was what we used to call a good read," he said. "Just between you and me, lad, I wasn't the world's greatest science-fiction writer. Lots of ideas, but sitting down there and typing was torture. Fortunately I could type sixty words a minute even dead drunk."

Somewhere behind the fog that was rolling into the forefront of Weller's mind, he sensed that Steinhardt's drunkenness was focused, that he was taking all this somewhere, that these self-deprecating revelations had a purpose. But he couldn't figure out what it was. Maybe another drink would help.

"What about you, kiddo?" Steinhardt said. "You gonna tell me that you were an ivory-tower aesthete? I mean, directing *monkey shows?* Did you really think you were doing anything but making a buck as best you knew how?" He winked and snatched back the bottle. "One old hack to another, Jack?"

Weller shrugged. Out here in the woods, his head reeling in the moonlight, all that seemed so far away and unreal, something he could be as detached about as Steinhardt apparently was. "Takes one to know one, I suppose," he admitted.

"Then why won't you come the rest of the way with me?" Steinhardt said.

"Huh?"

Steinhardt stood up, leaned against the tree with one hand, and looked down at Weller. "What you just admitted to me is not something you would have admitted to yourself before you had the benefits of Transformationalism, now is it?" he said. "You're not a hack mentality now any more than I am. I've brought you that far, now haven't I?"

Steinhardt's figure looming above him seemed huge and powerful, ancient and wise, outlined in the moonlight. "I suppose you have," Weller admitted quietly.

"So why not accept the next stage of your evolution like a man?" Steinhardt said. He sat down again and handed Weller the bottle. "I've gotten you off your treadmill to nowhere," he said. "So why don't you let me take you along for the best part of the ride?"

"Onta *your* treadmill?" Weller blurted boozily.

"I don't notice the ground moving backward under *my* feet," Steinhardt said. "Which is more than I think you can say for yourself right now, bucko."

"Offa the TV con and onta the Transformationalist con," Weller grunted stonily.

"So you really think it's all a con?" Steinhardt said in a voice gone hard and ominous.

The chirping of the crickets buzzed angrily in Weller's ears. "Fuck this!" he snapped. "Don't *you* think it's a con, John?"

Steinhardt clapped him on the shoulder. "Yer a kid after me own heart!" He grabbed the bottle and took a long, long swallow.

"Of course, it's a con!" he exclaimed. "It's the best goddamn con in the world! An income in seven figures, a billion dollars worth of capital to play games with. Learjets, Institutes, city townhouses, country retreats, Cuban cigars, and the devout dues-paying worship of millions. You ever hear of a better con?"

"You *tell* me it's a con, and then you expect me to swallow it?" Weller said thickly.

"Why not?" Steinhardt said. "It's such a good con that I swallowed it myself."

"Huh?" Weller grunted. His head was reeling, the half-hidden rooftops of the bungalows below seemed to flash and shimmer, and Steinhardt's eyes were a silver sheen of reflected moonlight. Words were becoming sounds that were hard to follow logically.

"That's the whole point," Steinhardt said. "I'm the best advertisement there is for Transformationalism because I *knew* it was a con when I took over Benson Allen's nut cult of the great me. Where I was coming from, everything in *Transformational Man* was drunken ravings I tossed off in six weeks for fifteen hundred bucks. I didn't see any potential at all. Harry and Maria had to browbeat me into taking over the movement, and even then the best I hoped for was to get my ass out of debt and get a few months ahead on the rent."

Steinhardt paused and took another drink. Weller couldn't believe where he was or what he was hearing, though he knew it was only confirmation of what he had always believed. But for John B. Steinhardt to be sitting there, drunk as a skunk, admitting that he was nothing but a sleazo con artist, that was totally unreal.

"But as the changes marched on, strange things began to happen in the old coconut," Steinhardt said. "Suddenly I woke up, and I was the leader of a mass movement, and I was rich, all off this low-grade scam. It put me beyond money, beyond the need to feed my ego; I had all of that I could ever want. So I said to myself: John, what the fuck is going on here?"

Steinhardt stood up and began pacing in small circles in front of Weller, punctuating his words with the bottle, like some bemused old rummy. "So I reread the Word according to me as if I were my own disciple—all the pamphlets and theories and bullshit encyclicals I had reamed out over the years to keep things going and create more product to sell."

He paused to take a long, rather slobbering drink. "Jesus, I was amazed at my own unsuspected brilliance, I kid you not," Steinhardt said with utter seriousness. "Somehow all this wisdom had come out of some place inside of me without my really even being aware of it. Even *Transformational Man* reads like the stuff of destiny now. And I had even previously explained *that* kind of transformation to my followers without realizing it. I couldn't see who I was until I was freed from that science-fiction-hack persona I had been stuck in. I had to become a phony guru to get enough changes between me and that to understand the previous level. And once I saw the process I had put myself through, I couldn't just be a phony guru either, because, goddamn it, the stuff I had used to set up the con was the real thing, and I had proven it on myself."

Steinhardt sat down close beside Weller and grinned at him crookedly. "Can you guess what I did then?" he asked rhetorically.

Weller managed to nod a woozy no.

"I put myself through all the bullshit processes I had invented," Steinhardt said. "I secretly had Benson Allen run them all on me. Partly to find out whether they really worked, partly I had some idea of breaking my writer's block. Well, I didn't break the block, but I found out I didn't want to. I found out that the thing I had become was the optimized me and all I had to do was accept it."

He handed the bottle to Weller, who drained what little was left. "I transformed myself through the Transformational processes I had dreamed up as a con," Steinhardt said. "Drink to that, laddy-buck! Drink to the ultimate self-made man!"

Shakily Weller dropped the empty bottle. The treetops were whirling through a starry sky. His head was roaring with the buzz of the crickets. His mouth could hardly form coherent words. Sweat was breaking out on his forehead. Steinhardt studied his face.

"Hey, you look awful, kiddo," he said. "Better walk you

306

home." He dragged Weller unceremoniously to his feet and steadied him around the shoulder for a moment with a sureness and energy which Weller, in his present condition, found amazing.

"Why . . . why . . . why are you telling me stuff like this?" he managed to say as they walked slowly toward the cabin, with his knees trembling and swaying as if he were on stilts.

"Because I want you to understand that *I* came into all this with at least as cynical an attitude as you did," Steinhardt said. "What's more, I don't *have* to believe that Transformationalism's the real thing to get anything I could ever want out of it. But *I* believe in it, even knowing a lot more shit than you do about it, sonny boy."

Halfway to the cabin a bubble of anger burst in Weller's reeling brain. He pulled himself away from Steinhardt's support and stood there, weaving, but standing alone on his own two feet. "What about the ripoffs, John?" he said. "What about what you've done to my wife? What about the mind-fucks and the control programs? What about the way you screw up people's lives?"

Oh, my god, Weller thought, after he had heard himself. What have I done?

But Steinhardt laughed, put his arm around his shoulders, and continued helping him back to the cabin, unruffled by anything. "Yeah, that's the bottom line between us, isn't it?" he said. "Somehow you got it in ya head that because I'm offering you the goodies of the world, that ya gotta fork over your soul."

They reached the cabin then, and Weller disengaged himself from Steinhardt and leaned up against the doorframe. His vision was beginning to go cloudy and a bubble of nausea was forming in his gut. "Yeah, well ain't that it?" he gargled.

"What the hell do I want your soul for?" Steinhardt shot back. "What am I gonna do with it, claim it as a tax deduction?"

"You wanna make me someone else . . . ," Weller woozed, really beginning to feel sick to his stomach.

"So what?" Steinhardt said. "I've done that to you already. Whatsa big deal, I do it to myself all the time. It's ongoing change, kid. You can't stop it, you can only try to find the best wave to ride. The one you got off of has already passed."

"I don't want anyone screwing around with my head," Weller said, holding onto the doorframe with both hands now. "It hurts like hell but itsa only one I got. I wanna stay me."

"Come, kiddo, you're not the old persona you're trying to cling to anymore," Steinhardt said. "You can't be. Too many changes. All you can choose is who you're going to become, there's no return-trip tickets on the train we're riding. The Jack you are now is twisting you up in knots trying to hold onto a past that's gone and can't come back."

Weller could only dimly understand what Steinhardt was saying now. Sounds and thoughts were crowded to one corner of his mind by the surging green demand of his guts, by a need to puke that was becoming his most immediate and fondest desire.

"Urrrrr . . ." he groaned.

"All you've got to do is let it go," Steinhardt said. "Accept the gifts of destiny. Be a fuckin' Transformational Man. Accept where you are now, and let yourself be what you're becoming. Let it all come out."

Let it all come out? That seemed like an idea of transcendental wisdom for sure at the moment. He was holding back an awful sour gag at the back of his throat. Steinhardt was absolutely right. There was on reason not to puke, no reason to hold it back any further.

"Goddamn it, you're a genius, and I'm an asshole," he groaned. "You're absolutely right, ya are. That's exactly what I'm gonna do right now, let all that stuff go, and get it the hell out of me."

Steinhardt stuck his face in Weller's. The smell of his breath made Weller gag, and he just barely held his gorge down. "Really?" Steinhardt said, blinking eyes as pink as elephants. "You're really ready, kiddo? No shit?"

"No shit," Weller muttered around a suppressed gag that this time seared the back of his throat with acid vomit. "Immediately!"

"Ya, well, we'll have to talk about it tomorrow when we're both sobered up," Steinhardt said. "Yer okay, kiddo!" He slapped Weller on the back, nearly causing him to lose his precarious balance. "But ya sure can't drink with the old master," he said. "You kids got no stamina."

"Uhhhh . . ." Weller grunted, half as a reply, and half a visceral reaction. "Gotta go. . . ."

He dashed through the door bent at the waist, staggered into the bathroom falling to his knees, and just managed to get his head over the toilet bowl as horrid sour puke exploded from his throat. Again and again he heaved his guts out, until he felt totally empty, until dry spasms made him clutch his stomach in pain, until nausea subsided into an overwhelming fatigue, an irresistible slide toward black nothingness.

He staggered into the living room half out on his feet, moaned as he felt his legs going out from under him, and just managed to flop facedown across the couch before his consciousness slid into sweet oblivion.

Annie looked narrowly across the breakfast coffee at him and for the third time said, "But what *happened*, Jack?"

Weller had choked down a big glass of eptifier as soon as she had awakened him in the morning from his stupor on the couch, so his pounding headache had just about subsided and the awful feeling in his gut had more or less faded away—not, however, to the point where he could face the thought of food with any equanimity. But the black, confused mood in which his mind had awakened would not go away.

"I told you twice, we got utterly shit-faced, and I don't remember what the fuck happened!" he snarled.

"Well, you don't have to snap at me about it!" Annie said. "I'm not the one that got drunk, puked, and passed out on the couch."

"But you're the one who's interrogating me about it!" Weller said. "That's your goddamn directive, isn't it, my little commissar?"

Annie's face went stony cold. "It has nothing to do with that," she said with exaggerated evenness. "It's strictly personal."

"I find it hard to believe that *anything's* strictly personal anymore."

"You don't trust me at all anymore, do you?" Annie said more softly.

Weller sighed. He didn't even know what he was arguing with her about. He half suspected that he was really arguing with Steinhardt, or perhaps even another side of his own head. Fact was, he *did* remember most of what had been said during his drinking bout with Steinhardt. Everything but the very end of it which was a vague green cloud of nausea, puking, and something which had happened between them. Somehow he had woken up with the feeling that he had won, that he had finally convinced Steinhardt of his sincerity. Or that Steinhardt had really won him over in his drunken state, at least to Steinhardt's own drunken satisfaction. He knew that *something* had happened, that the situation had been altered, but what and how were lost in the memory of a drunken blur.

And when Annie kept asking him about it, he had automatically taken it as a directive from Steinhardt; as if, through her, Steinhardt was trying to find out what he remembered, or maybe even trying to fill in a blank spot in his own memory track. But that was pure paranoia, wasn't it? Annie couldn't have spoken to Steinhardt yet this morning, now could she?

"I'm sorry, Annie," he said. "It's certainly true that you've been up front with me. At least I know where I stand with you."

Annie lifted her coffee cup to her mouth, stared speculatively over the lip. "And where do you imagine that to be?" she asked.

"Second place," Weller said, "to Transformationalism."

Annie looked down into the depths of her coffee.

"Am I wrong?" Weller asked.

Annie remained silent.

"If I'm wrong, I wish to hell you'd tell me so," Weller said. "If I told you I simply couldn't take this shit any more, that I was taking off, that you had to choose between Transformationalism and me *right now*, what would you do? Tell me you would come with me!" Fuck it! he thought. I've finally said it. We've finally come to the bottom line.

Annie slowly looked up at him. Her lower lip trembled. Her eyes filled with tears. "Is that what you're saying, Jack?" she whispered. "Are you finally issuing your ultimatum?"

"That's not answering my question," Weller said with awful coldness.

"And you really want an answer?" Annie said plaintively. A muffled mourning bell was already peeling in her voice.

I've got my answer, Weller thought. Haven't I known it all along?

But why the hell am I doing this? Paused on the brink of the final, irrevocable parting, the end of their marriage, the end of everything he had fought for and sacrificed for and suffered for all these months, Weller drew back again. What am I doing? he thought. I think I've finally won at least this round. I think I've sold myself to Steinhardt, somehow. I've bought time to work on her head, all the time I could ask for. Why the hell did I almost throw it all away?

"No," he said. "You don't have to answer me. I was just running a life scenario on you."

Relief, anger, and then puzzlement chased each other across Annie's face. "Why did you run a number like that on me?" she demanded.

"Because I think that John and I decided that I was going to work with him last night," Weller said. "And before I committed myself to that, I wanted to be able to feel that whither I goest, you goest too. So I could be sure I knew exactly why I was going to stay."

"Do you want me to lie to you?" Annie said quietly.

"No. You couldn't if you tried. I know where we stand."

"Well then," Annie said, suddenly brightening artificially, "then let's forget about it. Why torture ourselves with unreal negative life scenarios? Especially when the real news is so good!"

"You're so sure you know what's real," Weller said. "Maybe you'd like to tell me."

"We've got a life together here," she said. "You're going to work with John. There are no horrible choices to be made. Everything's coming out all right, isn't it? Isn't that what's real?"

Weller sighed. For the time being anyway, maybe that *was* reality. Certainly, at this moment, he lacked the courage to make it anything else. "Yeah," he said, squeezing her hand and forcing a smile. "I think I'm still hung over is all. Everything is coming up roses."

"Sure it is," she said, leaning over the table and kissing him on the lips. But deep inside him that mourning bell kept peeling, as if the essence of what he was still fighting to keep had already been lost.

Nervously alert, his mind racing with yet another dose of eptifier, Weller ascended the spiral staircase to John B. Steinhardt's domed lair. The summons had not come till noon, and he had had enough time to clear his head and think things through clearly. Steinhardt had displayed his dirty linen to him as if it were a badge of honor. Whether the intimacy it had established between them were real or not, it was obviously what Steinhardt had intended, and Weller had certainly told Steinhardt a thing or two himself. So if Steinhardt had really convinced himself that they had had a meeting of minds, why disabuse him of the notion? All I have to do, Weller decided, is keep my mouth as shut as possible and agree with everything he says. All I've got to do is let him con himself.

Steinhardt was lying in the big hammock in the center of the circular room, wearing only a kind of blue terry-cloth kilt. He unslung himself from the hammock like some ungainly walrus as Weller entered and stood there with his belly hanging out. "How's your head today, kiddo?" he asked brightly. "You were really fried last night."

Steinhardt walked over to the big oak desk at the north side of the room and perched on the edge. Weller dropped himself into a director's chair near the desk. "I'm more or less okay," he said. "That green goo sure works as a hangover cure."

Steinhardt took a cigar from the humidor on the desk, lighted it, and sent a nauseating puff of smoke in Weller's direction. "No blackouts?" he asked. "You remember everything that happened last night?"

"Clear as a bell," Weller lied forthrightly.

Steinhardt reached out his hand. "Well then, we have a deal, don't we?" he said. "You're going to be my personal director." Weller shook his hand and was able to beam back at him. For this was it, he had won, Steinhardt really trusted him now.

Steinhardt loped heavily toward the bar. "Care to drink to it?" he said.

"Thanks but no thanks," Weller grunted.

Steinhardt laughed. "Well, then I guess I'll just have to drink your toast too," he said, pouring about four inches of bourbon into a water glass and swilling down half of it with a smack of his lips.

He put down his glass, leaned against the bar, took a puff of his cigar, and became almost professional in tone, changing gears entirely. "Okay, Jack, we'll begin work next Monday. By then I want you to be ready to give me an idea of where you want to shoot your outside footage, how you think the testament should be organized, and I'll be ready to discuss when I do my raving for your cameras. Okay?"

"Okay," Weller said. "Except we really can't talk about when we're going to start shooting until we have a crew lined up."

"Don't worry about that, we'll just pick a date and I'll fly in whatever you say you need."

"Er . . . I don't know if Changes Production has good enough people for a project on this level," Weller said speculatively.

Steinhardt shrugged. "You be the judge of that," he said.

He laughed and took another gulp of whiskey. "For *my* immortality, I want nothing but the best, and I'm not going to limit my director to whatever Harry Lazlo has thrown together. You want pros, I will hire you pros. Consider your budget unlimited."

"Great!" Weller said. This might really turn into something after all.

"Well, I've got other fish to fry now," Steinhardt said, walking toward the stairs and ushering Weller along in tow. "You just relax and think until then, Jack, and hang loose."

He held Weller back by the elbow at the top of the stairway. "Just one thing," he said looking straight at Weller. "You *do* know what you're getting into? I mean, you already know a lot of things that aren't exactly for the masses, kiddo, and working with me on this thing, you figure to learn a lot more. Also, I don't want anyone in the movement who doesn't have to know about this project to get wind of it. The official story will be consistent with what got you here—we're just making commercials. Got it?"

"Sure, John," Weller said a little nervously. "If that's the way you want it."

"Good," Steinhardt said. "So you understand the need for reasonable security procedures."

"*Security procedures?*" Weller said uneasily.

"Oh, just standard stuff," Steinhardt said breezily. "Nothing to get excited about. You'll have to remain at the Institute throughout the whole project. No contact with outside parties. And a few other minor details."

He gave Weller a wink and propelled him on his way with a slap of the back. "We want to keep our little project under our hats, don't we, bucko?" he said conspiratorially.

I should be feeling that I've got it made, Weller thought, as he slowly descended to ground level. I *have* got it made. But something somehow told him that everything had gone too easily, that it was he and not Steinhardt who had just been had. It didn't add up logically, but he couldn't get rid of the feeling.

Twenty

Walking back to the cabin in the warm sunlight, Weller began to wonder whether his war with Transformationalism wasn't in the process of coming to a negotiated peace.

What if I just relax into the part I've been playing? he mused. Annie and I will be together, and maybe if we stop fencing over Transformationalism, we can be human to each other again. I'll have an interesting piece of work to look forward to, with an unlimited budget and a character like Steinhardt to play around with, and I should be able to come up with something that will turn him on without making me puke. And if I become John's fair-haired boy, maybe I can talk him into producing a feature. They've certainly got the money for it.

I haven't been able to change Annie's head anyway. Changes. That's my real life situation, and it could be a lot worse, so maybe I should just try to keep my consciousness eptified behind it and ride with what's happening for the best I can get out of it.

By the time he got back to the cabin, Weller was feeling almost at peace with himself. What the hell, he thought, what's so terrible about learning to love Big Brother when he's setting himself up as your benefactor, when he could even end up being your friend? What's not to like about that? What have I really been torturing myself over? Why not just relax and enjoy it?

He made himself a cheese and salami sandwich, ate it slowly with a glass of white wine, had another glass afterward on the couch, just sitting there, sipping, and mellowing out as he slowly digested the fact that the life decision had already been made. Looking at it at last from the other side, with the tension of suspense gone, it began to look not so bad after all.

About four o'clock, unexpectedly early, Annie burst into the cabin, dashed across the room, flung herself into his arms as he rose, hugged her tightly, and gave him a short hard kiss. "It's wonderful!" she cried. "Oh, I'm so happy!"

"Huh? Wha—?"

She bounced away from him, but still held both his hands tightly. "I've just been with John," she said. "He's told me all about it. Oh God, I'm so glad all this conflict is over! Ooh, I love you, Jack, and it's been so awful having to report on you and fighting with you. But that's all over now, isn't it?"

Weller paused. He took a breath. He looked at her, beaming at him from the balls of her feet. "Sure it is," he said, feeling a great gasp of tension soaring out of him, an enormous weight lifted off his shoulders and out of his heart. "You and me, babe!" He kissed her. He felt like giggling. He felt like a silly asshole. Goddamn it, Weller, isn't this what you really want? Isn't it what you've wanted all along?

Annie abruptly sat down on the couch, pulling him down beside her. "There's just one little detail to take care of," she said, pulling a sheet of paper out of her handbag and handing it to Weller. "I worked this list out with John, but we'd better go over it first to see if I missed anyone."

Suddenly uneasy, Weller looked over a long list of names of people that he knew—friends like the Shumways, business acquaintances like Johnny Blaisdell, his agent, his lawyer, his accountant, a long train of out-of-town relatives. "What the hell is this thing?" he said. "It looks like our Christmas-card list."

Annie nodded. "That's more or less what it is," she said. "Can you think of anyone I've forgotten?"

Weller felt all the dread and tension that he had thought he had just unloaded come back like a sock in the gut. What the hell is this? "Isn't it a little early to be worrying about Christmas cards?"

Annie giggled. "We're not going to send out Christmas cards, silly," she said gaily. "You're going to send out letters or postcards to the people on the list."

"I am?"

"Oh, I know it's going to be a drag writing the same thing a couple of dozen times, but they don't have to be very long, and I'll help you write them. You just have to sign them."

"What the hell are you talking about?" Weller shouted. "What letters? What is this shit?"

Annie looked up at him with innocent perplexity. "Didn't John tell you?"

"Tell me what?"

Annie shrugged. "I guess he didn't," she said. "This is just a security procedure for you to follow. We've worked out a good cover story, so you don't even have to bother yourself about that. What you'll do is tell everyone that you've landed an assignment to set up a state film company in . . . uh . . . Malawi and we'll be spending the next two years or more in Africa."

"WHAT?"

Annie continued to speak in a maddeningly robotic tone of absolute sweet reason. "You're going to be staying at the Institute for an indefinite time, so you don't want people to think you've disappeared mysteriously and nose around trying to find you."

"I don't?" Weller said numbly.

"Of course not, Jack," Annie said, as if she were stating something that they both knew was obvious. "And since you're going to be in such a high security level that you won't be able to contact even movement people on the outside, people *would* start getting suspicious and worrying about you if you just dropped out of sight without a word. With this African cover story, though, everything will seem natural."

Weller stared at her, utterly dumbfounded. He couldn't believe that his own wife was telling him a thing like this, and yet when he thought about it, the logic suddenly seemed inevitable. Electrified fences, guard dogs, security patrols, blackout of contact with the outside world. All the security measures of a concentration camp, so why *not* the old postcard-home schtick? What an idiot I've been today! The son of a bitch really knows how to rub your nose in it!

"I can't believe what I'm hearing," Weller finally managed to say. "Do you know that the Nazis used to run this same damned number with concentration-camp victims? They'd make them write predated postcards just before they shoved them in the ovens. Six weeks later the folks back home would get a card that said, 'Greetings from Scenic Auschwitz, wish you were here.' "

"Oh Jack," Annie laughed, "don't be silly. This is *serious*."

"SERIOUS? Fuckin'-A, it's serious!" Weller shouted. "Jesus Christ, Annie, don't you realize that the Nazis had those postcards sent home so that people could disappear without a warm trail? So they could gas them in ovens and no one would know."

Annie finally lost her infuriating good humor. "You're being infantile, Jack," she said. "Do you really think the movement is planning to kill you?"

316

"How the hell do I know? If I write those letters, I disappear and pull the hole in after me. They could snuff me or lock me in a cell for the rest of my life, or do anything else they pleased. How can I trust the good intentions of anyone who asks me to trust them *that* far?"

"Damn it, Jack, won't you ever stop being such a regressive?" Annie snapped. "Won't you ever learn to trust John?"

"*Trust John!*" Weller shouted. "How much trust do you think this fucking number shows in *me?*"

Oh, my God! Of course. Schmuck that you are, Weller, to believe that a guy like Steinhardt is going to take you on faith or swallow his own bullshit! This is the acid test, kiddo. You gotta prove your loyalty by putting yourself totally in my power, bucko! No way to con yourself through this one; it's either yes or no. He could all but hear Steinhardt telling it to him.

Weller forced some semblance of calm into his voice. "Don't you see what this is, Annie?" he said. "Damn it, are you totally blind? Goons, electrified fences, guard dogs, and now this. What's it going to take to show you where John's coming from? Gas ovens? Firing squads? Flaming toothpicks under your fingernails?"

Annie's lower lip trembled. Tears welled up in her eyes. "Oh Lord . . . ," she whispered. "Oh my God . . ."

Weller put his arm tenderly around her shoulders. "Yeah, I know," he said. "It's pretty hard when you get your nose rubbed in it."

Annie's whole body began to shake. She began to sob.

"Hey, it's not that bad, babes," Weller cooed, stroking her hair. "I'm not such a jerk that I walked in here without a ticket out. I can get us out of here. We'll be home soon, and before you know it, this will all be a funny story to tell at parties." He kissed her on the cheek and said with much more confidence than he felt: "It's a promise."

Annie choked back her tears, pulled away from him, and looked at him, dumbfounded. "What . . . ?"

"I've got 'em by the balls," Weller said, trying to pump as much confidence into his voice as he could muster. "I've got material John can hardly afford to have made public. They'll have to let us go."

Annie's eyes widened. "You're going to *blackmail* Transformationalism?"

"You could call it that," Weller said with a certain satisfaction.

317

Annie shrank away from him in loathing. "After all the transformations you've been through, haven't you learned *anything*?" she said.

"Haven't *you*?" Weller snapped back. And as he spoke, he was transported against his will to a cold clear mountaintop where he saw at once that he had lost her.

"Look, it's not too late, Jack," Annie said, her voice now trembling with desperation. "I can forget what I've heard. You've changed, you've grown, you've been transformed, you've been chosen to work personally with *John*. And you're going to throw all that away? For what? Because you can't let go of an old instantaneous persona that isn't even you anymore?"

But he was seeing her now from an anesthetizing distance, from the other side of the great divide. There she sat, lovingly beckoning him down into the pit. For how long had it really been over between them before this moment of truth had finally forced him to face it? She was his for the taking, but she had become something he did not want to love—a ghost, a horribly distorted *doppelgänger* of the lost Annie that had once been his. But that woman no longer existed. This was a stranger.

"It's over, Annie," he said. "You and me. Transformationalism. Mind games. All I want now is out."

"Won't you change your mind?" Annie pleaded. She got up off the couch and began pacing in small circles. "Look, all you have to do is sign those cards and letters now," she said. "That's all, I'll even write them for you. You don't have to change what's in your head now, all by yourself. There are processes that can help you. All you have to do is sign those cards, and we'll do the rest."

"That's what I'm afraid of," Weller said. "That's exactly what I'm afraid of."

A strange lassitude of spirit came over him. He had nothing left to love, nothing left to care about, nothing left of the life that had been. Only that pinpoint of consciousness within him that said, "I'm me"—and would not let itself be snuffed out—no matter what the cost.

Annie looked down at him with sad but patronizing sympathy. This was another person. This was his Comrade Commissar. "This is the end for us?" she said distantly.

Weller stood to meet her gaze levelly. "Unless you change your mind. Unless you'll come with me."

She reached out to him, pulled her hand back. "Oh, Jack . . ." She started, fluttered around the room like a trapped bird, shaking her head and muttering to herself.

"Oh God, I don't know. . . . I mean maybe . . . maybe there's a way . . . maybe this doesn't have to be. . . ." A wave of indecision passed across her face. She stopped in front of him and studied his face with an unreadable expression. "Look, I've got to think. I've got to be alone by myself for a while. I'm going to take a little walk. You wait here, okay?"

She started for the door, but Weller caught her by the elbow. "Wait for what?" he said. "For you to come back with a squad of Monitors?"

She turned and looked at him coldly. "Do you really believe I'd do that?" she said.

"I find it hard to believe you wouldn't," Weller said sadly.

"You think I'm going to rush off to get the Monitors to stop you from escaping, is that it? But you can't *escape*, Jack. There's no way out of here. The Institute is surrounded by—"

"I know, I know, a double electrified fence, guard dogs, and a fucking free-fire zone!" Weller snapped. It was true. She was right. There was no way to physically escape from the Institute, and even if there were, the long arm of the Monitors would reach out to grab him wherever he was. It didn't matter if she got the Monitors now, or if he surrendered to them himself. There was only one avenue of escape from Transformationalism, and that was with his mind, not his feet. *I've got to do what I've planned to do all along and use my insurance to talk my way free.* And the way through was John B. Steinhardt.

Weller looked at Annie speculatively, and, though he was totally conscious of the process, he started to *direct*. From where he was now, she was one more Transformationalist, she was part of the enemy, she had to be . . . dealt with. "Don't get the Monitors, Annie," he said. "Get John."

Annie blinked, then her mouth creased in a tiny ghost of a smile. "That's what I was really going to do," she said.

"I figured you would," Weller lied. Now that he thought about it, though, he should have seen it. He shouldn't have let his loathing for what she had become make him underestimate her like that. *Who else could decide this issue? Who else would she run to when she runs away from me?*

"John will know what to do," Annie said, opening the cottage door. "John will sync our optimum life scenarios together again."

"John is the answer, John is the way," Weller chanted sarcastically.

319

"You'll see," she said, as she closed the door behind her. "John will know what to do."

"And if he doesn't, I'll tell him!" Weller answered after she had gone.

"What's all this crap about refusing to carry out a simple life directive? What's this shit about blackmail threats? Why are you breaking the poor lass's heart, you cadly bounder?"

John B. Steinhardt, in all his worldly glory, stormed into the cabin with his mouth already going at cruising speed, and by the look of him, with a bit of a glow already on. Oiled to a sheen with suntan lotion, he wore only red satin swimming trunks and a black beach towel thrown around his shoulders like a cloak. He was still clutching a half-consumed mint julep as if summoned directly from his poolside pleasures, and Weller did not suppose it was his first of the day.

Annie trailed behind him like Lois Lane after some ungodly barroom parody of Superman.

"Fuck a duck, kiddo, what's wrong with you? I thought we had everything straightened out," Steinhardt said, collapsing into a chair.

How long Weller had rehearsed this confrontation in his mind and how blank he had become, now that he was faced with doing the whole scene in one perfect take! He had tried to rehearse it again in his mind while Annie went to fetch the Great I Am, but he couldn't come up with any scenario. He was going to have to improvise, he was going to have to be himself.

"That's right, Jack, isn't it?" Annie said, sitting down on the couch at the opposite corner, completing yet another angle of this twisted triangle. "You and John were going to work together."

"*Are* going to work together, Annie," Steinhardt declared expansively. He gave Weller a peculiar look. "Surely we're evolved enough to clear up a minor misunderstanding about a standard security procedure," he said. "And that's all this existential crisis is all about, isn't it?" There seemed to be a definite edge of threat to his voice.

Is this his way of inviting me to let him forget about any blackmail threat for the sake of my own health? Weller wondered. Does that mean he'd rather not deal with it?

"Yeah, this is an existential crisis about a standard security procedure, John," Weller said. "You've got too many standard security procedures. But when you borrow one from the

320

Nazis, even an unevolved type like me gets the point."

Annie shrank away from him in horror. Steinhardt gave him a look of what seemed like genuine hurt. "Come on, laddybuck," he said, "I've got to maintain security. This isn't a concentration camp, is it? It's more like the Manhattan Project. We're developing the atomic age of the mind here. We can't risk letting just *anyone* get ahold of what we have."

"Pardon me for being dense," Weller said dryly, "but why not? If you're supposed to be liberating minds, why don't you give all this wonderful benign knowledge to the world? That's what you'd be doing if you were what you pretend to be, John."

"Don't be a prick," Steinhardt said more harshly. "You know as well as I do that what we have would not exactly be benign in the hands of the current holders of worldly power. They'd just use it to sell dogfood to cat owners on TV and elect themselves to office. Universal Transformational knowledge is only benign in the hands of Transformational men. Before we can safely give it to the world, we have to create a Transformational world to give it to."

"The ends justify the means, right?" Weller said. "Pardon me for being so 1968, John, but you're talking like a fascist pig."

"Fascist pig!" Steinhardt exclaimed in wounded outrage. "I'm liberating the world from its frozen cultural matrices, its programmed consciousness, and you have the nerve to call me a fascist pig!"

"That's ridiculously awful, Jack!" Annie echoed.

"You're just replacing old programming with new programming of your own!" Weller said angrily. "That's what every fascist-in-liberator's-clothing says!"

Steinhardt leaned back into his chair, took a sip of his warming drink, and regarded Weller evenly and coolly. "I think I'm getting pissed off, bucko," he said. "I think I'm really getting pissed off."

"So am I," Weller said evenly, giving him a cold, level stare back. "That's why I want out of here. I look at what you've done to Annie and to me and to dozens of people I've met since I found out you existed, and I just wish I didn't have to know there was any such thing as Transformationalism. I don't care how much you like me, I don't care what you can do for me, I think what you're doing sucks, and I just want no part of it, okay."

Annie goggled at him in horror, bolted from the couch, and

perched herself on a chair across the room, clarifying the true geometry of the situation, even as he had finally made his rock-bottom feeling clear to both of them for the first time. And perhaps to himself as well.

"You don't want me for an enemy, Jack," Steinhardt said with more coldness than Weller had believed him capable of.

"You're right. I don't," Weller said. "I might if I thought I could do anything about you, but I know that I can't. You've taken my wife, you've pauperized me, you've cost me my job, you've messed with my mind, but you've also convinced me that you're too big for me to try to think about revenge. It's all too much for me, John. Just let me go."

Steinhardt took a sip of his drink. Annie exchanged glances with him as if pleading for Weller's boon. Steinhardt sighed, shrugged, frowned, shook his head. "Aw, come on, don't make me feel like a bad guy," he said unhappily. "You *know* I can't let you go. You know too much. I've unburdened the secrets of my soul to you. You've fucked my wife. And you're my favorite experiment. How can I give up on you? You're right, I've fucked you over, okay? So how can I leave you in this shape? I owe it to you to get you and Annie together, to eptify your messed-up mind, and to make you healthy, wealthy, famous, and wise."

"I don't want any of that, John. I just want out. I'd rather we shook hands on it, but I'll force you if I have to."

Weller held his breath as Steinhardt tapped his fingers on the lip of his glass. Now the cards were on the table and the final hand was about to be played.

"You're really going to try this blackmail thing on me?" Steinhardt finally said. "You're really going to reduce it to that level?"

"Only if I have to. If you'd just agree to let each other alone, the subject would never have to come up."

"The way you feel, it already *is* the subject," Steinhardt snapped. "How can I let you go after you've just spent so much energy convincing me you're a dangerous man with plenty of motivation for revenge?"

Weller's stomach sank. Oh my God, I didn't see that angle at all, he thought dismally. I just let my big mouth run off. "I . . . I didn't mean that at all . . . ," he stammered lamely. "I mean, I'm not an enemy of the movement. I don't want to end up like Richard Golden. I just want to live my own life and let you live yours."

Annie's mouth twisted into a moue of distaste. "You're groveling, Jack, it's disgusting," she said.

"If that's all it is," Steinhardt said shrewdly. He studied Weller. "How am I supposed to believe this live-and-let-live declaration from someone who admits he's ready to blackmail me? And from someone who's got some pretty good ammunition. I mean, Torrez is the expert, but it seems to me that Los Angeles's corporate Master Contact Sheet might really be potentially damaging. I'm supposed to trust you not to use it?"

"*You know?*" Waller gasped.

Steinhardt laughed. "You think the Monitors didn't search your house the night they grabbed you in Golden's apartment house? You think they didn't find it?"

"But . . . but if you knew, they why did you let me get this far, all the way to the Institute?"

Steinhardt took a drink, set the glass down, and floated up out of his chair. "Where better to isolate a maximum security risk?" he said.

Weller found himself scrabbling desperately for mental purchase. "But . . . but working on the film with you, getting drunk together, all the little games . . . ," he said. "You knew where I was coming from, and you played them anyway? Like a cat with a mouse!"

"You sell yourself short, laddy-buck," Steinhardt said, pacing the room ponderously. "And you sell me short too. All of that was sincere. I told you you were my favorite experiment, ever since you started screwing around with my wife. You've got balls, and you've got brains, and that's what I like even when it's fighting against me. You're a lad after me own heart. Which is now breaking because you're forcing me to deal with you like the stupid regressive blackmailer you're determined to be."

"Please, Jack, listen to him," Annie begged. "You don't know what you're saying. You're throwing the best thing in your life away."

Steinhardt perched heavily on the far end of the couch. "She's right, you know," he said. "But aside from that, think of what you're trying to convince me of. That you've got information so damaging to Transformationalism that we'll agree to leave you alone for fear that you'll make it public if we don't. Isn't that right?"

"That's just about the size of it," Weller said woodenly,

dazed by the way Steinhardt had pulled the rug out from under him.

"Well, isn't that an even better argument for fitting you with cement overshoes and taking you for a long walk on a short pier?" Steinhardt said, putting mocking menace into his voice, or perhaps making a very serious threat in a mocking way.

But whatever Steinhardt's true intent, he had suddenly given Weller something to cling to, he had revealed that the Great I Am knew everything in his hand but his high hole card. *He doesn't know* that killing me would just cause the Master Contact Sheet to go out to the whole wide world as a general press release in the worst possible circumstance! He doesn't know about the fail-safe mail drops.

"That's just what *my* little security procedure is meant to prevent, John," he said somewhat smugly. "I've multiple packets of press releases and letters to the authorities in secure mail drops. With instructions to drop them all in the mail unless they hear word to the contrary from me at short intervals. And the latest interval is almost up. If you don't release me or if anything should ever happen to me, the shit will hit the fan."

Steinhardt goggled at him. He seemed genuinely taken aback. "I'm supposed to believe that?" he said uncertainly. "How do I know it's not a bluff?"

"The only way you can find out is to call me on it," Weller said. "And neither of us would like the results of that, John."

Annie, who had shrunk back into herself during all this, now bolted from her chair, wringing her hands and looking pleadingly at Steinhardt. "I don't want to hear any more of this, John," she said desperately. "It's too awful. I can't stand watching this happen."

"I can understand that," Steinhardt said. "Why don't you just leave it to me?"

Annie nodded woodenly and started toward the door. She hesitated, looked back at Weller. "Jack, unless John can help you, this is the end, this is—"

"We've already said good-bye, Annie," Weller said softly.

Annie nibbled at her lower lip, sobbed once, and sighed. "I guess we have," she said. And then she was gone.

"Jesus," Steinhardt groaned. "On top of everything I had to witness that scene. You're making me feel awful. What a mess! What am I supposed to do?"

"Why don't you just give in and admit I've got you beat?" Weller said.

"Who says you've got me beat?" Steinhardt said distractedly. "When Fred Torrez tells me you can get away with it, I'll believe you can get away with it. Security matters I leave to security experts. But man to man, Jack, what am I supposed to do to eptify my own consciousness in this situation?"

"Huh?"

Steinhardt rose to his feet and began pacing again, his shoulders hunched forward under the towel he wore as a cloak; he seemed smaller, older, more human. "Look, kiddo, I'm not a monster. I messed up your life, I admit it. All I ever wanted to do was give you Transformational consciousness and reunite you with your old lady in eternal bliss and successfully find some way to bring creative people into Transformationalism without blowing out their lights. So what I've got now is a failed experiment and a guy who I've really hurt threatening to blackmail me in a way I cannot afford. How do I do what's right?"

"What do you think is right, John?" Weller said.

Steinhardt stood before him, threw up his arms, and suddenly grew expansive again. "What's right is I make up for what I've done!" he said. "I watch over you for the rest of your life like a guardian angel. I use my manifold connections to put your career on its feet. I prove to you that I'm sorry by never-ending good deeds. I win your forgiveness and successfully complete my experiment—"

Steinhardt stopped dead in mid-sentence. "Wait a minute!" he said. He sat down in his chair, swallowed down the remains of his drink. "I think I just heard me give myself an idea of cosmic significance," he said slowly. "Why not? Maybe that's the way to bring people like you into Transformationalism. Leave their minds alone until they're ready for the final transformation. Win their willing loyalty by being a benefactor, a facilitator, a lucky leprechaun patron of the arts."

He smiled benignly at Weller. "That's the life scenario I have in mind for you, bucko," he said. "Let you live your life and strew posies in your path to make up for what I've done and to prove to you that I really am the Way." He frowned. "I'd do it too, really I would, but—"

"But what?"

Steinhardt leaned forward, looked at him, and shrugged. "But you're a security problem," he said. "I mean, if you wouldn't trust me far enough to sign a few letters and postcards, why should I trust you to keep quiet about what you know?"

"How about my word on it?" Weller suggested quietly.

Steinhardt seemed to think that over seriously.

"How about because you believe I'm not dumb enough to want to end up like Richard Golden?" Weller said.

That seemed to sink in too.

"The risk you take by letting me go isn't as great as the risk you take that those press releases will go out if you don't," Weller suggested.

"I'd need a full Monitor analysis to be sure of that," Steinhardt muttered unconcernedly to himself. He seemed to have reached some decision.

Steinhardt beamed at Weller warmly now. "I'll do it, bucko," he said. "I'll do what's right if I can." He cocked his head, shrugged sardonically. "But I'm not taking any chances with my own ass. You're still a security problem. One that's too complicated for me to figure out without a lot more to drink."

He stood up, walked over to Weller, and shooed him to his feet. "Let's go," he said.

"Where?"

"To see Fred Torrez," Steinhardt said. "For technical problems I call in my technical experts. The deal is this, laddy-buck. I'm going to sit you in a room with Fred and listen to you convince him that the minimal-risk scenario is to let you go. If you can get Fred to admit that in my presence, I'll fly you back to L.A. first-class on my Learjet half an hour later." He clapped Weller around the shoulders and half dragged him out the door.

"But Torrez doesn't consider me exactly one of his favorite people," Weller complained.

Steinhardt winked at him. "For sure," he said. "That's why I'm willing to rely on his judgment. If you can convince him against his emotional bias, I'll know I've found the optimal scenario."

"And if I don't?"

"If Fred persuades me to hand you over to the Monitors, why then, I'll be persuaded to hand you over to the Monitors, won't I?" Steinhardt said. He laughed. "Out of habit, if nothing more, that's what he'll be trying to persuade me to do. If he succeeds, then you're in his tender hands. It should be quite a contest."

Seeing the outraged look on Weller's face, he stopped short

326

and turned Weller around to face him, nose to red-veined nose.

"Be a man, Jack," he said. "Think of it as a chance to prove yourself worthy of my beneficence. A chance to really show what you can do."

He slapped Weller on the back and gave him a bloodshot stage wink. "I'll be rooting for you, kiddo," he said.

Steinhardt rushed Weller over to Institute Central at a waddling near trot, then left him to cool his heels in what seemed to amount to a cozy little cell while he went off to fetch Fred Torrez. No glaring white walls and bright lights here, just a matched set of brown leather couch and chairs, walnut incidental tables, soft pastel yellow walls, and a thick navy-blue carpet. Given an assortment of magazines on a table, it could've been a dentist's waiting room. Given Weller's state of trepidation, he might as well have been waiting for a session of particularly unpleasant dental surgery.

While he waited for Steinhardt to return with the Monitor chief, Weller tried to dope out a coherent strategy for the upcoming final confrontation without much success. He knew that he had aroused Torrez's ire at least twice in the past—once by using Maria Steinhardt, and again after the Monitors had snatched him at Golden's place. Both times directives from John had prevented Torrez from doing his nastiest; first by allowing Maria to prevent Weller from being dealt with as a regressive after he had directly defied a Monitor life directive, and then by bringing him to the Institute after he was caught hobnobbing with a superregressive like Golden. Could he count on Steinhardt's support again, or had all of that been a scenario designed to inflame Torrez against him with this scene ultimately in mind? With Steinhardt, who could tell?

And what am I supposed to try to do here? Weller wondered in something of a daze. Convince Torrez that I'm really harmless? Or convince him that there's no way he can prevent those press packets from being released if they don't let me go? It seemed that Steinhardt had set it up so he had to do both simultaneously. And that seemed a contradiction in terms. Convince Torrez that a harmless nerd has Transformationalism by the balls? How the fuck am I supposed to do that?

Steinhardt returned fortified not only with a glowering Fred Torrez but with a fresh bottle of bourbon. He had thrown on a pale blue tennis outfit though his skin still glistened from suntan lotion, and he was carrying a clean-looking glass. Did that mean he intended this to be a little more civilized?

Steinhardt ushered the tense-looking Torrez to a chair opposite the couch on which Weller was sitting and took a position himself in a chair with a convenient end table, equidistant from both of them, poured himself a drink, and slapped the bottle down on the table like a judge's gavel calling the court to order. Was that some kind of statement too? Weller wondered. Or have I really reached an eptified state of paranoia?

"Now Fred here has been fully briefed on the details," Steinhardt told him, "so Fred will conduct this proceeding while I watch the show and get soused." He took a long drink to establish his intention and nodded to Torrez. "Over to you, Torquemada," he said.

"You may consider this a form of life analysis, Weller," Torrez said smoothly. But there was an extreme undertone of tension in his voice and a petulant annoyance in his expression that Weller sensed was partly directed at the forbidden target of Steinhardt himself. How is Steinhardt using this to run a number on *Torrez?* he found himself wondering. For suddenly it began to seem obvious that he was.

"I've been directed by John to recommend one of two alternative scenarios," Torrez continued. "Either you are to be terminated as a regressive and a severe security risk, or you are to be permitted to blackmail Transformationalism into letting you go free." He favored Weller with a vulpine smile. "Perhaps you can guess where my sympathies lie?" he said.

"Now, now, Fred," Steinhardt chided. "Do remember whose balls-up got us into this pickle."

Torrez flushed. So that's it! Weller thought. Sure, if I really *do* have a working fail-safe system for distributing the Master Contact Sheet to the press and the authorities, it means that the Monitors and Torrez let down the movement by not finding it out. In a way Torrez is on the carpet here too, and *I'm* interrogating *him* for John. He began to glimpse some light at the end of the tunnel.

"That's right, Torrez," Weller said. "You've got to certify me a liar to prove that you didn't screw up your job, don't you?"

"Well put, laddy-buck!" Steinhardt said.

Torrez glared at Weller.

"And you'd better put your feelings aside and be *right* this

328

time, because either way, if you're wrong, you really put Transformationalism in the shits," Weller said, bearing in on Torrez to Steinhardt's open amusement.

"Fortunately emotions and logic sync perfectly in this instance, Weller," Torrez finally said, maintaining his control with a visible effort. "Because the question isn't whether you're telling the truth but simply whether you're more dangerous to Transformationalism alive than dead."

"Two points!" Steinhardt said.

Torrez smiled. "If you are terminated, your dangerous knowledge is terminated with you," he said. "Whereas if we let you go, you'll always be a threat. I don't really think this decision is going to be all that hard to make. Do you?"

"You're forgetting that if you don't let me go, the Master Contact Sheet will certainly be made public in a few days," Weller said.

"A long assumption, Weller," Torrez said. "First I must assume that you're telling the truth about these secure mail drops in the absence of corroborating reports, and secondly *you* assume that even if you *do* have redundant mail drops set up, we *can't* extract the locations from you and recover the material before it can be mailed."

"After which, you can safely terminate me?"

"As you suggest . . . ," Torrez said smoothly.

"Well, then you've just admitted that I have no percentage in talking, haven't you?" Weller said. "I'm terminated either way."

"We have very swift and advanced ways of extracting information against your will," Torrez said, somewhat melodramatically.

"No doubt," Weller said. "But even if I told you who my mail drops were, you still wouldn't be able to do anything about it. I set it up that way." It was true. Wally Bruner's office was a fortress of security, what with all the borderline legal case he handled. My agent keeps his files in a safe because he's paranoid about industrial espionage. Bob Shumway is nobody's schmuck. And Uncle Bill is a gun nut. No way they could stop all the packets from getting through with only a few days to work in.

"But then if that's true, you'll always be a threat if we let you go," Torrez said. "Technically speaking, we're confronted with the same problem whether we terminate you or not, even if you're telling the truth. So we have no advantage in *not* terminating you."

329

Steinhardt laughed. "I love it!" he cried. "It's the sport of kings!"

"But that's not true," Weller said uneasily. "If you let me go, nothing will happen. Because I'm offering you a fair deal, Torrez. As long as you leave me alone, I leave you alone."

Torrez snickered. "No doubt you'll even give your word on it," he said.

"That's right," Weller said coolly.

"Well, your word isn't good enough, Weller," Torrez said. "The risk is still immeasurable."

"Well, what about Richard Golden?" Weller said off the top of his head.

"Golden?"

Torrez looked confused, and even Steinhardt seemed taken aback, which however, only seemed to intensify his interest and somehow amuse him.

"Sure, Golden has a thousand times the damaging material on Transformationalism that I do, yet you leave him alone," Weller said.

"You've met Golden," Torrez said. "Does he seem like someone who isn't being monitored, a free spirit?" It was meant to be menacing, but from the look on Steinhardt's face, it seemed as if Torrez was also trying to justify another unresolved mess to John.

"He's still alive," Weller said.

"Only because he'd be a bigger nuisance dead, maybe generating another round of investigations."

"Well, there you are. Let me go, and it's the exact same situation. It's the same situation already. I'm more potential trouble to you dead than alive. It's as simple as that."

Torrez seemed to unwind a notch. "Perhaps it is," he said. "We could handle you the way we handled Richard Golden." He smiled. He leaned back. "That's my recommendation, John," he said. "The same life scenario we worked out for Golden-type regressives."

He laughed. He beamed at Weller. "You'll like that, Weller," he said. "You'll be a free man. Just like Richard Golden. Afraid of your telephone, papering your windows with tinfoil, raving like a lunatic, and perhaps ultimately certifiable. There's your fair deal, Weller. You'll be an unemployable, discredited, raving paranoiac, but you'll be alive, and you'll be harmless. Congratulate yourself, Weller. You talked me into it."

Shuddering, but drawing courage from the horror of his predicament, Weller stared across the room at Steinhardt, the

330

ultimate arbiter of his fate, who was grinning like an asshole as he poured himself another in an endless procession of drinks. I'm pissed off at this drunken fraudulent egomaniac! Weller decided. Terrified, but pissed off too.

"That's not what you promised me, John," he said indignantly. "You said if I convinced Torrez here to recommend that you let me go, you'd put me on your Learjet for the Coast and do nothing but sprinkle my paths with posies for the rest of my life. Or are you too swacked to remember what the fuck you said from one drink to the next?"

Steinhardt suddenly seemed to snap into sharp focus, his vision clear as a clean glass lens as he stared Weller down. "I remember everything I've said back to the World Science-Fiction Convention of 1956," Steinhardt informed him with amusement. "What I might have meant at the time is a different story."

"Be a man, you sot!" Weller snarled, infuriated by Steinhardt's welching evasion. "Live up to your word, John. Or are you willing to admit to yourself in front of Torrez here that your word means nothing?"

Torrez cringed at this, he glanced back and forth between Weller and Steinhardt, not knowing how he was supposed to react. Steinhardt glowered indignantly for a moment. He frowned. He smiled. He took a drink, stood up, and orated at Weller.

"You're right, laddy-buck," he said, "and I'll take it like a man. I'll show you that John B. Steinhardt has a sense of honor. I'll do exactly as I promised." Pacing, he turned to Torrez. "Life directive, Jack Weller, effective immediately. Jack Weller is to be flown to Los Angeles on my private jet and released. Upon good behavior, he is to be treated as a friend of Transformationalism."

"*What!*" Torrez finally exploded. "You're releasing this dangerous regressive and making him your pet?"

Steinhardt held up his hand for peace. "*Upon good behavior,*" he said, "which is to be verified by monthly Monitor updates submitted to me. If he deviates from his part of the bargain, further disposition of his case will be at your discretion."

Torrez subsided; grievously disappointed and even shamed, but given an obsession for watching Weller for a hoped-for sign of regression that he could fester over for life. As John no doubt intends, Weller thought. Now I've got a lucky leprechaun and a bloodhound on my trail for the rest of my life to make sure I'm a good boy.

"You understand the scenario, Jack?" Steinhardt asked.

"Perfectly," Weller said. "I intend to give you no cause to ever notice me again. I hope you'll do likewise. I know you'll be watching, but please let me live in ignorant bliss."

Steinhardt laughed. He clapped Weller on the back. "Bliss, I promise you, laddy-buck. It will always be yours for the taking."

He took a sip of bourbon and shrugged sardonically as he started toward the door. "Ignorance, however," he said, "you'll have to handle on your own."

As Weller stood at the foot of the embarkation ramp between two Monitor guards, waiting, apparently for some luggage to arrive, a golf cart careened madly out of the woods at the edge of the landing field and made for the plane. On it were two suitcases, a driver, and Annie.

The cart pulled up in front of the Learjet. The driver started loading the suitcases onto the plane. The two guards moved to a discrete distance. Annie stood before him radiating a strange calm.

"I thought we had already said good-bye," Weller said. "Several times."

"But we never got it right," Annie said. "I don't want to remember leaving you all wounded and hurt. And hating me. I want you to understand that it can't be you and me anymore—not because I don't love you but because I feel happy and fulfilled now, and I can't lose that feeling or I'll die. I only hope you find your way to feeling like that someday, love. I'm sorry you're leaving yourself behind."

There was love, real love, in her heart, and Weller could not deny that to himself. But it was coming out all mixed in with Transformationalist programming. It was touching, it was horrifying; it was over, it was dead.

"And I'm feeling sorry for you, Annie," he said. "And that's no way to say good-bye either. So let's just agree that we're not the same people we once were and leave it at that. Two people loved each other once, and now they're gone."

"Thank you," Annie whispered. She touched his cheek for an instant and then darted away toward the woods.

Weller watched her recede in the distance for a long moment; then he turned his back on everything and boarded his getaway flight to the Coast.

Epilogue

Jack Weller paused at the threshold of the Shumways' big
sunken living room, swirling the ice cubes in his half-finished
drink, listening to them tinkle against the glass and watching
writers, agents, studio executives, minor acting talent, and
assorted hangers-on dance the Beverly Hills Pavanne, a/k/a
the Hollywood Hustle.

These days, what with Bob into writing features and an-
gling toward the idea of producing, Shumway parties were on
the way to becoming a minor industry institution, though to
Bob's annoyance, they were not yet deemed worthy of notice
in the trades.

Don't be snide, Clyde, Weller told himself. You're playing
the same game yourself. And don't forget you owe a lot to this
guy.

For Bob Shumway didn't forget his friends from the old TV
days now that he had hosted his way into upward mobility.
Bob, bless his goldfoil heart, had been his guardian angel
Hollywood style every since he got off that plane from his
previous incarnation. Bob hadn't given him time to think
about his blighted personal life and possibly twisted head. He
had pulled strings somehow and gotten him four cop shows, a
hospital show, and a schlocko TV movie about surfing to
direct before he could catch his breath. He suddenly found
himself working in prime-time TV which was a craziness all its
own. Which led him to the satori that the despicable old
Hollywood game was fun to play once you detached yourself
from the matrix.

When you detached yourself from the house rules and
played by your own scenario, you could also maintain an
Olympian attitude about the crap you had to work on to
survive.

At this level of irony the game was played against itself.
You didn't chase after any more crummy TV episodes than
you needed to make your nut. A reasonable man could live on
four episodes a year. If the stuff you did do was of decent

weekly TV quality, you got plenty of chances to *turn down* TV assignments with lordly disdain. This gave you Instant Mystique by creating the illusion that you were in such hot demand that you could pick and choose. Once word got around, you *were* in hot demand.

This career strategy had driven his agent screaming up the wall on several occasions, but when it got him the TV movie, Mort saw the light and was even beginning to use the scenario with other clients.

And on the phone Bob had muttered something about someone being at this party who wanted to talk to him about a feature-film project. Bullshit or not, that was the next higher level.

Weller took a sip of his drink and stepped back into the churn and swirl of the living room stock-exchange floor. Where the hell was Bob?

"Jack! Over here!" Bob was waving his arm over the mob scene from the vicinity of the bar. Weller followed this beacon through the sea of knees and elbows, but when he reached the bar he did a classic double take. Oh shit!

For sitting at the bar with Bob was . . . was *Morris Fender*. Morris Fender, the wormy son of a bitch who had been his producer on *Monkey Business!* The dirty little creep who had fired him without even giving him a chance to tell him to go fuck himself! A face he had dreamed of punching for years, the archetypal no-talent balding cartoon producer prick!

"I believe you and Morris know each other," Bob said dryly.

Weller stared at Fender not knowing what to say. Fender laughed. He seemed almost human. "We drove each other crazy on something I think we'd both rather forget about," he said. "We share a tragic past." He smiled at Weller. Suddenly he didn't seem like such a prick any more. Against his will Weller found himself almost liking him.

Bob did an imitation of a bleary drunk. "I'll just leave you guys here to reminisce about the good old days," he said with an evil stage chuckle. And he snaked-danced away through the crowd and disappeared.

What the fuck is this? Weller wondered. *Morris Fender?* Is *this* who wants to talk to me about directing a feature? *Morris Fender* making a feature film? *Morris Fender* thinking of hiring me?

"The last time I saw you, you were telling me I'd never

work in this town again," Weller finally said, by way of attempting to bring their relationship up-to-date.

Fender shrugged. "The last time I saw you, you had lost me my income by driving my chimpanzee crazy, and we were both playing zoo keeper to Barry the Brat," Fender said. "I'd just as soon not be reminded of the shit we were in together, wouldn't you?" He toasted Weller with his half-finished drink. "So I drink to the day Scuffles went apeshit and got us both cancelled out of the monkey house, and I say let's let dead dogs lie."

Weller laughed. He toasted Fender back silently, convinced that Morris Fender had gone through some changes of his own. Maybe in his present persona, Fender *was* a credible feature-film producer? After all, Weller, you're after directing one, and you both shoveled shit in the same zoo together.

Fender's eyes circled the crowded room. He nodded outward, toward the glass doors that opened out onto the Shumways' pool deck. "Now that we've got that stuff out of the way," he said, "maybe we could talk a little business?"

"Sure, Morris, let's get out of this crush."

They slithered through the crowded living room and out through the glass doors onto the pool deck. The Shumways' pool was sunk into a small shelf of land bulldozed like a rice-paddy terrace out of the hillside overlooking the city. The quiet summer heat was like a breath of the South Seas after the air-conditioned bedlam of the party. The city below flashed and shone like an electrified jewelry box. Weller rode a wave of confidence. Morris Fender, I can handle on this level. Besides, this guy has seen me at my lousiest, he realized. If he's still interested after that, it must mean I'm for real.

But now Fender, in this new environment, suddenly seemed a little more tentative. "You know, Jack, when this project began, you wouldn't have exactly been my first choice to direct it," he said half apologetically. "I mean, in the first place, bankable you weren't, and in the second place you were not exactly my favorite person. Frankly it was one of the backers who insisted I look at some of your later stuff, and that TV movie convinced even me you were no longer a schmuck."

"One ex-schmuck to another?" Weller suggested, not quite knowing how to take that.

Fender shrugged. "So one ex-schmuck to another, I've got a sweetheart deal here," he said. "My own independent production company. A script locked in. A five million dollar budget and a choice of three or four bankable stars. The day after I hire my director, we go into preproduction." He smiled slyly at Weller. "I know what a busy man you are, but you think you might be able to rearrange your schedule?"

Weller laughed in open glee. "I can see as how I might be able to squeeze in a feature-film project somewhere," he allowed dryly.

"Thought you might," Fender said impishly. He grimaced. "To tell you the truth," he said, "I've been having trouble finding a director who could sync with this script."

"Are you locked into a turkey, Morris?"

"No, no," Fender insisted. "It's a winner of a script. But it's got to be directed just right or it could bomb. And none of the directors I've talked to convinced me they could do it. It takes something special, something special it's been pointed out to me maybe you have, something that maybe came through a little on that TV movie. Want to hear what the project is and then try to tell me how you would direct it?"

"I'm all ears, Morris," Weller said. This was really turning out optimally. Figure out a good line of directorial bullshit about what a great movie you see in this script, and it's yours! If you can't do that, you don't *deserve* to direct a feature.

Fender slowly began walking along the chlorine-smelling edge of the pool toward the far end of the deck. "I won't kid you, this is going to be very commercial if it's done right, or an artsy-farsty box-office disaster if it doesn't have the right directorial touch," he said. "It's called *The Conspiracy*, and it's the ultimate phone-company-runs-the-world fantasy, but it's also got to be a kind of comedy to work right. You see the problem?"

"You haven't told me the story yet, Morris," Weller pointed out coolly, keeping a pace ahead of Fender.

"Huh?" Fender looked at him. He shook his head, and laughed. "I've told the story so many times lately, I guess I'm beginning to think I've told everyone in the world," he said.

Fender came to the low wall at the cliff end of the pool deck and leaned back against it. "Fade in on a crusading reporter, figure Redford or Reynolds at this stage, as he learns that his girlfriend has been kidnapped by parties unknown for purposes unfathomable," he began, pitching it like a writer in a story conference.

"So like Clark Kent is out to rescue Lois Lane," Fender continued. "That's the basic premise. But instead of there being no clues or leads to the kidnappers, there are dozens of them, and they lead off in all directions at once. The CIA. The Mafia. Moonies. Transformationalism. The KGB. It all seems to be part of one vast conspiracy, the *ultimate* conspiracy, get it? And as he probes deeper and deeper, the thing seems to grow larger and larger. Everything seems to be part of it. The police. The phone company. NBC. Winos in the street."

Fender paused, waved his arms, grinned, and continued again, obviously pleased with himself. "Finally we have a tour de force climax scene where *literally* everything becomes part of the conspiracy, down to license plate numbers, restaurant menus and the cockroaches in his crummy apartment. Hard cut to him being found dead the next day in this filthy room full of tapes and papers and files, dead from a cerebral hemorrhage. Impact, right?"

Down below them a dark overgrown ravine tumbled toward the city like a vein of darkness snaking toward the light. A cold wind seemed to seep up out of its hidden recesses though the actual temperature was pushing ninety. Oh fuck, Weller thought, this guy has a script about Richard Golden! It *can't* be a coincidence! Or can it?

"But we explain it to the less sophisticated audience in a final scene, if you're worried about that," Fender said, noticing that Weller looked a little uneasy. "His girlfriend finds the body and she tells the police she never was kidnapped. Our intrepid reporter went psycho when she gave him the ax."

Fender grinned at Weller as if he had just delivered a particularly juicy punch line, then wilted a little as Weller continued to stare at him dumbly. "Get it?" he said. "The guy was crazy from the opening shot. There never was a conspiracy. It was all in his head."

Oh my God! Weller thought sickeningly. This isn't funny anymore. A crack seemed to open in his bright shiny new Hollywood reality revealing something he never wanted to have to look at again. If this weren't the story of Richard Golden transmogrified into a cautionary tale against believing the ravings of such regressive paranoiacs, then he was one himself, just like the reporter in the script. Either way, the smell of Transformationalism was all over it.

"That's why I need a director with the right touch," Fender said with forced brightness. "The movie has to be dead serious while we're making the audience believe in the Conspiracy and then slowly fade into cuckooland till at the end they

337

realize it's black comedy that they've been believing in by the time he's arguing with his stove and getting messages from outer space off freeway signs. Then you've got to pop them right back into a tough street realism scene at the end. So now you know what the problems are . . ."

Oh man, do I see what the problems are! Weller thought. And I think maybe Steinhardt's found out how to solve one of them. If this thing gets made and released, they can terminate Golden without an investigation. He'd be a joke, alive or dead.

And so would I if I followed his vector, Weller realized. And here is this nerd offering me the script. Steinhardt certainly had a shitty sense of humor. He only hoped that was all it was.

Fender finally saw that Weller's attention was elsewhere. "You *do* want to see the script, don't you?" he asked somewhat petulantly.

"*Who* was it you said had told you to look at some of my later stuff?" Weller asked sharply.

"One of the backers. A guy named Harry Lazlo from some big conglomerate. What's that got to do with anything?"

"Do you mind if I ask you who wrote the script and where you got it from?" Weller said.

Fender seemed irritated by the way this was turning into some kind of interrogation. But he also seemed to feel he had been pinned for something; under pressure, he became a little defensive. "Look, this will maybe sound not so kosher, but I don't really know who wrote the script."

"*You don't know who wrote your five million dollar production?*"

"Yeah," Fender said with a shrug. "The agent who threw it to me told me that the name on the script was a closed pseudonym for a real heavy who needed money strictly off the books due to an alimony hassle. The deal came with it, so who am I to look a gift horse in the mouth?"

I wonder if Steinhardt wrote it himself, Weller thought; Or whether he had it churned out to order at the Colony.

"You wouldn't by any chance have gotten this deal from a little agency called Delta?" he asked Fender.

"Yeah! How the hell did you know that?" Fender exclaimed in surprise.

I've got a little list, Morris. "I get around," Weller said.

Fender studied him owlishly. "If I'm supposed to be

impressed, okay, I'm impressed," he said. "Ted Morisey at Delta put the whole deal together, not me, I admit it. Some money people came to him with the script, if you can imagine that, ready to go with the financing as bankers to an independent production. I got the sweetheart deal thrown to me because I'm a talented charming fellow and also because I've been giving a lot of work to Ted's clients."

"Lucky you, Morris," Weller said. Good God, it seemed that Fender thought all this was on the level, that he had no idea of whom he was dealing with. Maybe he was still a schmuck after all. "Just out of curiosity, do you know who your financial angels are?"

Fender inched away from the parapet and peered dubiously at Weller. "I don't know if I like that question," he said.

"Well, do you know?"

"What do you mean, am I involved with the mob or something?" Fender snapped, with some of the indignant pissantism that Weller had so known and loved in the dear dead days of *Monkey Business*. "Of course I know who my backers are, and they're all legitimate people! A savings and loan in East L.A., a book publisher who owns the novelization rights, and the parent company of the publisher, Utopia Industries. That's where this guy Lazlo comes from who recommended your stuff. You think I'm involved in laundering money for the porn mafia?"

Weller laughed hollowly. "Well, it *is* beginning to seem like an offer no one could refuse," he said archly.

Fender finally decided he was pissed off. "That's not funny, Weller," he snapped. "Maybe you're still an asshole after all. You're talking like you don't give a shit about getting to direct this movie."

Apparently even the new improved Morris Fender was capable of being a prick. Weller leaned languidly against the parapet and wondered whether he should tell poor Morris that he was involved with three or four Transformationalist fronts. If he's really what he seems, he won't believe me; he'll be sure I'm crazy. But if Fender *did* believe him, that would be worse. Because that would mean he was part of some Monitor operation designed to see if I'm still keeping my mouth shut. Or Steinhardt offering me one of his promised temptations. Or both.

He wanted no part of it, whatever it was. He only hoped that he could persuade it that it no longer wanted part of him.

"No offense, Morris, but I really don't," he said. "I'm sure you can find a director who can make a success out of this project, but it's not for me."

"What?" Fender exclaimed. "Are you out of your mind, Weller? You're turning down a chance to direct your first feature film without even looking at the script?"

Weller wrapped himself in his artistic Olympian mystique. "I just don't think I can get behind it conceptually," he said patricianly. "I believe it's important to select just the right vehicle for my feature-film debut. Perhaps your next project will be more my style."

"You *are* an asshole, Weller!" Fender snapped angrily. "Turning down a chance like this just to tell me to go fuck myself!"

"Nothing personal at all, Morris," Weller said, more or less truthfully. "I *would* really like to work with you on some other project someday."

"Well, don't hold your breath, Weller," Fender said nastily, and he stalked off nursing his wounded feelings.

Weller stood there alone in the darkness following the fault line of the deeply shadowed ravine as it crawled down the hillside like a black tentacle reaching for the city of tinsel and light. It seemed to him that something vast, amoeboid, and dark as the pit was insinuating its inky pseudopods into everything like the glob from outer space.

Pure paranoia! Weller shuddered and shook the vision from his mind. But also purely true, he couldn't stop himself from thinking. *And the best I can hope to do is keep out of its way.*

Mercifully Bob Shumway came out onto the deck, shaking his head and groaning as Weller knew he would.

"Jesus, Jack," he said, "Fender's under the impression you told him to get stuffed! How did you manage to screw up like that?"

"I just told him I didn't want to direct his movie," Weller said. "Don't worry, it'll just help my image."

"Help your image? But the reason you've been building your image in the first place is to get yourself a shot at doing a feature! Are you so into playing the game that you've forgotten why you're playing it?"

Weller studied Bob Shumway thoughtfully. This guy had been his guardian angel from the day he returned to Hollywood, every step of the way. . . . But *Bob Shumway?* No, it couldn't be. . . .

"Did you know that Transformationalism was involved in this project, Bob?" he asked. Not *Bob*, not just because Bob had introduced Annie and him to Transformationalism, not just because Bob had helped him out.

Bob rolled his eyes. "You're not going to start that shit again, are you, Jack?" he said, with a worried look on his face.

"You didn't know that Harry Lazlo was one of Fender's backers?"

"Harry *who?*"

"Harry Lazlo of Utopia Industries. A Transformationalist holding company."

"Look, Jack, all I ever did was hang around the Celebrity Center for a while," Bob said. "And believe me, I've wanted nothing to do with that outfit since you came home."

"I'm sorry, Bob," Weller said. The idea was ridiculous. Bob had stopped hanging out at the Celebrity Center and started throwing these parties as soon as Weller had returned to the Coast. He had made his contacts and gotten out. I'm not going to let them make me stop trusting my friends, Weller told himself.

"Let's go back inside and get another drink," Bob said. "I want one, and I think you need one."

Weller nodded. He followed Bob Shumway along the edge of the pool to the glass doors leading back into the party. He stood there for a moment, looking back into the darkness, and forcing himself to laugh at the image he got of a Japanese monster-movie blob reaching out to engulf him. He looked inside at the hustle and swirl of the wheeling and dealing party. If something *was* reaching out for him, it was in there in the neon, not out here in the dark.

"Could I ask you something, Bob?" he asked.

"Sure, kiddo."

"If you suddenly found out that Transformationalism or something like it had helped you secretly to your present success without ever asking for anything, would you want to keep letting them do it?"

Bob eyed Weller narrowly. "If I found myself thinking that, I'd go see a shrink."

"Just hypothetically . . ."

Bob stared right into Weller's eyes with as serious an expression as he had ever seen on the man's face. "Well, then just hypothetically," he said, "if I found out that someone powerful wanted to help me along, I'd bow to his good taste."

"Would you work for him?"

Bob's seriousness evaporated. He shrugged. "Who the hell cares?" he said. "Gulf and Western. Hot deutschemarks. Arab

341

oil sheiks. Transformationalism. You take your backing where you can get it, and then go do your project. I'm an equal opportunity employee. I recommend the same to you."

"You play your game, and I'll play mine," Weller told him. "I prefer not to play out of my league."

"You can't be afraid to ride the changes, boy," Bob Shumway said paternally, and led him back into the only game in town.

ABOUT THE AUTHOR

Norman Spinrad was born in 1940, graduated from the City College of New York in 1961, published his first story in 1963, his first novel in 1965, and has not held a job since. In addition to somewhere between twelve and fourteen novels (depending on the counting method used), three books of short stories, two non-fiction books, and two anthologies, he has published literary criticism, film criticism, political commentary, and essays on various scientific subjects.

He has been a literary agent, had a radio phone show, and is past President and Vice President of the Science Fiction Writers of America. He has written a couple of song lyrics and had a single record out as a singer in Britain and France which never came close to making the charts.

His novel BUG JACK BARRON was briefly banned in Britain and two of his novels, THE IRON DREAM and THE MEN IN THE JUNGLE are currently on the Index in Germany, where they are nevertheless selling quite well under the table.

CHILD OF FORTUNE

Norman Spinrad

Exhilarating, erotic, joyous, poignant, this extraordinary new novel by award-winning author Norman Spinrad is a remarkable literary achievement. Blending the magical wonder of A WINTER'S TALE with the vivid realism of ON THE ROAD and the mystical transcendence of SID-DHARTHA, CHILD OF FORTUNE is a masterwork of imaginative fiction by one of the most dazzling talents of our time.

"CHILD OF FORTUNE lifts science fiction to the next level. It's a literary masterpiece."

—Timothy Leary

"Spinrad is generously talented. CHILD OF FORTUNE is a magnificent read."

—Michael Moorcock

Turn the page for a preview of Norman Spinrad's
CHILD OF FORTUNE.

On the occasion of my fifth birthday, when the possibility of retreating into my own private realm was deemed necessary to my development, a fanciful playhouse was built for me deep in a patch of Bittersweet Jungle in the nethermost reaches of the garden.

Here as a young girl would I spend many hours with young playmates, and many more with no other companionship than that of the moussas I soon learned to entice from the trees with bits and morsels from the breakfast table. Of all the native creatures of Glade, these cunning little mammals, small enough to fit in a child's cupped hands, and willing enough to remain there for the pettiest of bribes, have cozened themselves closer to the human heart than any other, for they are the common pets of childhood.

Though in truth, perhaps, it is as much the little human children of Glade who are the pets of the moussas, for these golden-furred, emerald-eyed, monkey-tailed, leaf-eared, primatelike rodents never survive in a cage or as domesticated house pets, sullenly fasting unto death in any form of captivity. Nor, although they abound throughout Nouvelle Orlean and the surrounding environs, thriving amidst the habitats of men, will they ever deign to descend from their trees to frolic with gross and clumsy adults, even to accept the choicest dainty. But put a child in a garden with a few scraps of bread or a berry or two, and the moussas will soon enough come a-calling. Indeed often, when through negligence I appeared empty-handed, the moussas of the garden, though they might chide me in their piping whistles for my thoughtless lack of hospitality, would nonetheless come down to play.

And like a little moussa myself, I would often, in the late afternoon or early evening, emerge from my garden retreat to play the pampered and cunning pet of the clients and friends of my parents. As the children of Glade imagine that the moussas chattered and capered for their amusements, so, no doubt, did the adults of my parents' salons imagine that the fey creature whom everyone soon began to call kleine Moussa herself frequented their precincts to amuse *them*.

But from the moment their kleine Moussa knew anything of significance at all, I, like the moussas of the garden, knew full well that these huge and marvelous beings, with their extravagant clothes, incomprehensible stories, strange and mysterious perfumes, and secret pockets of sweets, existed, like the garden, and the river, and the myriad wonderous sights and sounds and smells of Nouvelle Orlean, and indeed the world itself, to amuse *me*.

Thus did the little Moussa frolic through young girlhood with the creatures of the garden and the clients of her parents' trades and the favored children of these denizens of Nouvelle Orlean's haut monde. Though naturellement I was not yet capable of appreciating the rarefied and elite ambiance of my parents' salon until my basic schooling was well under way and I was deemed old enough to travel to the academy on my own and venture forth into the city with my playmates.

Then, of course, my awareness of my favored place in the scheme of things became somewhat keener than the reality itself. As I became interested in the wider world around me, and began first to listen to word crystals and then learned to read them for greater speed, as I was taught the rudiments of esthetics, acquainted with the history of our city and our planet and our species, as my teachers introduced me to the sciences, the mutational sprachs of human Lingo, the basic principles of mathematics, und so weiter, I began to perceive that the discourse that had swirled about my little head like so much moussas' babble chez mama and papa was in fact in good part an elevated and rarefied version of my various teachers' discourse at the academy.

This inner perception of my true place in the world was not without both its negative and positive consequences. On the one hand, my respect for the authority of my teachers was eroded by my free and easy congress with their intellectual and social superiors, and I was not above hectoring them from time to time with what I imagined was superior knowledge gleaned from bits and pieces of table talk. On the other hand, I had almost from birth dined on intellectual haute cuisine, and much true learning had actually been absorbed as it were by osmosis; further, what little ambition I then had lay in the direction of acceptance as an equal by the denizens of my parents' salon, and so I was at least motivated to avoid the public intellectual embarrassment of the unprepared student.

The overall result was that I was a skilled if shallowly motivated and not excessively diligent student, lacking any true passion for scholarly pursuits, content to breeze through my studies with a parsimony of effort, and quite innocent of any perception of the educational process as connected to spiritual, intellectual, or karmic goals.

As such, though at the time I would have been mightily offended at the generalization, I was typical of the preadolescent stage of our species, for the biochemical matrix of passion—whether intellectual, artistic, political, spiritual, or sexual—simply cannot be generated by the prepubescent human metabolism. Thus does the wisdom of passing through the wanderjahr before contemplating that deeper education which must be informed by passionate dedication to some true life's work extend from the social and spiritual clear down into the molecular realm.

Which is also why the onset of puberty effects a tumultuous series of psychic transformations quite literally akin to the effects of ingesting powerful psychoactive drugs. While the earliest and most obvious social and psychological manifestation of this biochemical revolution is the awakening of that most presentient of human passions, sexual lust, once the biochemical matrix of passion itself has evolved in a young girl's physiology, that molecular hunger for novelty, somatic excitation, and adventure of the spirit seeks its polymorphous fulfillment in every realm.

Biochemically speaking, adolescence is a loss of endocrine innocence in that it opens the human spirit to all possibilities and dangers of passionate motivation denied to the juvenile metabolism. Yet at the same time, there is no more perfect naif than the newly pubescent creature, who all at once perceives the world through eyes, ears, nostrils, and spirit radically heightened and transformed by this psychochemical amplification of the childhood mind.

In many primitive Terrestrial cultures, before psychoesomics was a developed science or the bioelectronic basis of tantras elucidated, all sorts of bizarre and entirely counterproductive social mechanisms evolved, aimed at either "managing" these adolescent passions from the point of view of adults, suppressing their outward manifestations, or worse still, capturing, channeling, and perverting their energies in the service of theocratic dogmas, territorial aggressions, or the convenience of the adult body politic. Since the earliest, simplest, and somatically strongest of the nascent adolescent passions is of course sexual lust, most of these disastrous social control mechanisms revolved around delaying, transposing, or even entirely suppressing its natural amatory expression.

The results, of course, were exactly what modern psychesomics would predict—polymorphous adolescent rebellion against adult authority, violently sepatrist adolescent subcultures, excessive random indulgence in psychoactive substances without proper prior study of their effects, neurosis, depression, hysteria, the romanticization of suicide, militarism, cruelty to animals, and a scornful attitude towards scholarly pursuits.

Mercifully our Second Starfaring Age has long since put this torture of the innocent far behind it, and so my earliest experiments satisfying this new somatic hunger were conducted, as was natural, convenient, and esthetically pleasing, in the playhouse of my parents' garden.

Of course I hardly considered myself a clumsy young experimenter in the amatory arts even on the occasion of my first passe de deux in that bucolic boudoir. Was I not, after all, the daughter of Shasta Suki Davide, tantric maestra? Had I not grown up steeped in the ambiance of her science? Had I not, out of childish curiosity, ofttimes perused the catalogs of positions long before the illustrations therein were capable of arousing any but theoretical interest?

Indeed I was. Indeed I had. Moreover, I was not so unmindful of the benefits of motivated study that I neglected to delve deeper into the texts when the motivation for such studies grew deliciously immediate. Nor did I neglect to interrogate my mother for anecdotal expertise or to persuade my father to offer up both his lore on human nervous physiology and his more general knowledge of how men might be blissfully transported.

Verdad. I must confess that I had determined to gain the enviable reputation of a fabled femme fatale while still a virgin, for not only would such a mystique among my peers enhance my perception of my own centrality, it would also insure me the amatory services of most any boy who piqued my interest.

For my first granting of favors, I made the perhaps somewhat calculating choice of a handsome boy of fourteen known as Robi; not only did his slim and nearly hairless body and wide blue eyes arouse the proper spirit within my loins, though a year older than I, he was still charmingly tentative with girls, albeit something of a braggart among his male friends by way of compensation.

I was not unaware that a truly impressive tantric performance for Robi—especially, if, as I suspected, he was still a virgin—would speedily become common lore among the boys of our mutual acquaintance, thereby establishing my mystique as a lover of puissance from my premiere performance.

Enticing Robi into my bower was a simple matter of issuing

an unambiguous invitation in the presence of his fellows, though once we retired to my garden playhouse, his tentativeness was all too limply apparent despite his attempts at verbal bravado.

Undaunted by this phenomenon which was well reported in the word crystals I had perused in preparation, I applied a simple sequence of digital and oral remedies which at first seemed to further discombobulate the pauvre petit with their no-doubt-unexpected level of tantric sophistication, but which soon enough transferred his attention from the uncertainties of the virgin psyche to the naturally firm resolve of the youthful lingam.

Once the natural man in Robi had been properly aroused, he became an enthusiastic if rather hasty and clumsy participant, achieving his own satisfaction in the most basic of tantric configurations with all too much ease, and then satedly supposing that the performance had reached an esthetically satisfying resolution.

When of course it had hardly properly begun, for I was determined to essay certainly no less than a dozen basic positions with several variations of each, to enjoy several tantric cusps of my own in the process, and not to relent until I was entirely satisfied that he was thoroughly, totally, and finally exhausted beyond any hope of further arousal.

Though I lost count somewhere after the first four or five movements of the tantric symphony and probably did not achieve the first of my artistic goals, and though my still barely pubescent physiology left me far short of anything approaching platform orgasm, there was no doubt that the poor boy had been properly exhausted, for I was only persuaded to relent after his moans of pleasure had long since become pleas for surcease and his manhood openly confessed its surrender to the protoplasmic impossibility of rising to further challenge.

To say that Robi was constrained to crawl from our erotic encounter would be to descend to hyperbole, but in truth he staggered from the garden in something less than a triumphant strut, though to judge from subsequent events, his version of the affair would seem to have gained considerably more machismo in the telling.

For I was soon the smug recipient of numerous displays of male courting behavior, from which smorgasbord of possible swains I chose carefully, venturing not to offer up my tantric performances to older, more experienced, and hence more critically acute connoisseurs of the art until my mystique was well established and my store of experience sufficient to insure that it would survive congress with boys whose dedication to the mastery of the tantric arts was no less serious and diligent than my own.

Then, at last, I was able to enter into liaisons in which the pleasure I sought and ofttimes received was equal to that which I offered up in the service of my continued lofty self-appraisal, and genuine mutual affection was thereby enabled to bloom on the tree of passion, though I was still far too enamored of my reputation as a tantric adept and still far too hungry for new experience to even contemplate entering into any compacts of undying love or sexual exclusivity.

Thus through the sexual realm did the dimension of male companionship enter my life and with it the dyadic explorations of the possibilities of adventures and passions beyond those of the boudoir, for just as even the most avid and athletic of lovers can scarcely pass more than a few hours daily in actual embrace, so the passionate adolescent spirit cannot confine its sphere of attention and its hunger for novelty and adventure to the erotic realm alone.

In this manner did the boudoir door also open into the wide world around me, for each lover was also a person entire, possessed of interests, passions, and even obsessions beyond the object of his amorous desire, and more than willing to share them with a venturesome friend.

And so did the kleine Moussa, without noticing the transition, cease to be a child content to frolic in a child's world and become a true adolescent whose garden was no longer that of the parental menage but Nouvelle Orlean itself and the countryside beyond.

With Genji did I begin to appreciate the variety of cuisinary styles to be found in Rioville and learn to distinguish the masterworks of the true chef maestro from mere cuisine ordinaire; so too did I gain some modest sophistication in the products of the vintner's art. Pallo was fairly obsessed with music, and with him I must have visited a hundred or more concert halls, tavernas, al fresco performances, and the like. My passage with Cort was a stormy and brooding one and my parents were not at all displeased when I grew tired of his company, for he was an afficionado of psychoactive chemicals with much more enthusiasm and reckless courage than accurate lore or tasteful discrimination. Ali flew Eagles—great helium-filled gliding wings of gossamer, which took us over land, sea, and river with the magical exhilaration of unpowered flight, but not without a certain peril to life and limb. Perhaps the swain that my parents regarded with the most dubious eyes of all was Franco, who took me on expeditions, sometimes for three and four days at a time, into the Bittersweet Jungle, with only our feet for locomotion, stunners for protection against the more bellicose fauna, and simple covers over piled mosswort for a bed.

Let it not be said that I became merely the mirror of my lovers' passions, for I too had interests of my own which I shared with them, though none of them reached the heights of overweening obsession. To be my companion was to frequent galleries of the graphic arts and become conversant with the styles of worldbubbles, to power-ski the Rio Royale for a hundred kilometers and more upstream and become something of a jesting pest to the boat traffic thereon, and to play endless games of rather inexpert chess.

Moreover, there was much cross-fertilization of adolescent passions and interests in the circles in which I moved, which is to say Pallo gained cuisinary sophistication from dining with me. Franco was introduced to new psychochemicals, and even Cort was constrained to try his hand at gliding through the skies beneath an Eagle. In short, by the time I was seventeen I was a member of a society of my own, a circle of friends, lovers, rivals, former and future swains, which modestly mirrored the social coherence, shifting interests and relationships, and independent life of my parents' salon society, if hardly the seriousness of purpose, artistic and scientific attainment, or depth of scholarship to be found therein.

If I have given the impression that eroticism, intoxicants, athletics, adventure, and entertainment were far more central to our lives than were our academic studies, it is also true that the requirements of same, both in time and effort, were quite deliberately loosened by the mavens of the academy after one's sixteenth birthday. For the natural inclination of the adolescent spirit is to seek out just such pleasures as dominated our attentions, and to tie its wings to the nest of arduous study would be to teach only the entirely counterproductive lesson that scholarship is a grim and bitter task imposed by one's parents and one's society, rather than a joy and intellectual adventure to be avidly pursued as a heart's desire.

Indeed by the age of sixteen one's childhood education is all but drawing to a close; having learned to read, compose word crystals, comprehend basic mathematics, having gained some facility in shifting fluidly among the infinitely varied sprachs of human Lingo, having been acquainted with the history of the species and the various sciences, having been at least exposed to the variety of possible spiritual disciplines and physical arts available for individual development, und so weiter, there is really little else of lasting value for the nonself-motivated student to learn. One has been given the tools with which to develop the mind, body, and spirit, but until one finds one's own inner light, one's own self-generated image of what one wishes to become as an adult of the species, one's own true intellectual passions, more serious and specialized learning thrust upon the still immature mind is as pearls cast before swine.

Which is not to say that my friends and I were not slowly learning an important lesson as our schooling trailed off into an endless summer of ease and self-indulgence. Though some learned it more rapidly than others, and I was not to achieve this satori until I was eighteen, the lesson that our parents, teachers, and society were so wisely allowing us to teach ourselves at our own leisure was that the young adolescent's ideal existence of entertainment, intoxication, eroticism, sport, and easy adventure, unhampered by work, arduous study, or hardship, eventually becomes as cloying as an exclusive diet of the pastry chef's art. Through a surfeit of this endless frolic, one finally learns *boredom*, and once this karmic state is attained entirely by one's own efforts, one is ready to contemplate the next quantum leap of spiritual development, the wanderjahr.

Naturellement, I had learned something of the history of the wanderjahr in the academy, and had known from early girlhood onward that some day I too would take my turn at the vie of the Child of Fortune.

The first clear records of the wanderjahr as a conscious stage in human development come from medieval Europa, where students—alas, in those days only the male of the species—were set to wandering afoot along the highways and byways, either as subsidized Children of Fortune or as mendicants, before embarking on their studies at the universities, though some authorities claim more ancient and universal origins, such as the wandering monks of Hind and Han, the name-quests of would-be Indian braves, the years that Masai boys spent as tribal wanderers before their puberty rites, the Walkabouts of the Abos, und so weiter.

Be that as it may, the wanderjahr seemed to disappear for a time with the coming of the industrial phase of the Terrestrial Age, when the spiritual education of the young came to be regarded as an indolent frivolity in the light of what was seen as the practical economic necessity of processing idle youth into productive members of the workforce via an uninterrupted passage from the schoolroom through the university and into gainful employment as rapidly as possible.

Nevertheless, the wanderjahr, long-suppressed, reemerged at the dawn of the Age of Space in the rather chaotic form of youthful rebellion against this very concept. Alas, *these* Children of Fortune, far from being wisely granted a period of wandering freedom between schooling and serious study by their society in which to discover their adult callings and true names, fled from their parental venues of times at a far too tender age, or on the other hand had already embarked on serious university study before realizing that they knew not who they were, and broke off in medias res in a state of karmic crisis and confusion.

The unfortunate result was turmoil, angry conflict between youth and maturity, the spiritual and the social realm, between the universal quest for spiritual identity and the restraints of formal education, and between endocrine imperatives and the body politic. Many educations, having been interrupted in midstream, were never properly completed, others were never fairly begun, and those who had been restrained from ever following the vie of the Child of Fortune often awoke as if from a trance in their middle years to find themselves strangers to their own beings.

Once more the wanderjahr fell into social disrepute, for precisely the wrong lesson was learned by the unfortunate results of forcing the youthful spirit into chaotic rebellion rather than nurturing the Child of Fortune from whom the spiritually self-motivated adult of the species must emerge. Only the Arkies carried the torch forward in the First Starfaring Age.

But when the development of the Jump Drive reduced the duration of interstellar voyages from decades and generations to weeks, the wanderjahr reemerged again as the rite de passage of youth into maturity.

Naturellement, in our Second Starfaring Age, the Children of Fortune wander not afoot from town to town nor across the continents and seas of a single planet, but throughout the far-flung worlds of men, in the timeless sleep of the dormodules of the Void Ships, or as Honored Passengers in the floating cultura if parental fortune permits.

For the Children of Fortune of *our* age do not flee from home in rebellious defiance of parents and body politic; rather do they depart with the blessings, not to say necessary largesse, of same, since those who bid bon voyage have themselves lived out their wanderjahr's tales before choosing their freedoms in homage to the adults they have become.

To learn this sociohistorical lore as a young student in the academy is an abstraction of the mind, but the moment when you realize that the time has come to set your own feet upon the wanderjahr's path is a satori of the spirit, which can be neither arbitrarily determined by the passage of time nor forced upon the spirit from without.

Nevertheless, the decision is almost always made between the sixteenth and nineteenth year of life, and it cannot be denied that society plows and fertilizes the ground in which this flowering of the young spirit blooms. For it is the policy of society to ease off serious studies after the sixteenth year, and it is the endless idle summer resulting therefrom which teaches the lesson that this child's dream of perfect paradise is not the ultima Thule of the human spirit, that the time must come when of our own free will we must move on.

My first dim perception of this last lesson that we are taught, which is also the first we learn to our own, came as a certain sense of pique, a petulant feeling of betrayal as, one by one, the older members of my circle of friends and lovers first announced their intent to leave our garden of juvenile delights and then departed for other worlds. When those whose faces were no longer to been seen among us were a year and more my senior, the lofty airs and moues of condescension with which they said good-bye could be laid to the arrogance of peers who suddenly conceived themselves to be older and wiser beings than their comrades of the week before.

But when at last some who left began to be no more mature in years than I, when I began to see myself as no longer quite the precocious femme fatale sought after by older boys and instead found myself forever repulsing the unwanted attentions of what I perceived as callower and callower youth, my unease by slow degrees began to focus less and less on the decaying social life without and more and more on the growing mal d'esprit within.

As the esthetics of karma would have it, the moment when this spiritual malaise crystallized itself into satoric resolve came with the clarity and definition of a classic koan.

I was lying in my garden playhouse boudoir with Davi, a boy some several months my junior to whom I had begun to grant my puissant favors not three weeks before, more out of ennui and a sense of charity than any grand passion.

As we lay in each other's arms during what I then supposed to be a brief recumbent interlude between the acts, I could sense him becoming somewhat distant, withdrawing into himself. At length, he pried himself from my embrace and sat some small but significant distance apart from me on the cushioned floor, eyes downcast, shoulders hunched, as if nerving himself up to inform me of a rival for his affections.

"Qué pasa?" I asked, with no more than a careful petulance of tone, for on the one hand my primacy in his affections was a matter to which all save my pride was indifferent, and on the other, this would obviously best be served by the assumption of an air of superior calm.

"Verdad, you're the finest lover I've ever had," he muttered fatuously.

"Verdad," I agreed dryly, for given the modesty of his mystique in this regard among our peers and his no more than ordinary skill in the tantric arts, this was a pleasantry that left my girlish heart less than overwhelmed.

"Don't make what I have to say more difficult . . ." he fairly whined, meeting my gaze with a pout, obviously all too relieved to exchange his shy discomfort for a facade of pique with me.

"Relax, klein Davi," I said with quite the opposite intent, "if you're afraid to wound me with a confession of some other amour, rest assured, my pauvre petit, that I myself have a surfeit of lovers, past, present, and future, and will therefore hardly be crushed to learn of any pecadillos of yours."

But instead of flinching at the planting of this barb, he smiled at me most foolishly, or so it seemed. "Ah, Moussa, I *knew* you'd understand . . ." he fairly moaned in relief.

"Who is it then—Andrea, Flor, Belinda?" I inquired, with a nonchalance that was both feigned and sincere. For while the undying loyalty of this lover whom I was already regarding in the past tense would in fact have been a tiresome burden to my indifferent heart, the outré notion that this lout could possibly prefer the favors of some other to my own, while the ultimate proof of his callow unsuitability as a swain, was still an outrage of lèse majesté, which, nevertheless, I could hardly acknowledge with less than lofty amusement, even to myself. *Especially* to myself.

Once again, however, my perception of the situation proved to be at variance with the reality. "There isn't anyone else, Moussa," he said. "How could there be? Of all the women that I know, you're the only one who tempts me to stay."

"*Tempts you to stay?*"

"Verdad, you *do* tempt me to stay, but . . ."

"But *what*, cher dumkopf? What are you blathering and babbling about?"

He regarded me as if *I* were the one who could not find the sprach to make the Lingo of my meaning plain. "But I leave to begin my wanderjahr next week," he blurted. "Next week, the *Ardent Eagle* leaves for Nova Roma, and I'll be aboard. My parents have already bought my passage."

He beamed at me. He fairly glowed. "Fantastique, né?" he exclaimed. "The Grand Palais of the *Ardent Eagle* is presided over by Domo Athene Weng Sharon! My mother once voyaged with her, and she says that the decor is marvelous, the entertainments superb, the ambiance exhilarating, and the chef maestro, Tai Don Angelica, one of the half-dozen finest in the entire floating cultura!"

"You're . . . you're off on your wanderjahr next week . . .?" I stammered. "As an Honored Passenger?" Why did this entirely unexpected revelation cut me to the quick as no confession of human rival could have done? From whence this sudden pang of loss? What was Davi to me but a casual lover whose season had already passed? Why the desire to hold him here with me which I could not deny but which I could still less understand?

"Naturellement," he said gaily, answering my words with total obliviousness of the import of their tone. "My parents, as you are certainly well aware, can afford to pay my way from world to world in proper style with ease. Why would they have me stacked like so much meat in electrocoma when they can afford to buy my access to the floating cultura without even noticing the debit in their accounts? Surely your own mother and father will do no less for you?"

"Of course!" I told him, though the subject had never been broached between us. "But why such haste? Has life on Glade become such a bore? Will you not be sad to leave Nouvelle Orlean behind?"

"*Haste?* But soon I will be *eighteen standards*. Many are our friends who became Children of Fortune long before reaching such an advanced age . . ."

Such an advanced age? But this silly boy was younger than I! All my young life I had wished to be, or at least wished to appear to be, older and more mature than my years, and now, all at once, this . . . this imbecile was making me feel like some sort of eighteen-year-old crone! For the first time in my life, I wished, at least for the moment, to be *younger* than my years; there are those who would contend, nicht wahr, that that is precisely the moment when a woman ceases to be a girl.

"And as for Nouvelle Orlean . . ." Davi blathered on, entirely oblivious to my mood, entirely blind to the havoc his prattle was working on my spirit.

"*And as for Nouvelle Orlean?*" I demanded sharply.

Al fin, Davi began to dimly perceive that his discourse was being met with something other than avid enthusiasm, though the concept that he was being the cause of no little dolor d'esprit never seemed to penetrate his primitive masculine brain. He touched his palm to my cheek as one would console a child.

"As for Nouvelle Orlean," he said, "I'll miss you, Moussa, most of all. Indeed for nearly a year, I dreamed of nothing but being your lover. If not for that, I probably would long since have gone. Verdad, if we had not yet had our time together, I might tarry still. But as for the rest . . ."

He smiled, he shrugged, he cupped my cheeks and kissed me like a proper man, and for that moment at least, I saw once more the sincere and naive charm that once had won some small portion of my heart.

"Have we not tasted what there is to taste, seen what there is to see, been what there is to be, as children of Nouvelle Orlean, Moussa, you and I?" he said. "Nouvelle Orlean is the most marvelous city on our entire world, we both know and love it well. But having tasted it to the full and come to know it as well as we know our parents' gardens or each other's spirits, is it not therefore time to travel on?"

I regarded him in silence, glimpsing for the first time the sweet and noble man that this lightly regarded lover of mine might one day grow to become, and in this moment of farewell I do believe I touched depths that never before had been stirred within my heart.

"Next week I depart for my wanderjahr, and soon enough you'll be a Child of Fortune too, mi Moussa, né. Could I have remained here with you forever and never lived to learn my true name tale? Would you have stayed here with me until we both grew old and never walked of another world?"

"No," I said softly.

"Then may we part as friends? For truly of all that Glade has meant to me, the finest of it all has been my time with you. Should not the best memory of home be the last?"

"Truly and nobly spoken, cher Davi," I told him, with more sincere affection than had ever before filled my callow young heart. "Friends forever, Davi. May your road rise up to meet you. Bon voyage."

And I kissed him one last time, as much to hide my tears as to bid him good-bye. Verdad, my best memory of all the lovers that I had on the planet of my birth was my final sight of the very last.

After Davi left, I went out into the garden and sat for a time under the overhanging trees, deep in formless thought. The sky was cloudless, the air was still, and the sun was warm, and soon I became aware of the piping whistles of the little moussas in the treetops.

For a long time I sat there, staring up into the trees, catching quick glimpses of little golden shapes frolicking high in the branches. Now and again, or so it seemed, tiny bright emerald eyes looked down as if through the billowing green mists of the innocent past. Foolishly, I hoped that the playmates of my young girlhood would descend one final time to nestle in my hands, if only to bid a final farewell to the Moussa that had been.

Naturellement, they never came, not even after I took some crumbs of cake from the playhouse and sat there offering them on my open palms as I had not done for many years.

And as the sky began to deepen towards sunset over my parents' garden and still my little lost friends deigned not to call, I tried to remember when last it had been that the little Moussa had held one of her namesake in her childish hands. Verdad, when last I had even spared the moussas of the garden a passing living thought.

And failed. And in that failing understood that it had not been the moussas who had forsaken me but I who had forsaken them, as that little girl grew into the creature who short hours before had bidden the final lover of her childhood a fond and tender bon voyage.

At the moment of this wistful satori, a golden shape chanced to pause in a small bare spot among the branches; tail wrapped around a twig for balance, the moussa stood half erect, as if dubiously testing the posture of a little man.

Or was it chance? For a long moment, the moussa's wide green eyes seemed to lock on my own as if remembering back across time to my childhood years. As if to say, bon voyage, old friend, may your road rise up to meet you. As if to say, mourn not what has been but greet what is to come with a happy heart, and know that we of your childhood's garden wish you no less than your heart's desire. No blame, little Moussa that was, remember us sometimes out there among the stars, and hold our memory in the palm of a child's hand.

Then, with a little chirp of farewell, he was gone, and with him the little girl that longed to stay in her parents' garden, for in that moment, that wanderjahr of my spirit had begun.

THE DREAM YEARS

by Lisa Goldstein

"THE DREAM YEARS is fresh and stimulating . . . Ms. Goldstein brings to literature the sparkle of renewal that is needed in every enduring novel." —Han Suyin, author of THE ENCHANTRESS

Few novels have the power not only to contribute something fresh and new to the art of fiction, but to change the way we perceive the world as well. Lisa Goldstein's THE DREAM YEARS, the haunting second novel by the American Book Award-winning author of THE RED MAGICIAN, is just such a work.

Beginning in 1920s Paris, THE DREAM YEARS tells of a young Surrealist writer transported forward through time by a beautiful, mysterious woman to the 1968 Paris riots, where they must prepare the way for a visionary war of dreams in the 21st century. At once a tour-de-force of fantasy and a stunning recreation of history, THE DREAM YEARS is a groundbreaking work that challenges the boundaries of modern fiction.

THE DREAM YEARS will be available in hardcover beginning September 1, 1985.